Praise for Rose Lerner

"This rich and memorable Regency romance brings its setting and characters perfectly to life."
—Publishers Weekly on *Sweet Disorder* (starred review)

"…*Sweet Disorder* was a lovely read, enjoyable and engaging and cleverly drawn."
—Dear Author

"Lerner weaves an enchanting tale. The repartee between Nick and Phoebe is the icing."
—RT Book Reviews on *Sweet Disorder*

"…as thought provoking as it is spicy; a wonderful sequel to Lerner's *Sweet Disorder*."
—Library Journal on *True Pretenses*

"Rich in subtle characterization, deftly seasoned with danger, and tempered with just the right dash of tart wit and historical grit, Lerner's historical romance is to be savored."
—Booklist on *In for a Penny*

Look for these titles by Rose Lerner

Listen to the Moon

Rose Lerner

SAMHAIN PUBLISHING

Samhain Publishing, Ltd.
11821 Mason Montgomery Road, 4B
Cincinnati, OH 45249
www.samhainpublishing.com

Editing by Anne Scott
Cover by Kim Killion

First Samhain Publishing, Ltd. electronic publication: January 2016
First Samhain Publishing, Ltd. print publication: January 2016

Dedication

For Sonia
Let us share in joy and care

Acknowledgments

I'd like to thank Anne Scott, my editor, for helping my books live up to their potential, and everyone at Samhain for making them shine. Thank you to Kim Killion for another stunning, emotional cover. Thank you to my agent Kevan Lyon for being a rock, as always.

Thank you once again to the world's greatest critique partners, the Demimondaines: Alyssa Everett, Charlotte Russell, Vonnie Hughes and especially Susanna Fraser. Your support and insight make all the difference.

Thank you to my beloved and brilliant friends and first readers: Kate Addison, Tiffany Ruzicki, Greg Holt, Kim Runciman and Olivia Waite. (A bunch of you even read the first act *twice*, because you are angels!) Kim, you were the first person to want a Toogood book, back when you first read *Sweet Disorder*. Thank you. (I believe our initial concept was 007!Toogood but some ideas are too good for this world.)

And thank you to Marisha Banerji and Rukmini Pande for taking a look at Mrs. Khaleel's scenes. She's my first major Indian character and I appreciate you helping me do right by her! Any remaining errors of fact or judgment are of course all my own.

I want to thank my family, for always being excited about my work.

And finally and forever, thank you to Sonia for being willing to talk about this book more than any book should ever be talked about. <3

Chapter One

November 14, 1812
Lively St. Lemeston, West Sussex

Sukey Grimes, maid-of-all-work, gave the chipped mantel a last pass with her duster. Empty of furniture, the two attic rooms looked nearly a decent size. But on a rainy day like this, nothing could hide the leak in the roof. The boards in the ceiling swelled and rotted, and water dripped into a cast-iron pot with a constant *plip plip plip*.

Someone knocked.

"Mrs. Dymond, is that you?" Sukey called. "I've been over these rooms, and if your sister happens to be missing a hairpin with a lovely rosette on it, I simply can't *imagine* where it could have got to." She pulled the pin from her hair and held it out as she opened the door.

It wasn't Phoebe Dymond, former lodger in these rooms, or her new husband Nicholas Dymond either. It was a very tall, very well dressed, very— "handsome" wasn't in it. Oh, he was handsome; there weren't any bones to be made about that. But handsome was ten for a penny. This man had *character*. His jaw might have been hewn from oak, and his nose jutted forward, too large on someone else's face but perfect on his. His warm, light-brown eyes stared right into her, or would have if he'd seemed the slightest bit interested in her.

He glanced down at the hairpin, lips thinning. His eyebrows drew together, one bumping slightly up at the side. The tiny, disapproving shift brought the deep lines of his face into sharp relief.

Oof. He as good as knocked the breath out of her, didn't he? "I'm that sorry, sir, I thought you were somebody else." She tucked the pin back into her hair with relief. Mrs. Dymond's little sister had made the rosette from a scrap of red ribbon that showed to advantage in Sukey's brown hair. "Are you here about the rooms for let? They come with a bed," she said encouragingly, quite as if the mattress had been restuffed in the last half a decade.

The eyebrows went up together this time. "I am Mr. Toogood. Mr. Dymond's valet." The calm, quiet growl of his voice knocked the breath out of her too. Deep and powerful, it was made for loudness, even if he kept it leashed. Tamed, he probably thought, but Sukey didn't think you *could* tame a voice like that, only starve it into temporary submission.

She wondered what Mr. Toogood would sound like tangled with a woman in that lumpy bed. Were bitten-off growls all he'd allow himself there as well? She'd never find out—she had never tangled herself up with any man yet, and never planned to—but it was nice to think about nevertheless.

Tardily, her brain caught up with her ears. "Not anymore, are you? Or you'd know not to look for him here." She didn't expect Mr. Dymond could afford a valet now he'd married beneath him.

Mr. Toogood didn't flinch. If anything, he looked more calmly superior than before. "No, not anymore, that's correct. Can you tell me where I might find the Dymonds?" That voice rubbed up and down her spine.

She made a show of considering. "I don't know as I'd ought to tell you. How am I to be sure you are who you say you are?"

To her surprise, his lips twitched. He pulled a card out of his pocket. *John Toogood,* it read. *Gentleman's Gentleman.* His own card! Upper servants were another species, right enough.

She pocketed the card to show the maid next door. "Oh, that don't prove a thing. Anybody can have cards printed."

His lips curved, the lines between his nose and the corners of his mouth deepening in a very pleasant way. "And anybody can sweep a floor thoroughly, but I don't accuse *you* of doing it."

She laughed, startled. "You'd better not. I don't like having false rumors spread about me." So she'd missed some spots in the corners. Who cared? Mrs. Dymond wasn't paying her to clean this attic anymore. She'd done it out of the goodness of her heart, and to help lure a new tenant. Old Mrs. Pengilly, who owned the house, didn't seem in any rush about that, but Sukey needed the money.

She eyed Mr. Toogood. "*You* must need a place to stay now you're out of work."

He looked about the room. "I don't plan to be out of work for long."

"Nobody does." He was too tall for the place. He'd hit his head on the eaves dunnamany times a day. Sukey didn't say so.

"I don't need anything so large."

She smothered a laugh. "It's cheap. On account of the leaky roof. And Mrs. Pengilly might give you credit for furnishings, if you engaged to leave them here when you go."

"And what is your interest in the matter?"

She grinned at him. "It'll cost you threepence a week to have me clean and cook for a bit Friday and Saturday afternoons."

"I see. Are you a good cook?"

"I'm not *bad*."

He sighed. "If you give me the Dymonds' direction, I'll stop by again this afternoon to speak with…Mrs. Pengilly, I believe you said?"

* * *

Mr. Dymond surveyed his Cuenca carpet as if it could tell him what to say. This gave John Toogood, gentleman's gentleman, ample opportunity to observe that his former master's hair was growing far too long, that he had been consistently failing to shave a spot under his left ear, and that his cuffs were ink-stained. He did not dare look about the room.

"My mother's refused to find you another position, hasn't she?"

John kept his hands folded behind his back. "I wouldn't say 'refused', sir. She has not replied to my letter. Naturally the weeks after an election are a very busy time for her ladyship."

They both knew that Mr. Dymond's mother, the influential Countess of Tassell, never neglected any correspondence unless she meant to.

"I'm so sorry, Toogood," Mr. Dymond said. "I never expected this. I was sorry to have to let you go, but it never occurred to me that Mother would put you on the black list. You're bound to find another place, even so. You're an exceptional valet."

"Thank you, sir. Please do not apologize. I would not have troubled you in the first weeks of your marriage, had I not hoped for a letter of reference."

"Of course." Mr. Dymond went at once to a writing table and exchanged his cane for a pen. It became clear as he wrote that the pen needed mending.

John clasped his hands tighter together so as not to reach for the pen-knife. He wasn't looking forward to going about town, hat in hand, asking for work. He'd never done it before, having worked for the Dymonds all his life.

He hadn't even been Mr. Dymond's valet anymore. For the past four years, John had worked for his elder brother Stephen, Lord Lenfield, who sat for Sussex in the House of Commons.

But when Mr. Dymond sold his commission after a serious injury, the Tassells had judged a stranger's care too much for their son's nerves. The countess had asked John to serve him through his convalescence as a particular favor. She'd promised both John and Lord Lenfield that they'd be reunited in a matter of months.

Few politicians, asked what smoothed a man's way in government, would mention a close shave, clean linen and polished boots. Yet those things took subtle root in the minds of others, hinting softly, *This is a fellow worthy of respect, who knows how things ought to be done.* Lord Lenfield would be a great man someday, and John had thought to help him in his rise to greatness.

That was before Mr. Dymond married a poor widow and broke all ties with his mother.

Now the most glowing letter of reference wouldn't help John if the angry countess had really put him on a black list among her acquaintances. He had few connections outside that circle, and no man in it would alienate powerful people like the Earl and Countess of Tassell merely for an improvement—however marked—in his comfort, appearance and mode of dress.

And by the time Society trickled back to London for the opening of the new Parliament in a few weeks, news of Mr. Dymond's fall from grace would be through the entire *ton* like wildfire. Everyone would know John had been dismissed from the family's employ.

Unless he was minded to work for a Tory, which he wasn't, he'd have to seek a position among strangers who cared nothing for politics.

No, John wasn't pleased about the current turn of events. But unlike Mr. Dymond, it had occurred to him that the countess might punish him for failing to warn her of her son's inappropriate attachment. He'd done it anyway, and he regretted nothing. He would just have to venture into new spheres of greatness.

It came to him with a sinking feeling that many distinguished professions were famed for inattention to dress. Might neat attire even hamper the career of a scholar or man of science, raising suspicions that he couldn't be so brilliant as all that?

Mr. Dymond sanded his letter. "Stephen will stop in Lively St. Lemeston on his way to London. Mother wants him to make me forgive her. Maybe if you talked to him…"

John had written to Lord Lenfield already and received no answer to that letter either. His lordship would never rehire his valet against his mother's wishes, but a personal appeal might persuade him to help John find a position elsewhere. "Thank you, sir. If you might tell me when you expect him?"

"If you give me your direction, I'll ask him to come and see you."

Heat crept up the back of John's neck. He wasn't sure why this should be embarrassing, but he was embarrassed nonetheless as he said blandly, "I was thinking of letting your wife's old rooms, as it happens."

Mr. Dymond blinked. "Can you afford them?"

John (when employed) likely earned twice what the new Mrs. Dymond did with her pen. But Mr. Dymond saw only that he was a servant and she was a respectable lawyer's daughter. "I have a little money put by. And I am told the rooms are cheap, on account of the leaky roof." Told by that puckish maidservant, who didn't clean worth a damn and had a retroussé nose and pale blue eyes tip-tilted like a cat's.

That wasn't why he was taking the rooms. She was too young for him, and besides, the last thing he wanted was more scandal. Which there'd be if he was kicked out of lodgings for making advances to the maid. Or debauching her.

An image of her—naked, tossing back her unbound hair as she straddled him with a sly half-smile—appeared with startling speed and had an equally startling effect on him, though fortunately not to a degree visible to Mr. Dymond.

On reflection, John supposed it was only natural. While no Lothario, he enjoyed the company of women, both in and out of bed. He'd been accustomed to a healthy dose of it, living in London or traveling with Lord Lenfield to house parties that were nearly as convivial for the servants as their masters. Now for months he'd slept within call of a convalescent who barely left his rooms. There'd been few chances even to take himself in hand.

Lively St. Lemeston was full of women. He'd find someone older and more discreet.

Mr. Dymond nodded. "Be careful of the eaves. I've cracked my head on them more than once."

John grimaced. He was at least three inches taller than his former master. "Thank you for the warning, sir. Pardon me—" Unable to resist any longer, he reached out to tighten the uneven knot of Mr. Dymond's cravat. Their eyes met for a moment before John dropped his respectfully.

"I'll write to some of my school friends and see if any of them are looking for a valet," Mr. Dymond blurted out. "I really am sorry. If you ever need anything, you must come to me."

I'm richer than you are now, John thought. "Thank you, sir. You're very kind."

* * *

John held up three fingers. "And a few pieces of mace, if you will."

The North African peddler raised his tin spoon hopefully.

"Not spoonfuls. Three *pieces*." He pointed at the dry, lacy husks that had once tightly cradled nutmeg seeds.

With a sigh, the peddler wrapped three husks in a square of thin paper. "Two pennies and a farthing."

"Good morning, John Toogood, gentleman's gentleman," a voice said behind him. It took him a moment to place it. "How d'you do?"

John made himself count out the coins, tuck the mace into his pocket with his other purchases, and thank the peddler before turning to face his new maid-of-all-work. He hadn't seen her in the handful of days since he'd let his new rooms. It developed that she lived in at the boarding house just across the street, and came by two days out of the seven. Mrs. Pengilly had represented it as a blessed economy for both houses, and John had hidden his disappointment.

The young woman was even prettier outdoors, pale face reflecting the gray autumn daylight and brown hair soaking it in. In her drab bonnet, gray gown and dark pelisse, she suggested an apparition glimpsed and gone, a fleeting impression of dark and light a man might spend his whole life trying to prove he'd seen.

"Very well, and yourself?"

"Pretty tightish." She carried a basket full of market produce over one arm, and a cabbage and two parcels under the other. The basket was a third her height, and two or three times her width. "Fresh vegetables make my cooking eenamost good. Mind you, don't listen to Madge Cattermole if she tells you her winter broccoli are the best. Tories will say anything. Mrs. Isted's are just as good, and her carrots are sweeter." She indicated the stall with a jerk of her shoulder.

"Eenamost" was a contraction of "even-almost", used by uneducated Sussex folk to mean "nearly". *I could teach you to speak better,* he thought, and was promptly ashamed of it. Elocution lessons would help her to work in a great house, but not everyone wanted that. She seemed content where she was. "Thank you. I'm quite fond of pickled carrots."

"Brine all the flavor out of them, why don't you?"

"Your name wouldn't happen to be Mary by any chance, would it?"

Her eyebrows were short and flyaway, set wide enough not to touch the bridge of her nose when she frowned in puzzlement. With her pointed chin, they made her face seem not even heart-shaped, but outright triangular.

Then her mouth, already a touch crooked in repose, curled into a twisted half-smile so engaging as to seem a carnal invitation. "Because I'm contrary, you mean? I suppose I am, at that. But I was baptized Susan Grimes. Everybody calls me Sukey."

The name suited her. In France, she would be a Suzette. If he'd met her as a French lady's maid, he might have acted on this attraction. He bowed slightly. "A pleasure to meet you, Miss Grimes."

She looked touched and amused, as if she thought a show of respect for her sweet but a little ridiculous. "Thank you, Mr. Toogood. I'll see you Friday, then."

"If you'll wait for me to finish here, I'll carry your basket." His neck heated.

She looked indecisive. "Will you be long? Mrs. Humphrey don't like me to dawdle."

"I shall hurry," he promised. Hopefully she would think it manners and not eagerness.

"Well, I'd be a fool to turn that down, and my mother didn't raise any fools." She shifted the heavy basket on her arm and teased, "Maybe I'd ought to buy a few more potatoes."

Potatoes: the only thing denser than cabbages. John didn't react. "By all means. Where shall I meet you?"

"I'll be staying warm by the hot-gingerbread woman." A heavy drop of water fell from the sky and landed on her hand. "Or crowding under the Market Cross if it rains."

John hesitated a moment before offering her his umbrella, thinking regretfully of the damage to his wool overcoat if it were to be soaked.

"Of *course* you've an umbrella." She shook her head admiringly. "You keep it. I'll be all right if I can get to the Market Cross ahead of the crowd."

Before he could insist, she made for the ancient stone canopy. She went swiftly, for she gave herself no fashionable airs and wore thick-soled leather boots. Her stockings were undyed blue-gray worsted, her petticoats muddy and none of them a shade approaching white.

Her slim, tapering calves only appeared daintier emerging from her heavy boots. *She's a pharisee come to play tricks on me.*

Well, if she was a fairy disguising herself as a lowly maidservant to see what treatment she received at the hands of mortals, hopefully John's manners would earn him a gift. Human men ensnared by fairy women never ended well, but they enjoyed themselves along the way. Seven years in a green bower with her, drugged on fairy wine and subject to her delightfully cruel whims, would indeed pass like a day.

Before he could imagine much more than summer heat, her wicked smiles and tumbled hair and bare skin twined in grass-green silk, he set the fancy aside. Sussex fairies were a diminutive race who labored, drank beer and sweated; they had little in common with Sir Walter Scott's seductive elves. And it would serve a valet very ill to be cursed to speak nothing but truth, like poor Thomas the Rhymer.

A memory surfaced, of his father catching him listening to the maids' fairy stories at Tassell Hall and correcting his laziness and credulity with a fresh willow switch. He'd never heard how that tale ended. It had been something about a man who laughed at some pharisees, and nothing ever went right for him again. Maybe Miss Grimes would know the rest of it.

It was strange to remember that he'd believed the stories then. How old had he been when he stopped?

Don't let me ever hear you use the word pharisee, either, his father had said. It was an ignorant word—the product, presumably, of an ancient and widespread confusion between the Sussex double plural *fairieses* and the Christian gospel— but John liked the way it sounded.

He'd never hated the pain of the switch as much as the humiliation of being forced to present his naked buttocks.

Why should he think of all that now, when it was decades ago?

A drop of rain darted past the brim of his hat and splashed against his nose. John shook himself, laughing at his own distraction, and hastened to finish his shopping.

Chapter Two

There was a hole in Sukey's glove. Absently, she pushed it down until her bare fingertip protruded, then pulled it straight again, guiltily aware her fidgets were widening the hole.

She would have been home quicker and drier if she'd gone alone, instead of tarrying about while Mr. Particular haggled over his vegetables. He had a good face for haggling, didn't he? Unflappable. He looked liable to outwait stone.

But his smile was lovely, even if he seemed afeared it would wear out with use.

Sukey Grimes, why do you always crave the ones who are a challenge? Why can't you like easygoing lads who'll kiss the ground you walk on and laugh at all your jokes?

Actually, when she put it like that, she supposed she was keeping herself out of harm's way. If she fell for an openhearted man who adored her, what was to stop her bedding him? Marrying him? And Sukey didn't plan to marry.

Mr. Toogood raised one eyebrow at Mrs. Isted. Just a little incredulous curl at his left temple. That was a joke, that was. Mrs. Isted busted out laughing, and Sukey laughed too, even though the joke wasn't for her.

She wished it was, so badly her stomach hurt with it.

Marriage don't make you any less lonely, she reminded herself, turning her attention back to her worn glove. Anyone with eyes or ears knew that.

Sukey's aunt had told her once that her mother had been bright and laughing afore she married. That she'd dressed herself fine as fivepence. Sukey couldn't picture it.

"Miss Grimes."

Sukey started. "Mr. Toogood?" Lord, his voice had as many layers to it as the Dymonds' French wedding cake. She'd like to put a hand on his broad chest and feel it echo around before coming out his mouth.

Probably she'd have to slip her hand inside his shirt to feel anything. His skin would be hot and—smooth or hairy? Her fingers curled.

"Are you ready to return home?"

She held out a hand for his basket, so he might carry her larger one. He gave her his umbrella and took charge of both baskets. Domineering, wasn't he? It would serve him right if she held the umbrella over *his* head, but if she did that, great cold drips of water would run down the umbrella's ribs onto her shoulder and ear. She wasn't contrary enough for that, even to see the thwarted look on his face. She tucked the handle into the crook of her elbow so she could cradle the cabbage and wrapped-up herrings in her arms. "I'll never need a stepladder when you're around."

He set off towards home without asking what she meant. No doubt with that height, he took her meaning at once; people must ask him to fetch things off high shelves all the time.

"Are you from London, then?" she asked, nearly dancing along in the luxurious freedom of walking home from market without rain in her face and a heavy basket dragging at her arm. *It's not so bad*, she always thought, and then the last fifty feet were an agony that drove her to bargain with God.

He gave her a startled look. "My parents are the butler and cook at Tassell Hall."

The Tassell family seat was near Chichester, if she remembered aright. As far off as London, but in nearly the opposite direction. "I'd never guess you were from Sussex." What a shame! A homey burr would sound wonderful with that voice.

He didn't answer.

"You've been to London, though, haven't you?"

"I've accompanied my gentlemen there on many occasions, yes."

"What's it like?"

He considered. Water dripped from the brim of his hat, narrowly missing his jutting nose. She didn't understand why desire coiled hot in her belly at the sight. Somehow, she liked that he wasn't looking at her, that his amber eyes were focused like a hawk's in another direction entirely. "Loud. Sooty."

She waited, but that was all. "You aren't much helping me, are you?"

That seemed to strike him as funny. His forehead smoothed out and the corners of his mouth tucked in, hiding a smile. "I'm carrying your basket."

"So you are," she agreed, delighted anew by his unexpected willingness to joke. "I meant at making conversation."

"My apologies. Perhaps I might carry the groceries, and you might carry the conversation?"

What could she talk about all the way home that wouldn't require his participation? "I could tell you a fairy story, if you like."

His smile peeked out. "I don't believe in fairies."

"See if any help in *your* kitchen, then."

"Do they help in yours?"

She laughed. "I like to think so. There's *something* lives in my kitchen, anyways. It's forever moving the teaspoon from where I set it, and blowing on the coals, and drinking the last few drops of rosewater."

"Perhaps you'd do better without it."

"Hush! My bread would never rise again."

He eyed her, trying to decide if she meant it. He thought her a stupid country girl, that much was plain.

"Too clever and modern for your own good, aren't you?" she said. "You'll believe in God, I suppose, but nothing else out of the common way?" The thought struck her that maybe his chivalry wasn't chivalry at all, but courting. Maybe he thought her so far beneath him, he could ask her for a tumble without it hardly being an insult.

Had she been foolish, treating him friendly? She had to go into his rooms to clean them, and Mrs. Pengilly was going deaf. If he guessed she'd been happily imagining him poking her, he'd never believe she didn't want him to really do it.

His only reaction to the edge in her voice was a slight raising of his brows. "At Tassell Hall," he said drily, "maidservants who excel at their work sometimes find that the fairies have placed a silver coin in their shoe."

That was aimed at her, she supposed. He'd put her down as lazy, only because she'd left some dust in an empty set of rooms. Here she was suspecting him of designs on her virtue, and he lectured her like a disobedient child. The wash of relief left Sukey deflated. "Because raising a girl's wages would be too simple," she muttered.

"I see you've guessed the stratagem. It's an open secret that my mother distributes the coins at Lady Tassell's behest, but the custom is cheaper than raising wages, and results in a deal more gratitude."

Mrs. Humphrey also set great store by gratitude, so long as it was other people's to her. Sukey tightened her grip on the cabbage. Mrs. Humphrey would inspect all her purchases when she got them home, and ask how much she'd paid. Her mistress wasn't a bad woman, just a nipcheese, but Sukey wished she was more grateful for her maid-of-all-work's forbearance.

"Here we are," she said, in a worse mood than when she'd left. "Thanks for the help. I'll see you Friday." She held out his umbrella.

He gave a slight bow. "Thank you for the company. I'll carry this into the house for you, if you like."

She glanced towards the front windows of the boarding house. The curtains were shut for warmth, but that didn't mean no one was peering through. In the wintertime Mrs. Humphrey kept a meager fire in the parlor, and the boarders crowded in. "My mistress wouldn't like it."

He handed the basket over without argument, settling the umbrella on his shoulder as if he weren't already wet through. "Until Friday, then."

Sukey went in, setting the herring on the table. She rifled through the basket as she heaved it up after, to see what needed drying off.

"Who was that man you were dawdling outside talking to?" Mrs. Humphrey demanded behind her.

Sukey jumped and dropped the cabbage. Heart racing, she caught it inches from the ground and rose, clutching it to her bosom, shoving the teetering basket more securely onto the table with her shoulder. Mrs. Humphrey made the sound that caused her friends to sometimes call her Mrs. Harrumph behind her back. "Got a guilty conscience, have you?"

"No, ma'am. I beg your pardon, but you startled me." Sukey set the cabbage down and began laying the vegetables out on the table.

"I suppose that *man* is why you're late coming home from market. All my ladies remarked on it. Remember that this is a respectable house, and your behavior reflects upon all of us. Mrs. Stickles on Forest Road told me she was obliged to let her girl go, only for drinking a pint of ale with a footman staying at the Lost Bell."

Sukey would lay odds that if any of the boarders had remarked on it, it was only to note that Mr. Toogood was handsome. But she swallowed *I didn't dawdle outside even a bit.* She *had* waited at the market. What if someone had seen her and mentioned it to Mrs. Humphrey? She'd have to say she hadn't wanted the groceries to get wet, and likely Mrs. Humphrey would point out that a little water never hurt a cabbage yet.

She'd ought to have come straight home. Why did prudent thoughts always come when it was too late to do any good? One of these days the boarding-house mistress would stop gloatingly hinting at giving her the sack, and do it. Before Sukey, she'd never kept a maid past six months. "I'm sorry, ma'am, I tried to be as quick as I could. That was Mrs. Pengilly's new lodger I was speaking to, who used to be Mr. Dymond's valet."

Mrs. Humphrey's eyes narrowed. "And you'll be tidying up for him?"

"Yes, ma'am, as he lodges with Mrs. Pengilly."

"Lent you his umbrella, did he?"

"Yes, ma'am. He seems a very polite fellow."

Mrs. Humphrey turned a potato over in her hands, checking for sprouts. "Well, be careful, girl. He was giving you the eye. Men never do favors for free, and Mrs. Pengilly is deaf as an adder."

The general tang of fear in the kitchen turned sharp and metallic, slicing Sukey's throat as she breathed in. "I'm afraid I was thinking the same thing, ma'am."

Mrs. Humphrey set down her potato with a thump. "Wait here." She returned with a large wooden rattle of the sort carried by the constable and night watchman. "Take this with you. I'll listen for it."

Tears pricked at Sukey's eyes. *Don't be a sap,* she told herself, but it was no good. She felt grateful. "Thank you, ma'am. It's very kind of you."

Her mistress harrumphed and picked up the next potato.

* * *

Sukey let herself into Mrs. Pengilly's kitchen just after dawn on Friday, yawning.

"Good morning, Miss Grimes."

Sukey, half-asleep, nearly dropped her basket. At this hour Mrs. Dymond would be in bed with the covers over her head. But Mr. Toogood stood wide awake at the kitchen table, fine clothes covered by a truly enormous apron, rolling out dough in his shirtsleeves.

How would she have explained it if Mrs. Humphrey's rattle had spilled out from under her dusters and rags? "Good morning, Mr. Toogood."

He'd swept out the hearth and laid a good strong fire. "I know you normally do some cooking for Mrs. Pengilly and her lodger, but as I'm at loose ends, I've arranged to do that while I'm here. I've cleaned my rooms too, so when you're done with hers, if you'll come down here perhaps we can give her kitchen a…" His eyes smiled and that eyebrow curled a little. "A spring cleaning."

He was waiting for her to tease, *But it's November.* Yet her heart dripped down into her boots, that he was poking around doing her work better than she could and thinking to himself that *she* ought to do it better. To top it off, he looked crisp as a new banknote, and she'd barely remembered to comb her hair before jamming her cap on her head.

She turned away, pretending to fuss with the tie of her bonnet, and wiped sleep from the corners of her eyes. "There's only so much you can do in two part-days a week." Too early for archness, her words came out sullen as an infant. Sukey dwelt longingly on her pallet and blanket. "Mrs. Pengilly's never complained."

He faltered in his rolling. "I didn't mean to offend. I thought it would be something nice to do for her, and spring cleaning is always more cheerful with company."

She supposed that was all right. "Spring cleaning is never cheerful," she said, more to give him the chance to contradict her than because it was true. She'd never admit to it—getting excited about your work was for shoelickers like John Toogood, Gentleman's Gentleman—but spring cleaning was almost like a holiday, wasn't it?

He scraped up his dough and lifted it gingerly into the pie plate. "It used to be my favorite time of year at Tassell Hall."

"Better than Christmas?"

His eyes widened a fraction of an inch to signify being appalled. She didn't understand how he made that so droll. "Do you have any idea how drafty a country house is in December?"

"None at all." But she snickered about it all the way up the stairs, rich folk freezing their bums off in houses too big and gleaming for sense.

Sukey was unsurprised, when Mrs. Pengilly rose from her bed, to discover that she was charmed by her new lodger too. "A fine figure of a man, isn't he?" The old woman's eyes sparkled. "So tall."

Sukey winked at her. "He's got his coat off in the kitchen. Or he did an hour ago."

Mrs. Pengilly cackled happily. "Miss Starling told me he carried your basket home from the market."

All my ladies remarked on it, Mrs. Humphrey'd said. Miss Starling didn't mean any harm, but Sukey would thank her to mind her own business. She waved a hand. "You know men. Never forgo an opportunity to show off."

"Yes, for a girl they fancy."

"Oh, for goodness' sake." But part of her wanted to ask, *Has he said anything about me to you?*

"He's not as strong as my Harry was," Mrs. Pengilly said with satisfaction. "Harry could carry me from here to the Market Cross and not get tired."

Sukey laughed. "I expect there's less call to be lifting barrels in valeting." Harry Pengilly used to say he worked in shipping, but everybody knew he was a smuggler. Sukey still remembered her father pulling her close when they passed him in the street, whispering to her not to stare at his broken nose.

A knock came at the door. "It's Mr. Toogood. I've brought you a slice of onion pie."

Mrs. Pengilly beamed. "An excellent cook, that young man," she confided loudly to Sukey.

His landlady either didn't realize John could hear her through the door or didn't care. He tried to remember the last time anyone had called him a young man. Oh, he shaved closely enough to hide the gray in his beard, but…

It made him smile, how when he was younger it had been his heart's desire to look older, and at forty he was pleased by an old woman calling him "young man".

Mrs. Pengilly opened the door, looking like the cat that ate the canary. She was as proud as if she'd found such a useful tenant through her own shrewd practice, not happenstance and her maid's enterprising nature.

John held out the plate with its generous slice of pie, but she waved him in. "No, no, break your fast with me, sir. Sukey and I would be glad of some masculine company, wouldn't we, dear?"

Miss Grimes looked up from her silver polishing with a sunny smile. "Oh yes, and see that you don't roll down your sleeves."

An electrical shock ran through him, his body understanding before his mind did that she meant she wanted to ogle his arms.

Mrs. Pengilly laughed uproariously, and he realized that it was likely she who wanted to ogle, and Sukey was only playing along. "As you wish, madam," he said, ignoring their amusement. "I'll fetch another slice of pie. Mind you, it will be better when it's sat overnight."

"You know," Sukey said loudly as he ducked out of the room to fetch his pie, "I've been doing an imitation of a grand servant for years, and I never dreamed it would be so true to life." Was she pitching her voice for her hard-of-hearing mistress, or to tease him?

"Not much of a talker, is he?" the landlady said. "I'll see if I can get anything out of him." So when he returned, he answered Mrs. Pengilly's questions as briefly as possible, hoping to surprise a laugh—or at least a snicker—out of Sukey. But she kept her eyes on the silver.

"So you're from London, are you?"

Sukey had asked him the same thing. The corners of her mouth twitched, but she clamped down on them and didn't look up.

"Admiring my silver, eh?"

John started in his chair, and Sukey's cheeks flushed.

"Those candlesticks were meant for a duchess, you know," Mrs. Pengilly boasted. "Harry should have melted them down, but he knew how tickled I'd be to have them. Sukey, show him where Harry hammered out the coat of arms."

The maid was still, blinking hard. Were her eyes too bright?

"Are you well, Miss Grimes?"

She met his gaze. Too bright, without a doubt. "Yes, sir, tol-lol." She leaned towards him, tilting up the candlestick so a slightly rough patch caught the light. Her pale eyes warned him that if he said anything disapproving about what Mrs. Pengilly had just revealed, she'd cosh him over the head with it.

"Very nice. So your husband worked in…shipping?"

"Precisely." Mrs. Pengilly's eyes gleamed.

"That explains the ghost, then." Everybody he spoke to rushed to tell him about the woman who haunted his rooms with wailing and gnashing of teeth.

"Have you heard her?" his landlady asked.

So far he'd heard nothing but rain on the roof and the ping of water in the pot under the leak. "Not yet, but I'm sure she's there. Ghosts are very common in the homes of men involved in…shipping." And in their hidey-holes, and anywhere they didn't want people going after dark. Like the silver coins at Tassell Hall, it was too convenient to be credible. His eyes returned to Sukey by compulsion. Would she agree, or did she believe in the ghost?

The maid turned her back, rubbing the last of her fingerprints off a silver sauceboat as she settled it on the mantel. There was no way to guess her thoughts.

The row of silver gleamed and winked at him while she squeezed water out of dampened tea leaves, strewing them over the carpet to pick up dust. Tea leaves were entirely wrong for a carpet with so many pale patches; he could see the staining from where he sat. But she was quick and careful with her horsehair broom.

A cynic would say it was calculating and sneaky to do good work only where her mistress could see. But he judged it another sort of economy altogether: she apportioned her work where it would give Mrs. Pengilly most pleasure.

"That is a very handsome carpet, madam. How did your husband acquire it?"

"Aubusson," she said proudly around a mouthful of pie, not answering his question. Her blithe indiscretion of a moment ago seemed forgotten. "He knew I'd like it."

Beneath their chairs the carpet was protected by a sturdy green drugget, but she stroked it affectionately with her slipper through the serge.

Smuggling was a brutal business. John didn't delude himself that the late Mr. Pengilly's hands would have been anything but crimson, were the blood on them visible. But he and his wife had clearly loved each other dearly. John's parents, too, despite their differences, were like two pieces of a machine that no longer needed oiling, so smooth had they worn against each other.

When John was years in the ground, who would still think of him every day?

On market day he'd been fanciful, and today he was sentimental. But months cooped up with a silent master would make any man lonely. Perhaps instead of being wistful about a wife, John ought to look for a position in a married establishment, with a full complement of staff.

Sukey got on her hands and knees to go over the carpet with a clothes brush. Her bodice gaped, breasts small enough that he'd see her nipples if it gaped another inch. He averted his gaze, but out of the corner of his eye he still saw her turn, presenting her arse for his delectation.

He glanced as briefly as he could.

It was a slender, firm little arse, and her neat ankles were visible, her muddy boots changed for an ancient pair of slippers. He had a sudden vision of kneeling behind her to throw up her skirts and yank her bare buttocks against his hardness, while she shrieked with laughter and pretended to be indignant.

He stood abruptly. "Thank you for the company. I must get back to the kitchen before the beans stick to the pot." But he didn't go to the kitchen. It would be another half-hour at least before the beans began to stick.

No, he walked past Sukey's upturned arse and up the narrow stairs to his rooms, where he shut and latched the door. Mrs. Pengilly's loud voice carried through the floorboards, though not her words. So did Sukey's replies, pitched for her mistress to hear. Was he wrong in thinking he could still make out the muffled thuds of her knees on the carpet? Going into his bedchamber, he shut that door too, feeling distressingly visible despite the blanket he'd nailed over the window as a curtain.

Leaning against the wall, he opened his breeches and smallclothes. Too many buttons, damn it, surely they weren't all necessary.

With a smothered groan of relief, he took himself in hand. God, if she heard him, if she guessed—

Let her guess. Eyes closed, he slid down the wall until he sat on the floor, stroking himself with an insistent rhythm. He pictured the scene again, erasing Mrs. Pengilly without a qualm. Sukey and himself, tidying some room together, her on her hands and knees.

In his imagining they were old bedfellows, with no need to ask permission. When his knees hit the floor between her ankles, she'd glance over her shoulder, puzzled, but she'd only laugh at him when he threw her skirts over her waist, too impatient even to speak. He pulled her to him, his cock at her opening. *Someone could come in*, she said, her laugh breathless now.

I don't care. I have to have you. He drove into her.

She gasped and moaned, pushing her hips up higher. Accepting him, urging him on. She reached one hand past her bunched skirts to rub her fingers over her pearl. So eager already. *Harder*, she pleaded.

John pulled her towards him until she knelt upright, her back to his chest. Holding her tight with an arm around her waist, he pushed her bodice down to release her breast. Her nipple was small and brown and he wanted to taste it, but he couldn't reach so he rolled it between his fingers instead. She trembled as he fucked her hard and fast. He was so deep in her, so deep, taking her weight when her knees wouldn't hold her up. *Someone could come in*, she said again, but she frigged herself, moaning.

They'd see how much you like this, he said in her ear.

Yes, she gasped, *yes, I love it—*

John spent into his cupped hand.

He slumped, shaking, the wooden floor cold and unforgiving. Then he stood, washed his hands in the basin, and went downstairs to stir his beans.

Chapter Three

At eleven, Sukey finished in Mrs. Pengilly's rooms and went downstairs to the kitchen.

"Would you like a slice of pie?" Mr. Toogood asked, bland as ever.

She'd brought a hunk of cheese and some stale bread with her, but that pie was far more tempting. "Thank you. Aye, I'd love one."

He swallowed, his hand spasming on its way to the knife.

She squinted at him. "Be you well, Mr. Toogood?"

"Tolerably well, thank you." He glanced up at her with a frown, those light brown eyes boring into her. "And you? There was a moment upstairs when I thought you might be overset."

"There was?"

"When Mrs. Pengilly talked about her silver."

It had been hours, so it took her a moment to remember. "Oh. I—I worked for her two years afore I heard that story about the coat of arms on the silver. Even a year ago she'd not have told you. She grows forgetful, I think. Careless with age."

"Maybe she's only realizing that there's no longer much need for caution."

She nodded, seeing no reason to explain that Mrs. Pengilly's son was also in…shipping. Harry Pengilly junior liked to do more of the sailing, and was gone eleven months in twelve. "Maybe. I know it been't a grand tragedy for a happy old woman of eighty-five to become a little forgetful, but…"

"You're fond of her."

She nodded. "Are you fond of the Dymonds?"

"Of course." He said it without hesitation, and offered not a syllable more.

She shrugged and took a bite of her pie. Mmm. Roasted potatoes, sliced apples, hardboiled egg, onions and butter in a thick, rich dough. He really did know what he was about in the kitchen.

"Your boots could use a cleaning," he said.

She nearly choked on the delicious mouthful. "Beg pardon?"

"I could clean them for you, if you like."

She blinked, too surprised to even say "pardon" again. "Do you miss valeting that much?"

His face went blanker even than ordinary. "Cleaning leather isn't only for looks. It lasts longer when it's cared for, and needs less mending."

"I clean for my living," she said flatly. "On my day off, I'm not about to clean more."

"I didn't ask you to. I asked if you'd let me do it. If you'd prefer that I didn't—"

She threw up her hands. "I'd be a fool to turn you down."

"And your mother didn't raise any fools, or so I've heard." Not waiting for further encouragement, he fetched her boots from the door and set them on the table, going at the mud on them with a wooden scraper the size of a penknife. He made so finicky a job of it that he'd only finished one boot by the time she emptied her plate. As she was washing it, he said, "Would you begin by scrubbing the copper pots with lemons and salt, please?"

She sliced a lemon in two and dipped it in coarse salt, hoping he didn't notice she was near to mesmerized by his hands. Half the great copper kettle had been restored to a bright, pinkish shine before he'd finished scraping her second boot.

Next he set to brushing the leather with firm, careful strokes. "Were you born in Lively St. Lemeston, Miss Grimes?" He didn't raise his eyes from the falling particles of dust.

"Yes, sir."

"Have you any brothers or sisters?"

"No."

"Neither do I. Do you wish for them?"

Dunnamuch. She couldn't imagine the difference a sister or brother might have made to her when she was small and felt as if she and her mother could fall off the edge of this town with no one the wiser. She couldn't imagine the difference it would make now to have someone who shared her blood, who'd be with her through thick and thin, who'd help take care of Mrs. Grimes when she grew old.

"Now and again." She rinsed her kettle. "But it's a gamble, right enough. You can't rid yourself of a sibling, and from what I've seen, half of them are lovely and the other half so dreadful as to beggar belief."

"I suppose so." He sighed. "I've been reflecting that perhaps I would prefer my next situation to be in a house with more than one servant."

She looked up in surprise from feeling for stray grains of salt. Lonely, was he? Well, she supposed *that* wasn't much of a surprise, only that he'd admit to it. "One half-holiday a week isn't much to cram a life into," she agreed.

"No. At Tassell Hall, one was never alone."

Sukey wondered if she'd be happier in a house with plenty of other maids to gossip with. That was a gamble too, in her opinion. It might be nice, or it might be just more people making her eat carp-pie, more people to get her turned off without a character if they took a dislike to her, and more smiling and listening when she only wanted to put her head down and shut her eyes for half a tick. She was lucky Mrs. Humphrey had hired her, and she couldn't imagine trying to explain to her mother that she'd left because she was *lonely*. "I'm sure Mrs. Pengilly will let you hang around her as much as you please."

She was rewarded by an amused softening of his face as he came to fill a bowl at the sink. "Do your parents live here?" He stood politely at her elbow until she moved, instead of nudging her familiarly aside like an ordinary person.

"My mother lives just that way." She pointed. "She takes in laundry." He took that to mean her father must be dead, of course. She could tell by his face that he was puzzling over whether it would be impolite to say how sorry he was.

He went silently back to the table with his bowl, so she didn't have to decide between a lie and the truth.

"Do you see your parents much?" she asked over her shoulder.

Now he was scrubbing her boot with soapy water, neat round strokes with a little brush. "My mother and I exchange letters most weeks." He smiled at her boot, almost a whole smile. Her foot hurt with wanting him to hold it like that.

"I've sent her Mr. Dymond's pieces in the *Intelligencer*. She was always fond of him."

Mr. Dymond had been writing articles for the town newspaper on the terrible hardships of British soldiers in the Peninsula. The *Times* was sending him to Spain soon to write more of them. "My mum thinks the paper hadn't ought to print them. Her friend's son is in Spain, and the poor woman's been crying herself to sleep since they started." A thought struck her. "You didn't have to go with him, did you? When he was in the army?"

He shook his head, setting her boots down to dry. "I worked for his brother Lord Lenfield while he was away. Mr. Dymond is fond of joking that I would have had an apoplexy at the state of his clothes."

She laughed, relieved he hadn't been obliged to suffer the horrors Mr. Dymond described, and conversation fell off. Lemon juice stung her fingers as she restored the shine to Mrs. Pengilly's copper, while Mr. Toogood rubbed down the whitewashed walls.

But vigorous scrubbing, well…it got the blood pumping. Sukey was flushed and breathing hard, and all at once even looking at him seemed indecent. Muscles shifted under his breeches as he rubbed vigorously at a tomato stain that had been on the wall (Sukey reflected guiltily) since Michaelmas.

His big apron hugged half his wool-covered arse, leaving the central seam to her lustful gaze. He had one of the finer arses it had ever been her privilege to gawk at. The small of his back dipped nicely and then flared in a firm, commanding curve. *Even my arse is better than yours,* it proclaimed truthfully to the world. And the way it *moved…*

He turned away from the wall to pick up her boots. Face burning, Sukey dropped her eyes to the jelly mold she was cleaning. *I'd like a jelly mold in the shape of his arse.* She stifled a giggle. When Mrs. Grimes said hard work kept you warm in winter, this wasn't what she meant!

He opened a small tin, rubbing oil onto her damp boots with a bit of cloth. Catching her watching his hands, and thinking her curious as to his methods, he explained, "Neat's-foot oil and a bit of tallow." His voice as good as rasped across her nipples. She wanted him to look up from suckling at her breasts to calmly inform her of something in just that tone.

Examining the boot, he scooped a bit more oil out of the tin. "Don't use too much, for the leather needs to breathe. And always put it on when the shoe is still half-wet."

It set up some very peculiar feelings in her chest, the care he took with it. As if her old, ugly boots mattered. As if they were *precious*. Her merry lust turned wistful and aching. She couldn't remember the last time anyone had taken so much care with anything to do with her.

An old memory surfaced, of her mother combing her wet hair and cutting it carefully to bring out the curl, her fingers gentle in Sukey's scalp. Her hair had been golden when her mother used to do that. She'd thought Mrs. Grimes stopped because it grew dark, but looking back, her mother must have only been busy, finding herself on her own with a child to feed.

She drifted closer to Mr. Toogood, as if he could somehow make her feel like that again, safe and cherished and ignorant.

When she reached his elbow, he turned to look at her. Her mouth went dry. "How old are you?" he asked abruptly.

She froze. Why did he ask? How old was old enough for kissing?

She didn't want him to kiss her. Or, she did want it, but if she really *did* it, it'd make her a fool, and her mother a raiser of fools after all. "Two-and-twenty." She tried to sound unaware of any implications. Hopping up to sit on the edge of the table brought her a few inches closer to his mouth. *Fool.* "I made pickled carrots yesterday. The ladies devoured them."

He gave her that near-half-smile of his. A third-smile, maybe. "Did they?"

"Mrs. Peachey was the only one who didn't take any, and she won't eat anything that crunches."

He set her boot on the table, lips parting.

Please please, Sukey Grimes you're a fool, I don't care please, she thought.

"I'm sorry." His voice was about half again as deep as usual, and half again as gravelly. "My oil's to the other side of you." He might have said *You're the most beautiful woman I've ever seen* in the same tone and it wouldn't have been out of place.

"My afternoon off starts at three," she said, handing him his oil. "What would you like to do until then?" Her heart hammered in her ears.

He oiled one last dry patch and turned away. "They'll need to sit for a quarter-hour before I wipe away the excess. Then I can rub them with tallow." The front of his waistcoat was dark-patterned quilted cotton, but it was plain linen in back. She could see his shoulder blades bunch. "I think I've some sandpaper in my things. Why don't we clear off this table so we can sand away the knife-marks and oil it?"

A moment ago she'd been sure he wanted to kiss her too. He *must*. He'd— well, if he wanted it, he'd better self-command than she had, and she'd ought to be grateful for it.

Sukey was tired of being grateful. Of pulling back from boldness at the last moment. She was tired of keeping herself shut tight like a book no one wanted to read.

She'd seen some traveling players put on *The Sleeping Beauty in the Wood*, as a girl. She still remembered the princess's hand reaching for the spindle, enchanted and unknowing, while every child in Market Square shouted at her not to do it.

Sukey's hand came up ever so slowly and laid itself flat on Mr. Toogood's back, her palm just to the right of his spine. Her thumb touched one of the knobs in his backbone; she circled it, curious.

His muscles went rigid under her hand. Her sharply indrawn breath was the echo of his. "I'm old enough to be your father," he said.

She almost yanked her hand away.

But that wasn't a *no*. It was only an *I hadn't ought to*, and at the moment the difference between those two things was very clear to Sukey.

This was so stupid. She'd liked men before. She'd been slippery between her legs. But she'd kept her wits about her. Why couldn't she today?

It was those boots. He'd got her all soft and pliant with his hands on her boots, even if it was only because he liked things to be done properly and nothing to do with *her* at all, and now she didn't need any sweet words or petting to seduce her.

"I'm sure between the two of us we can contrive to make your cock stand, even so." She slid her hand down to the small of his back, eenamost to that flare she'd admired earlier. She hadn't quite the nerve to touch that.

When he's inside me, she thought. *When he's inside me I'll pull him closer with both hands.* God, she was on fire.

He turned towards her, cock obviously standing. She smiled, suddenly happy as well as eager, but he covered the smile with his mouth before she could finish it. His hand was flat on the table beside her, because he was too tall and had to bend to reach her. The other hand was steel around her upper arm. He growled, low and quiet like a dog giving warning, and she could feel him trembling.

So this was kissing. Real kissing, not just a peck on the lips. He tasted her upper lip, then her lower, the inside of his mouth scalding. She didn't know what she was doing, not really, but despite that growl he went slow enough to let her catch up. She shaped her mouth to his.

Somehow she'd never realized before what it meant, that their mouths would be touching, that she'd be so close to him. It was like last week's newspaper used for kindling, the past scorched over and gone in a blink, nothing left but bright blazing heat.

Something wasn't quite the way Sukey liked it. His mouth was open too far, she thought. So soon she discovered preferences! She held him still with a hand on the back of his neck so she could fix it. *She* kissed *him*, and he let her. His hair was soft. When she stroked the short bristling hairs at the nape of his neck, he moaned right into her mouth. That shocked her. She couldn't breathe for the thrill of it. She wanted—could she?—did she dare?—she tried to lick his lip. Catching the edge of his teeth, she faltered, feeling silly.

He broke the kiss, breathing hard. His light brown eyes stared into hers from too close. She had a dizzy fancy that he wasn't looking at her so much as letting her see right into him. She tightened her fingers on his neck for balance.

He ducked his head, leaned in and growled—there was just no other word for it—in her ear, "I brought myself to completion this morning, thinking of taking you."

She gasped. He'd *what*? Really? But there was nothing he could mean but frigging himself, was there? So when he'd gone upstairs after he left Mrs. Pengilly's, he'd... It was hard to imagine him doing anything so undignified, but of course he must. He *had*. Thinking of *her*.

And now he was telling her about it. She'd never felt anything like this wild pounding of her blood, spreading from her heart down her arms and into the soles of her feet and *there*, there between her legs.

"Do you understand me?"

She laughed a little wildly. "I may be a virgin, but I'm not *ignorant*."

He drew back, her fingers sliding from his hair and falling into her lap. "You're a virgin?"

Sukey glared at him. "Why wouldn't I be?"

John ran a hand through his hair. It was a mistake; his scalp was still sensitized. He spent half his life with his hands in other men's hair, but he couldn't remember the last time anyone had touched his. His skin had hummed and prickled delightfully under her fingertips.

Her virginal fingertips. "I don't—I just—I'm not taking a girl's maidenhead in a *kitchen*, for Christ's sake." His voice rose alarmingly.

She glared harder, those tip-tilted eyes narrowing. "I'm sorry I didn't bed half a dozen strapping young lads to make this moment more convenient for you," she hissed. "How inconsiderate of me!"

She might remind him of a spitting kitten, but she was two-and-twenty. A grown woman, and a strikingly appealing one. And now to find she'd waited all this time, for *him*? She'd made no bones about thinking John a square-toed stick-in-the-mud. "Why me?" he asked. "A girl like you—"

"And what kind of girl am I, pray?" She crossed her arms over her chest.

So square-toed that she assumed he must be calling her a trollop. "A very pretty one," he snapped. "I presume you've had offers. Christ, I can't believe I told you I'd—" He couldn't repeat it. This was the trouble with lust. It was worse than aqua vitae for loosening the tongue, and a man did and said things he'd never have dreamed of in a less fuzzy-headed state.

Reluctantly, her mouth curved. She tossed her head a little. "So what you're saying is I could have any man I like."

Their mouths were linked now. His curved in sympathy. "Well, I don't say *any*. That would be hyperbole."

It was plain on her face she didn't know what the word meant. But she said, "You're not so bad yourself." She hooked a foot around his legs, pulling him towards her, and Lord, he wanted to go.

He tilted her head up. It was a mistake. The underside of her pointed chin was sinfully soft. The ruffle of her cap lifted and settled, wisps of hair at her temple moving as if someone had blown on them. He wanted to blow on every inch of her. If he wasn't careful he'd say *that* too, and she'd die laughing at him.

"Miss Grimes, I'm sorry. I'm not saying this because you're a virgin. That only startled me, and gave me a moment to think of what we'd be doing. You work in a respectable house, and I am seeking a position, perhaps in a household with maidservants. Neither of us could afford the damage to our reputations if somebody walked in and saw us."

She sighed, letting go of him with a sad little nod. "I expect you're right."

John took up one of her boots and wiped away the streaks of excess oil gleaming on the surface, feeling a self-indulgent pang of disappointment. It was fortunate that virtue was its own reward, as few other rewards seemed to accompany it.

But he was only sulking. Virtue had many rewards. Take, for instance, the virtue of caring properly for one's boots: warm, dry feet, and money in one's pocket that one was not obliged to spend on new boots. The rewards of not dallying with the neighbor's housemaid were likewise self-evident and innumerable.

No, the proverb had it backwards. *Sin* was its own reward, its *only* reward. Its dreadful consequences lasted longer than any momentary satisfaction. He began to apply tallow to her boots, to keep off the water. It would have to dry for two hours.

Two hours he was trapped here with her, polishing this bloody kitchen to a shine. Perhaps it would be kinder to leave her to polish alone. But he'd been born into service; he could not idle while others worked.

She hopped off the table, not looking at him. "I suppose I'd better get to scouring."

"I think that would be best," he said quietly.

* * *

Storm clouds were rolling in. John sighed. Thus ended a few glorious drizzling hours during which water had dripped into the bucket in his parlor no more than once or twice a minute. This morning's unseasonal thunder had sounded like cannon, as if the Channel had overflowed its banks all the way to Lively St. Lemeston, and the French fleet were firing upon the town.

He pressed his face to the damp, chilly pane of his bedroom window, eying the rapidly approaching dark clouds. It was too early to begin dinner, but John couldn't bring himself to write one more polite note of thanks. His little table was littered with replies from Lord Lenfield's friends. Every letter said, *I'd feel uneasy, hiring a man the Tassells have turned off.* Not always in so many words, but the meaning was clear.

Some of those gentlemen had tried to bribe John from his place, once upon a time, but he'd been satisfied where he was and refused every offer with a virtuous pride that embarrassed him now.

A flicker of movement in the street below caught his eye. Sukey Grimes with an empty basket, gazing apprehensively up at the sky and walking towards the edge of town as quickly as she could without running. What in blazes was she doing out in this weather?

He ought to leave her alone. He'd expended the cunning of a Machiavel in not crossing her path since that disastrous Friday afternoon. But surely no errand could justify going out when such a storm threatened, unless it was to fetch a doctor. He threw on his greatcoat and hat and raced down the stairs with his umbrella.

Once in the street, he was conscious of several pairs of respectable female eyes in the boarding-house window. He waited to catch Sukey up until they were out of sight. "Good day to you, Miss Grimes."

She turned in disbelief. "Mr. Toogood? You'd better get back inside before the heavens open. Your lovely wool coat will swell."

"I had been trying not to think of that."

"What are you doing out of doors?"

"I saw you from my window. What errand could possibly be important enough to go out in such weather? You'll catch your death."

She shook her head. "It's St. Clement's Day. Didn't you hear them firing the anvils this morning? I've got to fetch apples for the blacksmiths."

St. Clement was the patron saint of blacksmiths, who celebrated their saint's day with zealous carousing and "clemmening", or parading from house to house collecting gifts of apples and beer. A bowl of apples had been waiting on Mrs. Pengilly's kitchen table for three days. "Firing the anvils?"

"Don't they do that at Tassell? The smiths put gunpowder in their anvils and set it off to frighten evil spirits." She smiled. "The horses hate it, but I always liked the noise."

Such quaint, pastoral customs. He wondered how many fingers had been lost in honoring them. "Give me your money and wait here. I'll buy the apples."

She snorted. "Am I going towards town? I haven't a penny. I'm to pick the apples."

"Pick them?" he demanded in disbelief.

She tied her bonnet on tighter and put her head down. "Mrs. Humphrey doesn't spend a farthing she been't obliged to."

"Surely she wishes to avoid the expense of calling the doctor for you."

"She don't think so far ahead. Miss Starling told me the first year she opened the house, Mrs. Humphrey didn't give out apples or beer at all. Said the blacksmiths weren't entitled to take food from the mouths of her lodgers simply because they'd decided to have a holiday. She was sorry when a clinker came through the front window and she'd new glass to buy."

"A clinker?"

She blinked. "Is that a Sussex word too?"

He pressed his lips together and didn't remind her that he was from Sussex.

"It's these sort of paving stones." She pointed at the small, hard bricks beneath their feet. "There's an apple tree a mile down the road. It's a favorite with little boys, but I'm taller than they are, praises be. I can generally reach a few they can't."

She meant to climb a tree in this weather?

"And your mistress knows you are on your way to go clambering about the upper regions of a tree in the blinding rain?"

Sukey nodded. "She were hoping the sun would come out, but it hasn't, and if I don't go now, it will be dark."

"This is madness. I'll buy you apples."

"I'd get the sack if I let you buy me apples," she said flatly. "No one would believe I didn't give you something for them."

"Then tell me where the tree is, and how many apples you require, and I will fetch them."

She gave him a pitying look. "When's the last time *you* climbed a tree?"

He'd been fourteen or fifteen. It didn't feel so very long ago, but looking at her smooth, youthful face, it struck him with great force that it *had* been. "I shall manage."

Her laugh had a nasty edge. "The branches would break under your great weight."

So she meant to go out on slender, slippery branches. "This is rank folly."

"No, rank folly would be losing my place by giving Mrs. Humphrey a piece of my mind," she said grimly. The wicker handle of her basket creaked under the pressure of her fingers, and he realized that she was not foolhardy in the least. She was frightened and putting on a brave face because she saw no alternative. "She wouldn't even give me an umbrella. Said I would let it turn inside out."

He held his over her head, silently.

"Thank you." She hunched her narrow shoulders. "But you should go back. You can leave me the umbrella, if you like." Her pelisse was too large, its upturned collar tailored to frame a profusion of linen ruffles she didn't possess. He could see water dripping down the back of her neck, plastering stray tendrils of hair to her cool, clean skin. He wanted to taste it.

"I like storms," he said calmly. "I find them picturesque."

"Do you now?"

"I'm a very poetical fellow."

"It shows," she said wryly, and let him take the basket. She stuffed her fingers into her sleeves, shivering, and for a mad moment he thought of taking off his greatcoat to serve as a muff for her. But the day was too wet and cold to do anything of the kind, so he merely kept pace with her—she was in such a hurry that he barely had to slow his longer legs—and waited to see how far she could go in silence.

A hundred yards, as it turned out. "Last year Mrs. Dymond came with me to pick apples," she said, a little sadly. "Mr. Dymond will take good care of her, won't he?"

"I have no doubt she is indoors at the moment, if that's what you mean."

She gave him an irritated look, her wet eyebrows small dark slashes in her white face. "It isn't."

He didn't know why her worrying over Mr. Dymond's wife should annoy him so much. "You would do better to save your tender concern for yourself. You are far more in need of it than Mrs. Dymond."

"I don't suppose anyone is in *need* of my concern," she said, heartily offended. "I can still bestow it where I like, I hope. You needn't behave as if I'm a loyal family retainer like you. Mrs. Dymond was a friend, of sorts. Someone to talk to, anyway."

John set his jaw, comprehending now why he was so annoyed. He had *never* wanted to be a loyal family retainer. He had liked and respected the Dymond family, certainly, and hoped to like and respect his next master. He hoped to achieve excellence in his field. He wanted his talents recognized and made use of to their full extent. But those were entirely different things.

His parents, on the other hand…they had always behaved as if they were the Dymonds' tender guardians and not their upper servants.

"You can't understand how rare it is for a girl who talks as much as I do to meet someone who holds her own in conversation," Sukey said ruefully.

John looked at her in surprise. "I didn't think Mrs. Dymond talked as much as all that."

She laughed. "Not if she don't know you."

Suddenly, he remembered catching sight of Mr. Dymond and his wife walking down the street not long before their marriage, heads together, lost in conversation. It had struck John peculiarly at the time, for he'd known Mr. Dymond since his birth and would not have described him as talkative either. But they had seemed to have a great deal to say to one another.

"I don't talk much…" But more than that, he rarely said anything of consequence. He and his mother filled pages with their letters, but it was all news and gossip. That was how they liked it. So now he trailed off, not really knowing how to continue.

"I noticed."

He sighed. What was the use in trying? He'd always be silent witness to others' conversations, like a statue in a bustling public garden.

"Was that all?" she asked.

"I seem to lack the impulse to confide in others. Sometimes I regret that."

She didn't know what to make of that. "You're lucky," she said finally. "Talking only gets you in trouble."

Another memory, this one much older yet more vivid: the Dymond boys begging food from his mother in the Tassell kitchen, early one morning before breakfast. Young Lenfield had been eloquently persuasive, while little Master Anthony, the baby of the family, had been confidently demanding. Even Mr. Dymond, at seven or eight, had chimed in with a winsome smile and a playful question of some kind.

Where had John been? In the pantry, to judge by the angle of sight. Polishing something, no doubt, while his mother smiled at the Dymond boys and sliced into a warm jam tart. He must have been almost twenty, too old to envy children, so he had told himself he was annoyed by the noise, and by the disruption of his mother's orderly kitchen at the only time of day when the servants could hope to work without interruption.

"Has it got *you* in trouble?" he asked.

She looked away. "I've lost a couple of places for talking too much," she said softly.

Every good servant deplored a chattering maid, and yet he felt hot anger on her behalf.

"I suppose you think I deserved it."

"No. I was merely thinking that when one works as closely with one's employer as a servant does, it is as necessary for one's personality to please, as one's work."

She gave him a sharp look. He was sure she was thinking he had solved that problem by not having a personality, but he hadn't provoked her enough to make her say it.

Somehow, he wanted her to say it. He wanted to hear the arch note in her voice that would take the sting from the words. He wanted to hear it even if she left the sting in. "Perhaps one day you'll find a mistress who is glad to have you fill the silence in her life."

She stopped walking abruptly. "Here we are."

The unleaved tree was beautiful, wide and rambling and perhaps thrice his height. High above them, a few twisted, gleaming branches were yet bowed with clusters of bright yellow-and-red apples.

Having taken the tree's measure, John glanced down at Sukey, who was pulling off her stockings. Her boots stood empty—and, he was touched to notice, she had set her bonnet atop them to protect them from rain.

That flash of bare foot and ankle was a shock. It took several seconds for his thoughts to flow again. "Miss Grimes—"

"It's going to start pouring any second. You stand below and catch the apples so they don't bruise." She clambered barefoot onto a low branch and very carefully pulled herself up to sit on a higher one. He wanted to tell her to come down, but she was right. He was far too heavy to climb in her stead.

Unreasonable commands were part of their profession.

Her bare feet dangled, shivering. He wanted to warm them in his hands. In the fraught, idle silence, that desire grew into a daydream of kissing her ankles, gently sliding up her skirts to expose white, slender calves downed with dark hair.

"Catch." She tossed him an apple. The distance was small enough that he caught it with ease. Two more followed. The black clouds were nearly overhead, and the wind was picking up.

"How many blacksmiths does Lively St. Lemeston possess?"

Sukey strained for a particularly fat apple hanging just out of reach. "Two, but they bring their apprentices and boys with them. What they don't take, I'll make into stucklings." Sliding along the branch, she levered herself up and yanked the apple free just as the skies burst open with a deluge of rain, a fierce gust of wind and a blinding flash of lightning.

She lost her balance and fell, screaming and clawing at nothing.

Chapter Four

John's breath stopped, but somehow he lunged forward and she plummeted into him instead of the ground. His arms locked around her, and her hands went around his neck. His pulse thundered in his ears, the sudden rush of blood making him dizzy. His cheek was hot and raw where her buttons had scraped it. Her breath came and went in heaving, whimpering gasps. Was she shaking, or was he? Or was it only the freezing rain hammering down on them?

Thunder rumbled, recalling him to himself. "Can you stand?"

"Thanks to you." She wiped water from her eyes with one hand. The other was still tight around his neck.

Reluctantly, he set her on her feet. "We ought to find shelter before the lightning reaches us." Another bright flash. Already the thunder came sooner, more lightning on its heels.

She drew in a deep breath. "There's a farm that way."

He made out the shape, a few hundred yards off but distorted by the heavy rain. His hat had fallen when he caught her. He set it on his head and picked up the basket and folded umbrella. "Take your boots and run."

His hands full, his broad-brimmed hat blew off again almost at once. He ignored it with a pang, but she turned back. "Leave it," he called sharply. "Will you be struck down for a hat?"

Heedless, she chased it down for precious seconds, fingertips catching at the brim. She only gave up when a gust of wind sent it soaring into the air. Lightning came again, turning the world colorless.

He stumbled through the rain, praying that nothing tripped them up. The wall of the barn rose up before him, and he was plastered against it before he could think. The door was round the other side; with her help he got it open. They slipped inside, shutting the door behind them just as lightning and thunder crashed simultaneously.

The sudden absence of rain on his skin and in his eyes, the distancing of the sound of it, left him disoriented. Blinking, he made out the barn floor on which he stood, just large enough for a hay wagon. To his left was a hay bay crammed to the rafters, and on the other side, a row of cow stalls, with haymows above.

Sukey appeared before him, plucking the apples out of the basket he still held and examining them for damage. That done, she peered up at John. With her pointed chin and narrowed eyes, she looked like a drowned ferret. "You'd better get out of that coat," she said, shrugging out of her own.

Her kerchief and shoulders were wet and her skirts waterlogged about the hem, but the rest of her appeared essentially dry. Nevertheless, she was damp and cold enough that her nipples showed clearly through her clothes.

She gave him a little shake, hands on his elbows, and undid the buttons of his greatcoat. "Here now. Say something."

I can see your nipples, he thought. The greatcoat's fitted sleeves wouldn't come off unless he removed his gloves. The soaked leather clung to his fingers.

Sukey was examining her own pelisse. Assessing the damage, he supposed, as she lingered on a dry patch in the lining, but then she lifted it up over his head and rubbed his hair dry. He was so startled that he let her.

When the coat went away and he could see again, she was smiling. "It's a good thing there aren't any mirrors here. I think you'd have hysterics."

He sighed and worked his gloves free, spreading them over a bale of hay with his wet greatcoat. There was a hard object in one pocket. He pulled it free, puzzled, and recognized with dismay the slim second volume of *Count Julian*. He'd slipped it into the coat on Sunday, in case it rained and he needed to linger in church. The edges were soaked, already rippling. He pressed it flat between his hands for a moment before he could resign himself.

He tried to wipe his coat down with his handkerchief, but the square of linen was quickly soaked and the coat little improved. He knew already that the weave would never look as crisp as it had.

"I'm sorry," Sukey said quietly.

He wasn't. If she had fallen, without him—"One ought not to fret over trifles." He could do nothing now for his possessions. What could he do for their health?

Sukey had sat on a bale of hay and tucked her bare feet into her petticoats. Probably that would suffice to warm them. Probably what he was about to do was entirely unnecessary.

But he crouched down and drew out one damp foot, cupping it in his bare hands. The other peeped out from beneath her hem as she shifted to look at him. They were so small. Fairy feet, meant to dance in the moonlight. He traced her anklebones with his thumbs and pressed his fingers into the arch of her foot.

Calluses lined her sole and ridged her big toe. She was no fairy, but a hardworking woman. That did not lessen his excitement.

He let go her ankle and chafed her toes briskly between his cold hands for long moments before heat began to build. Relief flared in his chest as she sighed and leaned back on her hands. Her toes relaxed between his fingers. When he was satisfied, he did the same to her other foot.

He didn't meet her eyes. If he did, this would be seduction and not aid.

When he released her, she hopped up and fished her stockings out of her coat pocket. "Dry as a bone," she said with satisfaction, thrusting her hand down into the toe of one and rolling it up in preparation for putting it on. She hesitated. "I suppose you'd better turn round." He obeyed at once, trying not to think of legs exposed or garters being tied. Was there a sound more provocative than rustling?

"All right, I'm fit to be seen."

Her nipples still showed through her bodice, and while her shivers had subsided and her lips had lost their blue tinge, she was white, her back kept straight only by her stays.

He sat beside her. *This is common sense, and not seduction.* "We are both thoroughly chilled. As one cannot safely light a fire in a hay barn, our best source of warmth is each other, unless we wish to cuddle with the cows. I give you my word I will be all that is respectful, if you will trust me so far as to..."

"Sit in your lap?" she supplied, amused. "But someone could come in."

At once he was on fire, thinking of everything he could do to her while she sat in his lap. How he could bare her breasts and warm her nipples with his hands. How he could turn her so she straddled him and warm them with his mouth. How he could enter her.

He deliberately recalled how he had said to her, *I brought myself to completion this morning, thinking of taking you.* Embarrassment drowned his inconvenient arousal. "The choice is yours. But I should hate for us to catch our deaths through immoderate modesty."

"Now that's an improving tale for the ages." Sukey took off her wet cap. "I'd ought to bring it to Mrs. Dymond's attention." (That lady made her money, what there was of it, writing literature with a high moral tone for children.) She hesitated, then pulled a pin from her hair, evidently intending to take it down to dry. It was a good notion, and John supported it wholeheartedly.

Damnation, this was laughable. Either he should fuck her, or he should stop thinking about fucking her, because he was in no position to satisfy himself any time in the near future. He leaned over and took up his book. He found his place without difficulty, but it was an effort to take the words' meaning in along with their shape when he could hear hairpins clinking together in Sukey's palm.

"I don't like being cold." She dried her own hair in her pelisse.

"Neither do I," he agreed mildly. Who did?

"It's one of the things I like least about being a maid. They get to stay in their warm beds until I've lit the fire."

John himself had never minded that. Discomfort was unpleasant by definition, but he hated excessive heat far more than cold. He peeled the page away from the next one and turned it carefully. A scrap of paper came off in his hand. He sighed.

"I won't be cold when I don't have to be," she said, and climbed into his lap.

He spread his legs to accommodate her, thinking she would turn her back to him, but she stayed curled up, resting her cheek on his shoulder and drawing her legs up to her chest, the back of her heels against his outer thigh.

She tugged at her skirts until they flowed straight from her gown's high waist over her shins. Her knees pulled at the gown, tugging the bodice away from her breasts so he saw the drawstring of her stays and a dark, bottomless gap that showed him nothing but that might, in better light, have revealed the busk of her stays, the swell of her breasts, and her thighs.

Her back was icy where it touched his arm. Unbuttoning his coat, he wrapped it around her as far as it would go. Her unbound hair, imbued with her scent, spread damp tentacles over her shoulder and clung to his arm as he lifted it to continue reading. She smelled of ashes and damp wool, tallow soap and turpentine, clean rain and lemons and sweat and skin. Seductive beyond reason. If he bent his head, he could bury his nose in her hair.

He tried to keep his eyes on his book.

Sukey made believe that Mr. Toogood was a very lumpy pillow. It wasn't easy, as he kept shifting about, his arms moving as he turned a page, his chest rising and falling under her cheek. It took long, clammy minutes, but at last a comforting heat built between them. It had been so many years since she was a girl sharing a bed with her mother, she'd forgotten how much better another person was than any warming pan or hot bricks or leaning against the chimney.

Even so, she wished they had a blanket.

Light flashed from outside, and though she knew the roar of thunder was coming, it made her jump a bit and burrow closer to him. He shifted again, uneasily. Blood rushed to her face as she became aware of something hard poking at her hip.

He must know she'd felt it. Would he speak? Would he kiss her? She held her breath.

He turned a page in his book.

Oh, it wasn't fair! He wanted her, and she wanted him, and why *shouldn't* they? Why shouldn't he lay her down on this hard, scratchy bale of hay and stick that cockstand right into her?

But he'd already refused her once. That and the damp chilled her enough that she could remember Mrs. Humphrey's kindness in giving her the rattle. Her mistress, who didn't trust her with a twopenny bit, had had faith in her virtue. Her mother had striven to bring her up to be smart and careful. It would be letting them down if she gave away her maidenhead like any featherwit.

How smug Sukey had been when Mrs. Dymond's sister had found herself with child last month. How sure she'd been that *she* would never be so foolish. Even after Friday in the kitchen, she'd thought, *Well, I'll be on my guard now.* Forewarned was forearmed.

He had lovely forearms.

Didn't pride go before a fall indeed? Sukey knew she should be ashamed of her weakness. But strength felt like a burden just now. She didn't want to die a virgin. She didn't want to go home and lie alone on her cold pallet in the kitchen and hear the moon whispering outside about what fun everyone else was having.

"What are you reading?" she asked, to have something else to think of.

"*Count Julian: A Tragedy.* It's a play about medieval Spain and the Moors. Mr. Dymond gave it to me after he'd read it."

She'd guessed as much from the expensive binding. "Do you like it?"

"I do." He shifted, the muscles in his legs tensing and relaxing. "It reminds me of Lear: a man who loves his daughter, yet puts his pride above her and so destroys a nation. But the author hasn't Shakespeare's gift for a story. I would have found the plot murky if Mr. Dymond hadn't explained the history of it beforehand."

She sighed. "There's been talk of building a theater here. A real theater that real companies would come and perform in. But I don't suppose it can happen before the next election, and who knows when that will be." Nearly everything in Lively St. Lemeston was built by elections, Orange-and-Purple Whigs and Pink-and-White Tories buying goodwill and vying to see who could subscribe more generously to the building fund.

He lowered his book, one arm coming to rest at her lower back as he put his hands on his knees. "Don't give up hope." His voice hummed through her where her side pressed into his chest. *I brought myself to completion, thinking of taking you,* he'd said. "I know the project is dear to Lady Tassell's heart."

It was dear to Sukey's too. By rights she ought to spend the next ten minutes sweating him for every last bit of information he possessed. But she couldn't frame one question. She couldn't do this. "I'm much warmer. I think I'd better…"

A still, charged moment—and he leaned away, his arms spreading wide to allow her freedom of movement.

She got to her feet, retreating to a nearby bale of hay. The parts of her that had shared his heat were soft and vulnerable. They felt colder than the rest of her, longing to press themselves up against him once more. She darted a glance at him and met his piercing amber eyes as he buttoned his coat, hiding the fall of his breeches. She guessed he was debating whether or not to apologize.

She'd ought to apologize to *him*. He was only in this barn, soaked through and denied release, because he'd helped her.

Knowing that Mr. Toogood was hard with wanting her and could set it aside and go on being kind—knowing that he was ignoring his own desires the way she'd ignore an aching back or sore knees—every bit of her strained for a way to thank him, to show him he hadn't offended her. And after a few frustrated moments she remembered that kissing a man wasn't the only way to tell him you thought he was splendid. *I lack the impulse to confide in others*, he'd said. *Sometimes I regret it.*

"Did you see many plays in London?" she asked.

He nodded. "I enjoy the theater. Lord Lenfield was kind enough not to object to my absenting myself of an evening, provided I was home before him."

That meant more than once a week, then, or he might have gone on his half-holiday. "What was your favorite?"

He hesitated.

"Please. I've never been to a real theater."

"Do you ever think of going to London? There's always call for a maidservant there."

Sukey knew girls who had left Lively St. Lemeston for London. She'd heard no news of them after. Maybe they were living lives much like her own, except that on their half-holiday they could go to the Opera. But maybe they were standing on some street corner with their breasts out, or they'd died of cholera or had their throats slit by thieves and were nothing but bones now.

"You hear stories about what happens to good girls like me in London," she said flippantly. "I'd like a theater, but for music and lectures and the like, here's as good as anywhere. There's a servants' ball most months, and the fair comes twice a year. I don't know when I'd have time for more diversions than that."

He smiled, startled and a little amused, as if he'd assumed she saw her home as a noplace too. Why, she knew a dozen girls who'd come up to Lively St. Lemeston from the countryside, and opened their eyes as wide to see a ball at the Assembly Rooms as Sukey would at ships sailing up the Thames.

"You're a snob," she said. "But I forgive you. You couldn't help it, growing up in a grand house like Tassell Hall."

"Likely not," he agreed. "Very well, last month I saw an English opera about fairies, adapted from one of Shakespeare's plays." It wasn't easy, but she did get him to talk, at length with genuine enjoyment. Lightning flared outside, the thunder lagging behind by several seconds now. For the first time today, Sukey felt only the excitement of a thunderstorm when you were safe inside, the small thrill of uncontrollable power, no different than the blacksmiths firing their anvils.

* * *

John hadn't forgotten Sukey's story about the clinker through Mrs. Humphrey's window. When he heard drunken caterwauling in the back garden that evening, and drunken pounding on the kitchen door, he hurried downstairs to make sure there was nothing dangerous about this little St. Clement's Day procession. It would be easy enough to find an excuse for crossing the street and ensuring no one offered Sukey any disrespect.

But what he saw reassured him. The two blacksmiths—one of whom was a stout widow woman of fifty—and their journeymen, children, apprentices, and assorted grubby assistants appeared boisterously drunk but well disposed towards their fellow men, not inclined to take liberties with person or property.

Therefore, after they trooped out of the kitchen, John went to a nearby cookshop and purchased two bottles of wine. These and a glass he carried upstairs, intending to get drunk—and perhaps imagine a more agreeable sequel to Sukey in his lap than her taking refuge across the barn from his awkward erection. He hoped he hadn't frightened her.

Surely not. For the space of a moment last Friday, she'd thought to give him her virginity in the kitchen. Christ, he wanted to take it. He wanted her to trust him with it, when she'd trusted no one else.

She wasn't careless or fearless; he'd learned that today. She was only full of bravado, and if she talked him out of his objections with a saucy tilt of her head, it would mean she'd weighed the risk and thought it worth her while. He yearned to bring her to such a pitch of desire that she *demanded* he deflower her, that she swore never to regret it.

She hadn't thought him worth the risk yet. Why should she ever? John drove in the corkscrew with a savage twist, yanking the cork free and pouring himself a glass with such haste that wine spattered his cuff.

Abashed, he set the glass down without tasting it. Wine should be allowed to take flavor from the air. He could wait a quarter of an hour to be drunk.

Suddenly he was annoyed, that in lieu of such cheerfully bawdy imaginings as filled engravings discreetly bought in printing offices—the sort he had entertained about Miss Grimes just a week ago—she had somehow inspired in him this brutal yearning. The moon gazed in the window, pale and sad and very, very far away.

He gulped a mouthful of wine and shut his eyes, resolutely conjuring the memory of her slight, maddening body curled against his. He reached down for his already stirring cock, ready to make believe his own hand was hers.

Footsteps rang on the stairs. Heavy, booted footsteps. What the devil? And damn, damn, damn.

John crossed to the door and opened it, shocked when the boots turned a corner and revealed themselves to be carrying Stephen Dymond, Lord Lenfield, up the stairs two at a time.

His lordship broke into a smile. "It's good to clap eyes on you, Toogood. I hope I'm not in the way." His pause was no stratagem. If John said he was, he would turn and leave again with no hard feelings.

"Naturally not, Lord Lenfield. May I offer you a glass of wine?"

Lenfield's eyes lingered on the two bottles, unfortunately the one thing in the room clearly illuminated by the candle beside them. "You're sure you're not expecting guests?"

John kept his face blank. Of all the people he would have preferred not to see him preparing for maudlin drunkenness, Lord Lenfield topped the list. "I only just returned from the Full Pot, my lord."

Lenfield sprawled into the only chair. "In that case, I could use a drink." He ran a hand through his hair. It was a habit John deplored, the primary reason he had always kept his master's hair cropped short, so it could not be too far disarranged. His hands itched to fetch a comb and bring order out of chaos, but he wasn't Lord Lenfield's valet any longer.

He fetched a clean mug instead and poured wine into it. "It is not quite orthodox, my lord, but it will do for this vintage."

Lord Lenfield swirled the mug anyway, sniffing it absentmindedly. Then he gulped it down without tasting it. "Thank you, Toogood. How do you do?" His eyes bored into John's, full of the concentrated Dymond concern that, liberally aided by their wealth, had made his family patrons of a good part of West Sussex.

"Very well, my lord. And yourself?"

He leaned back in the chair, helping himself to another mug of wine. "Oh, Mama's on a rampage. Not that I blame her. I've spent all day trying to make Nick see that you can't simply stop speaking to your mother because she vexes you, and he—well, he's being Nick."

John was glad he was not expected to express an opinion. While he himself would certainly never give his father—who could rival Lady Tassell for vexatiousness—the cut direct, he was disturbed at his own lack of censure for Mr. Dymond's behavior. He detected, even, a hint of envious admiration within his breast of which he was decidedly not proud.

"It's going to be a grim Christmas without Nick or Tony. I thought this year, with Nick back from Spain..." Lenfield sighed, his blue eyes fixing on John again. "I'm damned sorry you've been caught up in this mess. I'd hire you back if she were merely angry, but her heart's broken. I want her to know I'll stand by her. It's hard on you. Hard on me too. I was looking forward to having beautiful linen again when Nick was back on his feet." His smile didn't reach his eyes. John knew he was conscience stricken. Dymond concern, as far as it went, was genuine.

"I was not wholly surprised by this turn of events," John said gently. "I shall manage."

Lenfield's mouth formed a thin, tight line. "Once again, Nick considers no one but himself."

"Perhaps he was considering Mrs. Dymond."

Lenfield tapped his fingers on his mug and then, unexpectedly, laughed. "I never took you for a romantic, Toogood."

Mere silence, when being teased, would be interpreted as affront. John made a slight show of amusement. *What an incongruous notion! I, a romantic!*

"You might have saved yourself a lot of trouble by writing to my mother to warn her of Nick's infatuation."

John nearly asked, *Would you have?* He honestly didn't know. The way Lord Lenfield managed his mother was complex. But a lifetime's habit prevailed, of silence whenever possible before a Dymond.

"Whatever Mother says, it does your loyalty credit." Lord Lenfield's mouth quirked up. "If not your common sense."

John did not quite like the idea of his actions being taken for those of a—loyal retainer, as Sukey called it. He had merely kept his own counsel, as was every man's right. Growing up as the butler's son at Tassell Hall and finding his friends among his father's underlings, John had learned early to shrink from any appearance of tale-telling.

As a young footman, he had worked closely with his parents, as Lord Lenfield did with his, and been continually obliged to weigh his loyalties and what he ought to divulge to whom. His father had wanted him to continue on at home and one day succeed him as butler, but unlike Lord Lenfield, John had declined to fall in with his parents' wishes for his future. Now his loyalties were his own affair, and he liked it that way. Lady Tassell controlled his wages, but that did not make his conscience her property.

Lady Tassell hadn't lived with Mr. Dymond in London. She hadn't woken her son, cooked his breakfast and placed it within easy reach when he could barely summon the will to sit up in bed and read a book. She hadn't made sure to leave the lid off the chocolate pot so the smell wafted to him. She hadn't coaxed him to shave, changed his dressings, or laid hot and cold compresses on his wounded thigh. She hadn't taken off his boots, pretending not to notice it was an agony to him because the poor boy's pride couldn't have borne that. Neither had Lord Lenfield, for that matter. John had.

For months Mr. Dymond hadn't wanted *anything* but to be left alone.

Until he met that impoverished widow.

"Thank you, sir," he said at last, and left it there.

"I did ask around the town after employment for you. Unfortunately I don't think many people leave their posts this time of year. The vicar is in need of a new butler, but he was adamant that only a married man would do."

"Mr. Summers, my lord? I was not aware he supported the Tassell interest."

"No, he's been a Tory all his life. But I think he's softened in his old age. He was loyal as a rock to Lord Wheatcroft, but now that Wheatcroft's in the ground, he was quite ready to be friendly."

The vicarage was a handsome, modern house of brick with white trim, and John had always liked Mr. Summers despite his Toryism. His sermons, while making little effort to be profound, were consistently both entertaining and full of good sense, which rendered them remarkable in John's experience.

Mr. Summers was old, and when the living fell, a new vicar might want new servants, but until then the position would likely be a secure one. A steady, quiet one too, with a modest staff and no traveling. No more sleeping on cots in dressing rooms or pallets on hotel floors.

John had never wanted to be a butler, but a small house was different from a great one. There could not be more than five or six servants in all. How much more difficult than valeting could it be?

He was seized with a desire to manage that neat brick house, akin to the senseless but overwhelming lust inspired by a beautiful object in a shop window. "I take it he requires a new housekeeper as well? I could inquire among my own acquaintance."

Lord Lenfield shook his head. "No, he specifically wants a married fellow. I gathered the previous incumbent was turned off for persecuting the poor maidservants, and he hopes a staid paterfamilias will suit better."

"Did he say how much the position pays, my lord?"

His lordship frowned. "Forty pounds per annum, I believe. Why, Toogood? Have you been hiding a wife?"

John smiled. "No, my lord."

Lord Lenfield chewed at his lip, hesitating. As John had refrained for four years from remarking on his master's uncharacteristic dithering at the mirror before a certain political salon—a connection, by the by, of which Lady Tassell would decidedly disapprove—it was only justice when his lordship did not pry. "Well, you might pay the Reverend Mr. Summers a visit and have a go at talking him round yourself. Meeting you ought to make further recommendation superfluous, but I've written you a reference. If you really want the position, you may tell Summers I should be grateful to him for considering you."

This, from one of the acknowledged patrons of the town, was a promise of great practical value. John bowed his thanks. Lenfield fished two sealed letters out of his pocket and laid them on the table. "The other is from your mother."

"Thank you, my lord. Was she well when last you saw her?"

"Quite well." Lord Lenfield pushed himself to his feet. "Your father…"

John's heart raced unpleasantly. He knew his father must be ashamed and angry at John's disgrace. "Yes, my lord?"

"He's growing forgetful and irritable," Lenfield said at last, reluctantly.

John swallowed. Such a decline would be so hard on his father's pride. "I see."

Lord Lenfield paid minute attention to the fall of his greatcoat sleeves over his gloves. "I thought you ought to know." A button on one cuff dangled loose. John shut his mouth tight and said nothing.

He didn't see what he could do. He couldn't make his father younger—or make him do anything else, for that matter.

"If you wished to visit him, I would help you to arrange it when my mother is from home."

Oh. Of course. Visit him.

He could imagine his father's mortified fury at having to sneak his son in and out of his beloved mistress's house when her back was turned. "Thank you, my lord. That is very kind of you."

"Well, I shan't impose on you any longer." The loose button wobbled as Lord Lenfield held out his hand. "You know where to find me. Should you be looking for a position again in future, please write. Mother's too fair-minded to hold a grudge forever."

John thought the odds were even on that question. But he gave a small, warm smile back and shook his former employer's hand.

Chapter Five

The back door to the vicarage was opened by a woman of about thirty, who introduced herself with a faint, unfamiliar accent as Nora Khaleel, the cook. She was tall and very pretty, with large dark eyes, warm brown skin, and a commanding nose. When John explained that he had come to inquire after the butler's position, her friendliness turned wary. "And is your wife with you, sir?"

"I am a bachelor, madam." John tried to sound deferential but firm.

Her mouth set.

The previous butler had treated the female servants ill, Lord Lenfield said. How ill? It wasn't pleasant to know she was looking him over for signs of depravity, but he supposed it was still less pleasant for her.

"Larry," she called over her shoulder. Leaning against the jamb, she watched him in silence, waiting until he was safely under the eye of another servant. John silently commended her care for the security of the house. In the absence of a butler, management of the household must fall to her, as Mr. Summers kept no housekeeper. He would have liked a glimpse of the kitchen, to see if she kept it clean.

Presently a heavyset footman poked his head in, wig askew. "Yes, Mrs. Khaleel?" The youth—blond, to judge by his eyebrows—would not have found employment in a grander house, being a few inches under six feet, but with his breadth he made an impressive sight in rose-and-gray livery. The gold facings might be dull and the silk stockings spotted, but those were minor infractions. And he spoke respectfully to the cook, addressing her properly as "Mrs." as befitted her position.

"Mr. Toogood, this is Larry, our footman. Larry, kindly escort Mr. Toogood upstairs and inform Mr. Summers that he is here to inquire after the position of butler."

Larry frowned. "Where's his wife?" He looked at John as he said it, with nearly a glare. Protective of the female staff; a point in his favor.

Mrs. Khaleel raised her eyebrows. "That's for him to discuss with Mr. Summers."

Ducking his head, chastened, Larry realized his wig was loose and hastily straightened it. "Sorry, ma'am. If you'll follow me, sir."

The hallway to Mr. Summers's study supported the conclusion John had already formed: the servants here did their work *just* well enough. Everything was clean and in good condition, but like the scratched heels of Larry's buckled shoes, it could use a good polish. There were more servants than strictly necessary in a household of this size—not unusual in the homes of widowers with married children—and that bred laxity.

That was promising. There was something for him to do, and as yet he had met no one with whom he would dislike to share a household. In fact, he found himself taking a liking to Mrs. Khaleel's shrewd gaze and Larry's goodwill.

It was a snug, comfortable house. Even the churchyard a stone's throw from the door seemed...like a home, reminding him how long people had looked to this house for help and guidance. John's senseless lust for this position was only growing. He tried to rein it in, reminding himself that first impressions often lied. Perhaps he was overlooking the telltale signs of discord, cold drafts and mildewed cellars.

He did see dust and scratched, dull wood in the study, but as Mr. Summers's papers and belongings were scattered everywhere, the servants were likely not to blame. The vicar himself bent over his blotter, scribbling away with great crossings-out and mutterings to himself. But when Larry gave him John's card, he took off his round glasses and straightened with a welcoming smile. "Ah, yes, Lord Lenfield's valet. Thank you, Larry, that will do."

John had never seen the vicar so near. He was perhaps seventy years of age, thin lipped, the skin around his deep-set eyes faintly purple. With the silver hair that remained to him cropped so close that John was impressed at his barber's skill, he resembled nothing so much as grinning Death in an allegory, wearing the same expression of shrewd cynicism and good humor.

John liked him at once. "It's an honor to meet you, Mr. Summers. Your preaching is remarkable."

The vicar folded his hands. "You flatter me, but I thank you," he said with a hint of a smile. "Lord Lenfield recommended you very high, but as he must have told you, I have determined to hire a married man. I regret to have wasted your time."

No. This interview could not be over so soon. "A married man may be a rogue as well as a bachelor, sir," John pointed out, with all the sincere respect at his command.

"Mm." The cavernous eyes crinkled. "But I find that nothing illuminates a man's character so effectively as observing him with his wife."

"Very wise, sir." John, momentarily distracted by guessing what strangers would think of his father after watching him with Mrs. Toogood, searched for arguments that wouldn't reveal that Lord Lenfield had shared details of Mr. Summers's domestic affairs.

"But you disagree?"

"I don't disagree, sir. But I would respectfully submit that any man may dissemble anything for the space of an interview, and so may his wife. Lord Lenfield has known me since his birth, and he speaks for me. I can produce further references as to my good character, should they be desired."

The vicar steepled his fingers. "Why are you no longer employed by Lord Lenfield, then?"

John felt the prickings of something like despair. This would be the sticking point everywhere. He had been proud of having spent his whole life in service to the Dymonds. He had thought it a great recommendation should he ever wish another place, that he had given satisfaction so long. Now he could point to no other employers, no other situation but the one that had been tainted.

"I rose to first footman in the Tassell household at six-and-twenty. I became Mr. Nicholas Dymond's valet when he went to university, served his elder brother for four years while Mr. Nicholas was in the Peninsula, and reentered his service in July. But he has decided to no longer continue the expense of a personal servant. As Lord Lenfield has replaced me, I find myself at liberty. Both brothers have given me references, and Lord Lenfield said I might tell you that he would be grateful to you for employing me." He drew the letters from his pocket and held them out.

Mr. Summers raised eyebrows so pale and sparse they nearly disappeared into his face. "Now that *was* tactful. It speaks well for your discretion, if not your honesty."

"I consider discretion preferable to honesty when discussing my employer's affairs, sir."

Mr. Summers threw back his head and cackled. "A Daniel has come to judgment! I see you would best me in debate, Mr. Toogood, but fortunately I am not required to justify myself to you. I don't doubt you are an excellent servant, and were you married, you would head my list of candidates. But as you are a bachelor, I can only wish you the best of luck."

John ought to thank the vicar and be on his way. Parliament had opened. The beau monde was in London. If he went to town now, he could surely find a situation.

Instead, he gave voice at last to what he had been turning over in his mind ever since Lord Lenfield said, *He's adamant only a married man will do.* "There is a young woman…" He didn't know how to finish the sentence.

Mr. Summers looked highly amused and waited politely.

"If I were to find myself betrothed, would that change matters?"

* * *

After a lengthy discussion of the house and staff and an inquiry into John's experience and his opinions on a variety of subjects, Mr. Summers promised that if he returned to ask for banns, he and his bride would be granted a second interview.

As Larry escorted him out, John caught a glimpse of two adolescent girls watching from a doorway, a round-faced blonde and a scrawny brunette. Realizing he had seen them, they ducked out of sight. John's heart gave a thump. Poor girls, waiting to discover what new tyrant had been set over them.

Sukey would be kind to them. At the thought, his heart thumped again.

He wanted very badly to put this fearful household to rights.

It was a pleasant daydream, but he had probably wasted an hour of Mr. Summers's time with it, out of pure stubbornness. Did he really want the position badly enough to marry Sukey? Did he want to marry Sukey badly enough to take the position, and resign himself to a provincial vicarage? Then too, if he married he could never again be valet to a bachelor in lodgings, which greatly narrowed the field. He had never wanted to be a butler. Why was he even considering it?

John brushed off his hat, put it on, and went home to bake bread for his and Mrs. Pengilly's dinner, considering it all the way.

* * *

Sukey was at the market, haggling over onions, when a deep, familiar voice at her elbow said, "Good afternoon, Miss Grimes."

"Good afternoon, Mr. Toogood. I'm sorry, ma'am, but it's twopence or nothing. Mrs. Humphrey's orders."

Fanny Isted threw up her hands. "You won't find sweeter anywhere in Sussex. Nor cheaper."

Sukey felt the stirrings of panic. Would she have to forage for onions too? It was bad enough she'd likely have to go nutting after church this week, when everyone knew the Devil held down the branches for a girl who picked nuts on Sunday. "Oh, for heaven's sake," she said confidently. "Don't cut off your nose to spite your face. You'll be feeding half of those to the pigs. Market's almost over and they've started to sprout."

Mrs. Isted sighed. "You'll have to take the ones with soft spots, then."

Sukey felt Mr. Toogood's hand close around the handle of her basket. Instead of giving it to him as he seemed to expect, she held it out to Mrs. Isted, forcing him to let go. "If it's only a spot, and not half the onion. How much for broccoli?"

He stood, patient and silent, while she haggled over broccoli and cabbage, potatoes and turnips. His coat was as scrupulously clean as if St. Clement's Day had never happened, but Sukey flushed anyway, remembering it.

"May I buy you some hot chestnuts?" he asked when she had thanked Mrs. Isted and turned to go.

"I bought myself some, earlier."

"Some gingerbread, then."

Sukey loved gingerbread, but it couldn't warm the chill inside her. The new Parliament had sat yesterday. All the fine folk would be flocking to London, so that's where Mr. John Toogood, Gentleman's Gentleman, would go. She'd thought of nothing but him all week, hoping to see him and talk to him. It was only down to him she hadn't already given him her maidenhead.

She refused to be a forsaken maiden in a ballad. She refused to give her heart to someone who'd put it in his pocket and go whistling down the highway. *I did manage somehow before you came to town,* she wanted to say, but she'd only sound childish. "No, thank you."

"There's a matter I wish to discuss with you."

"As we live on the same street, I suppose I can't stop you sharing the road."

He tried to fall into step beside her, but his long legs kept striding on ahead without meaning to and having to fall back. A week ago she'd found it charming. Today it made her angry.

"I frightened you two days ago. I'm sorry."

She threw him an incredulous look. "The thunder frightened me, not you."

"I ought not to have suggested we warm each other in that manner. I hope you know that I would never take your agreeing to it as an invitation to overfamiliarity."

But she did mean it as an invitation. That was the trouble. "Is this what you wanted to talk to me about? You can't sleep until I tell you I know you're not one of *those* men? Never *you.*"

"I did frighten you."

"No," she said flatly. "You didn't. I'm just sick of men wanting to be petted and praised and admired only for not pushing a woman around." She *had* been grateful for it. And it wasn't fair. It wasn't right that simple respect should feel so rare and precious.

He nodded. "I'm sorry."

She didn't answer.

"That isn't what I wanted to talk to you about."

He obviously wanted her to express interest. *Well, bugger him,* Sukey thought. *Why should I?*

"The vicar is looking for a new butler."

Her heart began to pound. He was thinking of staying?

"Only he wants a butler who's married."

The conversation had now gone in two entirely unexpected directions. Sukey blinked, trying to guess the next one. "He—what? Why is that?"

"He thinks a married man more likely to be respectable, I believe."

"Ha!"

His mouth curved. "That's more or less what I said, but he was immovable."

"And why are you telling me this?" The horrifying possibility occurred to her that he was already married and meant to warn her of his wife's arrival.

He stopped walking. Part of her wanted to run off and leave him there, but she waited, meeting his gaze.

"I like Mr. Summers. I like it here. I told him…" He rubbed the back of his neck, looking discomfited. "I told him that I was fond of a local young woman."

Her heart leapt at that word, *fond,* even before she understood what he was suggesting. "Are you asking me to marry you?"

He spread his hands wide. "Not yet. But unless the idea repels you…" He sighed. "I thought we might talk it over. There wouldn't be any harm in going to see Mr. Summers together, to see if the thing is a possibility. My wife would be upper housemaid at the vicarage. It's a good position."

Her eyes widened, thoughts of marriage flying out of her head. Why, she'd never dare apply to be Mr. Summers's upper housemaid. The vicarage had *staff,* and a grubby maid-of-all-work couldn't possibly— His *upper* housemaid? She didn't know how.

"No harm?" she sputtered. "No *harm?* And if you decide afterwards you'd rather not, how could I ever go to church again?" Mr. Summer had baptized her. He'd baptized nearly everyone she knew under the age of thirty-five. And he had a way of gently skewering sinners that Sukey never, ever wanted turned on her.

He chewed his lip. "You're right. I'm afraid I'm not thinking clearly. I don't know what I want. Or rather, I do know, and it's this. But I shouldn't like to make a mistake."

It was only what she was thinking herself, but the words speared right through her. "I'm never going to marry. Never."

He didn't react to that at all. Not with surprise, anyway. With sympathy, she thought. As if he knew she must have a good reason. "Why not?"

"You thought my father died."

He drew back. Only an inch or two before he thought better of it, but he did. He didn't want to marry a bastard.

"He married my mother, all right. He lived with us until I was seven." She shifted her basket to her other arm. "He doted on me. He—" She shut her mouth on private memories of being carried on his shoulders, of being called *blue-eyed Susan*, of how he would sing a song over and over until she'd learned the words. "Well, he's living in Chichester now, with a new wife and five children."

Women talked as if you only had to be careful until the ring was on your finger, and then you were safe. But even if a man married you, if he meant to stay, if he did for a while—even if he loved you—it was never too late for him to change his mind.

"I'm sorry." Mr. Toogood waited, but when she was silent, he said, "I don't offer you certainty. Nothing is sure in this world, after all. I hoped you would talk it over with me, but if you're satisfied you don't want the position, and wouldn't marry me to get it, then there's nothing more to be said."

It wasn't his acquiescence that calmed her, but the *way* he said it, almost as if they were talking business. As if he was disappointed, but couldn't resent her for deciding his venture wasn't worth her while to invest in.

Her mother would want her to take him. *Not all men are good-for-nothings like your father,* she always said. *Don't marry a good-for-nothing, and you'll be right as rain. It's hard for a woman alone. You'll be old someday, love.* If Mr. Toogood wasn't the farthest thing possible from a good-for-nothing, he made a very fine show of it.

Maybe as his wife, she could stop worrying about ending her life in the workhouse. Then again, he was much older than she was. All right, so she could stop worrying about her mother ending up there.

Even if he left, he'd pay Sukey a maintenance. Oh, her father never had, not after the first year. But Mr. Toogood made a good living, and Sukey thought he'd pay, even just for the sake of his reputation. She promised herself she'd go to the parish and make him if he didn't.

If she thought of it as a business venture, and not marriage…

The road was so chilly, and she remembered clearly how warm she'd been curled up in his lap.

A very businesslike thought.

He walked along silently beside her, hands in his pockets. There was a peculiar lack of stickiness to him. Most people made you pay for it when you didn't behave as they hoped, with pinpricks or coldness or rage. But Mr. Toogood didn't snipe at her even though she'd just refused to marry him without so much as a thank-you. For all his airs of superiority, he generally knew how to share the road.

Indeed, the only thing he'd faulted her for yet was her housekeeping. "You'd be a regular tyrant of a butler." She glanced at him, trying to decide how disappointed he was, and trying not to think that if she married him, he'd bed her. "I don't know as I'd like to be a housemaid under you."

He looked a little sad, but maybe he was just cold. "Have you ever seen the inside of a clock? Or a watch?"

"Once or twice."

"It's beautiful, isn't it?"

She nodded, even though she guessed where he was heading.

"A home can be like that, when servants do good work. You might find you liked it."

It did sound nice when he said it like that, like being part of something bigger, being in church or having a family. But she fell asleep in church and sometimes she dreaded visiting her mother. "A home's not a clock. There'll always be more work than time to do it in, and there'll always be something out of place. If the books all stay on the shelves, it been't a home."

He shrugged and watched the clouds.

"I'm sorry," she said.

He shook his head. "It was a mad idea. I don't know why I bothered you with it. Please forget it."

But Sukey couldn't forget it, all that afternoon.

"I think you might add a little more water." Mrs. Humphrey stirred the cauldron. "It's soup, not pottage."

Any more water and the soup would *taste* like water. "I thought if they filled up on soup, they'd eat less meat, ma'am."

Mrs. Humphrey gave Sukey the narrow-eyed look of one who suspected she was being managed. "Well, add some more onion then, and send it up with plenty of bread." Bread, bought stale at the baker's, was the only thing cheaper than soup.

"Yes, ma'am." The soup, and then the roast, went up to the parlor, where Mrs. Humphrey would carve two thin slices of meat for each boarder and send the rest back down for tomorrow's pie.

In the kitchen, Sukey made the oatmeal pudding for dessert, still thinking about Mr. Toogood's not-quite-an-offer. Mrs. Humphrey had measured out the raisins and two scant spoonfuls of brandy before replacing both stores in a cupboard to which she held the only key. After an hour of soaking, the little heap of raisins was…not plump, but soft-looking, anyway.

It would only take another sliver of butter, a pinch more salt, a shade more sugar and brandy and raisins to make the pudding miles better.

An unsatisfying pudding wasn't much to complain about. Mrs. Grimes would even say it was virtuous—always thinking of tomorrow, always preparing for want and deprivation, always making sure no one got more than her share. But this last week, Mr. Toogood had reminded Sukey how a small kindness, a moment of generosity could transform an afternoon.

It made it seem awfully mean and joyless, the way Mrs. Humphrey took care to give you just *that* much less than you wanted. At the vicarage the pudding tasted like something, she reckoned.

As Sukey tipped the raisins into the pudding, two stuck in the bottom of the cup. She fished them out, and temptation seized her. She tilted back her head and dropped the raisins into her mouth.

There was a gasp from the doorway. Sukey turned to ice, the flavor trickling across her tongue bringing her no pleasure at all. She swallowed the raisins near whole and faced Mrs. Humphrey.

Her mistress's mouth had turned down so far it seemed to disappear into the lines of her chin. "Well, what do you have to say for yourself, girl?"

"I'm sorry, Mrs. Humphrey. Ever so sorry. It was only two raisins. I won't eat any pudding to make up for it."

She harrumphed angrily. "It was only two raisins today, but how much has it been over the years?"

Every bite she'd stolen over the years paraded before Sukey's guilt-stricken eyes. But she earned her board, didn't she, and dined on the boarders' leavings? Why was it stealing to eat food that would have been hers in an hour?

She couldn't say that. She couldn't think what to say. "I wanted to be sure the brandy hadn't soured." Oh, why had she said *that*? It was a patent lie. She'd ought to have said... But every sentence she thought of only made her look guiltier.

Mrs. Humphrey's eyebrows drew closer together. "And a liar too. I should have known as much, when you lied to me about why you lost your last place. I know you were sacked for your smart mouth."

But that was three years ago! Her heart pounded. "It was only two raisins, ma'am, I swear. You can take it out of my wages."

"Only two raisins." She harrumphed again. "You don't even blush. You don't know how good you have it here, you ungrateful girl. I never tasted a raisin in my life until I was nearly as old as you."

Shame swamped Sukey anew. How could she blame her mistress for scrimping? How could she have compared her to the vicar, who'd never wanted for anything?

"I know what's got into you," Mrs. Humphrey said. "It's that Toogood fellow from Tassell Hall."

Sukey's racing heart stumbled. "No," she said faintly. "He hasn't—"

"No doubt he's used to every luxury, and is throwing money around at Mrs. Pengilly's as if there's no tomorrow. I'm sure the Tassells keep raisins by the barrelful."

For a moment Sukey was relieved. But in Mrs. Humphrey's eyes, a spendthrift might be worse than a seducer. "I'll do better. I'm sorry—"

"Better safe than sorry, girl. I've ignored your insolence and laziness because I thought you loyal and obedient. But your lateness this week has been beyond anything." Her eyes widened in sudden dismay. "Did you really pay through the nose for spotty onions, or are you stealing, too?" She wrung her hands. "Oh, I've been played for a fool."

Sukey couldn't think or breathe. "You haven't. Mrs. Humphrey, please, I'll do better."

Mrs. Humphrey, having talked herself up to it, let the axe fall. "Maybe, maybe not, but you'll do better or worse elsewhere. And don't think about coming back here later to steal. I'll be watching for you."

"*Please*, Mrs. Humphrey."

Her mistress hesitated.

"Just give me another chance." Her voice shook. "If you still aren't happy with me at Christmas, I'll go—"

"Well, that *is* brazen. This isn't a negotiation, my dear."

Sukey saw her mistake too late, as always.

"I rather think you'll go now. I won't be ridden roughshod over in my own home, thank you very much. I'll have my door key back, and you may take your things and go. But leave the coat, I gave it you to use while you were in my service. Be sure I will warn Mrs. Pengilly of your behavior. You may stop by tomorrow for the wages I owe you. You see, I don't try to cheat you, though you have cheated me."

Hot words filled Sukey's mouth, but she swallowed them. Brandy lingered on her tongue, soured by fear. She untied the key from around her neck and held it out. Her things? What things? She put on her bonnet and changed her slippers for boots, and that was all she had in the world.

Mrs. Humphrey watched her out the door and latched it behind her, as if she might try to stuff things into her pockets on her way. Maybe she would have if she could, she felt that desperate. She kept her head high until she reached the street, and then she stopped, shivering. What a ninny she must look, with no pelisse and a pair of slippers dangling from her hand.

She'd have to go to her mother's. She'd have to tell her mother what had happened. Mrs. Grimes would be so angry and disappointed.

Why had Sukey been so stupid? So careless and self-indulgent? Had she really thrown away a good job, just for two little raisins? Her mother had beaten her black and blue after she lost that last place, so she'd remember the lesson.

Sukey was a grown woman now. Too old for a thrashing, surely.

Her mother had brought Sukey up to be cleverer than this. Sukey couldn't bear her mother to look at her and see a fool.

She scrambled to reassure herself. She'd find another job easy enough, wouldn't she? Mrs. Humphrey wasn't a popular woman. Tomorrow Mrs. Pengilly would laugh at the story, and she and Mrs. Dymond would inquire among their friends for a position, and that would be that. Probably. Two raisins couldn't turn every employer against her, even if Mrs. Humphrey advertised about them in the *Intelligencer*.

What if the new job was worse?

Oh, why did Mrs. Dymond have to be going to Spain?

She'd worry about that tomorrow. Tonight, she didn't have a penny in her pocket, and she hadn't eaten dinner. There was nowhere she could stay but her mother's, not without asking for charity. The Grimes women had never taken charity in their lives. They'd done for themselves.

A light flickered in the window of Mrs. Pengilly's attic. Sukey remembered what fear had finally succeeded in driving out of her head. She'd been as good as offered another position. Another home. Her mouth set in determination. It would be something at least to tell her mother, a way to say, *See, I'm not* entirely *a failure. I've got irons in the fire.*

Mr. Toogood had been angry with Mrs. Humphrey on her behalf, about the thunderstorm. She didn't know if he'd understand about the raisins, but maybe—maybe he'd be kind. Sukey wanted awfully for someone to be kind to her, just for a moment. She wanted to be out of the wind. Mr. Toogood's voice was so steady and so warm.

He'd lend her a coat, at least. Sukey crossed the street.

Chapter Six

John had sliced a hot baked apple for his landlady's dessert and carried it upstairs. As he sat to take a fork to his own, his back to the warm bricks below the little baking oven in the hearth wall, someone knocked timidly at the door.

Sighing, he set his plate down and went to the door. "How can I assist— Miss Grimes?"

She frowned up at him, hands tucked into her armpits.

"Come." He opened the door wider and stood back.

She hesitated before stepping into the light. Her whole face was tense and suspicious, jaw set, brows drawn as far together as they would go. She chewed at the corner of her pursed mouth. Where was her pelisse? Were those slippers poking out from under her arm?

"Are you angry with me?" He tried to think of what he might have done to make her glare like that. He tried not to want to kiss her until she stopped.

Her frown deepened. "Of course not. Why would I be?"

Because I asked you to marry me. "What is the matter, Miss Grimes? You oughtn't to go out in such weather without your coat."

She shrank away with an annoyed-sounding huff of breath. "Mrs. Humphrey gave me the sack."

He recognized her expression then: the tightly armored face and posture of a person who expected to be punished. He only just managed not to say *What did you do?* "What happened?"

She looked away. "I…"

"Here, come sit by the fire. Have you eaten?"

She shook her head hopefully, frown easing at last. Drawing her to the hearth, he let her take his spot below the bake oven. She removed her bonnet and huddled there while he ladled beef stew into a bowl for her and cut a thick slice of bread.

Some of the tension left her limbs as she gulped down her first mouthful. "*You* use enough salt. I can't remember the last time I had properly salted stew."

Inwardly, he prayed for patience. "The allspice makes it flavorful, really."

Her snort lacked its usual conviction. "I wouldn't know. Mrs. Humphrey doesn't let me use more than one berry at a time."

"To feed that whole house? That's false economy. Better to leave them out altogether, for you won't taste them."

She took an enormous bite of bread. Silence stretched as she chewed. Finally she took a deep breath. "I ate some raisins." Another pause. "Two raisins. Soaked in brandy. Well, I wouldn't say soaked. Sprinkled with brandy, more like."

He blinked. "She dismissed you for eating two raisins?"

The rest of her tension melted away. "It's ridiculous, isn't it?"

Probably he ought to make an effort to be fair. Raisins weren't cheap. He tried to guess at Mrs. Humphrey's weekly expenses—but he already hated Mrs. Humphrey, and he'd grown up in a kitchen. There were many things a servant never got: the prime cut of meat, the first piece of pie, an ice fresh from the mold. So many things had to go up to table pristine and whole. But in exchange, one might taste a meal as it grew, opine if the gravy needed more butter, pop a toasted nut in one's mouth on the way to the scullery. It was one of the great pleasures and privileges of belowstairs life.

Besides, he saw that Sukey had expected him to condemn her, and hated the picture of himself as haughty judge. Or worse, a loyal family retainer. "It's a disgrace," he said. "Your mistress is a shrew."

She laughed. "Harsh words."

He took down a new plate. Cutting his baked apple in two, he gave her half. "Did you wish to see Mrs. Pengilly?" That must be why she had come, mustn't it?

"Do you think she'd hire me in?"

"I don't think she's ready to admit she needs someone here," John said. "But her son will be here at Christmas, and it's his money."

She plucked the stem from her apple half, toying with it. "I reckon you're right." Her hands were small, every movement lovely. "I came to see you, in fact."

He took a sip of tea to wet his dry throat. He didn't dare eat his own apple, in case he might need to speak. "And how can I be of assistance?"

"My mother…" She trailed off. "I've got to go live with my mother until I find another place, and…" She rubbed at her arms.

There was no reason to take off his coat and hand it to her. He had another upstairs he might have given her, and it was hardly toasty in the kitchen. But his heart pounded as she slipped her slender arms into the sleeves, pulling it close to savor the warmth his body had given it. He wished her to know that he would freeze for her if she asked him to, and even if she didn't.

He also wished her to look at his arms in his shirtsleeves, and she did, a smile hovering at the corners of her mouth.

He took his overcoat from the peg and put it on, then sat cross-legged on the floor opposite her and waited, his skin on fire with impatience.

She looked terribly sad all of a sudden. "I think I want to marry you." Her eyes filled, a tear slipping down her cheek.

John didn't know what to say. "I never intended the idea to make you so unhappy."

"I meant to get by on my own. I ignored my mother when she said I'd end in the workhouse. I didn't want to need help. I don't want to get married only to have some man to take care of me."

"It isn't weak to wish for a helpmeet." Perhaps the coat had been the wrong gesture. "I wish for one myself."

She looked at him, and then she straightened, a little more cheerful. "That's right. You're lonely."

He had to fight a smile at the pleased way she said it. He widened his eyes and stuck out his lower lip, just a hair. "Terribly lonely," he agreed solemnly.

"And you want that job at the vicar's."

"Badly." He held his breath, waiting for her to decide that really, she was taking pity on him.

She turned up her little retroussé nose. "Really, I'm taking pity on you," she said slyly, eyes gleaming.

He met her gaze. "I hope you will."

Sukey caught her breath. She set her apple down, looking indecisive, and then launched herself into his lap, her cold hands at the back of his neck and her mouth on his. He gasped, kissing her, slipping his hands inside his own coat to circle her narrow waist. She was so eager she overbalanced him; he fell back on the floor. She sprawled atop him, slight breasts against his waistcoat and hipbones pressing into his stomach. He dug his fingers into her gown, feeling the quilting of her corset, so he wouldn't pull her cap off and yank the pins out of her hair.

Less circumspect, Sukey put a hand down and cupped his cock. Sensation shot through him, illuminating the dark kitchen.

"You don't have to growl at me between your teeth like that." She pressed down, her palm right over the head of his cock. "Mrs. Pengilly's deaf. Howl all you like." He let go of her waist and held his hands still for fear he would hurt her.

She shaped his length, the heel of her hand firm and her fingertips trailing after, and John thought, *Why not? What are the odds of someone walking in in the next half-minute?* "I'll spend," he warned her through gritted teeth, "and it would be highly imprudent to take the time for me to return the favor."

"I know," she murmured. "Someone could walk in. Do you want me to stop?"

If someone came in, they'd see his hair flopping about, his chest heaving. He lay flat on the kitchen floor, helpless against a pretty girl like any middle-aged fool. Sukey squeezed his ballocks clumsily between her fingers through his breeches. *This is the least dignified moment of my life.* He shut his eyes. He didn't want her to stop.

"Think of it as paying something down," she said. "In three weeks, you'll have it all."

This was payment? A promise that she wouldn't back out, or surety so that he wouldn't?

She nipped his earlobe as she dragged her nails up his cock, and he could barely find the breath to protest. He was soaking in pleasure like a raisin in brandy, every atom suffused. "I would keep my word for a handshake," he got out.

Her smile curved against his ear. "I know you would." She kissed his cheek and gave his groin an affectionate pat. "But where's the fun in that?" She rubbed her fingers over the tip of his cock.

He gave up and gave in, spilling into his smallclothes.

Sukey had never felt such a delightful sense of victory. Proper Mr. Toogood, with his iron self-control, wanted her to touch him so badly that here he was at the height of pleasure from only a few scrapes of her fingernails. He'd thought it his duty to say no and hadn't brought himself to do it.

So this was what it looked like when a man came. She arranged herself more comfortably atop him, propping her elbows to either side of his head, feeling better than she had all day. His hands, which had hovered inside his coat, settled gently on her hips.

She felt better, she realized, than she had in years. When had she grown so fond of his face? His high, frowning forehead was smooth for once. He no doubt thought his graying stubble slovenly, but Sukey liked it. A shame beards were out of style. She dropped a kiss on the end of his nose.

His eyes opened, startled. He looked even more startled when she grinned at him, but his mouth curved grudgingly. He lifted her easily off him and sat up, giving her a casually sensual kiss that reminded Sukey all at once that she wasn't his first. This wasn't the first time he'd had to find something to say to a woman after bedding her. Or *not* bedding her, as the case might be. He stood. "I'll get my coat and walk you home."

Once Sukey was left alone in the dim kitchen, doubts crowded in. But none of them were about Mr. Toogood, though surely they'd ought to be. No, she was suddenly eaten up with fear that the snooty vicarage servants would turn up their noses at her, and think her some draggletail that had ensnared poor Mr. Toogood with her wiles.

She smiled in spite of herself. Maybe she had. She polished her nails on his coat, and realized she'd left her gloves in the pocket of Mrs. Humphrey's coat. She'd have to ask for them when she went for her wages, and Mrs. Humphrey would give her such a look. She squared her shoulders. *You don't work for her anymore. Her looks can't hurt you.*

Mr. Toogood was so neat when he came downstairs. He'd been neat when he went up, his hair too short to really get out of place. *I would keep my word for a handshake,* he'd said even though his voice had gone deep enough to frighten a bullfrog. She'd somehow imagined he would shed his proper air with his clothes, but she was starting to think he could be starchy and buttoned-up without a stitch on him to starch or button. Happy and laughing, he'd still manage it somehow.

She was starting to find starchy and buttoned-up a handsome thing for a man to be.

Hand on the doorknob, he hesitated. "If you're sure about this, I'll call for you at nine o'clock tomorrow to go and see Mr. Summers."

"Let's shake hands on it." Sukey smiled at the hitch in his breath, tilting up her chin as if she were the kind of girl who was too rich to answer her own door. "I ought to be at home to callers at nine."

"You honor me," he said formally.

She thought he might only half mean it as a joke, and that got her through the silent walk to her mother's lodgings, and the silent climb to her mother's door.

"It's me, Mum. Open up." Sukey was glad Mr. Toogood couldn't see her nervesome face in the dark stair.

The door opened into more darkness. The room was heated, if you could say it *was* heated, by only a blank brick chimney. But the tallow candle in her hand lit up Mrs. Grimes. She was swathed in half-a-dozen shapeless layers of old man's coat and bedjacket and flannel petticoats, a knitted nightcap over her hair, hands shoved into gloves with the fingertips cut off. For a moment Sukey was just glad to see her mother, who was comfortable and familiar and didn't give a straw what anyone thought.

Mrs. Grimes frowned. "Sukey? It been't Friday yet. Is something wrong, child?"

Sukey's stomach turned over. She inched closer to Mr. Toogood. "Mrs. Humphrey sacked me, Mum."

Her mother sighed. "Oh, Susan Grimes. What did you do this time?"

"She didn't do anything, madam," Mr. Toogood said, taking Sukey completely by surprise. Mrs. Grimes too. Eyebrows flying up, she put her gloved hands in her pockets and rocked on her heels, waiting for a good explanation.

Mr. Toogood squeezed Sukey's hand where it rested on his arm. She felt strange and warm. Since her father left, there'd never been anyone to take her side with her mum.

"Mrs. Humphrey is an extremely unreasonable woman, and your daughter is far safer out of her employ than in. Did you know Mrs. Humphrey sent her out to climb apple trees during the thunderstorm last week?"

Mrs. Grimes's eyes widened. "No, I didn't," she said grimly. "Sukey, is that true?"

Sukey nodded. How many things had she neglected to mention to her mother about life at the boarding house, dimly ashamed, afraid to hear what her mother would say? She hadn't wanted to be told to leave, and she hadn't wanted to be told to stay. It was what it was, it kept a roof over her head, and there was no sense in being one of those dreadful complaining folk who never had a good thing to say. Better to be glad for what you did have, and hold on to it.

Her mother pulled her towards the candle. "Well, you don't look as if you came to any harm."

Sukey immediately felt foolish. "I didn't."

"She nearly broke her neck," Mr. Toogood put in.

"I was clumsy," Sukey said hastily, sure her mother was thinking it—but why was she so sure? "And I got the sack for stealing."

She could feel Mr. Toogood's puzzlement. She didn't care.

"I see," her mother said slowly. "Stealing what?"

"Two raisins from the pudding she was making for dinner, madam," Mr. Toogood said.

Her mother's face said she'd give her opinion later. Sukey wished she'd just say it and get it over with. "And who might you be? I don't believe we've met."

"This is John Toogood, Mum. He used to be Mr. Nicholas Dymond's man." She could see the sarcastic question on her mother's face: *Was he sacked too?*

Please don't say it, she begged silently.

"A pleasure to meet you." Mrs. Grimes held out her hand, looking entertained when Mr. Toogood bowed over it.

"I've just asked your daughter to marry me," he said, "and she has made me very happy by agreeing. I hope you will give us your blessing." Sukey couldn't decide if she wished he'd leave so she could talk to her mother, or wished he'd take her home with him so she wouldn't have to.

Mrs. Grimes's jaw dropped. "Sukey?"

"It's true." Regretfully, Sukey faced the fact that he couldn't take her home. "John, darling, you said you'd come and fetch me at nine o'clock?"

He hesitated, but he said, "Of course, Miss Grimes," kissed her lightly on the cheek, bowed to her mother, and vanished, leaving only a lingering odor of good manners.

"I can stay here until the wedding, can't I, Mum? It's only two and a half weeks."

Her mother walked back into her room, leaving the door open for Sukey to follow. "Come and get under the covers where it's warm. Good Lord, Sukey, the *wedding*? You never mentioned that man to me before in your life."

"I didn't think anything would come of it."

Her mouth turned up. "Ah, I see. And how long have you not thought anything would come of it?"

Sukey crawled under the blankets and huddled closer to her mother. "A fortnight," she admitted. Lied, rather. It wouldn't be a fortnight for a few days yet.

"An eternity, then." Mrs. Grimes held the candle up to inspect her face. "What do you even know of him?"

"He used to be Mr. Dymond's man. Mrs. Dymond told me her husband thinks ever so highly of him." Mostly she'd told Sukey he was a stickler, and that he'd got the stain out of her dress when her brother-in-law was sick on it. But a Dymond's word in Lively St. Lemeston was good as gold to a lot of folk.

Even Mrs. Grimes didn't turn up her nose at it, though she sighed gustily. "You'll do as you like, of course."

"So can I stay?"

"You can stay as long as you like if you help me with my washing. I'll take on extra work and you can have a bit of the money for your bride things. But where will you live when you're married?"

"Mr. Toogood thinks we can get work at the vicarage. He spoke with Reverend Summers this week, and we'll go and see him together in the morning." Sukey shrank from admitting she'd be an upper housemaid if all went to plan. If it didn't come off, her mother would think she'd been building castles in the air, and anyway, she might point out that Sukey had never had such a fine job before, and could she really do it?

"That's a nice coat." Her mother examined the inside of the cuff for wear. "Large for you, though. Who did you buy it from?"

"It's Mr. Toogood's. Mrs. Humphrey wouldn't let me take mine."

"Ah yes, she gave you the sack. Lucky you had a husband all lined up, eh?"

Sukey felt tears pricking her eyes. "Are you very angry?"

Her mother looked at her in surprise and then laughed. "It's for your husband to take a switch to you now, girl. Here, take off your cap and I'll braid your hair for bed."

He wouldn't, Sukey thought. *He wouldn't hurt me.* But she wondered. She'd only just met him, after all, and she'd never seen him angry. He was large enough to easily hurt her if he'd a mind to.

"Your father should be here to see you married." Mrs. Grimes pulled out her hairpins.

Sukey didn't know how to answer. They almost never spoke of her father. "Oh, pooh. It isn't as if we're fine folk who'll take up the vicar's time with flipper-de-flapper and waste money on cake for all our friends. I don't suppose you're planning to come yourself, even."

Her mother tugged her comb through a snarl, none too gently. But Sukey never had the patience to be gentle either. She had plenty of hair, no one would notice if she lost a few strands. "What of that? To think a daughter of mine would go to her husband in just her shift! Would you like my sea-chest? You always loved that chest."

"I couldn't." The old chest, on whose inside lid some sailor had painted a white-sailed ship on the waves, was the only note of whimsy her mother allowed in the room.

"Don't be silly, of course you could. Or you might take the mirror. It's only cracked at the very bottom. I've no need for such a large one, I only really use it to double the light of the candle. I won't have Mr. Toogood looking down on us, thinking he's done you some great favor by marrying you. Not when he'll have the keeping of me when I'm old."

"Mum, when you married Dad, did you think it might be a mistake?"

Sukey was afraid she'd let slip too much, but her mother didn't seem to think it a strange question. Maybe it was one she'd asked herself before. Chuckling, she combed the left side of Sukey's head into three parts, twisting each firmly between her fingers. It felt nice.

"Not for a moment. I thought the sun shone out of your father's arse." Her fingers slowed. "It's such a weight off my mind to see you married. Life isn't easy for a woman alone." She finished off the braids quickly. "Here, I have a present for you. Miss Makepeace gave it me last week."

She went to the trunk and took out a worn green ribbon. With a snip of her scissors she cut it in half, and tied up Sukey's braids with it. "I was never half as pretty as you, I'm sure," she said proudly.

Tears pricked Sukey's eyes. But was she making a dreadful mistake? *No. Mum never doubted, and you do. That means you're deciding with your brain and not your cunny.* She curled up under the covers in Mr. Toogood's coat and realized that it smelled like him.

It was hard to believe you weren't thinking with your cunny when you were tugging a man's lapel over your nose and mouth, breathing in deep and remembering him shuddering on the floor beneath you.

* * *

"Ah, little Sukey Grimes," Mr. Summers said. "Coming up in the world, I see."

John tried to unclench his jaw. He was wound tight as a spool of thread with nerves, for fear Sukey would say something ill-judged and lose them both the position.

"Yes, sir." She bobbed a curtsey. "I hope to be worthy of it, sir, if you'll give me the chance."

He blinked, surprised. But why? She'd never have managed years with Mrs. Humphrey if she couldn't curb her tongue.

"And how did you and Mr. Toogood meet?"

She'd been stealing a hairpin when they met. John hoped she wouldn't mention that.

"Well, sir, you know I worked for Mrs. Sparks that was, Mrs. Dymond now, and he worked for Mr. Dymond."

"It's a pity they mightn't have employed you in their own establishment," the vicar said with only a hint of sarcasm.

Sukey dimpled. "It *would* have been awfully convenient at that, sir."

Mr. Summers smiled at her. It had been a strange oversight on John's part to imagine that Sukey could not charm others besides himself. "Indeed. Tell me, what is your impression of your future husband's character?"

John kept his face carefully blank as Sukey threw him a laughing glance. "Look at him, he's afraid I'll say he's a stick-in-the-mud."

"I think any man of forty marrying a bright young thing like yourself would be afraid of that."

John wished, not for the first time, that employers felt obligated to be as tactful and carefully distant as servants did.

"Oh, he's spry enough," Sukey said. John could *see* her debating whether to wink. He cleared his throat, and she smiled at him instead. "I think he's the kindest man I've ever met, sir," she said firmly. "And the most generous." John's face heated.

"I don't imagine your experience of men has been large," Mr. Summers pointed out. "You have worked solely in female households, have you not? Too pretty for housewives to let you near their husbands, eh?"

Sukey shifted uncomfortably, and John realized it was probably the truth. "I'd not say that, sir. I *have* worked only for women, but it been't—isn't as easy to avoid men in this world as you may imagine."

Mr. Summers nodded. "So you think Mr. Toogood morally fit to supervise four women and train a young footman up in the way he should go?"

"I suppose I haven't known him so long as all that, but I do, yes. I think him morally fit for anything, sir."

The way she said it was only three-quarters a compliment. John smothered a laugh.

"I see. Have you letters of reference?"

For the first time, she faltered. "No, sir. I..." She looked at John.

"I think it is best to be direct," John said. "Miss Grimes lost her position at Mrs. Humphrey's yesterday. But I have no doubt Mrs. Pengilly and Mrs. Dymond would give her an excellent character if applied to."

"Mrs. Humphrey, yes," the vicar said. "And why did you lose your position?"

John nodded at her encouragingly.

"I was cooking the pudding for supper, sir, and ate two raisins. It was wrong of me, I know."

Mr. Summers gave that startling, delighted cackle of his. "Two raisins, I see. This *is* a terrible sin. But I am bound to remark that Mrs. Humphrey, while a very worthy woman, brings irresistibly to mind the passage, 'and though I have all faith, so that I could remove mountains, and have not charity, I am nothing'. Well, my dear, I do not keep the raisins under lock and key in *my* kitchen, so I hope you will not snack me out of house and home."

The worst was past, but to John's surprise, Sukey stiffened. "I'm grateful to you, sir, for saying it. But you know her family ate shorn-bugs for dinner when she was a girl."

"Very true." To John's relief, Mr. Summers did not look offended, thought he didn't look much chastened either. "There but for the grace of God go I. Now, Mr. Toogood, what do you think of your bride-to-be's character?"

"I think you have just witnessed it, sir. She is the kindest and most generous young woman I ever met."

Sukey flushed and clutched her hands together.

"She has not served in a gentleman's home before and has much to learn," John continued, "but I think if you will be patient, and have charity, the bread you cast upon the waters will be returned to you. Her care with Mrs. Pengilly is quite touching."

The vicar stood. "Well, the house has been rather quiet these last few years. Perhaps you will do something about that, eh, Miss Grimes?"

She shifted uncomfortably. "You must tell me if you think I'm chattering, sir."

"I shall not hesitate. Well, if Mrs. Dymond and Mrs. Pengilly do not contradict you, the positions are yours. Naturally I cannot have a courting pair living together under my roof, but there is no reason you, Miss Grimes, cannot start at once. If I read the banns Sunday and you are married—let me see— Monday the fourteenth of December, Mr. Toogood may take up his position then. Here, I will introduce you to the rest of the staff."

A girl appeared in the doorway in answer to the bell, out of breath. She was the round-faced blonde John remembered.

"Where is Thea? Never mind. Fetch her and everyone else to meet the new members of the staff." When the girl had ducked out again, Mr. Summers said, "You'll meet the gardener later. He's really an undergardener at Wheatcroft and comes once a week."

The blonde girl was soon back with Larry and the younger brunette. Mrs. Khaleel came in a moment later, a young gentleman on her heels. He was slender and very tall, dark haired, with bright blue eyes and an air of amused curiosity about him.

"I was just prevailing on your cook to warm up some mulligatawny for my dinner, sir," he said in a light, cultivated drawl, "and thought I'd meet the new servants."

"Of course, Mr. Bearparke. May I present John Toogood and his intended, Susan Grimes, the new butler and upper housemaid. I am sure you recognize my curate, my dear," he said to Sukey. "As his lodgings have recently fallen through and this house is far too big for one man, he will be taking up residence here very shortly."

John's eyes flew to the women in surprise. Mrs. Khaleel's mouth was a tight line. The vicar, no doubt, saw no contradiction in insisting on a married butler while allowing his bachelor curate the run of the place. John would have to keep an eye on the fellow. He cursed inwardly, hoping he wouldn't find himself at odds with his master's trusted associate so very early in his tenure at the vicarage.

"Once Twelfth Day is behind us," the curate confirmed with an infectious grin. "Christmastide is too busy for a man of the cloth to trouble himself with personal errands."

"Mr. Toogood, Miss Grimes," Mr. Summers went on, "this is Mrs. Khaleel, my cook; Margaret, my under-housemaid; Dorothea, my laundry maid; and Lawrence, my footman." Margaret, the blonde, gave John a hard look and stepped closer to Dorothea.

"It is very nice to meet all of you," John said. "Might I inquire your ages, Margaret, Dorothea?"

"I'm sixteen and she's thirteen, sir," Margaret answered for both of them. "You can call us Molly and Thea." Thea regarded him a little sleepily, smothering a yawn. He hoped very, very intently that the previous butler had not really hurt them.

"I'm eighteen," Larry offered helpfully.

"We look forward to working with you." John met each of their eyes in turn—except Thea, who was looking at her toes.

"Now you may show your betrothed to the door, Miss Grimes. I warn you, Mr. Toogood, my servants are not allowed to entertain visitors in my home, nor to gallivant about the countryside when they ought to be sleeping or working. You will have to content yourselves with meeting Saturday afternoons, when all of you take your half-holiday while I prepare for the Lord's Day in peace. Unless you do not subscribe to the country superstition that a man must not hear his own banns called, in which case you may see her Sunday mornings as well."

Sukey shook her head at him, eyes imploring, and John could almost hear her say, *It'll be church bells for your funeral next if you do.* "I am afraid I do subscribe to it, sir. But I look forward to returning to church services after the wedding."

Sukey sighed in relief, slight shoulders easing, and John wished he were not a servant and were not obliged to stand still and straight as an automaton instead of kissing her.

He felt disposed to linger in the chilly kitchen-yard, but Sukey still lacked an overcoat. "If I may see you Saturday, I will buy you a new pelisse," he said, and then was embarrassed by this small attempt at bribery.

"Bribing me with gifts, it's as if we're already married. I could use a good set of stays too." There was a forced note in Sukey's teasing, and he realized that while he returned to his quiet lodgings, he was leaving her in a new home alone.

"You'll do splendidly. And I would be glad to buy you stays. New ones sewn to your measurements, if you like." It would be the most intimate gift he'd ever given anyone.

For a second, he could see her talking herself round, and then she gave him a twinkling smile almost as bright as her usual. "Look at you throwing money about! Mrs. Humphrey was right about you. Tell my mum I won't be coming home and not to take that extra work, will you? I'll see you Saturday."

He didn't want to go. "If that curate bothers you at all, you must get word to me at once. Mrs. Khaleel did not like the idea of him living here."

She nodded. "I hope you know what you've got us into."

So did he.

Chapter Seven

"Owe no man anything, but to love one another: for he that loveth another hath fulfilled the law..." Mr. Summers's voice brought Sukey awake with a start, thinking he was asking her to fetch his tea or stir the fire. There was a special terror to nodding off in church when the parson was your master.

It was strange to be back in church with her mother, like every Sunday since she was a girl, when for nearly two weeks she hadn't left her new household. A servant's home was her world, and at the vicarage Sukey didn't even have the running of errands or going to market as an excuse to leave the house, for Thea, Larry and Mrs. Khaleel did all that. Except for her half-holidays and Sunday morning services, she'd spoken to no one but Mr. Summers and his servants. Sometimes she felt as far from her old life as if she'd gone to live on the moon, so it was a shock to see Mrs. Humphrey and the boarding-house ladies in the gallery opposite, and to remember she'd been less than half a mile from them all the while.

Below them, Mrs. Dymond and her family sat in their pew. She was relieved to see Mrs. Pengilly with them, looking well. John had promised he'd try to at least find her a new lodger before he left, but Sukey fretted.

"I used to think Nick Dymond was the handsomest man in the world," her friend Jenny whispered to her. "Now look how slocksey he is, with his hair in his face and his coat huddled on. It was all your man's doing after all."

"Shh. I can't talk in church anymore." *Your man.* She wished he were here, bad luck notwithstanding. She felt less and less certain she was making the right choice. True, she liked it tol-lol at the vicarage, though she was run off her feet learning the ways of a new house. Everyone was nice, the food was the best she'd ever had, and she and Mr. Summers got along fine. But marriage? If

Mr. Toogood were here, she'd feel safe about it again. She'd felt sure yesterday afternoon, when he was buying her new linen to match the brand-new stays that fit her like a dream. Sukey Grimes with a nightgown of her own with fine long sleeves to keep out the chill, imagine that! Now, without his quiet, sure presence, she thought, *It was only so I don't disgrace him before Mr. Summers.*

"I publish the banns of marriage," Mr. Summers read, "between Lydia Reeve of Lively St. Lemeston and Ashford Cahill of Blight's Penryth. If any of you know cause or just impediment why these two persons should not be joined together in holy matrimony, you are to declare it. This is the second time of asking."

Sukey peered down at Lydia Reeve, the Tory patroness, sitting smugly in her pew with her betrothed. *She* looked sure. Radiant. Everyone said it'd been love at first sight with the two of them. But for an heiress to marry a stranger and give him her money? How could she know it was safe so quickly?

"Don't they know he shouldn't hear himself church-bawled?" Jenny whispered. "Asking for trouble, that is."

"Funny how rich folk never worry about luck," Sukey whispered back. "Born with a surplus, I expect."

Fancying Mr. Summers was looking at her, she straightened hurriedly—and as he began to read her banns, she realized his eye *had* been on her. Drat. When would she learn to behave herself?

She looked around, proud in spite of herself to hear her name read out with John's and to have everyone know she was marrying him. Her gaze met her Aunt Kate's in the gallery across the way, and her heart gave a jolt.

She could still remember crying as Mrs. Grimes turned Kate away at the door after Mr. Grimes left. Sukey had liked her father's sister dunnamuch. Thinking herself very crafty, she'd said maybe Aunt Kate would give them money if they let her visit. Her mum had made her sorry for that.

Every week in church, Sukey wished she could talk to her.

Aunt Kate smiled at her. Jerking her gaze away before her mother saw, she caught Mrs. Humphrey glaring at her.

She checked her instinctive flinch, straightening to show off her new pelisse. It was finer than anything she'd ever owned, rust colored, with a high velvet collar and stylish frogging down the front. It was secondhand, but Mr. Toogood had paid for it to be altered, and Sukey looked fine as fivepence if she did say so herself. She could almost hear the *harrumph* from across the church.

* * *

The two and a half weeks before John's wedding passed with painful slowness. The exceptions were Saturday afternoons, which passed far too quickly. But Monday the fourteenth of December dawned at last. John presented himself at the church half an hour early, and read in an empty box pew until Mr. Summers and Sukey arrived promptly at nine, with the curate and Molly to serve as witnesses. John looked between them, trying to discern whether matters at the vicarage had been going as well as Sukey said, and how happy Mr. Summers was with his new upper housemaid.

"Have you a ring, Mr. Toogood?" Mr. Summers asked.

"Oh, I brought a napkin ring with me, sir," Sukey said.

John reached in his pocket and brought out the ring he'd purchased at the pawnshop. "I hope you like it." It looked improbably small lying in his palm, and he was suddenly afraid it would not fit and he had wasted his money.

"A posy ring? My, my. I thought those had entirely gone out of fashion since my boyhood," Mr. Summers said. Mr. Bearparke laughed, though without any malice, and John felt another pang of uncertainty.

Sukey gingerly took the narrow band of shining brass, with letters inscribed on its inward face. "*Let us share in joy and care,*" she read. "How sweet!" She tried it on each finger in turn until it fit snugly on her left middle finger. She held out her hand, fingers spread, with growing satisfaction. "Thanks. I think I'm the first girl in my family to be married with a real ring."

As she took it off and handed it back, their eyes met. Enough heat flared between them that John knew he wasn't the only one thinking of their wedding night.

He kept the ring in his hand throughout the ceremony so as to have it ready. He was glad he'd coated it in a fine layer of beeswax to protect Sukey's skin, for otherwise his sweating palm would have been entirely green.

Rose Lerner

After the wedding, they all walked back to the vicarage together—Sukey dropping his arm every few steps to feel the ring through her glove—and then John was obliged to throw himself at once into work. The house had lacked a butler for weeks now, and something needed his attention everywhere he looked. He went slowly through the house, making notes.

He tried not to be appalled at his list's length. These were surely sins of ignorance and not malice. Larry was not overwaxing the mahogany and scratching the mirrors on purpose. Perhaps the lad was nearsighted, and at least his mediocrity distracted John from thoughts of the coming night.

He glanced at the grandfather clock at the foot of the stairs to see how many hours remained in the day. Its painted face was so lovely and so begrimed that John went directly to the kitchen for a piece of white bread and a soft-bristle brush.

He heard Mr. Bearparke's low, happy voice before he opened the door. "…used to let me help in harvesting the mangoes. I can't really remember what they tasted like, but I know I thought it ambrosia at the time. I've toyed with the notion of begging the new Lord Wheatcroft to cultivate them in his hothouses. Do you think I ought?" The curate sat at a deal table in the corner of the kitchen, a sandwich and a stack of books before him.

Mrs. Khaleel gave John a nervous look from where she was cutting up a couple of chickens. "It's not my place to say, sir."

Mr. Bearparke's frown and glance in John's direction suggested it was not the sort of answer he had expected—or perhaps was used to getting—though he took it with a good grace, bowing his head over his books. John's heart sank. He liked the cook and hoped very much that she was not acting imprudently.

The painted hurrying ship, pink roses and gilt accents of the clock face were considerably brightened after an application of bread. John brushed the crumbs away with a smile and headed for the kitchen.

Through the open door to the kitchen-yard, he could clearly hear Sukey singing outside.

'Twas out of those roses she made a bed,
A stony pillow for her head;
She laid her down, no word she spoke,

Until this fair maid's heart was broke.

He went to the door. She was taking yesterday's ashes to the bin, skirts swaying jauntily with the motion of her hips. She was his wife now, part of him until Judgment Day. Tonight, and every night after, he could touch her to his heart's content.

Listening to her clear voice, John remembered with a sick jolt how much more energy he'd had at twenty-two. It struck him how gladly he fell into bed, how difficult it had become to open his eyes and clear the cobwebs from his brain after five or six hours' sleep. At her age he had stayed up until the small hours talking or drinking, and got up again before dawn and thought nothing of it.

Unlike valeting, this position did not allow for catnaps.

If Sukey wanted long nights of passion, he was unlikely to be able to oblige her. He was unsure, even, if he could satisfy her more than once in a night.

It occurred to him with a sort of panic that they had never discussed the possibility of children.

There is a man on yonder hill;
He has a heart so harder still.
He has two hearts instead of one...

Something else occurred to John. He stepped into the yard and waved her over.

She came readily. "How d'you do, Mr. Toogood?"

He couldn't help smiling. "Quite well, Mrs. Toogood, and yourself?"

"Oh, tol-lol."

John pointed at the neighboring window, fortunately closed. "That is Mr. Summers's study."

"I know."

"You had better not sing on this side of the house when Mr. Summers is at home. It might disturb him in his work."

Her face drained of friendliness. "Yes, sir."

John fought the urge to apologize. He was butler, and she was a housemaid, and however matters might be between them privately, he was responsible for running the house to Mr. Summers's satisfaction. Besides, it would put him in a damnable position if Mr. Summers took a dislike to his wife. "Thank you, Sukey."

She nodded and went quietly in, the spring gone from her step. John could not help going over the conversation as he continued his inspection of the hallway, searching for a more tactful way to give the same command.

He hadn't missed this particular dilemma of authority when he became a valet. Or any dilemmas of authority, for that matter. What had he got himself into?

He opened the narrow cupboard under the stairs, and thoughts of Sukey flew entirely out of his mind. Thea was curled up inside, fast asleep.

He cleared his throat once, then twice. She didn't stir. Her cheek was pressed to her knees, her mouth open and drooling. She looked heartbreakingly young and tired. Service was a difficult life for a young adolescent; later, it was easier to accept that one's life was mostly drudgery and always would be, and one grew more adept at fitting in enjoyment around the edges. But at thirteen, it still sometimes seemed monstrously unfair that one could not simply finish one's book when one was near the end, or—well, hide in a cupboard and sleep when one was tired. He glanced towards the closed study door.

"Thea," he said as loudly as he dared. Nothing. He laid his hand on her shoulder.

She jerked awake, trembling, and hit her head on the underside of the stairs in trying to get away.

John stepped smartly back from the cupboard door. She clambered past him, stopping as far off as she could without seeming disrespectful.

"Thea, you know you ought not to be sleeping during the day," he said gently.

"Yes, sir. It won't happen again, sir," she said almost inaudibly. A cobweb clung to her cap.

John jotted the cupboard down in his notebook as needing greater attention from the maids. "I will not mention this to Mr. Summers."

She gave him a darting, apprehensive glance. "Yes, sir, thank you, sir."

Not knowing what would calm her fear of him, and not wishing to distress her further, John said, "You may go back to your work."

"Thank you, sir." She fled, giving him a wide berth.

When the time neared for the servants' dinner, he repaired to the kitchen early, glad not to find Mr. Bearparke there. "Have you an inventory of your larder and pantry, Mrs. Khaleel?"

"I believe Mr. Summers has one of the pots and things."

"But none of the stores?"

"No, sir. I know how much of everything we have."

"Should you object to my taking one?"

She raised her eyebrows. "I'm not stealing, if that's what you mean."

"I did not mean to suggest any such thing." John felt exhausted. "I promise you I did not. I merely like to have things written down." He didn't point out the obvious, that in her absence or illness it would help the rest of them, for fear she would take offense at that as well.

She nodded, setting a large loaf of bread and a kettle of stew on the table. Curry wafted towards him.

"That smells delicious," John said honestly, hoping to please her.

"Thank you. It would be better if you English folk could tolerate cayenne." She said it drily, but he thought she meant it in a friendly way.

"Mr. Bearparke was brought up in India, I take it," John said delicately, coming round to his true purpose. "Does he enjoy cayenne?"

She didn't look at him. "Yes, sir, his father worked for the East India Company. I keep pepper sauce on hand for when he dines here."

There was a silence as John debated with himself. "If you like, I could speak to Mr. Summers about Mr. Bearparke coming to live here. I thought perhaps you might not like the idea."

She met his eyes then, defiantly. "I *don't* like the idea." She sounded hopeless of being believed.

He nodded mildly.

"He's a very nice young man, and a rich one, but I don't want a man to court me because I remind him of his ayah."

"His ayah?"

"His nursemaid," she said flatly, going to the hearth to examine the chicken roasting for Mr. Summers's dinner. As it had clearly been put on the spit in the last five minutes, he thought this a pretext to keep him from seeing her face.

"Would you like me to speak to Mr. Summers?" He didn't want to—it was his first day in a new home, and Mr. Summers was obviously on good terms with his curate and looking forward to sharing his home again—but he would.

"No, thank you." She poked at the potatoes baking in the drip pan. "Did Mr. Summers tell you why the previous butler left?"

"Not precisely."

"He was…he took liberties. The upper housemaid before your wife, Lucy, she couldn't stand it any longer and gave notice. She wept in Mr. Summers's study, and he winkled the whole story out of her." She gave John an imploring look. "I thought he was only a nuisance. I thought it was just me. I didn't know he was bothering the girls too. If I had, I'd have spoken out."

"I have no doubt you would have."

"We're lucky he believed us. I can't make more trouble. Twice in six weeks? He'd think I must be doing something to encourage them. That because I conversed with Mr. Bearparke sometimes, I…"

John hated that it was true. He'd seen it a dozen times in his career: a gentleman or lady taking a fancy to a servant, and a few weeks later the unfortunate person was out on his or her ear.

"Mr. Bearparke's been a gentleman so far," she said.

"Please tell me if he doesn't remain so. I will help you."

"Thanks."

He was debating what more he could helpfully say when Molly came in to lay the table.

Mrs. Khaleel walked by him with a pot. "If *you* don't remain a gentleman to the girls, I'll poison you," she said too quietly for Molly to hear.

"Understood."

* * *

The clock chimed eleven. Mr. Summers had gone to bed an hour ago, and

Sukey herself curled up beneath the blankets for half that time. *Like a human warming pan,* she grumbled to herself. *Everything nice and toasty by the time he gets here.* She had no notion what John could be about, other than avoiding her, but that made the fourth time he'd rattled the back-door knob to be sure it was locked.

This was the one thing about their marriage she was sure he *did* want. Could he be nervesome? No, she remembered the casual kiss he'd given her after she'd stroked him, how he'd taken in stride something entirely new to her. More likely his nerves were for his first day at the vicarage, and getting to bed was at the bottom of the endless list he was keeping. He must go through those little memorandum books by the dozen at this rate.

Sukey was tired and she had to be up at half past five. Serve him right if she just went to sleep.

But she'd been working since half past five this morning, all except the half-hour she'd spent getting married. Even that had been presided over by their employer. She didn't want to go to sleep without a few moments that were hers. She wanted Mr. Toogood to come and talk to her under the sheets. She wanted him to touch her. Oh, how she wanted him to touch her. She'd been waiting weeks for him to do it.

She thought about getting up to ask him to bed, but it was so cold. The butler's pantry, being a low growth at the back of the house without a room above, was the sole room with no chimney near it. Sukey was glad of the privacy, but the only heat came from the brazier in the far corner, holding coals that would start tomorrow morning's fire in the study.

Besides, she didn't want to beg him. She wanted him to want it as badly as she did, the way he had in Mrs. Pengilly's kitchen. *I brought myself to completion, thinking of taking you.*

She'd closed the sliding shutters except for one, cracked open to let in a beam or two of moonlight. She was alone in the pitch dark, on her wedding night. It was only good sense to prepare a little, so it wouldn't hurt if he was in a hurry. She skimmed her hands up to cup her tingling breasts.

Mmm. She rolled her hands, sensation spreading evenly through her breasts like a thimbleful of dye through water. Pulling up the hem of her nightdress, she reached underneath to tease one bare nipple.

In a flash she was frantic, her body restless and taut as if something was trying to get out. *I could go into that back corridor and ask him to fuck me right there against the wall,* she thought. But she couldn't, and probably he wouldn't, anyway.

Sukey had spent nearly three weeks in this snug little room by herself. If Mr. Summers rang the bell at night, it was up to Molly to answer it, not her. Three weeks of glorious privacy, and she'd held back from finally discovering what all the fuss was about venereal orgasm. It was part being worn out in a new job, and part embarrassment at being twenty-two and not yet knowing. But mostly it'd been a shy, mawky desire for him to give this to her, the first time.

Well, she'd waited, and he couldn't even be bothered to show up. That's what she got for relying on a man. She felt about between her legs. She slid a finger down her cunny and up again, and her mouth fell open. Oh yes, she remembered this from her few fumbling attempts in the past. Touching her slit was nice, but this spot above it was much, much nicer.

She petted it gingerly. Oh. Oh, yes. She went on, lost in sensation. *I'll go to sleep after this, legs spread, and he'll come in and stick his cock in me without bothering to wake me up first.* She imagined it, starting awake from sleep to unexpected pleasure, an unexpected weight on her body, tangled in the blankets and pinned to the straw mattress, his thrusts—

Suddenly everything was much, much better than before. A fever raged through her, a bright flash of lightning. She was hot, pins and needles all over, about to split open like a ripe plum. She did split open, her cunny convulsing, her body shaking and shivering.

It was so much more wonderful than she'd ever really believed it would be. She lay there, gasping and giddy, a wide foolish smile on her face.

The door creaked open, and her husband came in with his candle and began going around the room making sure the chests and cabinets were locked.

She giggled. "Come to bed." Her tongue felt thick in her mouth.

He went to the shutter she'd left open an inch or two. "This ought to be locked at night."

"It squeaks something awful. We'd hear if someone tried to get in."

His candle was near his face, so she could see his frown. "Then it ought to be oiled."

"But then I couldn't leave it open, and I like the moonlight."

"It lets in drafts."

"You wouldn't notice if you were in bed with me."

"The security of the house is my responsibility. Imagine a burglary my first night here."

"Is that what you've been imagining?" she asked tartly. "I've been imagining you in bed with me."

He went very still, turning towards her. "Have you?" he asked, a reluctant smile in his voice.

"Mm. For quite a while. Promptness is a virtue, Mr. Toogood."

"So is care," he said primly.

She sighed. "I don't have time for this. A minute ago I spent for the first time in my life, and if you don't come over here and make me do it again, I'm going to sleep."

He set the candle down. His face was in darkness, but she heard him swallow. "You did what?"

She blushed, wishing she hadn't said it. But they were married, and she was drunk and tingly all over, and she wanted that wonderful feeling again *now*. "You heard me."

"For the first time in your life?" He sounded more appalled than anything else. "You never...?"

She blushed harder. "You try being a girl. It isn't so very obvious what to do, and it takes a long time, and I always got bored or fell asleep before."

"But not tonight." He blew out the candle. Taking off his shoes and shrugging out of his coat, he began carefully arranging his clothes on a chair by the window. Which meant that, while she couldn't really see him, she could see the *outline* of him, moonlight creeping around the edges like sneaky fingers. *Good idea, moon.*

The gathered wool shoulder of his coat gave way to clinging, rumpled linen, which gave way—Sukey held her breath—to the smoothness of skin and muscle. As he turned to hang his shirt on a cabinet knob, she caught the edge of his hipbone.

"Not tonight," she agreed breathlessly.

He took a nightshirt from his trunk and pulled it over his head. For a brief moment his cock was outlined by moonlight. Too brief, alas, to see much but that it stuck out from his body, but Sukey tightened happily, everywhere.

"And how do you feel?" he asked.

"Oh, tol-lol," she said airily.

He huffed a laugh and crawled into bed with her. She turned towards him just as he landed on top of her, pushing himself down until his head was entirely beneath the quilt. Rucking up her nightdress, he pressed a hot, openmouthed kiss to her belly, and then took one nipple in his mouth.

Dear God. They had barely done anything but kiss before. Even when he'd spent, they'd both been fully dressed. Now his mouth was open on her bare flesh. This was more and strange and different and Sukey loved it at once.

"I was worried I wouldn't be able to satisfy you twice in a night," he confessed, his beard-roughened cheek scraping her soft skin.

"Were you really?" she asked, delighted that he'd been nervesome after all.

He nodded, pushing himself lower, and Sukey realized what he was going to do. Her legs were open and her nightgown already pushed above her breasts, if she was going to object she'd best do it quickly—

"Never mind, I don't object," she said. "But doesn't it taste—"

"It tastes like a woman. I like women."

"Stop talking," she ordered, and he did. Oh, that was wonderful, entirely different than fingers—*more efficient,* she thought, and almost laughed because her husband was so very efficient. Soon that lovely, unimaginable feeling rushed over her again. She couldn't believe her luck.

She felt every brush as Mr. Toogood moved up her body, his head emerging from the blanket to hover above hers. He was so much taller than her that his hips dug into her thighs. She tried to wriggle downwards, hoping even just for his cock to graze her tender flesh. "It's a good thing I didn't know about this or I'd have been married a long time ago." She wriggled again.

He laughed and reached down between them, moving so that...

So that his cock lay between her folds, the head over that particular spot.

He raised himself on his hands to keep his chest from smothering her. She moved a little. Oh, it was so *hard*, and that bump where head met shaft was such perfection.

"We never talked about children," he said.

She couldn't stop moving, but inside, she faltered. "I bought pennyroyal," she said breezily. "I'm not having children with you. Not for a few years, anyway."

Don't contradict me, she begged. *Don't. Don't make me stop doing this.*

"You can't brew pennyroyal here. Our master is a vicar, and it's a very distinctive smell."

"Fine," she hissed, rubbing hard against him. He groaned. "I'll keep it at my mother's."

"She won't mind?"

"She took me to buy it."

He moved down, *bump bump,* and then he surged into her. She'd thought she was split open before, but no, *this* was split open, this was being pried apart and helpless, so full of feeling she could hear her seams stretching. She gasped for breath.

"Does it hurt?" he asked, low as thunder.

She shook her head and pulled him closer, angry with his nightshirt. She pushed it up to claw at the hot skin of his bare shoulders. He shuddered and pushed his cock deeper inside her.

"I suppose you'd be flattered if I said something about how big you feel."

"I probably would," he agreed.

"It would be a lie, though," she said as mournfully as she could when her voice was trembling.

She felt his laugh, chest and hips shaking over hers. "Wrap your legs around me."

That got him even deeper, the bone in his groin hitting her in a really admirable manner. When he hunched forward to kiss her, the angle changed and she knew she'd spend again. She counted against his mouth, *One...two...three...*

Four thrusts and she flew apart, understanding now that her cunny rippled like that to draw him deeper into her. She was supposed to *work* tomorrow, knowing she could be doing this instead?

When her shaking stopped, she lay beneath him like a rag doll, head flopping back at an awkward angle. Part of her wondered if she could do that a fourth time, but mostly she was sleepy and happy and ready for bed. Still her husband thrust into her, grunting under his breath. She wasn't sure how to help him, now her own urgent instincts were quiet.

"John," she said. "May I call you John?"

He nodded jerkily.

"John, next time I'd like you to take off your nightshirt before we do this. Or perhaps wait to put it on until afterwards. That would be more efficient, wouldn't it?" She yanked and tugged until their bare stomachs touched, and then she raised her head and sucked on his nipple.

He made a sound like a shout sucked back down before it could escape. So men liked that too. She licked with the tip of her tongue—he shuddered—and nipped him with her teeth.

"Please," he said raggedly. "Again."

She did, feeling ever so smug. He froze, his groin pressed fiercely against hers, and spent.

Above them, a bell rang. She could feel John go alert, propping himself on his arms as if a few inches closer to the ceiling would help him hear. Long moments passed. Sukey almost fell asleep with him still inside her.

"Yes, Mr. Summers?" they heard faintly.

"That's Thea," John said. "Molly should answer the bell at night."

Sukey froze, much less sleepy. If he went upstairs to investigate, he'd realize what she'd found out over the last weeks: that Molly had got her hands on a key and was sneaking out at night, probably to meet a boy. And then either Molly would get the sack, or she'd think Sukey had peached on her and would make her life hell.

She tried to pull John down beside her. "You can shout at them about it in the morning."

He rolled off her, but he stayed propped up on an elbow. "Thea rises earliest of any of us. She must be allowed her rest."

Sukey's exhaustion left her no defenses against the affection that washed through her. He was so kind, worrying over Thea when he'd ought to be sleeping himself. She put her hand on his lovely, strong shoulder and yanked down hard. Surprised, he fell onto the mattress. "Sleep," she ordered.

"Yes, Mrs. Toogood," he murmured.

Sukey liked that.

* * *

John awoke in the dark. Either clouds covered the moon, or it had already set. Thea hadn't come to wake them, so it was not yet half past five. He rolled over and reached for his watch.

His wife stirred. "What time is it?"

John realized that his watch was still in his waistcoat pocket, hanging on the chair by the window. It was too dark to see the hands, anyway. "Not yet half past five." He turned back to feel for her face with his hands and kiss her.

A smile stretched his mouth of its own accord. Last night—well, he had satisfied her, that was certain. He couldn't remember the last time he'd been so aroused by a woman, so entirely consumed by enjoyment that no stray thoughts had intruded into their bed. He rolled his shoulder, feeling the scratch marks she'd left.

She curled an arm sleepily around his neck, pulling him down on top of her and spreading her legs. "I want to do that again."

When John's mouth fell open, she licked his bottom lip. He made a strangled noise, his body humming and still half-asleep, pleasure building as quickly and easily as in a dream. He pushed their nightclothes out of the way, feeling to see if she was wet. She was, and he entered her. Oh sweet Heaven, how she took him in. He moved slowly, unable to believe his luck at having married her.

She moaned and shifted, her small breasts brushing his ribcage. Supporting himself with one arm, he fondled them—for the first time, he realized. They fit neatly in his palm.

She reached between them to touch herself, already so damned wet he could hear himself slapping into her. He tried to match his thrusts to the rhythm of her fingers, tugging at her nipple with each one. She made straining, desperate noises. He wished he could see her face.

"Say something," she demanded.

He'd be embarrassed by this later, but at the moment, flattered by the request, he opened his mouth and said the first thing that came to mind. "You're insatiable."

She laughed breathlessly. "I'm what?"

"Never quotted," he said, using the country word. "How many times do you think I can fuck you today?"

"Five or six," she gasped. "I'll come and find you when I get bored of housework."

He shut unseeing eyes. "I'll be making an inventory of the pantry, and you'll just walk in and demand I put my cock in you."

"Yes," she said. "Yes, and you'd do it. You would."

"I would." He gave her a fierce thrust. "The shelves would be in the way. I'd have to give it to you on the floor, on your hands and knees."

She spent. John's arms gave out gratefully. He buried his face in his pillow, body half off her so he wouldn't crush her, and let his hips move, using her until he followed her into bliss.

She patted his hip. "Don't worry," she said teasingly. "I don't really expect you to fuck me five or six times a day. I know you're old and infirm."

John turned his face to the side so he could breathe. He didn't feel old and infirm at the moment.

The clock struck six. "What in blazes?" He sprang to his feet, waking soreness in unexpected places, and wrapped his shirt round his hand to snatch the lid off the brazier. The embers' light was barely enough to see by, but there was no time to fuss with his tinderbox. His shoulders twinged painfully as he pulled the shirt over his head. Damn. He *was* old and infirm.

"Thea must have overslept." Sukey pulled on her shift.

"Because Molly made her answer the bell in the night," he said grimly. Her silence struck him as weighted. He gave her a sharp glance. "You've been here nearly three weeks. Is this a common occurrence?"

"No."

"How uncommon is it?"

"I'm your wife, not your spy."

His fingers stilled on his buttons. "I'm not going to report them to Mr. Summers. I only want to know."

She frowned in surprise. Then she shrugged, combing out her braids with her fingers. The ribbons that tied them were frayed. He ought to buy her new ones. "Then wait and see for yourself. Do up my buttons, will you?" She glanced at him through her loose hair. "I'll get the girls up if you start the fires."

It stung to see her try to protect them from him. His mother had always shielded the underservants from his father's temper too.

It was his first full day here. He didn't want to start it by making everybody dislike him and think of him as a person one needed to be protected from. Yet he ought not to be lenient merely to curry favor, but begin as he meant to go on.

By making everybody dislike you? he asked himself sardonically.

So be it. "I'll wake the girls. You may start the fires and wake Mrs. Khaleel."

Her eyes narrowed. "Suit yourself." She tucked her hair into her cap. He wanted to do it for her. A few minutes ago, she would have let him.

He hadn't done anything to merit the change. He was entirely in the right. He raised an eyebrow back. "I shall, Miss Grimes, thank you."

Her pale blue eyes caught the light of the embers, fiercely smug. "I'm Mrs. Toogood now."

His neck heated. Damn it all to hell. He hated looking like a fool. "My apologies. I shall, Mrs. Toogood, thank you."

She snatched up the brazier by its handle and whisked herself out of the room, leaving him in the dark.

Chapter Eight

Molly and Thea were dim lumps when he opened the door to their room. "Girls?" Neither stirred. Anything louder would probably wake the vicar, and he had no desire to advertise their failing. He prodded a set of toes beneath the blanket with his foot. "Girls."

Thea rolled over with a small yelp, huddling under the covers. "Who's there?"

That woke Molly, who sat up and put herself squarely between him and Thea, crossing her arms across her full breasts in her nightgown. He carefully looked at the wall above her head, admitting to himself that he should have let Sukey do this. "It's six o'clock," he said in his mildest tones. "Get dressed and start your work. We'll speak about this later." He shut the door behind him and went to wake Larry.

When the maids were dressed and up and about the house, John found Thea in the living room. "Lost time can never be made up," he told her gently. "A day that might have been pleasant and easy is now a day of anxiety and haste."

"I'm sorry, sir," she said as if hoping it would make him go away. She dusted like an automaton. A slow one.

"Thank you. I accept your apology, and I'm sure the rest of the staff will also. Mistakes happen." He'd have liked to leave it there, but doing so yesterday hadn't noticeably reassured her. Sometimes discretion was not the better part of valor. "I gather that you and the other servants have had a difficult time of it, and that the previous butler was not kind."

She hunched her shoulders again, as if to hide that her breasts were growing. Her dress was too tight. He'd have to talk to Mr. Summers about a new one.

"I promise to treat you with respect," he told her. "And I hope that you will do the same for me."

She barely glanced up. "Yessir."

"Remember that we rely on each other in this house. If one of us falls, we all do, like dominoes."

"Yessir."

"I think you will find that the best medicine for trouble is to keep your mind occupied. Over time, the pain lessens, and the satisfaction in industry and self-reliance grows."

She nodded with an audible sigh. The magnitude of the situation seemed entirely lost on her.

"Thea, I've told you I won't mention this or your nap yesterday to Mr. Summers. But many more slips, and he will remark it himself." It was cowardly to shrink from sternness on his own account, and unfair to turn aside the blame onto another. But it was also the truth. He could not keep her from being dismissed if Mr. Summers found out she was sleeping in cupboards when she ought to be working. "I want to help you, but you must help me too."

"With what?"

He remembered her apprehensive reaction yesterday when he said he wouldn't tell Mr. Summers. As if, he realized with a burst of fury at his predecessor, she expected him to demand something in exchange. "With doing your work well. I will *never* expect more from you than that."

She sighed again, heavily.

"I know this morning was not entirely your fault. Last night when Mr. Summers rang, why did you answer, and not Molly?"

She froze. "She was sound asleep and I was up, sir. I thought there'd be no harm in it."

"I see. Is that the truth?"

She nodded frantically, the china Scaramouche she was dusting wobbling. She was lying or scared, but either seemed equally likely.

He moved closer to the mantel to catch the figurine if it fell, noting that Sukey, in her haste, had been obliged to sweep out the ash and light the fire without polishing the fire-irons or cleaning the inside walls of the fireplace. "Answering the bell at night is Molly's task, just as it is yours to make up the first fires and wake the other servants. You may wake her to do it, and if she does not like it, you may refer her to me."

"Yessir."

"If you ever wish to talk to me about any difficulties you have in this house, I will listen."

"Yessir, thank you, sir."

There was nothing else to be said. "If the alarm is not enough to wake you, you might try setting it at the opposite end of the room from yourself. Thank you, Thea, that will be all."

He went out of the room, unsure where to go. He was unfamiliar with everything, unable to simply do what needed doing himself to make up for that lost hour.

More than an hour. An hour for Thea, plus half an hour for each of the other servants, plus the time he was obliged to waste in chastising the girls. He went to find Molly, deciding to help Mrs. Khaleel in the kitchen afterwards, as that required no independent knowledge of anything.

His wife and Molly were in the study, so intent in whispered conversation that they didn't hear him coming. "I didn't tell him a thing," Sukey hissed, "but he isn't stupid."

Could this morning get any worse? He was sorely tempted to eavesdrop further, but that was no way to gain the girls' trust. He let his shoes click loudly on the floor.

They sprang apart. Molly gave him a wary look, but Sukey just tossed her head and hastened from the room. He had felt so close to her a quarter of an hour ago. He wanted that feeling back.

"Thea overslept this morning because she was doing your work in the night," he said plainly. "Why is that?"

"I must have been sound asleep. It's hard to wake me."

What on earth was the secret? Was she bullying Thea into doing her work? Could she have found a means of leaving the locked house at night? Or was she trysting with the footman? A terrible suspicion struck him—but surely Mr. Summers himself could not be molesting Thea. "Did Mr. Summers request that Thea attend him?"

He could see that she took his meaning at once. "No, sir," she said firmly. "It were my fault. I was sleeping too sound."

"It had better not happen again, or you will be getting up at five to light the fires yourself."

"Yes, sir."

"I hope you will speak to Thea and give her leave to wake you in the night if necessary."

"Yes, sir."

"You may work through breakfast today, to make up for lost time."

"Yes, sir," Molly said. "But Thea shouldn't have to miss breakfast, she didn't do anything wrong."

First Sukey trying to shield everyone from his terrible wrath, and now Molly? "As it happens, I did not ask her to. But if you wish to protect her, you would do better to encourage her to do *her* job, and not yours."

She hung her head. "Yes, sir."

"Thank you, Molly, that will be all." Before going to the kitchen, he glanced in at Thea. She was staring blankly at the full ashpan, not moving. How tired *was* the poor girl? He itched to take the ashpan from her, get her on her feet again with a quiet word. The room would not clean itself. But he refrained with an effort.

* * *

"You didn't eat breakfast, Mr. Toogood," Sukey sang out as John carried the breakfast silver past the kitchen door. She stood at the sink, washing Mr. Summers's plate and cup.

Relieved she wasn't holding a grudge, John quashed the urge to snap, *When would I have done that?* He'd been run off his feet ever since his conversation with Molly—first laying out Mr. Summers's clothes and shaving things with

Larry, Molly underfoot emptying the chamberpot and bringing up water when that ought to have been done first. Then he'd helped Thea finish preparing the morning rooms for use, then shaved himself in the near dark before waking the vicar and dressing him. He'd laid the breakfast things, some of which had had to be returned to the kitchen because there were bits of yesterday's butter and marmalade on them. Now if he could just polish this damn silver, he could finally consult with Mrs. Khaleel about the day's remaining meals and what wines to bring up from the cellar...

"Shh," he said, coming closer, and not dulling the edge in his voice as much as he'd hoped to. The tray was heavy. "Mr. Summers has a visitor, and very likely neither of them are fascinated by my eating habits."

Her teasing smile faded. "Oh, I see," she said drily. "Well, I've got an urge to start singing. Aye, there's a *very* bawdy song rattling around in my head trying to get out."

He regarded her impassively, inwardly mystified and vaguely hurt. Was she holding a grudge after all?

"Or you can eat that." She pointed with her elbow, almost knocking Mr. Summers's teacup against the side of the sink as she set it on the drying board. "Won't take but a minute." John glanced in the direction indicated, and saw two fat slices of toast dripping with butter and marmalade.

He opened his mouth to tell her he was busy—but he couldn't. Something wobbled in his chest, and probably in his face too. Sukey ducked her head, blushing and trying to say with every line of her body that it was nothing and why was he making such a fuss?

John set the tray on a nearby table and took a slice of toast. He caught the edge of Sukey's smile as she turned away to check the rising of a bowl of dough. Her apron pulled against her curves, and suddenly John was thinking of last night. And this morning. He blushed too.

Tonight he'd leave the candle lit so he could see her breasts and hipbones and crooked mouth.

But an hour later, watching her through the open door as he cleaned Mr. Summers's dressing room, he thought, *She won't even let me into bed tonight.*

She and Molly were making a hash of the bed. What did they imagine was the purpose of making a bed with two people, if not to pull the sheet quite tight and straight? Reluctantly, he went to explain it to them, hoping against hope they would be glad of the knowledge.

"I've made a bed before," Sukey said, frustrated, the third time he had her pull the sheet out because she absolutely refused to use her entire arm, held perfectly straight, to tuck the corner under.

"Yes, but likely not such a big one, and you were on your own in a boarding house. A man of Mr. Summers's stature expects to get into a smooth bed and have his corners stay securely tucked through the night." Besides, what was the pleasure in making a bed if it was wrinkled and uneven after? But she would undoubtedly mock him if he said so.

She flushed, and Molly said, "There's no need to be unkind."

Sukey froze, and John flinched inwardly. He hadn't meant to be unkind, only state the obvious. But he couldn't allow Molly to think she could dictate how he spoke. He raised one eyebrow, not very far, and regarded her until she slitted her eyes at him and went back to her work.

Sukey let out a breath at having avoided a quarrel. He heard her whisper as he went back to the dressing room, "I didn't mind. Don't get yourself in trouble on my account."

Tomorrow is another day, he told himself as he finished his hasty cleaning of Mr. Summers's shaving things, wishing he could spare a full day for the vicar's wardrobe, which was peppered with stray bits of dirt and old meals, particularly at the cuffs and knees. As he wrote it down in his notebook, he passed Sukey dusting another figurine.

She held it carefully in her apron to get at the back and beneath the folds of the girl's skirt. The vicar must be fond of them—there was one in each room in the house—and she was taking care that they would gleam for him, just as she had polished Mrs. Pengilly's silver.

"They're all part of the same set," he said—an uninspired observation. He hoped she wouldn't think he was trying to condescend to her, when he only hoped to worm his way back into her good graces.

She glanced at him warily. "I like them, they're bright."

"Lady Tassell has a set. They're from Bavaria." He drew nearer to her. "Characters from the commedia dell'arte."

Wrapping a corner of apron around her pinky finger, she wedged it between the figurine's arm and body. "What's that?"

"What Italians have instead of our harlequinade. You're holding Columbine." He ran a dust cloth over the empty mantel for her, and she replaced the little china girl on it, turning her to find the prettiest angle and stepping back to admire her.

"I don't know what a harlequinade is either."

Of course. Lively St. Lemeston had no theater. "It's a kind of play using the same characters over and over in new situations." He took his courage in his hands. "I didn't mean to be unkind earlier."

"Oh, Molly's a mother hen, that's all. You were right, I'm not used to anything so grand." She sighed, looking about the modest bedroom, plainer and smaller than anything at Tassell Hall. "If you'd tried, you probably could have got one of the housemaids at Lenfield House to marry you."

John knew several beautiful and accomplished women who worked at the nearby Tassell estate. "I had no wish to try," he said quietly.

Her face brightened with one of her confident smiles that was half-bravado. Impulsively, he put his hands round her waist and lifted her onto the nearby footstool (intended for the more pedestrian purpose of dusting the ceilings). When he kissed her, she kissed back, her mouth soft and hot. The anxiety of the day curled into a ball and settled at the bottom of his stomach, out of the way.

Her hands curved over his shoulders. "I can't half wait for tonight," she whispered, and nipped at his jaw. "Please don't dawdle locking up."

The door swung open. "Now, now," Mr. Summers said, dry amusement in his voice. "I know you're new wed, but there are impressionable young women in the house."

The ball of anxiety stretched and clawed at him. Of all the people to catch them! John stepped away, resisting the urge to look down at his apron for any telltale bulge in his trousers. "I beg your par—" His voice cracked.

Mr. Summers chuckled.

"It's not his fault, sir." Sukey bobbed her head with a hopefully sly smile. "I'm irresistible."

John cringed. He hated that her insouciance charmed him so much when they were alone, and mortified him so before their master. It was bitterly unkind to wish her quiet—especially when she was a better judge of the situation than he, for Mr. Summers cackled.

"So you are, my dear. Perhaps you had better remove yourself from her orbit, Mr. Toogood. Accompany me to my study, as I wish to discuss the Christmas brandy with you."

In the study, Pantaloon leered at him from the mantel, a ridiculous old lecher.

* * *

That night, John came to bed prompt as anything. He left the candle lit while he made love to her. At first Sukey thought it was because he wanted to see her body—but he got up after and went out of the room, checking the doors and windows again, and then sat down with his blighted notebook and pencil!

"It's bedtime." Was it her wifely duty to drag him to bed, just as she'd had to force breakfast down his throat? No, one must draw the line somewhere. "What are you even about?"

He smiled at her. "I'm creating a list of tasks for everyone on the staff, so that things may be done more efficiently."

Her heart sank. It would be nothing but quarrels and chidings as far as the eye could see. "It's your first week. Can't you let well enough alone for now?"

He put down his pencil. "I don't set much store by well enough, I'm afraid."

"Of course you don't." She flopped back against the pillow. She didn't like that after one night of being married, she already missed having him beside her in the bed. "Don't blame me when you fall asleep and drop the tea tray on Mr. Summers's foot."

He smiled tiredly, the gray in his beard catching the candlelight. She'd kissed that stubble just a minute ago. "I won't. Good night, Mrs. Toogood."

She rolled away from the light, tucking the blankets so snug around her that when he did at last come to bed, it woke her. He curled up on his side of the bed, and his hand—she fancied his hand hovered between them, the blankets lifting as if he would place it on her hip. But a moment later it landed heavily on the pallet and stayed there.

* * *

"I can't read this," Molly said flatly, looking at the list of tasks, arranged by hour of the day, that John had neatly written for her. Sukey read her own, feeling cold and small. It began,

Half past 5 a.m. Clean fire irons and black-lead fireplaces in rms. not used in morning.
Clean all marble hearths.*

A note was written at the bottom of the sheet: *(*) denotes tasks to be performed once per week.*

They each held like papers, with faces that bespoke a like dismay. John seemed unfazed. "Can you read at all?"

Molly flushed. "Print, a bit. Not flourishy writing like this."

"I can make you another, writ in block letters, with sketches to help you make it out," he said calmly. "When you've followed it a week or two, you won't need the paper anyway."

Sukey was grateful he didn't make a fuss; for a moment she'd been afeared it hadn't occurred to him how many working folk never learned to write. Nor read, for that matter. As a child she'd hated her mother sitting her down with a slate to copy out the alphabet, and later the Psalms, for an hour at a time, boxing her ears when she got it wrong, but she was grateful now.

Molly dug her heels in. "You've given Thea too much, sir. She can't do all that and fetch and carry for the rest of us. We do well enough as we are, sir, don't we? Why the change?"

"Because I think we can aspire to better than 'well enough'."

Sukey sighed inwardly.

"I have remarked over the last week that many important tasks are regularly forgotten or omitted because you have no time for them or have not been in the habit of doing them. With increased efficiency, more could be accomplished. Of course I hope you will let me know how you find your lists, and in a month's time we may change them should they prove really impossible."

"Has Mr. Summers complained?" Molly demanded, voice rising. Sukey winced.

John regarded her steadily.

"Sir," Molly added, bowing her head mutinously.

"If you like, we may go to Mr. Summers and ask him whether I have the authority to set you household tasks."

The girl's mouth set.

"In fact," he said, "I believe that as under-housemaid, you are obliged to obey myself, Mrs. Khaleel and Mrs. Toogood."

"Yes, sir." Molly gave Sukey a glare. She writhed inwardly. *Don't drag me into this, John.*

"I have no wish to set myself up as a tyrant," he said to them. "The alteration will be difficult at first, but I think that if you will try to follow the course I have laid out, you yourselves will find that your work becomes easier. I hope we may all treat each other with courtesy and respect in the meantime. If you have no questions, you may go, and if you wish to stay and discuss your list with me, you may do so."

Everyone hurried out of the butler's pantry but Larry, who filled the next half-hour with anxious requests for explanations. John gave them patiently, feeling more and more discouraged. When the footman was satisfied and John could get back to work, his spirits sank further to see his wife and Mrs. Khaleel talking quietly in the kitchen doorway, heads bent over their lists. *Talking sedition,* John thought. When Sukey saw him, she stepped back with a guilty flush.

"You've put thorough cleaning days on Wednesday, sir," the cook said.

"Yes, Mrs. Khaleel?"

"That's market day, sir."

His shoulders sagged a little. "Ah, yes. Thank you for bringing the matter to my attention. Will Friday do?"

Mrs. Khaleel looked at Sukey, who looked back as if to say, *Don't drag me into this.*

"On Friday, I make refreshments for the parish vestry meeting," the cook said, "and Thea goes with Mr. Summers to serve them. They only didn't meet last week because of Advent."

"Of course," John said, feeling a fool. He could not help thinking that Sukey might have spared him this. There she went, scurrying out of the room while he was occupied. "I remember now. Mondays, then?"

"I think Mondays would serve admirably, sir, thank you."

"Wonderful. Thank you, Mrs. Khaleel." John went to find his wife. He could not decide whether he was irritated or hurt that she hadn't been willing to talk to him herself. He was hardly a Judge Jeffreys—or a Mrs. Humphrey.

He found her at once, airing and dusting the upstairs bedrooms in compliance with her list. *Are you afraid of me?* He couldn't ask that. "Mrs. Khaleel and I have agreed to change general cleaning days to Monday," he told her. "Is there anything else on your list that must be altered directly?"

"I don't think so, no."

"I did not mean them to be an unalterable proclamation," he told her. "I said I welcomed suggestions."

"But you didn't, when Molly—"

"I objected to Molly's tone, not her opinions."

"She's worried about Thea."

"So am I."

She came closer and put a hand to his lapel, trying to coax a smile from him. "You worry more'n you ought. We all know Mr. Summers didn't complain. I don't know what the countess expected at Tassell Hall, but you can relax a fraction here."

His face stiffened until it felt like a mask. She just wanted everyone to relax and be friends, but sometimes things needed to actually be *accomplished*. "A master who is made to suffer for indulgence soon learns to be harsh."

She threw up her hands. "Maybe Mr. Summers rates charity and mutual goodwill above efficiency." She spat out "efficiency" like a curse, and then looked appalled at having done it.

I see no reason to assume Mr. Summers's priorities align with your own. John struggled with his temper. "A month isn't so long. If you all still hate it in a month, I'll come up with something else."

She hesitated, an expression he couldn't read flitting across her face. "Now you've finished writing the lists, will you stay in bed instead of jumping up as soon as…as soon as you're satisfied?"

John was startled. He had been sure she was busily wishing she'd found a quiet position somewhere else instead of marrying him. For the first time this morning, he felt his mouth curve up. "Does it really matter to you?"

She beamed back, looking immensely relieved. It came to him that perhaps she wasn't afraid of him. Perhaps she only wanted him to like her as much as he wanted her to like him. "Oh, I only want to know if you'll be out of the way when I receive my lovers," she said, drawing away an inch—but only an inch. Still within easy reach.

He glanced at the door, then leaned down to whisper in her ear. "How many lovers?"

"Oh, not above half a dozen. One doesn't like to be greedy."

His eyes flickered to the door again. "I think Molly is leaving the house at night. That's why I've been staying up. I heard Thea answer Mr. Summers's bell again last night."

Every night, though, he wished he were in bed with his wife instead. If Molly wasn't sneaking out, he was losing sleep for nothing, and if she was, catching her would force him to decide if he could conceal it from his employer.

After all, what did he care if Molly had taken a lover? She looked terribly young to him, but at her age he'd lost his virginity to a chambermaid at a house party. Though it had always been a fact of life that if a servant was caught engaging in an affair, he or she—and more especially she—would likely find herself out on her ear, John had never yet made it his business to carry tales.

Blast these small households where they kept the maids walled up like nuns! In a large establishment, with plenty of menservants and visiting back and forth with other large establishments, it was easy enough for a girl to find a lover without filching keys or shirking work.

Perhaps they would all be better served if he asked Sukey to whisper a discreet word in Molly's ear about the virtues of pennyroyal tea.

He should have stayed a valet.

Sukey's heart sank again. She'd been feeling so cheerful for a moment there! All week she'd been worrying that John regretted marrying her, as it became clearer and clearer that she was not in the least what he was used to in an upper housemaid.

A minute ago, she'd read in his face everything he'd have liked to say—about how ignorant she was, and lazy, and how the word "efficiency" shouldn't be mocked. Her idle worries had grown to an awful lump just below her ribcage. If she could have blurted out *You still like me, don't you?* without sounding clinging and whinging, and not the sort of wife men liked at all, she would have.

And then he'd said, *Does it really matter to you?* and she'd realized he wanted to ask her the same thing.

Now what should she do? Say he was mistaken about Molly? "Why did you not go up and catch her gone?"

"Thea would only make up a plausible excuse for her, and besides..." He hesitated. "When I went to wake them the first day, they were frightened to have me in their room. I had rather catch her coming or going. I waited until three this morning for her to return."

She looked at him. Good Lord, he'd barely slept. He was worried indeed. And, she guessed, he hoped to keep this from their master. If he had gone up and spoken to Thea, Mr. Summers would have heard him.

"Then it's no use staying up again," she said. "You'll get circles under your eyes, and all Mr. Summers's guests will remark upon it."

He lowered his voice even further. "If she gets herself with child..."

If Molly got herself with child, there would be nothing either of them could do to keep it from Mr. Summers for long. And Sukey was getting fond of the girl. She reminded her of Mrs. Dymond a little, always crossing her arms and glaring, and she drew good-luck talismans on scraps of paper. Sukey had a sketch of a holly leaf tucked into her shift right now.

"Do you really think she's meeting a man?" She could come up with no better explanation herself. "She's so hardheaded."

He shrugged.

Oh, why should Sukey fret herself into an early grave for a girl who'd never thank her for it? *Molly's job is Molly's lookout,* she told herself, *and no reason for John to stay up at night when he could be in his warm bed.*

"I suppose sometimes it's difficult to be hardheaded," she said mournfully. "When a gentleman is very handsome."

His mouth twitched. "Is it?"

She widened her eyes. "I hope you don't think I meant you!"

He laughed. Feeling very daring, she took his hand and placed it on her breast. John glanced at the door and moved towards her, turning as if to push her against the wall—and then he stepped away. "You win, Mrs. Toogood. Tonight I'll stay in bed with you."

They'd been married a week already, and they'd be married many more, and yet all that day Sukey counted down the hours to nighttime, skin crawling with eager frustration. The novelty hadn't worn off of lovemaking, but that wasn't all. He'd promised to stay with her. She'd convinced him. She was a siren.

She daydreamed through supper about falling asleep with his strong arms around her, safe and cherished, instead of trying to nod off to the pencil-scritching sound of him thinking hard about nothing to do with her.

"What are you doing on Saturday, Molly?" Mrs. Khaleel asked.

She tried to listen to the conversation. If she ignored the other servants, they'd think she was getting above herself. John was off serving Mr. Summers's tea and answering the bell so the rest of them might eat in peace, having taken his own hasty meal during Mr. Summers's dessert. He did that every day, and every day his kindness sweetened Sukey's supper.

"After the mummers' play, I have to help my friend Sarah with her washing," Molly said glumly. "She's been ill and not able to keep up with the work." Groans of commiseration went up around the table. She sighed. "All our other friends are going nutting. I asked them to help us, but..."

"I'll help," Larry said. Sukey was impressed. You'd never catch her making an offer like that.

"Oh, you don't have to do that," Molly said, taken aback. "It's your holiday."

Larry shrugged, helping himself to some more rice pudding. "I don't mind."

"What about you, Thea?" Sukey said before Molly, who looked about to break down in tears of gratitude, could nobly insist she didn't need him.

Thea shrugged. "Dunno."

Sukey remembered being Thea's age and hating to be asked about anything, so she didn't press her. "And you, ma'am?"

Mrs. Khaleel smiled. "Imogen Makepeace's mother always makes soup from the remains of her goose, and I'm to make the dumplings." She looked happy about it, so Sukey didn't say it didn't seem like much of a holiday to her.

John walked in. Sukey felt as scalded as a biscuit dipped in coffee, even though he'd only come to fetch a taper.

He scowled at a candle-end, no doubt weighing if it *was* a candle-end now and his perquisite. She'd seen him fussing over this question a time or two already, afeared both to take a candle not his by right, and to give Mr. Summers one that would burn out during use.

"Mrs. Toogood?" the cook said.

"Beg pardon? I'm sorry, I was sowing gapeseed."

Mrs. Khaleel shot an amused glance between Sukey and the object of her gaping, who was slipping the candle-end into his pocket. Maybe tonight he'd light it while they— "I asked what your plans are for Saturday."

Sukey dragged her eyes back to the table. "Going to the mummers' play, but after that, I'm not telling. That's my time to be free of all of you."

* * *

She'd barely closed the shutters when he shut their door and pressed against her from behind, his arms making a cage when he set his hands on the table. "Don't move," he whispered, taking his lit candle-end to the iron chest that held the silver. Then he was snug at her back once more, already hard.

"You'd better check the locks," she said.

"I checked them all twice."

"Even the windows?"

He faltered, and she cursed her heedless tongue. But he undid her buttons, holding her gently but firmly in place when she tried to turn towards him. He pushed her gown off her shoulders and had her step out of it, pausing to lay it carefully by. Then her flannel petticoat, and her linen one.

For a moment Sukey wished she hadn't been working since half past five, and smelled sweeter. But he must have not minded it, for his hands shook on her corset laces. At last he lifted her stays over her head and set them aside.

She drew in a glorious gulp of air. The first breath after unlacing was always free and heady, a small perfect moment, and when his hands cupped her bosom through her shift, the first thing to touch her so close all day, she gasped a second time and arched her stiff back. He teased her through the linen, pinching her nipples until she was whimpering.

Then he teased her between her legs, unbuttoning his breeches with his other hand. She was so excited, so eager for him—she reached up and pinched at her own breasts, because she had to and because she'd learned he liked it.

But he set his hands on her hips, hefting her off her feet and pitching her forward until she clutched at the table for balance. She fetched up flat on her belly, breasts crushed against the pine.

She cried out when he pushed up her shift and slipped a finger into her, testing her wetness, and cried out once more when he drove into her. It wasn't what you'd call a comfortable position, but maybe that was why she liked it. She liked the way her legs dangled, her arse in the air. She liked how the table slid when he thrust. She liked feeling small and helpless under his onslaught, under the onslaught of pleasure. He surged into her over and over, and just as she thought he'd spend, he stopped, thighs trembling between hers. She wriggled, but he put a hand on her back to stop her. "Don't move or I'll come."

"Why don't I want that?"

He breathed in and out, lodged deep within her, and—this was nice too. Being joined, and aching, and not so urgent. When his fingers slid firmly up the back of her neck, her shiver made him shiver in answer. Untying the strings of her cap, he set it aside. The easing of that slight pressure on her scalp was near as glorious as taking off her stays—and then he began feeling for her hairpins.

She moaned in surprise and sank forward, resting her cheek on the wood as he skimmed his fingers over her hair and burrowed in, until every last pin was out. He combed through her hair, loosening and fluffing it, and fanned it out on the table. She stretched and shifted like a cat, striking sparks of pleasure where his hard length was still buried inside her.

"You filched this pin from Mrs. Dymond's sister, didn't you?" He dragged the twin tips of the curved hairpin down the left side of her spine and up the right, tickling and tingling and better than any backscratcher.

"Does it have a little red rosette?"

"It does, yes."

"I did indeed. Are you going to punish me?"

There was silence behind her. He continued to trace whorls and lines lightly across her back with the hairpin. She shook with pleasant chills, crying out at the way it pushed her up against him. "Please," she begged.

"Please punish you? Or please have mercy?"

"Either."

His big hand spread flat on her lower back. He dragged it up her spine and into her hair, where he clenched his fist, pulling her head up so her back arched and her breasts jutted out. It changed how he entered her, every thrust suddenly unbearably delicious. She moaned, words gone, and he leaned down and cupped one breast, closing and opening his fist in time with his thrusts so her breast squeezed through his fingers, her nipple catching at the last with a painful, wonderful tug.

"Ahhhh," she cried, out of her mind with pleasure. His hand twisted tighter in her hair as he bent over her, curving his body around hers and crushing her to the table. He made that bitten-off growling sound right in her ear and then—oh—he bit her ear, his teeth trembling as he spent.

Every part of her throbbed. Every part of her wanted him. When he softened and began to slip out of her, she moaned with disappointment. When he stood, she felt his effort in the table beneath her.

His hand smoothed over her arse and delivered a light, stinging slap. "That doesn't look very comfortable for you," he said, breathing heavy. "I'll roll out our bed if you fetch the pillows."

Her cunny squelched emptily as she obeyed him. He moved the candle-end to the table and knelt on the bed. "Lie here." She did it.

"Touch yourself," he said. "Bring yourself to completion."

It wasn't the first time he'd asked to watch her do this. It still embarrassed her to take a pleasure in which he had no part, but she liked it too. She pulled up the hem of her shift, exposing her wet cunny to him. He watched without expression as she trailed a hand over her belly, sliding her fingers between her legs, down and up. Teasing herself and making a show.

How quickly this luxury of pleasure had become familiar, almost a necessity. How quickly he'd made her hunger for his cock, his hands, his voice, his gaze. Well, so did he hunger. Look how he watched her. Here, he never thought she ought to do things different or better.

"Put your mouth on my breasts," she said impulsively. He ducked his head with a sharp breath, mouthing her aching nipples through her shift. So hot, his mouth was.

She moved her fingers with more purpose as he pushed her shift up roughly to suckle one breast and then the other. He rolled her nipple carefully between his teeth, and it drove her mad to know he did it with the single-minded purpose of helping her spend, because she'd demanded it and he wanted to obey. She curled a possessive hand over his skull. "Good boy."

Joy racked her at last. Her nipple stretched through his teeth one last time, and he kissed her. "I'm going to check the locks once more, but I'll be back directly."

True to his word, he crawled into bed before she'd even dozed off. She'd thought maybe they'd talk quietly for a bit, but she snuggled up to his big, warm chest and fell asleep at once.

* * *

On Christmas morning, Sukey awoke in darkness. She listened carefully but could hear no one. John didn't stir as she buttoned her pelisse over her nightgown, took his house key from his pocket, and went into the hallway, cracking open the shutter to read the tall clock at the foot of the stairs. Four o'clock.

Sukey grinned to herself. She was the first awake, and the luck of welcoming Christmas into the house and sweeping trouble out the door would be hers. She'd been afeared that she'd lose the privilege she'd always had as maid-of-all-work.

She thought of John in their bed, his tall, commanding form relaxed in sleep. She wanted that luck for herself. She wanted to be happy this year. She tiptoed into the kitchen to fetch the broom.

A door within the room eased open. Instinctively, Sukey flattened herself along the wall, and Mrs. Khaleel—it must be her, as she slept in a closet by the pantry—padded right past her in the dark and into the hallway, not quite shutting the kitchen door behind her. *Stealing my luck,* Sukey thought. But Mrs. Khaleel had no house key. How would she open the door?

Sukey heard the door open.

"Mr. Bearparke," Mrs. Khaleel said, yawning. Sukey's eyes widened, and she peered through the crack of the door. The cook wore her flannel night-rail, her hair in a thick braid over one shoulder. She leaned sleepily against the doorjamb, bathed in the pale light of the waning moon. Meeting him in her bare feet, no less! "Is everything all right?"

Chapter Nine

Mr. Bearparke was a tall, slender shadow in trousers and a man's hat. "I've asked you to call me Ned."

Mrs. Khaleel was silent.

"It's Christmas morning," he said softly. "I thought I'd give you the luck. Where's your broom?"

"Mr. and Mrs. Toogood are just there," she answered softer yet, pointing towards the butler's pantry. "If anyone sees us, they'll think—" She hadn't planned on meeting him, then. But she'd come to the door when he scratched at her window.

Of course, he had a key to the house. He could have walked right in and pulled her out of bed if she hadn't come. Sukey shivered.

"Nora," he interrupted her.

She went entirely still.

"Nora, don't." He stepped towards her, moonlight flashing on his pale, sincere profile, and Mrs. Khaleel retreated until she hit the kitchen door. Sukey drew back. Now all she could see was the cook's hand on the knob. "Nora, you must know I love you."

"I can't. You know I can't. My position—"

Sukey dithered over whether interrupting would be welcome or otherwise, and just how much Mr. Bearparke would resent her for it.

He laughed. "Oh, of course, you don't know. Nora, among my people that's a declaration. I mean, a proposal of marriage."

Mrs. Khaleel drew in a sharp breath. Sukey's own jaw dropped. Marriage? To a gentleman? "No," Mrs. Khaleel whispered. "No, I can't."

"Of course you can, darling." Mr. Bearparke laughed again, rather shakily, as if his own uncertainty was absurd. "You *can*. I'll even take you home if you like. They're saying the East India Company will have to give up its monopoly to convince Parliament to renew its charter this year. Missionaries will be allowed into India at last."

"Missionaries?"

Sukey heard a kiss and, screwing up her courage, inched closer to the door, hoping she'd still be in darkness. Only the cook's hand was pressed to his lips, her face turned away—from Sukey too, praises be.

"Nora, you're shivering," Mr. Bearparke said tenderly. "Let's shut the door."

She broke away from him in a single burst of motion and stood, trembling violently. "I can't. I'm sorry. Ned—I'm sorry."

There was a long silence. "You can't?" he said at last, quietly. "Or you don't want to?"

Sukey squeezed her eyes shut. If he became angry, she'd have to go out there and stand up to her master's friend. She wished she'd stayed in bed and didn't know about any of this. *Please don't be angry,* she thought. *Please be as harmless as you act.*

If she needed to, she could wake John. Or would that make things even worse?

"I don't want to." Mrs. Khaleel's voice was a thread.

Another silence. Then Mr. Bearparke laughed once more, as if his pain was absurd too. "I don't believe you." He did sound angry. "I don't believe you for a moment. You do love me."

She didn't answer.

"You need time to get used to the idea, that's all," he said, his light touch almost restored. "I didn't mean to spring it on you like that. I'll ask again at Epiphany. Think it over, won't you? And don't forget to welcome Father Christmas when I'm gone. It's good luck, you know." But Sukey heard the doorknob and the key rattle in his hand as he went out and locked the door behind him, and it was a long moment or two before his footsteps headed away from the house.

Mrs. Khaleel sank down to the floor, still and hunched.

The safest thing to do would be to wait it out, and then go back to bed and pretend she hadn't seen a thing. Mrs. Khaleel wouldn't be best pleased to know she'd been eavesdropped on. So Sukey waited, listening to the hall clock *tick* and *tock*.

She thought about John. Being tall and self-contained didn't really mean you never needed somebody to look after you. Sukey was already here. She might as well make herself useful.

She eased open the kitchen door. The cook tensed, her head snapping around. "Who's there?"

"It's me. Mrs. Toogood. I couldn't help—well, I expect I could have helped overhearing, but I thought you might need me, and besides, curiosity killed the cat. How are you?"

"Tol-lol."

Sukey was still a little startled every time Mrs. Khaleel talked like a Sussex girl. But the cook had lived in the neighborhood more than fifteen years, having come over from India as nursemaid to a local family when she was a little younger than Molly. Sukey was afraid to go to London, and here Mrs. Khaleel had gone halfway round the world. Sukey sat on the hall floor beside her. "Did you know he wanted to marry you?"

Mrs. Khaleel sighed. "I was afraid he did. It's harder to say no to marriage." Sukey nodded.

"I can't be a reverend's wife," she said, as if Sukey had argued. "I can't."

"Is that all? Why not? If he were a missionary in India, you wouldn't have to worry about embarrassing him before his congregation." Maybe that hadn't been a tactful thing to say. And did she want to go home, as Mr. Bearparke thought? Or had she been glad to get away?

Mrs. Khaleel snorted. "Why does India need missionaries, Mrs. Toogood?"

"Because they're heath...ens." She grimaced. "I'm that sorry. I meant, because they aren't Christians."

"Precisely. I am not a Christian. It doesn't seem to have occurred to Mr. Bearparke any more than it occurred to you."

That brought Sukey up short. Sedate Mrs. Khaleel, a—a what? Did she worship idols? But she went to church every week! "Does Mr. Summers know?"

Mrs. Khaleel shrugged. "I was baptized when I came to England. In India it never troubled my employers, but here—I suppose people talked, and they didn't like it. I go to church. That's enough for Mr. Summers."

Sukey felt a little relieved to hear that. "Then you *are* a Christian, aren't you?"

Mrs. Khaleel looked at her. "I hope not," she said at last. "And my name isn't *Nora*, either. Ned Bearparke is a darling"—her voice wobbled a little over the word—"but I wouldn't be happy with him." The corner of her mouth turned up. "Maybe at first. But I'd hate him after a while. He doesn't know it, but I do."

"Your name isn't Nora?"

"No. It's Noor. But even before I was baptized, no English folk could be bothered to learn it. It isn't even difficult to pronounce, any more than Khaleel! But half the time people get *that* wrong. If you knew how many times I've thought about giving in and calling myself Collins—" Mrs. Khaleel broke off at Sukey's expression. "Sorry."

Sukey was too self-conscious to ask if she'd been mispronouncing it without knowing. "You did the right thing, turning him down," she said, feeling surer of her ground here. "My… This is a secret, so please keep it." There were people who knew. But nobody official. Nobody like Mr. Summers. You could hang for bigamy. That was part of why her mother had never tried to go on the parish, no matter how hungry they got. Sukey shouldn't say anything.

She turned John's ring on her finger, a nervesome habit she'd got into. It comforted her for no reason at all. Mrs. Khaleel's eyes followed her fingers. A little wistfully, Sukey thought. "A ring's nothing," she said, holding hers tight to protect it from any listening pharisees with a sense of humor. "My father, he left my mother. He's got another wife now in Chichester, and me and my mum have been getting by as best we could since I was a kid. People think, 'Oh, marriage, you're a fool to turn that down, you'd be set for life', but you aren't really."

"We will keep each other's secrets."

Sukey nodded, feeling a little proud that Mrs. Khaleel trusted her.

"Would you like to sweep the trouble away from the door? I'm sure your husband would loan you his key."

Sukey dangled the key before her eyes, and they smiled at each other.

The door had been opened already. The luck was gone, wasn't it? But maybe the trouble wasn't. As Sukey took up the broom, a thought struck her. "But he's moving into the house."

Mrs. Khaleel's hand fisted in her lap.

"You should tell John. He could—" Sukey had no idea what he could do. But he knew a lot of things she had no idea of. Why not this? "He could talk to Mr. Summers."

Mrs. Khaleel huffed a laugh. "He told me that too. I daresay he would, for all the good it would do me."

Sukey privately agreed. Mr. Summers seemed kindhearted enough, but Mr. Bearparke was his curate and friend, and Mrs. Khaleel was just his cook. She swept the broom hard across the floor and out the door, and hoped it was really so easy to banish trouble.

* * *

Boxing Day is my favorite day of the year, Sukey thought as the mummers' play began in the taproom of the Lost Bell. She wasn't sure if it was true or if she was drunk on cider and the feel of three whole crowns in the purse between her breasts. Two were wages for the last few weeks, paid on the quarter day yesterday, and one was her Christmas box, given to her by the vicar with festive ceremony this morning.

They'd each got a crown, and John and Mrs. Khaleel a guinea. And the upper servants had already received several presents from the tradesmen with whom they managed Mr. Summers's accounts. Sukey couldn't get over it. Two crowns was a whole quarter's wages at Mrs. Humphrey's, and usually half of it was held back for things broken or scratched or burnt.

Terrified of losing her purse, she kept touching her bodice to be sure it hadn't fallen out. She'd ought to put it somewhere in the butler's pantry, but... well, she'd never say so aloud, but what if another servant stole it? She mostly trusted them, but how could you even blame someone for stealing something so tempting, when it was in such easy reach? It was for the best John was taking his guinea to the savings bank this afternoon, or she'd have run through it in a flash.

He'd offered to share it with her. But she'd said no. Why? What was she so afraid of, that she'd turn down half a guinea for it? What could he expect in return that she wasn't already giving him whenever she had the chance?

But maybe that was the problem: he didn't expect anything in return. She didn't want to be anybody's charity case.

He'd said he'd buy her new gloves without holes too. She'd need them come January, so she'd thanked him and tried to feel smug about her luck in landing him. But even that galled a little, not less because he'd scolded her again five minutes later about making the bed.

She ought to put her own coins aside for a rainy day, but maybe she'd buy something pretty for the servants' ball on New Year's Day. A new cap or a shawl.

She'd never much minded wearing her only gown before. When you dressed for coal-stains and dust every day, it was exciting enough to be clean and curl your hair and leave off your cap and neckerchief. She'd always felt pretty. But she hadn't been married then. She'd had nobody to impress.

John had laughed up his sleeve at her when she'd bragged of Lively St. Lemeston servants' balls. God only knew what the servants he'd been used to living among got up to at the New Year. They drank champagne, most likely. They owned evening gloves and dancing slippers.

She was tired of feeling small and young and country mouse, and as if John had done her a favor by condescending to marry her. She wanted him to pay her court, and feel smug about *his* luck. She wanted to be better than pretty. She wanted to be beautiful.

Mr. Foley cut a particularly funny caper, and Sukey nearly spilled her cider laughing. The grumpy bookseller's Quack Doctor was always the drollest part of the mummers' play.

But all the actors were very gay, capering about with bright patches and strings of spangles pinned to their coats. This year Mr. Whittle from the Lost Bell did the rest one better, sporting an entire coat of bright patchwork. Lord, that must have taken weeks. Did he sew it, or his wife?

It made her think of Mrs. Dymond's sister, bent over her needle from dawn to dusk through all of election season when she'd come, pregnant and unhappy, to live in Mrs. Pengilly's attic. Mrs. Dymond's wardrobe had been unrecognizable afterwards, embroidered and trimmed and dyed to within an inch of its life. Sukey supposed everyone distracted herself in her own way—

That was it! Sukey had meant to go round the shops herself after this, but Mrs. Gilchrist—the girl was Mrs. Gilchrist now, because when you were that beautiful, gentlemen overlooked a little thing like another man's baby on the way—knew the inventory of every Whig milliner and dressmaker and pawnshop in town by heart, and she'd read enough fashion magazines to carpet Market Square. She'd know exactly what Sukey'd ought to buy.

Sukey fidgeted with her ribbon-trimmed hairpin. It would be a fine excuse to visit, but could she really bear to give it up? She'd had it in her hand the first time she'd seen John. He'd trailed it up her back last week.

She shivered, remembering, and John put his arm around her to keep her from cold, as if the crowded taproom wasn't the warmest place in town.

"I'll take you to the Honey Moon after this if you like," he murmured in her ear. "I've heard the mince pies are to die for."

She gave her hairpin a little pat of farewell, and set her hand over his. "Saturday afternoon is my time to be free of all of you, you know that."

So when the play was over, Sukey walked up Cross Street, passing the Honey Moon's delicious smell of brandy and ginger without going in, and waited nervously in the Gilchrists' kitchen while the maid-of-all-work went to inform her mistress of Sukey's visit.

That poor girl must be worked to the bone, Sukey thought, for the kitchen was neat as a pin. Mrs. Gilchrist was the finickiest soul she'd ever had the misfortune to meet.

"Sukey? Happy Christmas. Is everything well with you?"

Sukey recognized Mrs. Gilchrist's rose gown (which must have been let out at the bodice, for the girl's graceful bust had never been so large before), but the great gold shawl wrapped about it with such aplomb looked brand new. So did the snowy linen at her neck and wrists and the frothy cap atop her dark hair. Dashing young matron was a style that suited her.

Sukey bobbed a quick curtsey and held out the hairpin, feeling awkward. "You left this at Mrs. Pengilly's, ma'am."

Mrs. Gilchrist's perfectly arched brows went up, and her lips twitched. "And you finally decided to return it?"

Sukey's awkwardness faded into annoyance. "I'm sorry, ma'am. It slipped my mind."

Mrs. Gilchrist looked at the hairpin. "You keep it. I probably wouldn't wear it again anyway."

Sukey's jaw dropped. "I don't have *lice.*"

"I'm sure you don't," Mrs. Gilchrist said hastily. "I didn't mean to suggest any such thing."

"Of course you didn't." No, she hadn't meant to *suggest* it, but she'd been thinking it. Probably wouldn't borrow a hairpin from her own sister, that's how particular she was.

The girl waited with an air of faint puzzlement as to why Sukey was still there.

Sukey shifted nervesomely. "Could I ask you for some advice? About clothes?"

Mrs. Gilchrist's face lit up. "Please do!" Something about her big dark eyes and the shape of her mouth made her forever look as if she might start crying. But if she cried about fashion, they'd be tears of joy.

"I got married."

"Oh, yes, I heard the banns. I wish you joy! You married Mr. Dymond's valet, didn't you? Who hates puns on his name and is very good with stains?"

Sukey smiled fondly. "That's him."

"It's splendid being married, isn't it?"

"Yes, ma'am," Sukey said at once, determined Mrs. Gilchrist should have no inkling of her doubts on the subject. "And there's to be a servants' ball for the New Year. I want to look my best. I have a few crowns, and I hoped maybe you'd seen something, at the pawnshop or somewhere." She took off her pelisse. "Something to spruce up this old gown a bit."

Mrs. Gilchrist looked critically at the plain serge. It wasn't even clean, not really. Sukey hoped very much that no coal dust was actually visible. Then she looked at Sukey's face. "You're very pretty. I've always thought so."

That was a pleasant surprise. "Thank you, ma'am."

"We're about of a size. Well, you're a little taller, but that's all right. I'll dress you if you like."

Sukey's jaw dropped. She was sorry for every uncharitable thought she'd ever had about Mrs. Gilchrist. "Would you really?"

The girl smiled broadly, just such zeal in her eye as Bonaparte must have when he looked at the map of Europe: *You won't even recognize yourself by the time I'm through.* "Come upstairs and let me see what I have in my workbox."

There were three gowns in the bottom of Mrs. Gilchrist's workbox, neatly folded and waiting for a glorious resurrection. The girl held each one up against Sukey, eyes narrowed, and Sukey forgot how to breathe.

"This one," Mrs. Gilchrist said, nodding to herself. Sukey was glad to have the momentous decision taken out of her hands. "It brings out your eyes, and I don't think it looks *too* outdated. I copied it from the September 1810 *Ackermann's Repository.*"

The chosen gown, of soft ice-blue worsted wool, was cut *very* low. Sukey had taken it for an underdress, as there wasn't even a seam at the waist; darts gathered it under the bosom—in other words, scant inches from the neckline. "Your mum let you wear that?"

"Oh, there's a chemisette for underneath." The girl waggled her eyebrows. "But I promise it's still very daring. Watch the pins don't come out if you dance in it." She rubbed at a crease in the wool, mouth twisting. "Don't worry, I'll get that out before Friday."

"I'm not worrying," Sukey said, more understandingly than she might have before her marriage. She was beginning to think it a heavy burden, to see only the smudges and not the silver. "It's beautiful."

She crossed town to Mrs. Pengilly's next, to see how she was getting on. To her surprise, as she climbed the stairs she heard John's voice from within. But why was she surprised? True to his promise, he'd found a new attic lodger before taking up work at the vicarage.

Her first instinct, strangely, was to sneak off. But she rapped on the door.

John opened it, of course. He smiled broadly when he saw her, deepening the grooves that laughter had cut in his face. "Come. We were just having a glass of cherry bounce." His flushed face told her he'd already had a glass or two. His voice, raised so Mrs. Pengilly could hear, thrummed through her.

It wasn't *un*splendid, being married.

Harry Pengilly junior poured festive red brandy into a delicate glass and handed it to her.

"Ooh." She breathed in deep. "Smells like summer."

"Smells like Christmas," Harry Pengilly boomed.

It tasted like both, shot through with cherries and cinnamon. Warmth spread through her like sunshine and a crackling wood fire. "Have you still got any of the cherries? Those are my favorite part."

"A girl after my own heart." Mr. Pengilly passed her a bowl of brandy-soaked cherries. She dropped two in her mouth, moaning as the taste spread across her tongue.

John watched her, amber eyes bright, and Sukey wanted to taste cherry bounce in his mouth too. Last Boxing Day—she remembered it with a wince. She'd had some of Mr. Pengilly's cherry bounce, but she hadn't enjoyed a drop, for Mrs. Humphrey had given her a single penny for her Christmas box along with a lecture on why she didn't deserve more.

Every year Mrs. Humphrey had fed her carp-pie with her coin, and every year Sukey had let it ruin her holiday. She'd got Christmas boxes from the boarders, from Mrs. Pengilly and Mrs. Dymond, and yet that penny had sat like a stone in her pocket, sucking up her joy.

"So," Mrs. Pengilly said with a grin. "How's married life treating you, girl?"

Why not make the old woman happy? Sukey put her arms around John's neck and hopped up, aiming for his mouth. He caught her instinctively, as she knew he would, holding her steady against him with her toes off the ground. She pressed her mouth to his, and he kissed her back with fervor, until she grew too heavy and he had to set her down. "Oh, tol-lol," Sukey said, draining her glass.

Mrs. Pengilly cackled and her son whistled, and John flushed and beamed at her. "I bought us a bottle of brandy." He pointed at a green glass bottle on the table, corked and sealed with red wax.

Sukey wouldn't have expected her upstanding husband to buy smuggled spirits, but Harry Pengilly in a selling mood was hard to resist. "Shall we save it for ourselves, or go snacks with the others?" Her instinct was to hoard it, sharing a glass before bed all through Christmas and making love in a warm, tipsy haze. But she found she liked the idea of sharing even better, hosting a late-night party in the kitchen and staying up late, laughing and talking with their new friends. High life belowstairs, indeed!

His mouth curved mischievously. "I thought you might like to give it to Mrs. Humphrey as a Christmas gift."

Sukey made a startled noise. He'd bought a whole bottle of brandy just so she could lord it over her former mistress? Oh, but she wanted to do it!

Mrs. Pengilly burst out laughing. "A fine idea! Did you know she's gone through three maidservants in the last month? The new one's a proper toady. Don't trust her as far as I could throw her, myself."

"That's no matter, Mum," Mr. Pengilly said. "I told her not to come round anymore. I think Mr. Toogood has the right of it. It's high time I found you a nice girl to live in."

"Pooh, it's a waste of money. I do well enough on my own."

While the Pengillys argued among themselves, Sukey whispered, "Thank you."

"I generally strive to avoid pettiness, but a little gloating now and then is good for the spleen." He handed her the bottle.

She flushed, grateful all over again that he had taken her side so easily. "I didn't mean that. Thanks for talking to Mr. Pengilly about his mother."

His fingers lingered on hers. "Of course. I know you're fond of her. By the by, I believe the Dymonds mean to leave for Spain in a few days, should you desire to wish them a safe voyage."

"Do you want to come with me?" She remembered he'd been puzzled she considered Mrs. Dymond a friend of sorts. But he'd been with Mr. Dymond so long.

He hesitated, then shook his head. "I'm foxed, and I'd only distract from his packing. I'll give him good wishes in church tomorrow."

So they left Mrs. Pengilly's together, but he went north towards the vicarage while she held the smooth curve of her brandy bottle in her hands and crossed the street.

She nearly went round the back by force of habit—but she tripped right up to Mrs. Humphrey's front door and boldly seized the knocker.

Miss Starling answered the door. "Sukey!"

The boarders were collected round the fire in the front parlor. "Where's the spinet?" she asked, startled.

Miss Starling sighed. "Mrs. Humphrey sold it. It's all right, I still have my guitar."

Sukey was struck, as she never quite had been before, by how bare the room was—not only because the wallpaper was ancient and peeling, but because there was not a single attempt at decoration of any kind.

Like my mother's room, she thought, unsettled.

Today it looked cheerful enough, bedecked with greenery she was sure the boarders themselves had gathered and hung, but there were no pictures on the wall, not even an old fashion plate put up with tacks. The mantel piled with pine boughs was ordinarily quite empty.

Sukey had never thought much of it. Empty shelves and tables were easy to clean, and she wasn't expected to fuss about with oil and wax for the furniture. But it struck her how much more like a home it might appear, with only a few minutes and a penny here and there.

She supposed it didn't matter much to the boarders. They had their own rooms, and gussied them up to their hearts' content. Only she and Mrs. Humphrey had spent their lives keeping everything that mattered locked where no one could see it.

"Come, come." Miss Starling took her arm. "Happy Christmas! We've missed you on our musical evenings. Sing us a good Robin Hood song."

Sukey had meant to give the brandy to Mrs. Humphrey privately, ever so sweetly, with a poisoned barb or two about making up for any little thing she might have wasted. She'd wanted to rub Mrs. Humphrey's nose in how well she'd done since she left, make her old mistress have to be grateful to *her*. But if she did that, the bottle would go in the locked cabinet and be stretched out over the next two years.

She held out the bottle. "Happy Christmas! Shall we open it?"

"Oh, we couldn't," Miss Starling said. "That's yours."

"I brought it for you ladies." Sukey grinned at her. "I've come up in the world, you know."

"Don't look a gift horse in the mouth," Iphigenia Lemmon called. "Shall

I fetch glasses?"

They looked at each other, thinking of going down to the kitchen to ask Mrs. Humphrey for the use of glasses. Sukey remembered now that breaking one of the set while washing it had been the pretext for omitting a Christmas box altogether on her first Christmas at the boarding house.

Getting the sack here was the best thing that had ever happened to her. Why hadn't she left on her own? Why had it been so easy to stay?

"We shall drink from the bottle," Miss Starling proposed to a chorus of agreement.

"Songs I don't mind, ladies, but shouting—" Mrs. Humphrey froze in the doorway of the room. "Sukey."

"Ma'am." Sukey bobbed a curtsey from habit.

Mrs. Humphrey drew herself up. "If you need to speak with me, you may come round to the back door."

Sukey drew herself up too. It was small and mean, but she hated her old mistress. She hoped her new toady of a maid was stealing.

"She came to see us," Miss Lemmon said. "She's going to sing to us about Robin Hood."

"Happy Christmas, ma'am." Sukey gave her a defiant smile. "Have a glass of brandy at my expense, if you like."

Mrs. Humphrey looked at Miss Lemmon, industriously opening with the bottle with a corkscrew she had produced from somewhere about her person. "I don't drink smuggled brandy," she said abruptly, "and neither should you. It's unpatriotic. What would Lord Wellington say?" She went out and slammed the door.

Sukey felt ashamed—of the smuggled brandy and her own unkindness.

Miss Lemmon passed her the open bottle. "Never mind her," she whispered. "What difference does it make?"

Sukey took a swig. None. It made none at all.

* * *

After leaving the Pengillys', John had meant to buy a secondhand book at

Foley's Folios, but as the proprietor was a mummer and had closed up shop for the day, he had spent a leisurely afternoon by the kitchen fire with one of Mr. Summers's histories. He could wish for more stimulating reading matter, but it was nice to have nothing to do.

Even if he had secretly hoped, as he had the Saturday before, that he and his wife might contrive to share more than a few moments of conversation. But no, this was her chance to get away from him.

"Johnny?"

There she was now, in the doorway of the kitchen. He smiled at her. "Mrs. Toogood."

A few steps into the kitchen made it obvious she was quite drunk. "Mr. Dymond hopes you'll send over your recipe for curing headaches." She spoke very loudly. John hoped the vicar couldn't hear.

"My father swore me to secrecy when he taught me that recipe, I'm afraid. Mr. Dymond celebrated the birth of our Lord rather heavily, I take it?"

"Hadn't even shaved," she confirmed, and laughed at his wince. "He and my poor mistress both were in a bad way. I left them to it pretty quick. I'd have felt sorry for them, only Mrs. Dymond said it was justice for how happy they'd been last night."

She smiled at him, evidently well pleased with him and the world in general. "Wake me up when it's time for my bath, will you?" And she was off again, leaving him to his dull history.

A half-holiday ought to leave one feeling rested, but when Sunday dawned, John only felt discontented and unready to begin another week. A morning spent in church made things worse. This was the first time regular church attendance had been positively required of John by an employer, and today he resented it, as nearly another half-holiday stolen from him. On returning to the vicarage, he was obliged to give himself a stern talking-to before he could go briskly about his duties.

They had all left for the morning service too early to clear the breakfast things; he went to the dining room to make sure that Molly had since done so.

She was rolling up the hearthrug, presumably to take it outside to shake it out. A task Thea ought to have performed that morning.

"Molly?"

She threw him an apprehensive glance before standing, the rolled rug under one arm, and attempting to look blank. A piece of folded paper poked out of the neckline of her gown. On drawing closer, John recognized his own handwriting. A terrible suspicion seized him, a hundred small indications from the last week, overlooked at the time.

"What is that paper?"

"It's the list of chores you gave me, sir." She stood as tall as she could, which wasn't very.

"May I see it?"

There was no way to refuse. She handed it over with a defiant look. Unfolding it confirmed his worst fears. "This appears to be the list I gave Thea." Thea had copied it out again on the back in block print, so Molly could read it.

She frowned. "Is it? We must've got them swapped."

John felt very tired. So, no doubt, did she, attempting every day to accomplish two full days of work. On very little sleep, if his suspicions were correct. Had she taken Thea's tasks in trade for answering the bell at night? It was an uneven bargain, if she had; and Molly had been at him to lighten Thea's work from the moment he'd written the lists.

"You're a good friend, Molly. But one day you will learn that you do others no favors in doing their work for them, instead of encouraging them to do it themselves."

Her eyes narrowed, and he remembered that she had spent Boxing Day aiding a sick friend with her washing. "I'm just helping Thea out for half an hour," she insisted stalwartly. "Mrs. Khaleel sent her into town for some onions."

There was nowhere to buy onions in town that would be open on Sunday, and the hearthrugs were meant to be shaken out in the early morning, when Thea had decidedly not been on an errand. This could not continue.

Mr. Summers was presently at the church, leading the afternoon service. "Thea," John called, loud enough to be heard all through the house. Thea did not appear. "Dorothea Maddocks, where are you?"

He went through every room, opening cupboards and chests, and found her scrambling out from under the bed in one of the guest bedrooms. It was at least a credit to his staff's work that she was not sneezing or covered in cobwebs. "Thea, I found this in Molly's possession." He showed her her list.

She gave him a panicky glance and said nothing.

"I know you are very young," he said gently. "You are evidently in some distress as well. But that is no excuse for allowing others to do your work for you. Poor Molly has been run off her feet."

Out of the corner of his eye, he could see the other servants gathering in the doorway. He went to shut the door, and then reflected that perhaps privacy would not reassure Thea in the way he hoped. "Mrs. Toogood, kindly attend me."

Sukey stepped reluctantly into the room. "Go back to your duties," he told the others. "I do not suppose you would like everyone gawking at *you*." He shut the door, under no illusions that they would not still be there when he opened it again.

"Thea," he said, "if there is anything you would like to say in your own defense, I would be glad to hear it."

She shook her head hopelessly.

"I was your age once, you know. I might understand."

She snorted.

He didn't know what to say that wouldn't sink and vanish into her lethargy like a pebble dropped in a pond. "There have been plenty of times when I have not wished to do my work. But you and I were born into a station where we either work or starve. Do you wish to starve?"

She sighed noisily.

"Thea?"

"Of course not, sir."

"Then you must work."

"Yes, sir." The dull defiance that often underlay her monosyllabism was more pronounced than usual. She had never even thanked him for the new dress that she wore. He hoped she had thanked Mr. Summers.

"Thea, you cannot collect wages indefinitely without earning them," he said, more sharply than he meant to. "Do you understand that?"

"Yes, sir."

"Then from now on, Molly will go on errands and you will stay here where I can keep an eye on you." He looked at Sukey, relieved to find that her face mirrored his own frustrated incomprehension. Without that, he couldn't have said, "And if I find you hiding in a cupboard or under a bed again, I shall be obliged to bring the matter to Mr. Summers's attention."

Her face twisted resentfully. "I can't help it," she said hotly, tears brimming in her eyes.

"What do you mean?"

"N-nothing. Never mind."

"You *can* help it." If he could not make her see, she would be turned off by Epiphany. "You must try harder. Self-command is never easy, but it is always possible."

"You don't understand."

"Then explain—"

The door burst open and Molly barreled in. "You beast," she said furiously to John. "You *beast*. Can't you leave her alone? I don't mind a spot of extra work. Just until she's feeling better." She put her arms round the crying girl, who clung trustingly to her in a manner both touching and maddening.

"She will never feel better if you all coddle her like this. The only cure for malaise is exertion." He realized the next moment that he ought to have objected to her tone instead of deigning to quarrel with her.

Molly curled a hand around the girl's head. "You've assigned her too much work with your bloody lists. You've given us all more work than there are hours in the day. We know how to do our jobs, but no, you think—"

Sukey came forward and tugged at her arm. "We'll all be calmer later. Let's—"

She was right. John was not calm in the least. "Good Christ," he said in disbelief, "what is wrong with all of you? I told you to give it a month. A month! You will be used to it soon, and do it faster than you can at present imagine. But no, you are all so damned lazy—"

"John," Sukey said in as quietly reasonable a tone as one could manage through gritted teeth. "No one is lazy."

Why did she always take their part against him? He was no tyrant. He was the opposite. His father would have told Thea to get her things and go after that first nap in the cupboard, no matter what the girl had undergone.

He turned on her. "Oh no? Then *why*, after a fortnight of being constantly reminded, do you still never look at anything in the light after cleaning it? The number of dishes I have had to polish streaks off does not bear thinking on."

She glared at him. "I'm trying. I've never cleaned such fine china before."

"There is lack of expertise and then there is lack of common sense. How much experience do you imagine one needs in order to open a shutter and tilt one's head to catch the light?"

"No one has ever complained of my work before," she said passionately.

It was low, he knew it was low—but he raised one eyebrow and let the silence stretch. *Haven't they?* Her face flushed bright, bright red, and her mouth trembled.

"Stop feeding her carp-pie." Molly's voice shook. "It's low, to be nasty to your own wife."

John flushed with shame.

Sukey forcibly shoved the two girls out the door, as if afraid of what John would do. "We'll talk later, when we're all calmer," she said, not looking him in the eye, and shut the door.

There was nothing pressing requiring John's attention. He would occupy himself for a few hours in repairing Mr. Summers's neglected wardrobe, and perhaps by evening he would have decided how to proceed. He strode to Mr. Summers's room, jerked open the wardrobe, and began laying out coats and pantaloons with shaking hands.

Chapter Ten

Thea headed for the laundry, sniffling and wiping her streaming eyes and nose on her sleeve. Sukey and Molly followed, but she said, "You shouldn't help me anymore. You'll get me in trouble with Mr. Toogood."

Sukey thought this was the most sensible thing she'd ever heard the girl say, but Molly stopped as if she'd been shot. "I didn't mean to get you in trouble."

"I *told* you to leave me alone. No one ever listens." Thea stamped off to the laundry and began sloshing water about.

"John's just trying to keep her from getting the sack," Sukey said.

"So was I!"

"Then you're on the same side, aren't you?"

Molly went still, surprised. And then, to Sukey's shock, her face trembled and tears brimmed in her eyes.

"What's the matter? What did I say?"

Taking her by the arm, Molly dragged her through the kitchen past poor Mrs. Khaleel, who must be dying to know what had gone on upstairs but couldn't leave her kettles and roasts, and shut the pantry door behind them. "If I tell you something, do you promise not to tell your husband?"

Sukey bit her lip. First Mrs. Khaleel, and now this? But she was deadly curious, and after all, if Molly were stealing, she could break the promise with a clear conscience. She nodded.

"It's my fault Mr. Perkins touched Thea," Molly whispered, her face crumpling further.

"How could it be your fault?"

Molly's voice sank still lower. "I—I'm so ashamed. I *did things* for him. I

Rose Lerner

touched him."

Sukey's eyes widened. "You mean you liked him?"

Molly shook her head as if to shake off the very idea. "I'm still a virgin," she said fiercely. "I can still get married. I—he told me if I didn't do it, he'd make Thea do it instead. But he was putting his hands on Thea anyway. I should have gone to Mr. Summers. I should have told, and instead I committed awful sins, I let him live here—I didn't *know* he was at her. I swear I didn't know." She rubbed her hands on her apron. "I can still smell him on my hands."

Sukey had no idea what to say. "You did it to protect Thea. You meant well."

A tear slipped down Molly's cheek. "I wanted a house key. He gave me one. I'm a monster." She hid her face in her hands.

Sukey wished very hard that someone else, who knew what to say, were here instead. But for some reason, Molly was talking to her. She put a hesitant hand on the girl's shoulder. "Why did you want a key? Are you meeting a boy?"

Molly gave a strangled laugh. "Meeting a boy? You think I'm sneaking out to have *fun*? Sarah has consumption." She bit her lip, hard, and squeezed her eyes shut for a moment. "She has consumption and she can't work in the cold and wet. She'll starve if I don't help her. I'm so tired. I just want—I'm so tired."

How many people's work was Molly *doing*? Sukey put an arm around her. "You can't carry the whole world on your shoulders. You're not tall enough."

"Thea hates me."

Sukey thought of last week, when she'd wanted to ask John if he still liked her, and then realized he wanted to ask her the same thing. "Have you talked to her about what happened?"

"I can't. She must hate me. I can't."

"You should talk to her." Sukey squeezed her shoulder. "Better to know for sure, one way or the other. But I don't think she hates you."

Molly drew in a deep breath. "You promised not to tell your husband."

Sukey felt cold. She'd learned why Molly was sneaking out—not to get herself pregnant—and she couldn't tell him. He'd be furious if he knew she knew, and he was so worried. "I won't. But he'd understand. He understands

140

thinking he has to do everything himself."

Molly's eyebrows drew together. "I do have to help Sarah. I'm not following her around telling her the china is streaky. I'm helping her."

Privately, Sukey thought Molly's friends would never get off the teat if Molly didn't pop them off, but she didn't say so. She didn't say, *At this rate, maybe you'll get yourself sacked and you can help Sarah all day every day.* She didn't say that helping Thea hadn't worked out so well. It seemed like kicking Molly when she was down.

Besides, she felt ashamed. *She* would never go without sleep to do extra washing or risk her job or touch someone she disliked to help *anybody*. She was self-serving, when you got down to it. Cold, maybe. She looked out for herself, and wished other people would do the same.

* * *

She spent the rest of that long, awful day following her neatly written list.

One o'clock p.m. Staff dines in the kitchen. John appeared, looking tired. Thea did not. John went and fetched her, and they all ate in silence.

Half past one. Needlework. Sukey was hemming a new drugget to protect the carpet under the dining room table. The wool had been embroidered by one of Mr. Summers's married daughters.

Embroidery—thinking of pretty things and creating them—was for ladies, and hemming was for Sukey. She'd no desire to trade places; you could hem and think of something else.

Unfortunately, today she mostly thought about that nasty look on John's face, saying clear as words, *We both know you've got the sack a few times, because you're a lazy slattern.*

Half the time she shook with indignation, and half the time she wanted to cry. He'd been so kind about Mrs. Humphrey. He'd trusted her to do him proud at the vicarage, and she'd tried. She really had. But she didn't know how to do anything *properly*, and he didn't see the trying, only the failing. Usually she and Molly chatted a bit, or sang while they stitched. But today Molly didn't say a word as she darned the household's stockings.

Half past four p.m. Verify that fire has been lit and dressing room prepared for Mr. Summers to change for dinner. Help Mrs. Khaleel in the kitchen. Put plates in warmer by the oven. Remember, dinner must be served HOT.

"Hot" was in block letters, underlined twice.

I'm not an idiot, she grumbled to herself. *I don't go about thinking dinner would be better cold.*

Mr. Summers was dining out anyway. The staff ate a silent tea together in the kitchen at six. "Mr. Summers will return late," John said. "After nine o'clock, when you have prepared his rooms for the night and put everything in readiness for tomorrow, you may all go to bed early if you like."

Sukey carried her workbox into the butler's pantry for the evening, along with a branch of candles and a stack of Mr. Summers's clothes, on which John had marked tiny tears and frays by pinning scraps of old linen to the fabric.

At nine o'clock she rolled out their pallet and changed into her night things. The house was silent, except for someone pouring water in the kitchen. John, refreshing Mr. Summers's pitcher so that whenever he chose to come home, his wash water'd be neither too cold nor too hot.

Sometimes it felt like all the care he'd given her when they met—Mr. Summers got it now. She hated it. But it was pitiful, too.

John wouldn't agree. He'd say, *It's a quiet time to read, waiting up for Mr. Summers.* But she knew if she went upstairs, he'd not be reading. She'd see him fussing with Mr. Summers's nightshirt and banyan and slippers and nightcap: Were they warm? Were they hanging too near the fire? Were the coals in the warming pan still hot, and should it be moved to another part of the bed?

Hours of work for a half-second less of chill, and would Mr. Summers even notice the difference? And John had worn himself out, nothing left for his wife.

She wrapped the pelisse he'd bought her around her nightgown and went into the kitchen.

He turned at the sound of her footsteps. "Mrs. Toogood."

"Mr. Toogood."

They stood looking at each other a while.

"I'm glad you came in," he said slowly. "I wish to apologize for earlier. Molly was right. I was low, and nasty."

She hadn't expected that. "Then you didn't mean it, about my lacking common sense? About my never looking at things in the light?"

He frowned, annoyed again. "I don't think you lack for common sense at all. That's why I can't understand… But that isn't what I wanted to say. Thank you for stopping the argument. I should not have lost my temper with you or with Molly. It was undignified, but worse, it was unkind. Especially to you. I have already spoken with her, but I wished to… I thought you might like an evening to yourself."

She blinked. He'd been fretting over this all day too? It broke her heart all at once, the endless pains he took. The way he'd written *HOT* like that, and underlined it. The way he'd probably spent hours thinking of the right words to describe his behavior: *Undignified, unkind, which is worse?* She hid a smile. Maybe Mr. Summers didn't get all of it, after all. "You *were* low and nasty. Don't forget it."

He nodded.

"But you were right," she admitted reluctantly. "I'm used to being maid-of-all-work in a boarding house for eight women, where there's never time in the day to do everything I need to do. So I learned to do things halfway. Good enough. I know that it isn't *really* good enough. Not for you."

He sighed and sat at the kitchen table, pressing his forehead into his fists. "I don't want to be like my father. Do you know what the servants used to say at Tassell Hall?"

She shook her head.

"Not 'The room looks well' or 'Dinner is excellent'. It was always 'It's *too* good'. And they smirked when they said it. Because they meant it was done to my father's standards, and it wasn't a compliment to him. But I— It itches at me when something is askew, or spotty, or dusty. It itches and nags until I have to speak."

"Your father isn't going to inspect your work here."

He waved a hand impatiently. "That isn't it. I'm *like* him. I inherited his fussiness, and I don't know how to stop it. I hate it when things aren't done properly."

She pulled out a chair and sat opposite him, tucking her chilly hands into her armpits. "Everyone in this house wants things to be done properly."

He sighed. "Except Thea."

"Except Thea," she agreed. "We'll protect her until she gets back on her feet. We will."

"But *ought* we to? What if by shielding her from consequences, we're preventing her from improving? And don't we have a responsibility to Mr. Summers, not to allow him to be imposed upon?"

"I don't pretend to understand her." Part of her still wanted to give Thea a good slap. "But…"

My mum would beat me black-and-blue if I got myself in trouble like that, Sukey'd said once about Mrs. Dymond's poor pregnant sister. But when she'd met a man who tempted her, Sukey hadn't been any better than she should be, herself.

Mrs. Grimes would beat her black-and-blue if she slept the day away in self-pity too. But Sukey had never been in Thea's place, and she wanted to be her mother about as much as John wanted to be his father. Just because they'd never received much toleration didn't mean they couldn't give it. "Mr. Summers also has a responsibility to her. She was insulted and abused under his roof, by a man he put over her. It wouldn't be very Christian to turn her off for being unhappy about it. We'd have to make him see that."

He let out a breath. "Yes. You're right. He would see that. Eventually."

"Everyone wants to do things properly," she said again. "It isn't the carp-pie we mind. It's being made to feel small. We're all of us working hard, doing the best we know how, and you don't seem to know it. You never notice what's done well, only what isn't."

He nodded.

"Do you remember the raisins? You said it was false economy."

He licked his lip. "It was."

"Hoarding praise is false economy as well. And I told myself I didn't want to live where everything was weighed and doled out, that I wanted to be where people were generous with each other."

His lips parted as if he wanted to speak, but she hurried on, wanting to get it all out before she lost her nerve. Wanting him to hear her in this brief space where she seemed to believe she deserved it. "I thought you'd give me that, but lately it seems as if the only time you think I'm good for anything is when we're—when I'm spreading my legs for you."

Even now, saying it, she wanted to do it. Her cunt ached just looking at him, so handsome and strong, and he'd make her feel safe and happy and as if he worshipped her. As if he was glad to have married her. *I didn't want an evening to myself,* she could say, and wrap her arms around his neck, and he'd…

He got out of his chair and came to kneel by hers. "I know you work hard. Do you want to know something I admire very much about you?"

She nodded.

"At Mrs. Pengilly's, you hurried in the kitchen, but you polished her silver with great care. And here, those porcelain figurines—you pay attention to what your employers love most, and you make it shine for them. It's one of the kindest things I've ever seen."

She blinked. "Truly?" He didn't think her a lazy good-for-naught after all?

He tugged her hand from her armpit and kissed her knuckles. Then he pulled off her wedding ring and wiped it with his handkerchief, so his spit wouldn't tarnish it. "I should have said so before. I'm sorry." He slipped the ring back on as if…as if he worshipped her.

She blinked back unexpected tears. He didn't own anything to polish, but on a sudden she wanted to make the *world* shine for him. She felt almost as if she could. Or—as if she could help him see that the world *was* shining already, despite the smudges. "That wasn't so hard, was it?" she said cheekily. "Now try that on the girls."

* * *

As he went about his work over the next days, John tried to look for things to praise in others. It was difficult. His eyes always went first to the scratch, the uneven wax patina, the faint stain left on the marble. His ears caught a dish clinking against the sink, or furniture scratching the floor.

He watched and listened for mistakes without conscious thought, and when he saw them, everything in him leapt to correct them with the same instinctive urgency that sent one darting forward to catch a falling vase.

He told himself, over and over, that a small lump of wax would cause no disaster. That Mr. Summers had never once in the weeks John had presided over the staff complained to him about the quality of service. He made himself bear it at least a few times in ten and smother his criticisms. And he tried, awkwardly, to pay his underlings compliments. He prowled the house, forcing his eye to linger on what was correct instead of sliding over it in search of what stood out. "The bed was perfectly made today, Mrs. Toogood, thank you," he said, his face flaming hot.

He'd known it embarrassed him to receive compliments—he never knew what to say or do—but he'd been surprised to discover giving them was nearly as bad. Sukey ducked her head, brows drawing together.

He'd annoyed her. His heart misgave him. Of course he had. In her place he'd be thinking, *Not the bed again! Trying to get into my good graces now, are you? I know I did it right, and I don't need any pat on the head from you.*

A compliment, he realized, required mutual esteem in a way a correction did not. It required him to believe that Sukey cared for his opinion. And why should she care for it? Why should any of them? There had certainly been no signs that they *did*. But then a smile spread across her face and she said shyly, "I think I've got the knack of it."

Hoarding praise is false economy as well. Why had he denied them both this small pleasure, this moment of charity? Because he was embarrassed? Because he'd never had it growing up, perhaps; it felt as awkward and unnatural as the first time he'd held a razor.

At least, unlike with the razor, his father wasn't here to tell him he was doing it wrong and snort when he cut himself. Learning new skills was always embarrassing, but one had to soldier on, just as he expected his staff to soldier on with their lists.

He could not stop himself from hating to see things done incorrectly. But he could stop himself from withholding praise when it was due.

Mrs. Khaleel, straightforward woman, responded to his careful compliments (*The larder is wonderfully neat* and *You always trim the roast so carefully* and *The soup smelled so good Mr. Summers caught my stomach rumbling*—oh, that one was hard to admit! In future he'd eat a sandwich before serving dinner, to prevent a recurrence) with a nod of acknowledgment and a "Thank you, Mr. Toogood." But she began setting aside morsels of his favorite foods for him, and he was careful to always eat them with a show of gladness.

Larry was easy; he soaked up praise like a sponge, face glowing. To John's secret surprise, it seemed even to inspire not laxity, but more care in him. The wax on the mahogany furniture grew smoother and the lampwicks more neatly trimmed—evidently in hopes of further praise, which John bemusedly gave—and Larry took to bringing John his mother's letters the moment they arrived.

Molly was a harder nut to crack. She responded to every compliment with a sharp nod of her head and a muttered, "Thank you, sir." John would have liked to give up, as it was entirely evident that she *was* thinking, *I don't give a damn for your opinion.* But he made himself continue, contriving to find some private amusement in pretending not to notice her snub, and in her annoyance at that.

It was difficult to find things to praise in Thea's work, as she continued not to do most of it. But at least he could find her when he looked for her now; he thanked her for that. He reminded himself that he could not expect a sea change overnight and went on as best he could. But sometimes he remembered vividly why he had never wanted to be a butler. He had wanted to be a valet, and answer to no one, and have no one answer to him, and do his own work and be done with it.

* * *

Sukey looked at herself in the mirror after three hours of hard labor. Earlier, twisting her wet, clean hair up in curl-papers with the other girls, she'd almost been sorry not to stay at the vicarage and get ready together. Mrs. Khaleel had promised to dress everyone's hair.

(The servants generally bathed Saturday night after their half-holiday, to be fresh for church, but today, as it was Christmastime and the New Year and they'd all petitioned for it, bath and half-holiday alike had been moved to Friday to allow for the New Year's Day ball.)

Staying at home would have been more fun. Sukey was cold, and stuck with pins, and her head hurt from Mrs. Gilchrist pulling at her hair. But she didn't understand why Mrs. Dymond always kicked up such a shindy about that because it was *worth* it. "You were right. No one will recognize me."

Mrs. Gilchrist drew herself up. "I never said any such thing. Naturally everyone will recognize you. You always look like this. The gown merely calls attention to it." She said it with the confidence of one quoting revealed religion.

Sukey smiled at her. "I never argue with a compliment."

"Nor should you."

"Then I'll give *you* one: you're a sorceress."

Mrs. Gilchrist blushed, but she didn't argue. "Thank you." She'd pulled Sukey's hair into a high, tight twist, pinning her curls smooth along her temples to dangle in a row over her ears and neck, no ringlet allowed to overlap its neighbor. Now she deftly pinned Sukey's cap flat and dainty and settled it on her head. Stepping back, she eyed her critically. "Something's missing." She raised her voice. "Reggie?"

Mr. Gilchrist popped his head through the door like a jack-in-the-box. "You called, soul of my soul?" His eyes lighted on Sukey, who squirmed for fear he'd think she looked ridiculous.

Mr. Gilchrist pressed both hands to his heart. "And who is this vision of loveliness? Alas, I married too young!"

His wife laughed. "I just told her she looks exactly like herself, you bufflehead."

"Only more so," Mr. Gilchrist concurred at once. "Good evening, Sukey. Marriage suits you, and if I may say so, so does that dress."

It was impossible to feel self-conscious in the face of such silliness. "Thank you, sir." She swept him a curtsey, the blue wool swishing like a dream.

"There's something missing," Mrs. Gilchrist told her husband, waving an urgent hand in her direction.

He looked Sukey over with a more critical eye, kindly not remarking on her boots. She supposed she could change them for slippers at the ball, but if she did her toes would be black and blue tomorrow.

"Blue ribbons on the cap, I think, to tie it together."

Mrs. Gilchrist's eyes widened. "Reggie, you're a genius." She beamed at him.

"I'm glad I could help," he said with unabashed sincerity, dropping a delicate kiss on his wife's cheek as if it still amazed him that he was allowed. Sukey felt jealous of such open adoration; even if John wanted to, which she didn't think he did, he couldn't behave like that at the vicarage. "Unless you need anything else, I've got to deliver oranges to the workhouse for the Cahills."

Mrs. Gilchrist shooed him out, already fastening two bands of blue velvet to Sukey's cap and tying them behind her ears.

"*Thank* you," Sukey said. "I don't know how to begin to thank you."

Mrs. Gilchrist smiled. "Have a good time at the dance, and tell me your husband swooned at your feet. And bring back my pins. You're currently wearing thirty-seven of them."

Sukey's heart swooped inside her. Did she mean...? "I'll return the pins with the dress next Saturday," she said, testing. "That's my soonest half-holiday."

Mrs. Gilchrist's smile widened. "Return the pins, the necklace, and the ribbons. Keep the gown."

Sukey fingered the blue wool. "Are you sure?"

"You love it, don't you?"

Sukey nodded, smoothing over her hips. They didn't feel like hers. They were too graceful and sleek.

"A dress should be with someone who loves it. And—thanks for keeping my secret." She put a hand to her belly, her smile nearly as exuberantly joyful as her husband's.

"Now I know how you repay favors, come to me if you ever need a murder covered up, do you hear? Mr. Toogood's wonderful with stains." But Sukey's eyes stung. The baby hadn't been a *happy* secret a few months ago, and now it was. It was nice to know things did sort themselves out in life sometimes.

* * *

John was early to the servants' ball. He generally was early when he went places on his own. At the servants' dances he'd been accustomed to in London, that was the best part of the evening. He could help mix the punch and talk with friends before it became too loud and crowded for conversation. But tonight he didn't know a soul. Not wanting to ruin the line of his gold-buttoned coat, John hadn't even brought a book.

In previous years he'd worn his beloved set of evening clothes, but that was too fine for his new station. He saw that even his Sunday suit overshot the mark. Slipping off his kid gloves, he eased them flat into his pockets.

When he'd traveled here at Christmas with the Tassells, he'd attended this ball, but talked mostly to the Lenfield party, who didn't seem to have arrived. John shifted uneasily, remembering his extremely pleasant liaison with the undercook, spanning two or three Christmases. He'd broken it off when she'd started to hint at marriage. He prayed seeing her wouldn't be awkward.

He hoped Gil Plumtree, Lord Tassell's valet, would be here tonight. One of John's favorite people since earliest childhood, Plumtree was expansive, cheerful and cosmopolitan, always with five minutes and a lively anecdote to spare for a little boy. Whenever the elder Mr. Toogood had taken the valet to task for idling, he'd shrugged and said, *So take it out of my pay.*

He heard Sukey laugh behind him. She must have come in at the far door. Turning, he saw her embrace a group of friends, chattering and laughing. She shook her head at something one of them said. "Don't mind him," he caught. "Men are beasts."

She was dressed to the nines in an ice-blue gown she must have borrowed. Men *were* beasts, or at least John was, because he wanted to rip her out of that knot of happy young people and drag her somewhere they would be alone—to talk to her, to kiss her, or just to sit quietly, he didn't care which. The crowd already had him on edge. A fiddle tuned up, screeching, and he wanted his wife all to himself with a ferocity that disturbed him.

Instead he pasted on a smile and went to her, holding out his arm. He'd been to balls before. He could drag himself through one more. "Mrs. Toogood."

"Johnny!" Empty punch cup in her hand, she drew to the side and posed, tilting her chin up and pointing her toe in her worn boot. "Do you like my dress?"

It's two years out of style, he thought, and hated that his first instinct was always to be unkind. "Wait." He pulled her to him by her hand, pressing his palm into her wedding ring. She smelled strangely of lavender and starch, but when he kissed her, her mouth was friendly and quizzical. After a moment she sucked in a breath and went up on tiptoe, tasting of lemons and nutmeg and rum.

John drew in a deep breath and let it out. Yes, one could tell the gown was copied from a fashion plate. While the seamstress had got the darts right, the real trick to a seamless waist was how it fastened in the back, which wouldn't show in a magazine. But that didn't matter, any more than the boots did. Sukey looked trim and fantastical, slightly out of step with the world as he knew it. The pale wool turned her eyes a pure, clear blue, as if they reflected northern skies.

Beginning *just* above her nipples, the dress skimmed over her breasts and flowed to her ankles like water. The bodice gaped in the center, held taut with a bit of silk lacing that John guessed to be stronger than it looked.

The illusion of indecency was preserved from the reality by a linen chemisette rising snowily over Sukey's bosom and curling into a wide collar of pointed lace, one of those fashionable antique touches.

"You look as if you'd wandered out of a faerie ring."

She touched the starched collar self-consciously. A loop of tiny blue beads nestled in her collarbone, a second falling to the *V* of her collar. "It's a bit much, I expect."

"I love it." God, he wanted to cup one of her breasts. He'd feel three layers of linen and her stays, but the soft gown tricked him into believing it would be only her under the wool, soft against his palm.

She drew closer. "It's held together with thirty-seven pins," she murmured in his ear. "They belong to Mrs. Gilchrist. I'll need your help getting them out later."

He put a hand to her shoulder and felt for the head of the first pin. "I'll start with this one." He trailed his finger down. The fitted arms of the gown were slashed and puffed, the full sleeves of Sukey's shift coaxed through three rings of slits in the wool and pinned into place. The shift was yellower than the collar; he'd offer to bleach it for her later. "Then this one."

She shivered, biting her lip, and John felt all at once that he could face the party with equanimity, because after it she'd go home with him.

"Come on," she said. "I want to introduce you to all my friends."

Her friends struck him as young and rattlepate, but they were nice enough, even if they did try to winkle gossip about the Dymonds out of him. And soon enough the fiddle struck up, and he could lead her out onto the floor.

* * *

Sukey had always mostly danced with girls she knew. There just weren't enough footmen and grooms to partner all the maids—and if she was honest, she'd avoided dancing much with men. Especially ones she liked, so as not to give them any ideas.

It felt wonderful to take her place on the floor with her hand in John's, in her beautiful new dress, and see women up and down the set making sheep's eyes at him.

He knew the steps and performed them competently. A little stiffly, but that was John. She snickered to herself. Later, he'd be competent and stiff as a poker in their bed.

She turned and dipped and came up to take his hand again. Her skirt swirled about her legs, ice blue and fine. She loved dancing, but this was something else again, this flow and eddy of desire. This was the magic of a faerie ring.

The punch she'd drunk warmed her skin, and the room looked friendly and welcoming. The world looked friendly and welcoming, as if tonight she didn't have to be careful. She didn't have to watch where she stepped or what she said or how she said it.

Farther down the room, Mrs. Khaleel was dancing with her friends, all of them giggling. It was startling and lovely to see her without the reserve she generally wore at the vicarage. Sukey wondered if she could make John giggle. He laughed sometimes, but she wanted to see him giggle uncontrollably. She'd missed her chance on Boxing Day, when he was bosky on cherry bounce.

"Have you had any punch?" she asked him when next their paths crossed.

"Not yet."

"Let's get you some after this set."

He smiled easily at her, flushed from dancing. "If you like."

* * *

The punch was well made, sweet and strong, flakes of nutmeg drifting through John's glass and warming the dark taste of rum.

"John?"

He turned. Blast. "Maria," he said with a smile. "You look delightful."

She did, in an olive-green silk with gold beading that brought out the green in her eyes and the gold in her freckled skin. "Thanks. So do you." She smiled at him, turning her cup round in her hands. Her smile was wonderful, he remembered now. Broad and frank, as if she was about to laugh at some private joke.

He tugged on Sukey's arm, linked through his. She turned to look at him. "Sukey, I'd like to introduce you to a friend of mine from Lenfield. Maria—Miss Granby," he said, wishing there were some way to soften it, "may I present Mrs. Toogood?"

Maria's grin faded, her eyebrows going up. Sukey, seeing it, raised her chin.

Maria held out her gloved hand a little unsteadily. John suspected the Lenfield party had begun celebrating before their arrival. "Nice to meet you. I heard John had the banns read." That was a relief, anyway.

"I own I was surprised," she continued. Now he could hear the wine in her voice, a touch slower and more tuneless than usual. He would have found it seductive in other circumstances. "I wish you every joy, of course. But John always told me he wasn't interested in marriage."

John gritted his teeth. There was no polite way to say, *No, I told you I didn't want to marry* you.

Sukey shrugged. "I was never interested in marriage either, until I met John."

Maria laughed. "No, I don't suppose you were old enough."

Sukey straightened sharply, and he remembered that she was not precisely sober herself. "I'm twenty-two!"

"You don't look it." She snorted and looked at John. "I should have known that when you said you'd marry once you were settled in your career, you didn't mean a woman of your own age. After all, *you* can wait to have children as long as you like."

"Maria," he said, "this isn't necessary. Let me take you back to your friends."

She put a hand on Sukey's shoulder. "Let me give you some advice, dear. He didn't mind bedding me. He *loved* bedding me. He *married* a provincial little nobody barely out of her teens because he wanted a wife he could browbeat."

A wash of red filled John's vision. "That is *not* true." Sukey was a grown woman. He *hadn't* taken advantage of her. He hadn't. And he didn't browbeat her.

You make me feel small, she'd told him.

Sukey wrenched away from both of them, her eyes glinting dangerously. "No one browbeats me."

Maria laughed pityingly. "Don't they? You've got maid-of-all-work written all over you."

Sukey started forward, and stopped. "If I wasn't wearing a new gown, I'd make you sorry."

Maria calmly poured her cup of punch down the front of Sukey's dress.

Chapter Eleven

Sukey made an awful, heartbroken wheezing sound, staring down at the spreading stain. Her hands hung helplessly at her sides. John froze, torn between fetching a napkin and staying to make sure no one did murder.

"You *bitch*," Sukey shrieked, and threw herself at Maria. "I'll kill you!" She went for Maria's eyes.

Fending her off with one arm, Maria pulled her fist back, clearly about to plow it right into the side of Sukey's head.

John shoved between them, hoping he wouldn't be badly damaged. "Maria," he said, taking her wrists. "You're drunk. You're going to be mortified in the morning. Go away."

"You're right, I should have spilled my drink on *you*. Walk me to the punch bowl for another?"

Sukey charged around him. He let Maria go to grab his wife by the waist. Kicking his shins, she struggled and fought. "I can get the stain out if we do it now," he said in her ear. "We'll get it out. I promise."

Maria looked greatly cheered. "This is what you get when you marry a child," she said smugly, and swanned away.

Sukey yelled curses after her, still struggling in John's arms—but more, he thought, as an outlet for her feelings than because she really wanted to get free. In a few more moments, she sagged against him. Her friends crowded around her, congratulating her and making nasty remarks about Maria.

"It's ruined," she whispered. Raising her fingers to her gown, she looked at them as if they were wet with her own blood. "I ruined it."

"I'll get it out," he said again and kissed her ear. "Come into the kitchen with me."

There, John introduced himself to the Lost Bell's cook and gave her a shilling. "Hot and cold water, hard white soap if you have it, distilled vinegar and spirits of wine, and as many good clean rags as you can spare." Another shilling, and the sink was theirs. "Come here."

He felt for that first pin at Sukey's shoulder. Not how he'd imagined the moment, but wishes, alas, were not horses. He drew the pins out quickly, sticking them in his lapel. She stood very still and let him do it. She did look young just now, young and lost and trying not to cry.

"Why did I say that? I'm so stupid. She wouldn't have done it if I hadn't told her it was new."

"It wasn't your fault, any more than you fell out of that apple tree because you were clumsy." John lifted the stained chemisette over her head. "I should have gone to talk to her before now. I didn't think. I didn't think she'd care so much." He unpinned her sleeves.

"You forgot she existed," Sukey said sadly, and he winced, thinking of her father. Then her eyes narrowed. "You did forget she existed, right?"

He stepped behind her to undo her buttons. "I did," he admitted—or reassured her, he wasn't sure which. "I'm sorry."

Her outer petticoat was stained too. She slipped it off before it could soak through. "Of course, she doesn't know you only married me for your career."

He blotted the stain, careful not to press it into the fabric. Carrying the gown to the sink, he trickled water through the wool from the back. The grated nutmeg would be a difficulty.

"You were supposed to contradict me," she informed him with an attempt at her usual impudence. He glanced up in surprise and saw her shivering by the fire in her single petticoat, hugging herself for warmth.

Taking off his coat, he tried to help her into it, but she grabbed it and thrust her arms in the sleeves, scowling. "I'm not actually a little girl."

"I know. A man is supposed to do that for a woman."

"I've got perfectly good arms. I don't need help with my coat. I'm not useless like some stupid lady's maid."

John didn't say, *If you don't want tender consideration, why take the coat at all?* He didn't say that Maria was a cook. Sukey's curls brushed the dark blue velvet collar of Lord Lenfield's old morning coat. With those pale blue ribbons in her cap, it almost looked like an ensemble. He'd have let her keep it, but her pelisse was longer and warmer. He gave a penny to a passing scullery maid to find Sukey's friends and collect her things.

"I'm sorry," Sukey said when the girl was gone. "I'll pay you back." She fished her purse out of her décolletage.

"Sukey, you don't have to repay me, but you do have to let me work." He diluted vinegar and alcohol with water and moistened the stain, rubbing the soap in. Then he folded clean rags, dampened them with the vinegar mixture and laid them over the dress. "That will draw it out. In a few minutes we'll change them out."

"I was looking forward to this party. I wanted—" Sukey glanced at him. "I wanted it to go well."

John's heart smote him. "I'm sure some of your friends would be happy to keep you company. Shall I fetch them?"

She gave him an incredulous look, as if he'd said something obtuse. Then she sighed and shook her head. "You should go back. I'll stay here and change the rags."

He laughed. "I'm having a much better time in here than I would be out there."

Her face brightened. She looked at him through her eyelashes. He hid a smile. What an incorrigible flirt he'd married. "Really?"

"It's noisy and crowded out there." He started on the chemisette's stain, though he wasn't worried about that one. The collar itself was untouched and could be sewn to a new shift if necessary.

The scullery maid brought in Sukey's pelisse bundled neatly around her everyday gown. Sukey pulled the gray serge over her head with a sigh. "I didn't have time to go and drop it at home. Turns out it was for the best."

John accepted his coat back with undeniable regret. "You did nothing wrong," he said, buttoning her dress for her. "She shouldn't have behaved as she did. It isn't your fault when other people are cruel to you."

"That's worse," she said, her voice a little thick. "Then there's nothing I can do to stop it." She rubbed the rough serge discontentedly between her finger and thumb. "Why did you marry me, anyway?"

"I was terribly lonely," he reminded her, the corners of his mouth curving up in spite of himself. "And I badly wanted the job at the vicar's. You took pity on me."

"No." She looked up at him, her tip-tilted blue eyes brimming with tears. "*I* was terribly lonely, and *I* wanted the job at the vicar's, and *you* took pity on *me*."

John felt sick. Was it true? Had he taken advantage of her after all? She'd said she wanted to marry him, that she wanted a helpmeet. A tear slipped down her cheek, and he scrambled for a way to cheer her. "If you like, you could go back to the party and I could stay here and finish with this. Since you have a dress, it seems a shame to waste the occasion."

She drew back, shocked. "And leave you here alone? I don't think so."

"Thank you. But I wouldn't mind." He changed the rags, remarking with satisfaction that the punch seemed to be coming out.

"If I leave, you might as well be at work. I'm not going to let you work seven days in the week."

At least her tears seemed forgotten. He dried his hands carefully on a clean rag and tipped her chin up. "It's not work when I do it for you."

She glared at him. "*Yes*, it is."

He didn't know how to explain that it mattered to him, that these skills he'd acquired for pride and coin could comfort her. It sanctified something temporal and mundane. "Don't you think there's a difference between doing something for love, and doing it for money?"

When her frowning brows went up and her narrowed eyes rounded, John flushed scarlet. *For love or money* was a set phrase, and all he'd meant. If he left it there, she might think—well, that was better than hurrying to correct himself.

He'd been quite eager to correct any misconception Maria had had about their connection. Overeager, he supposed. He'd never meant to be unkind, only to have things clear between them. Because while he'd liked her very much, he'd never thought he might want to spend his life with her.

It was too soon to be in love with Sukey, and certainly far too soon to say any such thing. But he could imagine it being true one day. He saw her flaws—more clearly than was any credit to him, sometimes—but none of them seemed untenable.

She'd been silenced by his slip. Now she seemed to be trying to regain her balance. "Would you leave me in a kitchen laundering your clothes while you went to a party?"

He smiled at her. "I suppose not. But—"

"There's no but," she said, exasperated. "If you wouldn't do it, why do you think I would? If it's not because you think I need your charity. Being a provincial little nobody barely out of her teens."

John felt as if she'd slapped him. He tried to be kind, and she threw it in his face.

"You *don't* think of me as your equal," she said. "Why should you? I hate how much I want you to take care of me. But you don't have to do it just because I want it. You can expect more of me."

His ears rang. So it was his fault he thought she might want his help, *and* his fault that she did want it? She wished him to—what? Withhold it from her so she could feel independent? Perhaps she should try having some backbone instead. A grievance, carefully suppressed, broke free and leapt from his tongue.

"I can expect more? More what, precisely?" he demanded. "I would love your help in supervising the staff, but as far as I can glean, your chief concern is that none of them ever be annoyed with you."

"Quarreling doesn't solve anything."

"Neither does ignoring problems and hoping they go away on their own."

Her chin went up. "I'm ignoring less problems than you are. And I am helping supervise the staff. I—" Her mouth snapped shut. "I can't break confidences, or I'd tell you about it," she said, clearly aiming to wound. "But I'm doing plenty to help you."

Confidences? What did she know? Who Molly had been meeting?

Whatever it was Thea insisted he wouldn't understand? How much better might he manage the house, if he knew what she knew!

Of course she had a right to her own counsel, just as he did, and she would hardly be the recipient of confidences long if it was realized they were being repeated. But it was easy enough for her to make friends with everyone if he was obliged to give all the reprimands.

"Whatever you may think, I have never expected you to spy for me," he said. "But as you seem to have no difficulty leaving the unpleasant part of our work to me at home, you cannot blame me for thinking you might wish to do the same here."

For a moment he wondered how his father felt, seeing his wife universally adored. And he *hated* that he wondered it. There was no comparison; there could not be.

Her hands fisted at her sides. "Well, I told you I didn't! I'm here, aren't I?"

"Yes, and see how much my evening is improved thereby."

He heard her sharp intake of breath. Her eyes slitted, shooting cold blue sparks. "I do believe you'd be happier slaving away alone in here. I think that's pathetic."

"You've made that very plain," he clipped out. Even as he said it, he knew it *was* pathetic, that he liked her so much and couldn't seem to be agreeable to her. It was pathetic how wistfully he imagined working in here alone, quiet and steadfast. A man ought not to long to express his affection to his wife without the inconvenience of her actual presence.

She crossed her arms. "You asked me to marry you," she said. "I suppose you'd never have blushed for *Maria* before Mr. Summers, or had to tell her how to make a bed. So elegant and worldly she is—ha! *She* started a fight, not me. Well, she'd have married you. But you picked me. I suppose you thought with me around, you'd always have someone to feel superior to. And now I expect you're sorry and wish you'd picked someone better. Someone you'd like spending a quiet evening with."

It felt like something heavy had smacked into his chest. "You don't have any idea how I feel."

"No? Then tell me, Mr. Upper Servant!"

He knew she was right. It was like making the bed or polishing the silver; he told her the bad and expected her to guess the good on her own. He expected it to be obvious. How could it not be obvious?

He could not manage to tell her more plainly how much he liked and admired her, because that required him to believe she'd be pleased to hear it.

Maybe she would be. Maybe she wanted desperately for him to say he loved her. Somehow that idea was worse. Because he'd picked her, just like she said. He'd looked all over England, he'd had more lovers than he could count on both hands, and he'd never found anyone he liked so well.

Nearly every man she knew was in the next room.

She'd been lonely and afraid, young and inexperienced, and he'd used it to talk her into a marriage that she'd turned down when she had a job.

The more he wanted her, the more he needed her, the more he asked her for—the less chance she would have to be the woman she'd wanted to be, who stood on her own two feet, who had nothing between her and the sun. The less chance she'd have to discover what she really wanted. He'd been collecting his burdens for forty years. Even if they'd grown heavy for him, she was too young to be asked to shoulder half.

If he hadn't married her, she'd be out there enjoying herself instead of trapped in here, miserable.

"Faith, it's like being married to a rock," his wife muttered as she turned her back on him, stubbornly staying even though there was nothing to stay for.

* * *

"Is everything all right?" Larry asked Molly at breakfast.

Molly frowned sharply, looking up from the sandwich she was making out of a slice of plum pudding, a goose's wing and a stale dinner roll. "Why?"

Larry shrugged. "I didn't see you dancing at the ball last night."

John felt guilty. He'd spent most of the ball in the kitchen with Sukey and hadn't looked in on his staff at all.

"At least I went," Molly said. "Thea, you promised to meet me there."

Thea shrugged. "I fell asleep."

Molly frowned again, this time in concern. "Do you think you ought to see a doctor?"

Thea rolled her eyes. "I'm a growing girl. I need my rest."

"I don't know, Thea, you've been sleeping dunnamuch."

John noticed that this had successfully turned the conversation from her own behavior at the ball. He tried to meet Sukey's eyes, but she was staring at her plate.

"You'd ought to find better friends, Molly," Mrs. Khaleel said. "They all look like watering pots to me."

"They're having trouble," Molly flared up. "They need me."

"Yes, but do you need them?" the cook asked.

Molly pressed her mouth into a tight line. "Of course I do. They're my friends."

"A friend is a joy, not a burden."

"Everybody's a burden sometimes," Molly snapped.

Sukey sighed heavily. *I hate how much I want you to take care of me,* she'd said.

John set down his own toast and marmalade, unable to take another bite. He didn't see her as a burden. He needed her as well. He did. If she knew how much—if she knew how false his appearance of calm, competent certitude could be—

His stomach turned over. She wasn't much older than Molly, really. They both should be enjoying themselves, not worrying about anyone else.

After breakfast, he caught her as she was leaving the kitchen. "Mrs. Toogood?"

She squared her shoulders, clasped her hands behind her back and fixed her eyes firmly on the middle distance. "Yes, Mr. Toogood?"

He blinked. "Might I see you in the butler's pantry for a moment?"

It was also their bedroom, though the pallet was rolled up in the corner now and the room was his place of business. Last night had been the first night since their wedding they hadn't coupled on that pallet.

He didn't mention that. "I wish to apologize for my sharpness last night. It was unfair to reproach you for not taking more responsibility here at the vicarage."

Her mouth twisted like she'd bitten a lemon—but then it smoothed out. She still didn't look at him. "No matter, Mr. Toogood."

"I've been thinking about when I was your age. I was fourth footman at Tassell Hall." He'd been ambitious, his eye on valeting and escape, but quietly so. "My days were long and my work demanding, but it was not a position of responsibility. I worked under more experienced men and gave orders to no one. It was a pleasant time in my life, if rather devoid of sleep."

She didn't look at him. He could feel the point he was trying to make slipping away. If she would only smile! "Young people sharing living quarters— well, I can tell you that the amount of wine I consumed on an average evening would probably kill me now."

Her lips didn't so much as twitch.

"My point is that it is Mrs. Khaleel's task to manage the female staff. I should not have reproached you for not doing what is not yours to do. I want you to be happy, not give yourself gray hairs." He rubbed at his chin. He had no gray hairs on his head yet, thank goodness, but his beard was slowly but surely frosting over.

Her mouth compressed. "Yes, Mr. Toogood."

"Sukey, what are you doing?"

"I'm sure I don't know what you mean, Mr. Toogood."

He felt like a mouse talking to a brick wall. "Is there something you would like to say to me?"

"No, Mr. Toogood."

"Stop saying my name," he said in exasperation. "What have I done to offend you?"

"Nothing, Mr. Toogood."

He threw up his hands and went to the silver chest to begin his midmorning work.

"May I go, sir?" she said behind him.

He glanced at her in surprise. "Of course."

She bobbed a curtsey, actually bobbed a curtsey at him, and enlightenment dawned. She wasn't just standing stiffly and refusing to look at him. She was mocking him by pretending to be the sort of highly trained, impassive servant she imagined he wanted her to be.

"Is this about Maria?" he said, relieved to think that her anger was only jealousy, after all. "I assure you, I would *not* rather be married to her."

Now she did look at him, a contemptuous, pitying look. "I don't think you listen when I talk," she said, and walked out.

John stared after her, a frightened, sorrowful, empty place in the center of his chest. But anger quickly rushed in and filled it. She punished him for not *guessing* what she wanted? She parodied him to his face? Was that how she thought he spoke? He knew that anger towards her served no purpose, but the more he tried to crush it, the harder and denser and hotter it became, a stone inside his ribcage.

By dinnertime his jaw ached, he had compiled a list of approximately four hundred counterarguments and he was quite incapable of being civil to her across the table. He kept his eyes on his bowl as he filled it. "I'll take my dinner in the cellar, thank you, Mrs. Khaleel."

* * *

Sukey had been fuming all morning. The gall of him, the pigheaded blindness, to give her a speech about how young she was and how she'd ought to be gamboling about like a little lamb, when just yesterday she'd told him she wanted to be treated as an equal.

She was angry because last night he had just stared woodenly at her when she asked him to tell her how he felt about her, and he thought she was *jealous*? Of a woman he'd thrown over and forgotten?

But a pit opened in her stomach as she watched him disappear through the door with his bowl of stew. He was avoiding her?

If she made him hate her, he could leave town and go anywhere. Would *she* have to leave town? Lively St. Lemeston was her home. But would an abandoned wife dismissed without a character by the town vicar be hired anywhere respectable?

And that would be it. Her one chance at marriage, because *she* was no bigamist. She twisted her ring on her finger. *Let us share in joy and care.*

She'd never have anyone to share in her joy and care again.

"Are you well, Mrs. Toogood?" Mrs. Khaleel asked. Everyone looked at her.

"Oh, Mr. Toogood and I had a little quarrel, that's all," she said with a nervesome laugh.

Mrs. Khaleel put a hand briefly to her shoulder. "Married people quarrel. Don't take it to heart."

Molly frowned. "He's not kind to you. I don't know how you put up with it."

"Shh." Sukey glanced at the kitchen door.

Molly's frown deepened. "You shouldn't be afraid of your own husband."

Sukey threw her hands up. "I'm not. You'll hurt his feelings terribly if he hears you. And he's very kind to me."

"Not that I've noticed," Thea muttered.

"He's been kind to me," Larry said, but very quietly. Molly gave him a withering look.

Sukey stabbed at a piece of beef with her spoon. "He is. That's what we quarreled about. I told him…" It was so stupid. "He's just so much older than me."

"Too old," Thea agreed in an undertone.

Sukey ignored her. "He behaves like I'm a child who needs taking care of. He doesn't listen to me."

"Uch," Molly agreed. "I hate it when men don't take me seriously."

"Why did you marry him?" Thea asked.

Because he made me feel safe. As if I didn't have to do everything on my own. "I think I wanted someone to take care of me," she admitted miserably. She could remember being small and feeling safe and warm and loved. She remembered her mother's hands in her hair, her father lifting her onto his shoulders. She missed it with a howling, childish grief.

She felt sick and disgusted with herself. Had she wanted a father all along, and not a husband? How could she be angry with John for giving her what she'd wanted?

"Don't we all?" Mrs. Khaleel said wryly. But Sukey knew that she'd been strong. She'd sent Mr. Bearparke away and stood on her own two feet. *A friend should be a joy, not a burden,* she'd told Molly. Surely that was doubly true of a wife.

Molly snorted. "Women need to stop expecting men to take care of us, because they won't. We need to take care of each other instead."

Sukey was a little overwhelmed. At Mrs. Humphrey's, she'd seen her friends at the servants' balls, and now and then on Friday afternoons. She wasn't used to having women about, whom she could talk to whenever she liked.

She hadn't ought to have confided in them about John, not when he already thought she was making friends with them at his expense. But she'd done it anyway, because she craved their kindness so much. Just as she'd been unable to resist those two brandy-sprinkled raisins. She was weak—and contrary besides, because the more they sympathized, the more in the wrong she felt.

At a sign from the cook, Thea fetched a pan of baked dried apples out of the oven. Later they'd be piled in a pretty china bowl with whipped cream, nutmeg and toasted almonds for Mr. Summers's own dinner. There was none of that at the servants' table, but Sukey still marveled at the luxury of soft, sugary apples spooned onto her plate, bubbling from the oven. There were a dozen plump rum-soaked currants just in her portion.

This was exactly what she'd craved and imagined when she left Mrs. Humphrey's. She'd imagined generosity in practical terms, rich food and people giving each other things, doing things for each other. But she hadn't done these women any favors, and they hadn't done any for her. They'd listened to each other, that was all. And it mattered more than the apples.

Meanwhile, John had tried to do something for her yesterday, and it had made her angry. Because that sort of kindness was a parent's kindness for a small child. It went all one way. She'd thought that would make her feel safe, but it didn't. She wanted a husband, not a father.

Maybe generosity wasn't about giving or receiving. Maybe it was just about the sharing. In joy and care, whichever happened to be in the offing.

John had arranged it again so she was with her friends and he was working alone somewhere. Could be that was what he wanted, but she didn't believe it. He'd been the one who wanted to work in a house with staff.

"I'll take some down to Mr. Toogood, Thea." Sukey stood up to fetch a bowl.

"Eat yours first," Mrs. Khaleel chided, pushing her plate towards her. "They'll get cold."

Gratitude closed Sukey's throat. "Yes, ma'am," she mumbled. "Thank you."

Stomach comfortably full, she made her way down the cellar stairs. She felt like an intruder as she eased the door open. Was it too late to turn back? The wine cellar was the menservants' domain. It was surprisingly cozy. Brick arched overhead and a fresh carpet of sawdust held in heat from the big covered brazier, set in a brick circle at the center of the room. Casks sat in scalloped wooden racks along the wall.

John was trickling a bottle of white wine through a cambric-lined strainer and a funnel into a crystal decanter, arms rigid and eyes fixed on the sediment in the bottle as if trying to set it ablaze. "Shut the door, please. The heat's going up the stairs."

She did as he asked. The heavy door and the brick overhead seemed to cut off all sound from upstairs. "It's nice down here."

He made a disgusted sound. "I need to overhaul the whole mess. My predecessor was a lazy idiot as well as an abuser of defenseless women. When I started here, the claret wasn't properly insulated, the sawdust was ancient, the casks months overdue for reracking, and the red wine so badly pricked I've almost given up hope of recovering it."

The tension in his deep voice set her to vibrating with it, the way one guitar string set off another. He was furious with her, even if he was trying not to say so.

Maybe she should leave and let him come to her. But—he hadn't even asked her to. She refused to behave like a servant hiding from her master. Yes, he was angry. What was so terrible in that? So had she been angry. Married people quarreled, like Mrs. Khaleel said. She was sure by now he wouldn't hurt her, and he couldn't sack her without losing his own post. She'd spent enough of her life backing down and begging for forgiveness. He was more miserable than she was, looked like, and she was going to fix it.

She ventured closer. His dinner bowl had been emptied, at least. "I brought you some dessert."

"Put it there, on that keg. I can't set this down until it's finished."

She pricked up her ears. "Really?"

"The sediment is already disturbed. If I set the bottle upright, it will slosh about and mix with the good wine."

She slipped behind him. "So if I wanted to do…say…this, you couldn't stop me?" She ran her hands over his thighs. They were nice thighs, and he'd be a sight more relaxed after, that was certain.

She couldn't feel him jerk, but she heard the trickle of wine falter and begin again. "Stop that at once," he said through his teeth. "For God's sake. Can't you understand this is delicate work?"

She resisted the urge to give him a hard poke. "I don't know why you always do delicate work when you're angry."

"Because it requires my entire attention," he said pointedly.

She came round to his front again so he could see her rolling her eyes. "Pouring wine, even very slowly, doesn't require your entire attention. Maybe you should smash a few things instead."

He snorted like an outraged bull. "And who would clean them up after I'd smashed them?"

"I could."

His breath caught with a sound almost like a laugh. "And then Mr. Summers would take it out of my pay. I find it hard to believe it would be worth it." At last he set the bottle down, peering at the cambric with a shake of his head and at the decanted wine with grudging satisfaction.

He needed this. They both did. She cocked her head and tried to sound sure of herself. "I can think of something that would require your entire attention."

His jaw clenched.

"You'd feel better after." She stepped closer, though her stomach plummeted an inch for each second of his silence. "Shut your eyes if you like." She thought of something she'd done twice now that he seemed to like very much. Her mouth watered with eagerness, her nipples tightening. *Don't let him refuse me.* She knelt in the sawdust.

Ah yes, the front of his trousers moved a little at that.

She licked her lips and winked at him. "If you don't want me to, now's the time to say so."

He was holding his breath, by the looks of him. His amber eyes were hot. Maybe with anger, maybe with lust, maybe with both at once. The bulge in his breeches was growing. "Take out your kerchief," he bit out at last.

She'd been holding her breath too, she realized. She let it out and tugged the kerchief out of the neck of her dress.

He leaned down, his hand burrowing under petticoats and stays in one quick, efficient movement, yanking her left breast up to balance on the shelf of her bodice. Her right breast followed it, and there they sat, high and exposed. He didn't touch them. He only looked.

"Go ahead," he said, his voice rough and deep with anger. And it didn't frighten her at all. It excited her.

She undid his buttons, not making any particular show of it. Pushing aside his smallclothes, she took hold of his cock and sucked the head into her mouth.

He gasped, hips jerking. She hadn't learned to take him in as far as she wanted to yet. But when she rubbed her tongue against the flat tip of him, he inhaled so sharply it echoed off the curved brick ceiling.

"Harder," he said. "Faster."

She obliged him, though it made her dizzy. She'd taken to this at once. It was like plain speaking, somehow; you couldn't make it pretty or decorous.

His animal part twitched against the back of her throat, and his scent filled her nostrils.

But after a minute or two he put a hand on her head and moved her away, taking his cock in his own fist and pleasuring himself with fast, brutal strokes.

Unsure what to do, she stayed on her knees watching him. Her bare breasts should have been chilled, but instead they felt hot where his gaze touched them.

His lips pressed tightly together and he panted harshly through his nostrils. "Show yourself to me."

She gave him an inquiring look.

"Lift your skirts."

"Yes, sir," she said with a complete lack of deference, and maybe that annoyed him, but he liked it too. She could see his fingers tighten on his cock as she followed orders, reclining on her elbows and hiking her skirts above her waist.

"Spread your legs." She did it, face so hot she must be scarlet. Would he fuck her? But he didn't, only looked her over like a naughty French engraving.

Sukey glanced at the door—but no one would come in. Why should they? They'd ring the bell if they wanted anything. Still, she liked how sinful and daring this felt. Like that first time in Mrs. Pengilly's kitchen. She shifted lazily, watching his breath catch.

"You're wet," he said.

She flushed hotter, that he could see that. "That's because I like having your cock in my mouth," she said crudely.

He spent, seed dripping down over his fingers. Grimacing, he pulled out his handkerchief with his clean hand. Sukey rose to her knees. "No need to launder anything," she said, and licked his seed off his thumb.

His cock fell from his startled fingers. Catching it, she licked it clean, then did the same for his hand. He twitched, ticklish, as her tongue flicked between his thumb and forefinger. She glanced up at him. His shoulders weren't vibrating anymore.

"Why did you push me away? I could have kept on."

He sighed. "I would have used you roughly."

Oh, he was too sweet. She bit his thumb. "I'd not have minded."

He gave one of her nipples a friendly tweak, mouth curving tiredly. "Evidently not." He handed her the wineglass he'd been using to test the wine. Swallowing the remaining mouthful, she stood, tucking her bosom and kerchief back into her dress.

He looked embarrassed now, buttoning his trousers with unnecessary care and fidgeting with his cuffs. He always seemed to feel he'd made a fool of himself after bedding her.

"You don't have to be embarrassed." He was too tall for a quick kiss, so she kissed her fingertips and pressed them to his lips. "Not even you can be dignified all the time."

He covered his eyes with the back of his hand. "Did I look *very* silly?"

She laughed. "No more than I did, I'm sure." She smoothed her bodice and shook out her petticoats.

"*You* did not look foolish."

"Only because I didn't spend."

He looked remorseful. "I'm sorry. Come here."

She shook her head. "Dinnertime is over." She patted her stomach, reminding him what she'd recently swallowed. "Half past one is needlework." And she swept out of the room and up the stairs, carefully shutting the door behind her.

* * *

John knew they'd resolved nothing of their quarrel. But how could it be resolved? She was young, and he was old *and* stuffy. He'd try to be less stuffy, and she'd be older by and by, and there was no profit in talking of it. His relief that she wasn't angry—hell, his relief that *he* wasn't angry—was a tangible thing, sitting at the bottom of his breastbone and wanting to—to *move*. Shout, sprint, jump, weep, *something*.

He hated being angry at her. He hated, also, that he'd needed her help to stop, and that it had been no dictate of reason that swayed him, but only an animal relaxation, as if he'd resorted to drink.

It felt splendid nevertheless.

It was a long afternoon, but when night came he finally understood why people said there was nothing like falling into bed after making up a quarrel. Every kiss was a revelation, every inch of her skin a benediction. Each time she spent was a miracle.

* * *

John's unusual lack of exhaustion on Twelfth Night was likely why the noise woke him. Mr. Summers had gone to a celebration a little ways out of town and, as there was barely any moon to travel by, meant to stay the night. John and Sukey spent most of their evening in bed, dozing off shamefully early.

John lay blinking in the dark, unsure what he'd heard. Nothing, perhaps. He hoped it was nothing, so he could go back to sleep.

But there it was: a creaking stair. He'd been meaning to tighten those treads for weeks. John slipped out of bed, finding his greatcoat by feel and fumbling it on over his nightshirt. Tiptoeing to the door, he cracked it half an inch and waited, eye to the crack though it was too dark to see. It might only be someone looking for a snack. He heard footsteps creeping down the corridor. A shadow paused between the doors to the kitchen and the kitchen-yard.

John heard the tumblers of a lock turn. He flung open his own door and sprang.

Chapter Twelve

But he was too late. There was a muffled squeak, the kitchen-yard door slammed open, and footsteps pounded into the yard. If he didn't catch the figure at once, it would be lost in the inky darkness that filled the world. He raced after it, the uneven, frozen ground agonizing to his stocking feet.

There was a painful thud and a scrabbling sound. John, putting on a burst of speed, tumbled headlong over something soft and whimpering. Ice and gravel scraped his hands, but he seized her tightly round the waist and said, "Molly, you are caught. Give it up before we both break our necks."

There was a long silence. "Fine," she said tightly. "Get off me."

"I beg your pardon." He released her, feeling ridiculous and guilty. She scrambled to her feet. Her skirts brushed his arm with her out-of-breath inhalations.

"If you come inside with me now, I will hear you out before I decide whether to speak with Mr. Summers." There was a long, blind silence. "Mrs. Khaleel or Mrs. Toogood may be present if you like."

There was a pause. "I want Mrs. Khaleel," she said hoarsely.

He lit a candle and built up the fire while Molly roused the cook, who fussed silently over Molly's scratches while John put on water for tea. The women looked very solemn in the dim light; Mrs. Khaleel's fingers on Molly's face were sorrowful and resigned.

"Mrs. Khaleel, if you would unlock the tea caddy."

She glanced up at him. "I have some used leaves put by for us. I'll fetch them."

He looked at Molly's bowed head. "Tonight we'll use fresh. Mr. Summers can take it out of my pay." Gil Plumtree's old phrase sprung to John's lips without thinking, probably comforting him more than Molly.

Lord Tassell's valet had always regarded the household's strictures as a set of formalities to be followed or disregarded to suit his purposes—the first person to show John that being a good man was not entirely about following rules and pleasing the Dymonds. He would think nothing of hiding a stolen house key from his employer to save a good-hearted young girl. Knowing that made John feel a little less nervous about the idea.

"You don't have to be nice to me," Molly mumbled. "Just give me the sack and get it over with."

John sat at the table across from her. "I told you I would hear you out. So tell me, where were you going?"

The girl looked at Mrs. Khaleel, behind John. He couldn't see what the cook did, but Molly nodded at her. "My friend Sarah, she's sick. Awful sick. I was going to help her with her washing."

"In the middle of the night?" John didn't conceal his horror. "In January? And then walk home? Good Lord, both of you will catch your deaths."

Molly started to cry. "She's already dying. She's got consumption and our friend Jack threw her over." Her lip curled. "He said it would be *too hard* to watch her waste away. The cur." Mrs. Khaleel came to put a hand on her shoulder. Molly buried her face in the older woman's night-rail, her stifled sobs sounding as if they were being ripped out of her.

"And is that the only reason you've been leaving the house at night?"

Molly shook her head without looking up. His heart sank. It was already risking his position to hide this. If Mr. Summers discovered he had winked at her meeting a man, he would never work again.

"I look in on my dad," she said, her voice muffled. "Make sure he's eating."

"Is he ill as well?"

Molly emerged from Mrs. Khaleel's skirts, eyes red and swollen. "He's a drunk," she said bitterly, and wiped her nose on her sleeve.

John drew in a deep breath. "I see. Anything else?"

"No."

"Have you been doing anything immoral?" *If you have, don't tell me,* he thought.

Molly drew her key out of her pocket and set it on the table, face set. She looked at the cook. "I did immoral things to get this," she said in a hard voice. "He was hurting you and Thea and Lucy, and meanwhile I *willingly...*"

Mrs. Khaleel's lips parted, her knuckles going white on Molly's shoulder. "You're just a girl," she said fiercely. "I should have protected you. I should have known. He only—grabbed at me a bit, and said some nasty things. I didn't realize he'd go farther. I didn't think he'd bother a little English girl."

"No, *I* should have known. He swore he'd leave Thea alone and I believed him. Like a dolt. As if I didn't know what a worm he was." She looked at John. "I *should* do Thea's work. It's my fault she's like this."

"Neither of you are at fault," John said firmly. He thought once more of Sukey telling her mother she was clumsy for falling out of a wet tree in a thunderstorm. "The blame is often put on women in such cases, but that is hardly justice. Mrs. Khaleel risked losing her position. You risked the same, and you risked, as you believed, your friends' safety, both here and elsewhere. You had a choice between two evils, and you chose what you believed to be the lesser. Mr. Perkins, on the other hand, voluntarily chose evil over good. The blame is entirely his." He reached out and pocketed the key. "You know I can't allow you to keep this."

"But I need it." Her swollen eyes were desperate. "Sarah will *starve.*"

"Sarah will not starve. And neither will your father. Let me fetch my memorandum book."

Returning, he poured hot water into the teapot, then flipped the book open to a new page and picked up his pencil. He started, looking at it.

It had been sharpened.

Not to a perfect point, unfortunately, but someone had sharpened his pencil, which had been, he remembered now, nearly down to the wood. There was only one person who might have done it: his wife. It was a strange, new feeling, and it made the responsibility before him seem less dire. "So. Your friend Sarah. I'm sorry she's ill."

"Thank you."

"I apologize for asking, but are you quite sure her illness can't be cured? We might approach doctors first."

"Her little brother and sister died of it already, a few years back. She says she knows it can't be cured, and she doesn't want to be bled and starved and dosed and fed false hope until— But it could be months and months."

"Can she receive assistance from the parish?"

"She's tried to get a settlement in Lively St. Lemeston, but the parish won't give her one. She moved here from Nuthurst after her family died. She'd have one if she married Jack, the reptile."

John wrote *no settlement* in his notebook. "I see a number of avenues to assisting her. Would she like to go home to Nuthurst? The parish here will pay for her journey."

Molly shook her head emphatically.

"Very well. Is she Orange-and-Purple or Pink-and-White?"

Molly made a face. "Pink-and-White, of course, sir."

"Of course."

Molly's face changed. "Oh, I'm sorry, I didn't mean to be rude."

He smiled, although he had hoped she was Orange-and-Purple, since his own connections were on that side. "It's quite all right. Might I point out that Mr. Summers has a great deal of sway in the parish vestry? You might prevail on him to help your friend get a settlement."

Molly made an apprehensive noise. He didn't blame her. Mr. Summers could be very sarcastic when he'd a mind to, and it could be hard to guess when he'd have a mind to.

"Should that fail, we may try approaching others with influence," he said matter-of-factly. "Mrs. Toogood, I believe, is friendly with the wife of the Pink-and-White agent Mr. Gilchrist. Sarah is a laundress, is she not? Has she many customers?"

"She did."

"If we fail to get her on the parish, perhaps she could find another young woman who would care for her in exchange for inheriting her business."

Molly's face brightened. "I never thought of that."

"Two heads are better than one." John poured her a cup of strong tea. "Now. Your father. Has he any money of his own?"

She warmed her hands on the cup, hunching to breathe in the rich smell. John felt a little calmer himself at having done something positive to cheer her. "He does get money from the parish. He was a carpenter, but he lost his leg on a job a few years ago."

"And when you say that you make sure your father is eating, do you mean that you buy him food?"

She nodded shamefacedly, her mouth a tight line. "Every quarter day I give some of my wages to a neighbor, and she puts bread in the cupboard on Sundays."

"Because his own money is spent on drink."

"But he still doesn't eat it if I don't remind him." Her voice was hard, even argumentative, but her eyes were pleading. "I have to visit. I have to. He could die in that hole and no one would find him until Saturday. Just fall down the stairs and lie there bleeding." She gulped down her tea as if hoping it would make her feel less tired.

"Could the neighbor look in on him?"

"He doesn't listen to her. He only listens to me." She glanced despairingly at Mrs. Khaleel. "He loves me. He's a good father and I can't just let him…"

John didn't like what he was about to say, but it had to be said. He leaned forward, keeping his voice impassive. "Perhaps it is time for him to go in the workhouse. He would be safe and fed there." Unfortunately, it was an option not open to Sarah, as neither workhouses nor hospitals would take consumptives.

She bit her lip. "He'd hate it. He'd be miserable. He might even—he's sick when he *don't* drink now." But John would have sworn a flash of hope crossed her face.

"His existence does not sound particularly happy at home," John said gently. "How much worse could the workhouse be? And perhaps after some time without strong drink, he will do better and go home again. Or we might be able to find him a place in an almshouse."

That was definitely hope on her face now, but she sighed, shoulders slumping. "He'd never go."

"*You* cannot go on like this. Believe me, I know what it is like to feel responsible for—for everything. I spent many years as a valet precisely to limit my obligations. But you cannot be in three places at once and do the work of three people, any more than I can."

"There's a difference between worrying over my father's life and worrying over how neatly a *bed* is made," the girl snapped.

Mrs. Khaleel made a warning murmur, and John sat back, startled. "I like things to be done properly, yes. A well-made bed is a satisfying object to look upon. But my real concern is that we give Mr. Summers satisfaction and all retain our positions."

"Mr. *Summers* never complained about how I made his bed."

No. John supposed he hadn't.

"You believe I should worry less about you and the other servants, and do my own work. That I should leave you to make your own mistakes."

"Yes!"

"If I go back to bed and permit you to continue to leave this house in the night, and you are caught and sacked, or catch your death from walking about at night in wet clothes, would you really hold me blameless?"

"*Yes.*"

"Then how can you be blamed if your father chooses not to eat?"

She glared at him, clearly feeling that he had somehow cheated.

"It is a hard lesson to learn, and I have not entirely learned it myself," he said quietly, "but we cannot be everywhere at once. *But it will be left undone if I don't do it,* I think, and it's very difficult for me to accept the answer, *Then it won't be done.* Sarah and your father—I hope and believe we can find ways to help them. But whether we do or not, you do not owe it to anyone to risk your livelihood or to go without sleep dunnamany nights in the week. You look tired. Aren't you?"

She shut her eyes in defeat, then laid her head in her arms on the table. "So tired," she confessed in a whisper.

"You are a good friend, a good daughter and a good servant," he told her. "You will still be all of those things when you are sleeping and safe at home at night."

"Thank you, sir," she said glumly.

She reminded him terribly of himself. "Have you given any thought to where you wish to be in ten years?" he asked her. "Would you like to manage a household of your own one day?"

"You mean get married?" She half-laughed. "No one's asked me yet."

He dropped his eyes to his notebook, a little embarrassed at having misspoken. "No, as a matter of fact. I meant, would you like to be a housekeeper, or a cook like Mrs. Khaleel?"

He supposed that few people would consider the vicarage his household. He supposed it was *not* his household. But while Mr. Summers might be master, in his heart he felt, nevertheless, that the place really belonged to them. The servants.

She blinked. "Do you think I could?"

"Why not?"

"I can't even read."

"I think Mr. Summers could be prevailed upon to allow you to attend Sunday school."

"R-really?" She sat up a little straighter—and dropped her head in her arms again. "He never would. The Quakers run the Sunday school, and Mr. Summers says Quakers are anarchists."

"It might be a battle," John allowed, "but I believe I could win it."

She shook her head. "I'm too tired to think about this now. I can't think about this."

He nodded. "Of course. Get some rest. But think about it tomorrow. Think about yourself for a change."

She looked uncertain.

"Would you like me to talk to your father about the workhouse? He loves you. When he understands how much he's frightening you, perhaps he will feel differently."

Molly hesitated, and gave a tiny nod. "Thank you," she whispered.

"You are welcome. Would you like me to speak with Mr. Summers about Sarah, or would you rather do it yourself?"

"I'll do it myself," she said with a decided bravado that reminded him of Sukey. She stumbled a little with weariness as she stood up and made her way out of the room.

John remained at the table, jotting down a list of future tasks relating to Molly in his notebook.

"Thank you," Mrs. Khaleel said.

He looked up in surprise, having forgotten she was there. "You're welcome. Please, have some tea."

She poured herself a cup, sitting in Molly's vacated chair with a sigh. "I have said the same thing so many times. Of course when a man says it, she believes him."

John, already unsure and wishing he had said a hundred things differently and better, felt supremely uncomfortable. What could he say to that? Was it true? "She considered herself responsible for a hurt you suffered. I imagine that was part of why she could not allow herself to believe your assurances."

Mrs. Khaleel wrapped the end of her braid around her finger. "I was too ashamed to speak to her about it. And now I'm ashamed of *that*."

"Life is full of shame," John said ruefully. "Would that it were not so."

Her fidgeting hands stilled. "Could you ask Mr. Summers for me not to have Mr. Bearparke to live here? I don't think—I think it would be a disaster."

He nodded, surprised and grateful. He must not have done too badly tonight if she trusted him enough to ask him that. If she believed he had a chance of success. "Of course."

"What will you say to him?" she said apprehensively.

He rubbed at his temples, wishing for his bed. He had not had any tea himself. "I'll give it some thought. But I don't anticipate needing to say more than that I have observed the curate is overpartial to you, and that I believe it extremely unwise for him to live here. Perhaps…perhaps I might add something to the effect that while I have the utmost faith in both your virtues, it is best not to rely solely on one's fortitude, but to avoid the temptation and opportunity for sin, as far as possible."

Her eyebrows went up admiringly. "You should have been a vicar yourself. He'll eat that up."

He was surprised into a laugh. "Thank you, but I can't agree that planned hypocrisy is a good recommendation for the surplice."

She smiled. "That's a matter for debate."

He smiled back. "Is there anything else we ought to speak of?"

She shook her head. "Go back to your bed. Thank you again."

He stood, and then thought that perhaps he ought to say more. A compliment. "I should rather offer you thanks. I am very grateful to have someone on whom I may so completely rely as my partner in managing this house."

Her face glowed.

When he got back to the butler's pantry, he found Sukey waiting for him with a lit candle. "What happened?"

"I caught Molly sneaking out."

"I know. I eavesdropped for a minute or two. You were terribly kind to her."

He ought to disapprove, but he only felt warm. And it was hard to mind that she had probably known about all of it first, when Molly and Mrs. Khaleel had finally trusted him. Her pointed face was flanked by loose, lopsided braids, and she had acquired an old linsey-woolsey striped bedgown at least twenty years out of fashion that she wore as a sort of dressing gown. All in all she had a charmingly sleepy, havey-cavey air. He leaned down and kissed her. "I'm doing my best. Thank you for teaching me how to pay compliments."

"Thank you for teaching me how to kiss," she murmured, her teeth catching at his lower lip.

He tugged at her braid. He'd meant to buy her new hair ribbons, but he liked these old green ones. "I compared her fear for her friend with my fear when work isn't done properly. And I was shocked when she pointed out that it wasn't the same. Because it feels the same to me. It feels like averting disaster. Why is that?"

"It seems to me like you generally expect Mr. Summers to leap out from behind an end table and give us the sack."

"I suppose I do." It should have been a humiliating observation, but there was no condemnation in her tone. He could think of no one else in the world he could have talked to about this without expiring of embarrassment. The answer to the riddle was obvious, now he thought of it. Perhaps that was most embarrassing of all, that he'd never thought of it. "You may have gathered that my father could be very harsh when things were not done as he liked."

Her eyebrows said, *You're a chip off the old block, then.* But her mouth said, "I have gathered that, yes. My mum—well, she could be harsh enough, but she had less rules."

He took a deep breath, and then another. "I knew how he liked things done, and I had an unfortunate tendency to impart my knowledge to others. It didn't always make me very popular outside my own circle of friends, as you can imagine. But I really did feel a sense of panic, because I knew that if they made enough mistakes, eventually one would be their last at the Hall."

She nodded. "I still count the coal when I light the fires, even though I know Mrs. Humphrey isn't going to check the scuttles."

He sighed, pinching out the candle and drawing her down into bed with him. "I'm sorry, I'm keeping you awake."

"I like it when you keep me awake."

"Tomorrow morning I have to talk to Mr. Summers."

"What about?"

"About Mr. Bearparke coming to live with us."

She didn't ask why. So Mrs. Khaleel had confided in her. At the moment, he didn't mind it. "Take this with you for luck." She sat up and felt through her clothing, pressing a scrap of paper into his hands.

He couldn't see it, but he knew it was one of the little talismans Molly was always drawing, pencil-drawn flowers and twopenny bits and cups of tea with steam rising out of them. The maid had never offered him one.

He didn't believe in talismans. But he believed in gifts, and he believed in good wishes. "Thank you," he said, and got up to tuck it into his coat pocket so it wouldn't be lost.

* * *

He said it just as he had told Mrs. Khaleel he would. "It is best not to rely solely on one's fortitude, but to avoid the temptation and opportunity for sin, as far as possible," he finished, looking at Mr. Summers' blotter so he wouldn't have to see the vicar's face grow grave.

"I see." There was a world of disappointment in the words.

John waited, tense and hopeful, to see what he would say next.

The vicar toyed with his pen. "Are you sure?" he said at last. "I know him to be fond of her, but I have always thought it because she reminds him of his childhood. He was born in India, you know."

John kept his face blank. "As far as I know, there is nothing to reproach him with. But perhaps he has been less guarded around me, or perhaps his thoughts tend more towards the mundane. I thought the nature of his interest quite unmistakable. I'm sorry, sir."

Mr. Summers's long sigh was silent, but John could see his thin chest collapse slowly and his shoulders hunch. "Well then. It would be a sin on my own part to put him in the way of further temptation. Thank you for bringing this to my attention."

"Thank you, sir." He hesitated. "If I might be so bold, sir…"

"Please do." Mr. Summers now sounded resigned rather than amused.

"I apologize if I do either you or Mr. Bearparke less than justice. I wish only to say that I would be sorry to see Mr. Bearparke blame Mrs. Khaleel for his disappointment."

Mr. Summers's eyebrows shot up. "I believe you do do us less than justice. You have placed the matter in my hands. Rest assured I will deal with it."

John nodded. "Yes, sir. Thank you, sir."

"You may go, Toogood."

John bowed. His hand was on the doorknob when the vicar called him back.

"How is Thea?" the old man asked quietly.

John hesitated. Thea was at least reliably where she should be when he went to check on her, but he regularly caught her sowing gapeseed out of the window, or else working at a glacial pace. It had been too much to hope that the vicar could remain blind to it. "She is unhappy, sir," he said, hoping his delay in answering had not been obvious. "There is no mistaking it. But time is said to heal all wounds."

Mr. Summers rapped his knuckles on the desk, his mouth turning down.

"Will that be all, sir?" John said, trying to behave as if there was nothing more to be said—as if talk of hiring a new laundry maid had no place here and had not so much as crossed his mind.

"She used to sing while she worked. It brightened up the place, even if most of her songs were gruesome in the extreme."

John remembered that he had chided Sukey for singing and felt ashamed.

"Thank you for your patience with her," Mr. Summers said at last. "Pray continue it. That reminds me, Mrs. Toogood is said to know a wide selection of local ballads. I'm told she was much in demand when Mrs. Humphrey's lodgers had a musical evening."

John hadn't known that. He couldn't suppress a pang of jealousy that the vicar did.

"I fancy myself something of a local historian," the vicar said. "I should like to try to write some of her songs down, if she might sometimes sew in the living room by the spinet."

The pang of jealousy turned to a dull ache. John would like hours of the week to sit quietly and listen to his wife sing, but such luxury belonged to their master, not to him. "Yes, sir. I shall inform her."

"That is very obliging of you," the vicar said, an amused twist to his mouth. "It is not a command, however, but a request."

"Yes, sir." John felt embarrassed and in the wrong, and even more resentful at having been made to feel that way.

"Thank you." The vicar nodded, dismissing him. But he called out once more, just as John was at the threshold. "Toogood! The temperature of my dinner has increased remarkably since you came to work for me."

"I'm glad to hear it, sir."

"Thank you for your dedication to your work. That will be all."

John was embarrassed by his rush of emotion, but tears pricked his eyes all the same. "You are very welcome, sir. Very welcome indeed."

He shut the door behind him and leaned against it. It was foolish to be so affected by a simple compliment. It felt like relief, an intense relief belonging to something greater than the temperature of dinner. He headed for the kitchen to give Mrs. Khaleel the good news, but as he neared it, the side door opened and Sukey came in, a large pineapple cradled like a babe in one arm and mud caked on her boots. Stamping her feet on the mat did little to remove it.

And there the anger was, his father's anger, hot and sure of itself. "There's a boot scraper in the courtyard," he said, trying not to sound short. "Scrubbing this floor is the one real task I've seen Thea undertake this week, and she was proud of it when it was done." He'd even caught her smiling at the damp, smooth stonework.

"I used the scraper."

Why did she argue instead of even looking at her boots? "I couldn't tell."

She raised her eyebrows. "It's lovely to see you too."

He took a deep breath, and then another, trying to calm his instinctive irritation. It receded obediently, like the sea at low tide—baring, to his surprise, a sad uncertainty that clung like seaweed to his ribcage. Ugh. Anger was a deal more pleasant. *I was terribly lonely, and you took pity on me:* it had seemed a flirtatious falsehood once.

Even at Tassell Hall, servants had not lost their places so easily as all that. What was he so afraid of?

"I'm sorry," he said, wanting to take her in his arms and feel her warmth. "Please don't be angry with me."

"I thought you were angry with *me.*"

He shook his head.

She smiled at him, always more ready than he to let a grudge go. "I brought you these." She held out a fistful of—of flowers, many-petaled and opulent, rose-pink and startling white. At first he could only be dazzled; after a moment he recognized hothouse camellias.

"Where did you get them?"

She hefted the pineapple. "Mrs. Khaleel sent me to Wheatcroft for this. His lordship showed me about. I'd never seen a pineapple growing. Did you know they grow one to a plant?" Her eyes shone. "It was the drollest thing I ever saw, a spray of leaves peeping out of a pot with a pineapple plumped atop them."

As Tassell Hall had a pineapple stove, he had seen it many times. But he was overwhelmed by her charm. He could imagine how gratifying her pleasure and amazement must have been to the new Lord Wheatcroft, an enthusiastic hothouse gardener. She should have hurried home, of course, but Mr. Summers could hardly fault her for politeness to a peer of the realm.

There he went again, creating excuses and explanations for a calling to account that would never come. He had not been required to explain anything to Mr. Summers in all the time he'd worked here. It was Mr. Toogood senior before whom he had constantly had to defend himself and his friends.

He took the flowers she had brought him. She had thought of him. He felt again that foolish, disproportionate gratitude, throat closing and eyes stinging.

She removed her bonnet with her free hand. "They're called camellias, his lordship said. The pink one is new to England and supposed to be very fine."

John put the flowers to his nose, though he knew camellias had little scent. To hide his face, perhaps.

"Do you like them?" A hint of uncertainty crept into her voice, a mild plea for reassurance.

"Thank you." That wasn't enough. "I was feeling rather melancholy, and they cheered me." There. That didn't sound like the enormous confession it felt like, did it?

She smiled sunnily, going on tiptoe and turning her face up for a kiss. He picked her up and kissed her, breathing in the fresh air that clung to her. He set her down in a moment, knowing anyone might see them. "Thank you. I'll put these in water. Please—don't forget to clean the mud off your boots."

Sadness was more unpleasant that anger, but it occurred to him that it might be easier soothed.

* * *

Sukey slipped into the kitchen. "Here's your pineapple, ma'am."

Mrs. Khaleel looked up. "Oh, it's not mine. It's Mr. Summers's contribution to the Twelfth Day dinner he's going to later. You might bring it to him, if you please."

Sukey nodded, hovering a moment, unsure if she ought to say anything or not. The cook looked calm enough, making cakes for the wassailers who would come tonight to howl Mr. Summers's apple trees, but...she kept glancing out the window at the churchyard to see if anyone was approaching that way.

"He said he'd ask you again on Epiphany."

Mrs. Khaleel pressed her lips together. "Maybe he'll forget."

They both knew Mr. Bearparke wouldn't forget. But maybe he'd think better of asking where he'd already been told no. The cook glanced out the window and went still.

There he came, picking his way through the snow-covered graves. Seeing them, he stopped to make a snowball and throw it. It spattered the window, and Mrs. Khaleel's mouth turned up, just a little.

"You're sure you don't want to tell him yes?"

She slipped her cakes into the oven. "I asked your husband to speak to Mr. Summers about him." She wiped her hands on her apron. "He'll hate me."

How much had Mrs. Khaleel actually told John of what had passed between her and the curate? Sukey herself hadn't breathed a word. But now she thought maybe she'd ought to have, so John would be prepared for whatever Mr. Bearparke was about to do.

"Let him in, will you?" The cook smoothed her hair into her cap.

"Do you want me to leave you alone?"

"Don't you dare."

But when Mr. Bearparke brushed past her with a cheery smile and said,

"Would you be a good girl and ask Larry if he'll see to my boots?" Sukey didn't know how to refuse him. She was a servant and he was a gentleman.

She had to do something, though. And she was abruptly quite sure that John would know what that ought to be.

She found him exactly where he was meant to be at this hour—thank God for lists!—in the cellar, decanting the wine for dinner. "Mr. Bearparke is going to propose to her again," she said urgently. "She told him no already, on Christmas morning. I'd ought to have told you, but she swore me to secrecy. He said he'd come back on Epiphany. He's in the kitchen with her, and she asked me not to leave her alone but he sent me away—"

He nodded. "Thank you for telling me." He took the stairs two at a time, straightened his waistcoat, and strode directly to Mr. Summers's study and went in.

Sukey felt immensely reassured. But that still left Mrs. Khaleel alone in the kitchen. She wavered. Larry, at this hour, was pressing Mr. Summers's evening clothes in his dressing room.

Sukey went back into the kitchen. "I couldn't find him, sir," she said loudly. "If you give me the boots, I'll take them to him."

Mr. Bearparke straightened from where he had stood very close to Mrs. Khaleel, leaning in to murmur to her in a way that looked half commanding and half pleading. He looked past Sukey to something behind her.

She turned to see the vicar standing in the doorway, John a respectful few paces farther back.

"And here I thought my curate came to my house to see me," he said drily. "A word in my study, if it wouldn't incommode you."

Mr. Bearparke flushed a dull red, spine straightening. "Certainly, sir."

Chapter Thirteen

They all hovered around the kitchen door, wishing they could make out the low voices in the study. For once, John said not a word about idling. Time passed. Mrs. Khaleel pulled cakes from the oven and put another tray in and then, after more time had passed, broke a cake apart and handed it round.

"They might have spent a minute or two more in the oven, I think," John said. "But the flavor is remarkable."

The criticism ought to have annoyed Sukey, but it was such an ordinary thing to say that it reassured her instead. She thought it had the same effect on Mrs. Khaleel, who gave him a small, anxious smile.

Mr. Bearparke's voice rose passionately. "But sir—"

The study door opened. "My key, if you please," Mr. Summers said. "And you may consider yourself at liberty to look for another curacy. Should you wish to, that is."

The blood drained from Mrs. Khaleel's face. Mr. Bearparke drew a key from his pocket and handed it to the vicar with bowed head. Sukey couldn't help feeling sorry for him. It was no fun getting the sack. "I am sorry to have disappointed you, sir. My intentions—"

The vicar raised his eyebrows. "Were honorable, yes, yes. I'm sorry too. You're too clever a boy to make such a cake of yourself."

Mr. Bearparke came and stood before Mrs. Khaleel, who held herself very straight and met his eyes. "You'll regret this," he said intently.

Sukey gasped. Beside her, John tensed. "Are you threatening my cook?" Mr. Summers demanded.

Mr. Bearparke looked aghast. "No! Good God, no. But, Nora, you'll regret it. You'll wish— *Think*."

Sukey thought maybe the cook would have liked to speak. Her mouth opened and closed, her color came and went. But in the end she glanced at her watching master and said nothing.

Mr. Bearparke gave her a bitter look. "Well, if you're content with your lot, there's no more to be said." He put his hat at its usual rakish angle on his head, shoved his hands in his pockets and slammed the kitchen-yard door behind him.

"Mrs. Khaleel, if I might have a word with you," Mr. Summers said.

She nodded grimly. "Let me take my cakes out of the oven."

"Sir," John said quietly while she was doing it. "If I may—"

Mr. Summers sighed. "Have some faith, Toogood."

Why should he? Sukey thought with instinctive anger, and was startled at herself. Mr. Summers had done all right so far. But employers always wanted you to trust them as a child trusted its father, blindly, when the truth was, some fathers couldn't be trusted and servants were old enough to know that.

She trusted John, she realized with surprise. She didn't just want him to take care of her; she knew he would, and she knew he would know how to. He'd take care of all of them. When had she become so sure?

She almost didn't like being sure. It felt dangerous, like walking across a chasm on a plank bridge without looking down. It might seem sturdy, but you could fall easy enough.

John subsided, but he touched Mrs. Khaleel's shoulder as she went past and nodded at her, not caring that Mr. Summers could see him. Sukey thought maybe, even, he wanted Mr. Summers to see, and know that he was on the cook's side. That she was his, that she was all of theirs, and they'd stick together.

"I do believe I pay you to make yourselves useful," the vicar said with an ironic glance round, and they dispersed—but not very far.

At last Mrs. Khaleel came out. She went into the kitchen, took up a warm cake, smeared a healthy dollop of pink icing over it, and brought it back into the study. Sukey, contriving to dust the clock, saw Mr. Summers smile sadly at her.

When she followed the cook back to the kitchen, John was waiting for them. "What did he say?" he asked quietly.

"He told Mr. Bearparke he couldn't live here. Mr. Bearparke said his intentions towards me were honorable. Mr. Summers said it would be a dreadful match." Mrs. Khaleel laughed a little. "It was not the most flattering of conversations. But Mr. Bearparke said I would make a fine wife for a missionary to India, and Mr. Summers said he'd thought he was training his replacement here in Lively St. Lemeston, and if Mr. Bearparke meant to go to India, then he'd better start training someone else. Mr. Summers said he thought I had a right to know. And then he told me to avoid undue intimacy with unreliable young men."

Her mouth twisted, and she hugged herself. "I never wanted him to lose his place over me. I *told* him it was no good."

"If you told him you did not love him, that ought to have been an end of the matter," John said. "You have nothing to reproach yourself with."

The cook looked between the two of them. "You make things sound so simple. Thank you."

But she didn't sound comforted, and Sukey knew why. She'd never told Mr. Bearparke she didn't love him. "Here, let me help you with those cakes," she said, bumping hips with her as she came to stand by the table.

Mrs. Khaleel bumped her back. Her mouth trembled. "They need to cool before we ice them. I have some things to attend to in the pantry." And she fled.

"Should I go after her?" John asked, sounding unsure of himself.

There was a high, muffled sound from the pantry, and then another.

Sukey straightened. "I'll go after her. You'll only embarrass her. Go on."

John leaned in to kiss her. "Thank you." And Sukey felt, despite the seriousness of the moment, rather important and very motherly and not at all as if she was walking on a plank over nothingness.

She knocked on the pantry door. No reply. "May I come in?" Another high, muffled sound. Sukey opened the door. Mrs. Khaleel sat on the floor, her face pressed into her knees and her shoulders shaking. She had not even brought a candle.

Sukey shut the door behind her, feeling her way in the dark to lean her head on the cook's shoulder. "I'm sorry."

They sat like that a long time.

* * *

"I'm meeting Gil Plumtree, Lord Tassell's valet, at Makepeace's Coffeehouse," John told Sukey on Saturday afternoon. Having heartily admired the man since childhood—indeed, "loved" would not be too strong a word—John was glad they had finally managed to arrange a meeting before the Tassells removed to London. "He's—well, I suppose he's a sort of uncle to me."

He had never said so aloud before. He hoped if she met Plumtree, she would not repeat it. "Would you like to come along and make his acquaintance?"

Her fingers slowed as she tied her bonnet, hesitating. "I don't think so," she said at last. "I like having Saturday afternoons all to myself. Do you mind terribly?"

"Of course not," he said, wishing it were true.

She kissed him on the cheek and hurried out the door. By the time he'd put on his hat and gloves and followed her out, she was halfway through the churchyard, and passed out of sight before he reached Market Square.

John went on to Makepeace's.

"Johnny, my boy!" Plumtree enfolded him in a warm embrace redolent of pipe smoke. A beanpole in his youth, he had broadened in middle age into a mountain of a man, one of the few John knew who topped him by inches. His good-humored face with its large and crooked nose beamed down at John. "It's wonderful to see you. Is it true what everyone says?" He made a show of peering over John's shoulder. "I don't *see* a Mrs. Toogood."

"She cherishes her afternoons off."

Plumtree sighed gustily. "A woman after my own heart. It's for the best. A coffeehouse is no place for a woman."

The servingwoman snorted as she set two steaming cups of coffee on the table. "Good Lord, you must be older than you look." She was the proprietor's daughter, a pretty black woman with her hair pulled into a cluster of curls at the crown of her head. John had been buying coffee from her for years, but today the playful slant of her eyes made him think of Sukey.

Plumtree laughed. "Now, now, Miss Makepeace, I look ancient. But it's kind of you to flatter a dotard."

"Can I get you gentlemen anything else?"

"I believe I spied some darling little cakes when I came in? Are they new?"

Miss Makepeace smiled proudly. "You remember Peter. He's apprenticed to a confectioner, and I finally talked Papa into selling some of their sweets here."

"Peter? That grubby little infant?" Plumtree said with mock horror. "Good Lord, how old *am* I?"

John found he didn't mind, after all, having Plumtree to himself. He felt comfortable in the way one could only be among people one had known all one's life. Sipping his coffee, he listened contentedly to Plumtree and Miss Makepeace rattling on about cheesecakes and meringue. He hoped his wife, wherever she was, was enjoying her peace and quiet after a long week.

Cake and sandwiches were brought, and Plumtree steepled his fingers. "Now, my dear boy. Of course I wish you every joy. Tell me all about her." He smiled mischievously. "I saw Maria make quite a scene."

John covered his eyes. "Don't remind me."

"We'll say no more about it. I'm only sorry you left early, for I was looking forward to seeing you. Are you quite mad for her? I hope you are, or you'll be pining for London by Midsummer."

John sighed. "You two would get on like a house afire. You have a similar irreverent ease."

"Can't keep up with her?" Plumtree said with a twinkle. "We old men—"

"That isn't it," John interrupted firmly. "But I—I never thought I would be a butler. I never wanted to give anyone orders."

Plumtree laughed. "Pish tush, I never saw such a bossy child."

John reflected unhappily that that was true. He had hoped to be a less bossy adult. He looked down at his coffee. Water had condensed on the table under the hot china cup, shimmering as he turned the cup between his hands. The oak was scarred with rings left by coffee cups past, and yet he fought an urge to take out his handkerchief.

"I don't know how to do this," he admitted. "I—well. I suppose you know I aspired to be like you. But I find I'm like my father after all."

"That's not so bad," Plumtree said quietly. "Nor is it surprising. He sired you, and he's a good man."

John laughed. "Plumtree."

The valet fussed with his meringue. "I hate to speak ill of your father to you. You've always been so hard on him."

"He's always been hard on me."

"I know. And I suppose it's no secret that I find him—irritating. I've… well, I've been avoiding him lately. He isn't well, you know."

John nodded. "Lord Lenfield said the same thing in November. But I don't see what I can do. I can't leave my post, and Lady Tassell…"

Plumtree rolled his eyes. "Ah, yes. I don't know how she imagines you could have stopped Nick Dymond from thinking with the head in his breeches. And so I told her."

John choked on his coffee. "You *told* her that?"

"Not in so many words, but of course I did. She was making a cake of herself. Does she really think her friends aren't laughing at her behind her back over it?"

John cringed. "Did you say that too?"

"What was she going to do, sack me? Not with everything I know about that family, she wasn't. I told her to take it out of my pay."

John wondered if he would ever be so brave. "Meanwhile, I'm sure my father didn't say a word in my defense."

"I believe he has privately. I know *I* didn't take her to task before witnesses."

John did not put much stock in that.

Plumtree leaned forward. "Your father *is* a good man, and a good butler. A better butler than I could be. Lord, that house would be a mock-beggar hall inside a fortnight if I had your father's position!"

John clenched his jaw. His mother and Plumtree both always insisted that John was being unfair to his father. Somehow it had been up to John to be reasonable, even when he was twelve years old and his father a grown man.

"I'm not saying that to take his side. But you're a good man too. If you share some qualities with him, that's nothing to be ashamed of."

"I don't want to be disliked behind my back the way he is."

Plumtree raised his eyebrows. "Then don't be."

"I wish it were that simple. But I nag at them, I get angry…my wife finds out everything before I do." In the end, though he had talked to Mr. Summers about the curate, it was Sukey who had comforted Mrs. Khaleel, because John would just embarrass her.

John hadn't done much, in fact. Mr. Summers had been trustworthy after all, and his own guardianship mostly unnecessary. "I don't want them to be afraid of me."

"Afraid?" Plumtree looked surprised. "I suppose the henhearts among the staff are afraid of getting shouted at, but I don't think your father is quite the Ivan the Terrible you make him out to be. It's only natural to be a *little* afraid when someone has the power to dismiss you. You can't expect to be their *friend*, any more than Lord Tassell can expect to be mine. If you don't like it, you should have stayed a valet. We're every servant's friend. Unless they're shits."

Some of that was very good advice, and some of it was nonsense; John couldn't sort out which was which. Plumtree was impervious to intimidation, but John had seen footmen's hands shake when Mr. Toogood came in a foul mood to watch them work, and grown women burst into tears at his sarcasm.

John admitted that he had been afraid. It seemed both disloyalty and melodrama—his father, after all, was no ogre. He loved his son. But John could remember begging his mother: *don't tell him I dropped the ice cream pail, don't tell him I was rude to Lord Tassell, don't tell him I was drinking, please, please don't.* He remembered his father towering over him when small crimes could not be concealed. Much of John's long-ago childhood was indistinct now, but those memories were etched cleanly into his mind.

What had *he* been afraid of? He had known quite well his father wouldn't give him the sack—would not even seriously harm him. The worst he faced was the switch and a little mortification.

He had been an oversensitive child, that was all, just as he was an oversensitive adult. Knowing he was a disappointment to his father, that he didn't measure up, had filled him with awful, hollow panic, like stepping on a rotten beam and plummeting through the floor.

That, he acknowledged at last, was the impending disaster he truly feared when he saw something ill done. Not Mr. Summers's displeasure. Not the loss of his or anyone else's position. Nothing real. It was only an echo of his terror of his father's disappointment, established by long force of habit. He always felt as if someone was about to pop out from behind an end table and tell him he had failed.

It angered and humiliated him that he'd left the Hall and his father, that he'd purposely made himself a life where his father's disappointment had no place and could not touch him, and then had promptly begun where his father had left off, blaming and upbraiding himself for every failing, and blaming and upbraiding others in turn. Why? Why in the name of God was he so perverse and so impressionable?

"I'm sorry. I'm sure you're as tired of this old tangle as I am. Tell me, how is everyone at the Hall?"

Plumtree's eyes gleamed. "Well, you'll be happy to know that Notts has a new light-o'-love." Notts, the head gardener at Tassell Hall, was something of a Lothario among the local widows despite being now in his seventies. He would fall madly in love, plant the object of his affection a new garden, and then find his enthusiasm unaccountably waning. "A new one? I really thought he might marry Mrs. Fry."

"Oh, I knew it wouldn't last. He finished building her trellis and 'his love, Lord help us, faded like my gredaline petticoat'."

Anecdote followed anecdote, and then, when John was laughing helplessly at a story about stealing peach stucklings, Plumtree said, "Your father still wants you to succeed him, Johnny."

John stilled. "*What?*"

"I told you, he's not well. Even your mother isn't as young as she was."

John felt a pang of fear. Mrs. Toogood was seventy-five. Still hale and active, she might live another twenty years, but there was no denying she was old.

"Lady Tassell has asked them to manage the Rye Bay house, but your father won't go."

The Rye Bay house stood on a tiny estate on the East Sussex coast, far removed from the Dymonds' political interest in the western part of the county. It was used purely (and rarely) for pleasure jaunts and would be a charming retirement for his parents.

"That's not my fault. He knows I never wanted to be the Tassell Hall butler."

"Yes, but he also knows you never wanted to be a butler at all. And now you are one, aren't you?"

John rubbed at his eyes. "My mother hasn't said a word in her letters."

"Hasn't she? I daresay she doesn't want to press you, and I ought not to have brought it up."

"Sukey would hate Tassell Hall."

Plumtree winced. "Terribly provincial, is she?"

"That's not what I meant." It hadn't been. He'd meant that Tassell Hall was chilly and full of a sense of its own importance.

Rather like me, he thought unhappily. "It doesn't matter. Lady Tassell won't consider it." He'd never expected to be glad of that.

Plumtree smiled at John. "It's funny, really. I always thought you would succeed *me*."

"As Lord Tassell's valet?" John asked, startled. "Are you thinking of retiring?"

"Oh, heavens, no. As the *next* earl's valet."

John felt warm. He had hoped the same thing, he admitted to himself. That one day Lord Lenfield would succeed to the title and he himself would stand as beloved uncle to the younger servants. But perhaps he wasn't suited for that. "I hope you aren't disappointed."

"In you, my dear boy? Never."

* * *

Sukey, walking down Cross Street after a delicious penny plate of Scotch collops at the Robin Hood, glanced in the windows of Makepeace's and saw her husband clasping the hand of an older man. So that was Gil Plumtree, the reason John had become a gentleman's gentleman. They looked very cozy together, and he probably knew all sorts of darling stories about when John was a kid.

She wished she'd agreed to go along—and didn't much like that she wished it. Her half-holidays were the only time she had apart from John—nearly all she had apart from him at all, excepting one set of clothes and a few coins. Give them up, and…

She didn't know what she thought would happen, except that maybe they'd get sick of each other. Was she really still on about *what if he left her?*

Well, but he might. Someday. And then she'd better have something left of her own.

Even so, she almost went in. She'd been invited, and she knew John would be glad to see her. But Mr. Plumtree looked even more like a gentleman than John did: dandyish, with gold rings on his fingers. She could tell just by the way he held his face that he spoke beautifully. What if he didn't think she was good enough for his adoptive nephew?

Not wanting them to catch sight of her, she quickened her steps until she was before the broad stairs of the boarding house next door. A well-dressed lady leaving the circulating library on the ground floor ran smack into her. She looked Sukey up and down with a sniff. "Mind where you're going."

"Yes, ma'am," Sukey muttered, and then wished she hadn't. But she couldn't be rude. What if the lady recognized her at church and complained to Mr. Summers? Maybe she'd ought to have begged her pardon too. The Scotch collops stirred queasily in her stomach.

The woman went her unmerry way, but Sukey stood there, struck by a thought. John liked to read. He used to borrow books from Mr. Dymond, but now…

How much did a subscription cost? She'd never inquired, knowing she didn't want one. A friend of hers split a single subscription with a dozen other girls, so it must be expensive. On the other hand, she still had most of her

Christmas money burning a hole in her shift, and on Lady Day she'd have three whole pounds coming to her.

But she couldn't make herself walk up those steps. She wasn't rich enough or clever enough. Everyone inside would turn up their noses as soon as they saw her boots. And that was before she opened her mouth and broad Sussex came out.

So she trudged on to the Gilchrists', where she gave back the necklace, ribbons, and two neat pin-papers, counted over three times on the pavement outside. "Thanks so much for letting me borrow them. And thank you again for the dress."

"You're very welcome," Mrs. Gilchrist said. "So, did he swoon at your feet?"

Sukey flushed. "I—"

The girl's face fell. "He didn't?" She patted the blue beads as if to soothe their wounded feelings.

Sukey thought back to before the disaster. "No, he did," she said, surprised to remember it. *You look as if you'd wandered out of a faerie ring.* "Right at my feet."

Mrs. Gilchrist looked very relieved. "As he should have."

He'd swooned at her feet, and he'd cleaned her dress, and he'd told her he'd been wrong and that she ought to enjoy herself because he wanted her to be happy. He asked her every week to spend Saturday afternoon with him.

She'd been worrying and worrying that he'd leave her, that she'd make him not want her. But she'd started every quarrel. *She* was angry with *him*. *She* was dissatisfied with their marriage. *She* wanted something different from what they had. How had she got it so backwards?

And what on God's green earth did she want?

"Ma'am, you used to work at the circulating library, didn't you?"

Mrs. Gilchrist put a worried hand to her belly. "I still do." Once a lady grew round, she wasn't supposed to go about much. Just another way the gentry had of making their own lives difficult. "I wonder if Mrs. Potticary will still give me the first look at the fashion magazines when I'm only a subscriber."

"I'm sure she will," Sukey said. "Can I ask you how much a subscription costs?"

The girl sniffed. "Surely Mr. Summers isn't going to subscribe after all his preaching against novels."

Mr. Summers was indeed severe on the subject, fond of jokes about the soggy tipsy-cake a girl's brain came to resemble when she read them. "No, I think my husband might like to become a member."

"Oh, of course, I'm sorry. It's fifteen shillings and sixpence per annum." Mrs. Gilchrist tried bravely to sound as if she thought maybe Sukey could afford that.

Sukey tried to sound as if she thought so too. "I see. Thanks!" Too bright by half.

"It's only a crown for two months, though," Mrs. Gilchrist said hopefully.

That was almost twice as much yearly—but Sukey had a crown.

She'd been screwing up her courage to open a bank account, so she'd have something to fall back on if John left her. But for God's sake, she hadn't been married a month yet. It was too soon to plan for John leaving.

No, it's too soon to stop *planning for it,* she thought. But she'd *wanted* to go with him today when he asked her, and she hadn't let herself. She'd told herself she couldn't have what she wanted, and that it was for her own good. In fact, she'd been miserly with herself, and miserly with him, and she was sick of it.

Maybe that was why she'd been so discontented, why she never quite felt as she ought. It wasn't John's fault after all. It was hers, for keeping her heart in a locked cupboard instead of sharing it with him.

She was going to put her money on them.

Walking back down Cross Street, her dirty boots stood out against the smooth flagstone sidewalk. Once, she'd have taken no notice, but now they'd been clean, it ate at her to see them caked with mud and water.

John would clean them for her if she asked him.

She remembered that first time in Mrs. Pengilly's kitchen, how she'd been seduced by his hands on her shoes before he ever touched her. It still frightened her, how soft and open she'd felt.

She'd liked it though, hadn't she? So maybe instead of insisting he'd ought to stop taking care of her, she should give her all to taking care of him back.

* * *

Sukey went home early, a pasty in hand for her supper, not surprised to find John reading by the banked fire in the empty kitchen. She'd been slowly coming to understand she liked doing other people's kindnesses: polishing Mrs. Pengilly's silver and making John eat his breakfast and comforting Mrs. Khaleel. But today felt even better than that, because she'd chosen and planned it. Her anticipation of John's happiness was a lantern burning in her chest.

"How was your afternoon?"

"Molly's father was insensible with drink when I went to speak to him about his health," John said. "I'll have to go again next week."

Oh dear. Poor Molly. "What are you reading?"

He wrinkled his nose, turning the book over. "A history of the Anglo-Saxons. Mr. Summers has generously allowed me the use of his library, but I'm afraid his taste runs to…histories of the Anglo-Saxons."

She beamed, drawing the little card from her bodice and handing it to him.

"This card entitles the bearer, John Toogood, to withdraw two books at a time from the Lively Library," he read slowly.

"It's good until Lady Day. They have more than a thousand books."

He turned the card over. "Thank you, but…you bought it for the quarter? Libraries charge twice as much that way."

Her smile wobbled. "I know, but I didn't want to spend more than seven and six."

He looked sick. "You spent seven and six on this?"

The light in her chest guttered. "Yes, because I thought you would like it!"

He looked at her, and his face cleared. "I do. I do like it." Standing, he took her in his arms. "I hadn't even thought of a circulating library."

"You thought we were too small."

"*You're* too small," he teased, leaning very far down to kiss her. "I'm sorry,

I only—the difference in our wages—you ought not to be buying me presents."

"With the difference in our *ages*, you ought not to strain your back carrying me to bed, but I don't try to stop you," she retorted.

He took the hint.

Afterwards, she said, "When you asked me to marry you, I told you I didn't want to get married only to have some man take care of me."

"That wasn't when I asked you to marry me," he said. "That was when you said yes. There were some intervening hours."

"Which I'm sure you spent nursing your broken heart."

He sighed. "No, I suppose not. But I was disappointed."

Pleased, she nestled closer to his side. "The point is, *you* said that it wasn't weak to want a helpmeet. That you wanted one yourself."

He nodded.

"I want to be a helpmeet to you. You were right at the servants' ball; I've been asking you to treat me equal, but I haven't taken equal responsibility." She put a hand over his mouth when he tried to interrupt. "Not at the vicarage. In our marriage. Well, I mean to try. And you've got to let me. You can't scold me for buying you a present."

He bit her palm. "If you insist."

"I do." She wiped her hand on his shirt. "And I think—I think we should take our dinner alone two or three days in the week. I think it would be nice for us, and nice for the rest of the staff."

He sighed. "Plumtree told me today that I can't expect to be their friend, any more than Mr. Summers can expect to be mine." He sounded sad. *I was lonely, and I wanted the job at the vicarage, and you took pity on me,* he'd said. There was at least a little truth in it.

"That doesn't mean you can't be *friendly* with them," she said. "I was friendly with Mrs. Dymond, even if you laughed at me for it. But we both remembered she paid me wages, so she didn't put me in awkward positions and I didn't tell her aught she could use against me."

He nodded slowly. "I suppose." He turned to face her. "Very well, but we ought to spend those dinners talking, and not…" He trailed a finger down her belly. "Sometimes I think we talked more before we married."

Well, wasn't that a lovely thing to say? He'd rather talk to her than take his pleasure. She sat up, pushing him down on his back and straddling him. Her heart fizzed like ginger beer. "Lord love you, Johnny," she scoffed, "I didn't marry you for your mind." She settled herself comfortably atop him, chin planted on her folded arms. "I miss talking to you too," she confided. "I saw you and Mr. Plumtree at Makepeace's. Do you think you'll see him again before he goes to London?"

He shifted her so that his stiffening cock lay along the juncture of her thighs. "We made plans to meet again next week."

"Could I come along?" She squirmed her hips, making him grow until every movement mashed her pearl into him.

"Would you really like to?"

She dropped a kiss on his shoulder. "Not for the whole afternoon, mind. But I wouldn't object to a cup of coffee before I shake your dust off my feet."

His happy grin caught on a gasp. "Did I ever tell you about Mr. Notts, the head gardener at Tassell Hall?"

To her surprise, they found it was possible to carry on a conversation and take their pleasure, all at once.

Chapter Fourteen

On Tuesday John's throat ached, on Wednesday he was sniffling, and on Thursday morning when he tried to get out of bed, he stumbled and fell to one knee, steadying himself on the wall. His head felt stuffed full of cotton wool—and other substances less pleasant. A great exhaustion weighed him down.

"John?" Sukey asked sleepily.

I'm fine, he tried to say, but no sound came from his throat. He cleared it. This time, the words were a croak.

She held the candle Thea had brought them up to his face. "You look awful. Suety. Go back to bed."

It sounded like a splendid idea. The morning air made him shiver fitfully, though he felt it dully, as if his body and brain had left off communicating with one another. But it was only a cold. He had no wish to indulge himself in malingering. "I'm well enough. I just need to drink some tea, and I can…" He lost the thread of the sentence.

"Go to bed," she said firmly. "We managed somehow before you got here. We can manage without you for a few days."

He felt *that.* It was a sharp pang of mingled humiliation (at his own egotism in supposing anything else) and fear (that he was indeed superfluous). "Sukey—"

"Sleep. You'll make all of us sick if you try to work."

That was good sense, wasn't it? Fuzzily, he decided it *was* sense and not laziness. Crawling back under the covers, he lay there, grateful for the warmth and wishing he could breathe. He wanted nothing more than to fall back asleep, but he didn't know if he could.

"Molly," Sukey called softly at the door, "come and help me with my stays.

John's ill."

Molly came in. "What's he got?"

"A cold, I think." There was a pause. "Had we ought to call the doctor?"

John tried to decide if it was worth the great effort to speak.

"For a cold?" Molly snorted. "Probably not."

Thank you, he thought.

"It'll drive him mad not working," Molly said after a moment.

"Too bad," Sukey said ruthlessly. "Where's his list?"

"His what?"

"You know. His list of things he has to do every day. He must have made one for himself. We'll go snacks on it between us."

"Psh, we don't need to do that," Sukey said. "It'll only be a few days."

"Aye, and the first day he's on his feet he'll kill himself trying to finish four days' worth of work in one," Molly said bluntly. "He'll fret less if he knows his work is being done, anyway."

Sukey sighed. "Sad, but true." Cloth and paper rustled as she extracted his list from his coat pocket. He half-wanted to snatch it back—none of them knew how to do his work—but instead he pulled the blankets over his head and concentrated very hard on sleeping until, finally, he managed it.

* * *

Later, John remembered little of that first day. He woke only to relieve himself and blow his nose. The second day, he rose at one, very weak and hungry. He went into the kitchen to find the servants at dinner, arguing over the location of Mount Parnassus.

Thankfully, Mrs. Khaleel caught sight of him before he could enlighten them. "Stand back," she said. "I don't mean to catch cold."

Sukey took up a plate that sat beside her and brought it to him. Instead of the nice hot stew he could *nearly* smell simmering over the fire, it held a cold and faintly jiggling sheet of calf's-foot jelly.

"Can't I have some curry?"

She shook her head. "You're an invalid. This will give you strength and not upset your digestion. Besides, it's delicious."

John made a sad, defeated noise.

"Me and Thea already ate some for breakfast, and Mr. Summers will have it with whipped cream for his dessert at dinner," she said cheerfully. "Mrs. Khaleel uses dunnamuch lemon and sugar. Just the thing for a winter cold." She handed him a spoon. "Now go back to bed and I'll bring you in some tea. If you're good, later you can have beef broth."

"You're enjoying this, aren't you?"

She patted his cheek. "Only a little."

He glanced past her. "Larry, have you repaired the lining of Mr. Summers's hat? I meant to—"

Sukey gave him a gentle shove, shaking her head.

"This will only take a moment—"

The shove was less gentle this time.

When she brought him the beef broth a few hours later, he was sitting up in bed reading. "I could work," he said, setting down the book guiltily. "I'm not so very sick anymore."

"Is dat so?" she said, imitating his stuffy-nosed croaking. "You're dot so berry sick eddybore?" She laughed. "I can't possibly make my voice that deep but you get the idea. Mr. Summers asked us to bring you these, with his compliments." She set a stack of clean handkerchiefs by him.

"You really don't mind that I'm spending days in bed with a book?"

Sukey looked at him as if he'd gone mad. "It's been a day and a half. I'm not jealous, if that's what you mean. I hate being sick. Ugh." She crouched down to pass him the bowl of broth.

"You should go. I wouldn't want to make you ill. Maybe you could share a bed with Mrs. Khaleel tonight."

Her forehead wrinkled, her mouth going more lopsided than usual. "My mother never kept clear of me when I was sick. I thought it over, and I reckon the same thing holds for married people." She leaned in to kiss his forehead. "Good, still no fever."

That was a relief, because John felt pretty damn warm.

"Here are some lozenges for your cough." She set them on the chair.

The broth was good, salty and rich, but his energy was exhausted after a few sips. He fell back on the pillow. "I hate being fussed over." As a valet, when he was too sick to work, he'd been allowed to mope in peace and solitude.

"Make the best of it." Sukey took the broth out of his shaky hands.

"No, I—I like it from you."

She preened a little. "That's because I'm your wife."

Lord, he liked everything from her. "My father always wanted me to succeed him as butler at Tassell Hall." John had told her so many things, but somehow never that. He'd spent his whole life distancing himself from the possibility. But nothing, not even Lady Tassell's disfavor, could make his father forget about it.

She blinked. "You didn't want to?"

"At six years old I evidently informed my mother that butlers didn't have any fun."

Sukey laughed—no doubt at the incongruous idea that John Toogood, gentleman's gentleman, had once wanted to have fun. Now here he was, a butler. And he liked it. Was suited to it, even. *I never saw such a bossy child,* Plumtree had said.

"He didn't want it said I was his favorite, or that I received any special treatment. As I was to one day lead them, it was vital the other servants be given no excuse to resent me. I was ten when Lord Lenfield was born. I always knew I was too old to envy him and his brothers. But I did. If they came into the kitchen, my mother fussed over them and gave them treats. If my father came upon them roughhousing, if they scratched the marble of the fireplace, he only laughed and said that boys would be boys."

So many words brought on a fit of coughing. He took the bowl from her, gulping down broth to soothe his throat.

"Surely your parents only did it to please the Tassells," she offered.

"I know. Even then I knew. It didn't help."

"You're taller than the Dymond boys."

He nearly choked. "So I am," he said when he could speak again, thankful he hadn't spat broth on the bedclothes. Grease was the very devil to get out of linen. "Thank you."

"And handsomer."

"Now *that* is a very kind lie."

She huffed a laugh. "Lie about so serious a subject as male beauty? God would strike me down."

He fell back into his pillows, wheezing. "Stop joking." It was hard to feel handsome in a sickbed. But she obviously didn't mind his appearance or the repulsive sounds he was making. He'd barely felt self-conscious about them himself.

She waved a hand. "They're good-looking enough, and I didn't object to seeing Nick Dymond in his shirtsleeves, but they've got ice-cream faces. No character. Nothing to stick in the mind."

"They have character," John said, curiously affronted. *And when did you see Nick Dymond in his shirtsleeves?* Then he remembered drying Mr. Dymond's coat after he'd soaked it helping the present Mrs. Dymond with her laundry at their first meeting. It unsettled him to realize that Sukey must have been there, and to remember they had been nothing to each other then.

"I never said they didn't. I thought we were talking about their faces."

John's face, and its effect on women, had never been a particular source of dissatisfaction to him. But the Dymonds—they were golden. Even when he remembered them as boys in the kitchen at Tassell Hall, there was a shaft of light limning their blond heads, like little angels.

"I was only coddled when I was ill," he said, coming to the point at last. "As a small boy I enjoyed it, but when I was older…I had ceased to want their favoritism. I was ashamed to be indulged above my fellow servants. My mother would make delicacies to tempt my appetite, and I'd push them away and say I didn't need them."

His throat was painfully sore. Why had he suddenly been compelled to tell her all that? It was strange how one came upon memories of childhood unexpectedly, as if the mind were a closet one could lose things at the back of.

"When I was eight, measles swept the town," Sukey said. "I was taken bad. I actually—I refused to eat. I thought if I was ill enough my father would have to come home and see me."

John caught his breath in sympathy. "But he didn't?" he asked through the resultant coughing fit.

She shook her head. "I almost died, though." Eyes averted, she pushed the cough lozenges towards him. "When you're ill, take care of yourself as best you can. It's the only sensible thing to do. No matter what."

He caught her hand. "I'm sorry. I will."

She kissed his temple again. "Please do."

* * *

By the third day he was restless. Everyone insisted he needed fresh air, but he was only permitted to walk in circles in the kitchen-yard, and hustled back inside after a quarter-hour. The truth was, by then he was tired and light-headed enough to be grateful to go. But his book no longer held his interest, and he felt wronged that he was to miss his half-holiday that afternoon. The only bright spot was Mrs. Khaleel's milky, buttery gruel, delicately flavored with cardamom and treacle.

A knock came at the door. "Come." He sat up and tried to look dignified in case it was Mr. Summers.

It was Molly, with a bundle of paper. "May I speak to you, sir?"

"Yes, of course. I'm sorry I can't speak to your father today, but next week I certainly shall."

"I don't blame you for being sick," she said with a little smile. "You can't be everywhere at once."

"Thank you." They shared a moment of mutual understanding—but she looked nervous as she sat in the chair by his bed. He wondered if he ought to rise, himself, but there was no other chair and his legs were bare beneath his nightshirt.

"We made new lists," she said.

"Yes, to cover my work while I was sick. The thought showed both kindness and an instinct for authority. I thank and commend you."

She clutched the papers tighter. "You're welcome. But I mean we made new lists for after you come back as well. I hate cleaning the coal scuttles, and Thea likes it, and Sukey detests sweeping up cobwebs and I don't mind it. The looking glasses had better be cleaned on Wednesday when Mrs. Khaleel is at market, because the smell makes her ill…"

She spoke from memory, not referring to the lists in her hand, which she couldn't read. John didn't doubt that they had been her idea, nor that she had insisted on bringing them to him herself to spare her fellow servants any resulting wrath.

He listened gravely, feeling both ashamed and proud. "It sounds as if you have done an excellent job," he said when she was finished. "Thank you. I ought to have made up the lists from the start with assistance from all of you. You know the house and each other better than I do. I will look these over, and if I see a need to alter them, I'll discuss the matter with you first."

She handed him the lists. It threw him curiously off-balance to see they were in Sukey's handwriting. She hadn't breathed a word of this conference among the servants to him. She'd given him no warning. She had never voiced a single complaint about her list—and here Molly was, telling him his wife hated sweeping up cobwebs.

"You did say all along we could give suggestions. But we didn't know yet if…" She trailed off, flushing.

"I'm glad that, being better acquainted with me, you found me worthy to be trusted with your ideas." John smothered his momentary frustration with his wife—his secret wish that she had come in to see him herself, instead of hiding behind Molly's more forceful will.

"The lists are a good notion, though," she said, with an unprecedented desire to conciliate him. "It's good to think about things, and not only do them the way you always have."

John remembered what he'd said to Sukey, so long ago now, about a well-run home being like a clock. He'd tried to manage the vicarage as if the other servants were cogs and wheels he could rearrange to improve its workings. But Sukey was right. A home wasn't a clock—and neither was a marriage. They grew and blossomed at their own pace, in their own manner, and he must be patient and allow it.

He smiled at Molly. "My sentiments exactly."

"And I've thought it over," she said. "I think I'd like to be a housekeeper some day. Did you mean it, about Sunday school and learning to do figures?"

* * *

Sukey came into the laundry to fetch John's handkerchiefs. Thea had wiped a clear patch on the fogged windows and pressed her forehead to the glass, staring out the window at the snowy garden.

"Good morning."

Thea spun round and tried to look as if she'd been working, but it was more or less impossible.

They had all been trying to ignore Thea's sadness. A week ago, Sukey wouldn't have dared to bring it up. But nursing John this week—such a little thing, but she felt different. She saw that she was a grown woman and Thea was a child, and it was foolish to demand the girl speak first. Cruel, even.

She thought of John confiding his jealousy of the Dymond boys, even though on St. Clement's Day—the memory was almost distant now—he'd said he lacked the impulse to confide in anyone. Even the most standoffish people sometimes wanted someone to listen to them.

"Thea, may I speak to you for a moment on a personal matter?"

"Yes, ma'am."

"Let's sit down." Sukey found a dry spot of floor and lowered herself to it. "You've been unhappy, I think."

Thea shrugged, sitting down and fussing at a bit of dirt on her apron.

"I haven't wanted to speak to you about this, because I didn't want to embarrass you. But I know that Mr. Perkins, who held Mr. Toogood's position before he did—he hurt you, didn't he?"

Thea looked at her lap, acutely uncomfortable. Sukey almost stopped talking. But what could be worse than this silence? Tact was a fine thing, no doubt, but she'd never had a gift for it.

"You've got nothing to be ashamed of," she said. "It weren't your fault. 'Tweren't any of your faults, excepting his. My last mistress, she wasn't very kind to me. And I never wanted to talk about it, because I felt...I felt as if I deserved it. Sometimes I thought she didn't treat me any worse than I deserved, so what did I have to complain about? And sometimes I thought I deserved it because I didn't complain, I didn't do anything to stop it. It's easy to feel small and stupid and ashamed and as if you should have known what to do. But it's never your fault when people are cruel to you. It's always theirs." John had said that to her, and she believed him. "You didn't do anything wrong."

"He didn't *hurt* me," Thea mumbled. "He just touched me. It could have been a lot worse."

Sukey nodded. "How do you feel about what happened?"

Thea shrugged.

"Was I right when I said you were sad?"

Thea hugged her knees. "I don't know why I'm so sad." Her voice was soft and fierce. "He's gone, and he barely touched me, and you and Mr. Toogood are nice and there's nothing to be so sad about. But I can't stop."

Sukey blinked back tears. "I'm sorry. That sounds hard." After a long silence, she said, "You could talk to Mrs. Khaleel and Molly, if you wanted to. They might understand what happened better than I do, since they were here."

Thea made a doubtful face. "I don't think they want to talk about it."

"They feel bad, like you do. Maybe they aren't sure you want to either. From the outside, it's hard to tell the difference between not wanting to talk and being nervous about it."

"Have you ever been sad and not able to stop?"

"Not like that. Not so I couldn't work. But do you know Mrs. Piper? Her daughter Betsy works at the Honey Moon."

Thea nodded. "I've seen her in church. She wears that hat with the stars embroidered on it."

"My mum told me she was that sad once. After Betsy's little sister was born. They had the doctor in and everything. He said it was called melancholy. And she's better now."

"Did the doctor give her medicine?"

Sukey tried to remember. "Well, he said her circulation was sluggish and her blood thick, so he bled her. But she'd been sad longer than you. He said in the early stages, light foods, exercise and cheerful conversation help more than anything else."

Thea rolled her eyes.

"You haven't been going out much, even on Saturdays," Sukey pointed out. "You didn't go to the servants' ball."

Thea picked at her apron some more. Then she mumbled something.

"Beg pardon?"

"I didn't want everyone to look at me," she said loudly.

"Everyone? Or mostly men?"

"Men."

"Do you think you'd feel safer if you went in to town with me?"

Thea's eyes narrowed. "You always spend Saturdays alone. You say it's your time away from all of us. I don't want your pity."

"It's not pity when people like you. Anyway, I don't always spend Saturdays alone. I stayed here this Saturday with John, didn't I? And the Saturday before, I came home early."

Thea snickered. "I know. You're loud."

Sukey blushed and played her trump card. "It's not pity, because I want something in exchange."

"What?"

"Mr. Toogood told me you like bloodthirsty songs. I collect songs, and I thought you might teach me some of your best ones."

"Hmm. I expect I could do that." Thea's mouth curved slyly. "Do you know 'Thomas the Rhymer'? There are *rivers* made of blood in that one."

* * *

John heard an unfamiliar voice singing in the laundry room. Did one of the girls have a visitor? Mr. Summers didn't permit it. He would have to get rid of her, and quickly.

He'd done some work that morning, but he'd tired himself out and was back in bed now, trying to catch up on accounts. He heaved himself up and opened the door. "He made fiddle pegs of her long finger bones," the voice caroled, sounding a little self-conscious.

Mrs. Khaleel poked her head out of the kitchen. Seeing him, she smiled brilliantly, as if to say, *Isn't this wonderful?* John blinked, puzzled.

Mr. Summers peered around the hallway corner, saw them and smiled as well, putting a finger to his lips.

"Sing it again," Sukey said. "I want to learn the words."

"I could write them down for you," the voice said.

For a moment John was so shocked he couldn't move. It was Thea.

"Mm-mm," Sukey said sternly. "I learn better hearing it. You promised. Sing."

Sukey had made her sing again, when John had despaired of helping her. Maybe she was a fairy after all.

He felt a pang of guilt, that he'd despaired. That he hadn't been the one to talk to Thea. He had told Sukey he lacked the impulse to confide in others, but perhaps what he lacked was the ability to invite confidences. He'd confided in Sukey much further than she had in him—than anyone ever had.

Was he doomed, like his father, to work alone in the butler's pantry while his wife was surrounded by her friends?

Good Lord, illness made him maudlin! He was glad for Thea. That was the main point. He wasn't foolish enough to suppose that one song would banish months of inveterate misery. But it was a beginning.

* * *

A lovely week followed. Sukey remained determined on showering him with wifely care and affection, leaving him little notes and sprays of holly. Thea began bringing hot shaving water to the butler's pantry, and John was sure Sukey had put her up to it. It was extra labor for Thea, for nothing, when he had always been content to use cold—but it was such a luxury not to shiver and worry about slicing off gooseflesh that he couldn't countermand the order.

And twice they dined alone in their room, conversing with surprising ease. John found himself nearly chattering away, as if he'd been storing up thoughts apurpose to spread out before her now.

He told her about Plumtree teaching him to take out blackberry stains when he was six years old, his struggles with Nick Dymond's dreadful smoking chimney at Oxford, scandalous house parties and the bleak months after Mr. Dymond came back from Spain.

And she told him about Mrs. Humphrey's lodgers and learning new songs from peddlers and her friends' misadventures in love. She didn't talk much about her childhood, he noticed, but he remembered that a marriage blossomed at its own pace and didn't pry.

And at night they began coupling again, now he was recovered from his cold. Some of the urgency was gone, the newness and wonder, but in its place came familiarity. John had always liked his lovers, and had known some of them a long time. But there was something about bedding his wife—no, about bedding *Sukey*—that seemed entirely different. Surely he would have remembered this comfort, this ease and surety. Not the kind that came from a friendly tumble, but from *knowing* her. From sharing with her in joy and care.

Trust, he supposed, was one word to describe it. But that didn't seem right. Intimacy, then? Affection?

One night it was very late and they were both tired, and they looked into each other's bleary eyes and laughed a little and went to sleep without anything more than a kiss. John lay in the dark, exhausted and fuzzy-brained, and felt terribly happy. They didn't have to couple tonight. Because they both knew there would be tomorrow, and the day after, and the day after that.

There was another word men used to describe their feelings for their wives. After his slip of the tongue at the servants' ball, John had not allowed himself to use it, out of some obscure sense of propriety.

He did not think the quality of his sentiments needed to change for the word to be apt. Yet there must be some reasonable interval of time, some duration of feeling, before the thing was named, even in the privacy of one's own mind. One ought not to risk a mistake. Her father had said he loved her and her mother, and later he had left them.

Besides…

The surety and ease in bed, the confidence that she would accept his touch, and not laugh at him—it didn't extend to this. She wouldn't laugh, but she might be dismayed. She might draw back. She might say it was too soon, and she would be right.

They had married shortly before Christmas. Lady Day would be plenty of time to contemplate saying the word aloud.

John could only imagine how Sukey would laugh if she knew he was ordering his declarations by quarter days. He smiled in spite of himself.

* * *

Sukey, on her way to airing out the guest rooms, was stopped by the sound of crying. It was coming from Thea and Molly's room. Drawing near and peering through the keyhole to see if she ought to go in, she saw Thea, her face in Molly's lap, weeping as if her heart would break. "I felt better yesterday," she sobbed. "And today it's as bad as ever."

Molly smoothed a hand over her hair. "Convalescents have good days and bad days. Everyone knows that."

Sukey crept away, hoping Molly was right.

* * *

John left Molly's father's lodgings with a wretched, crawling sort of feeling. The man had agreed to think about the workhouse. He had wept, in fact, at the idea of distressing his daughter. He had been very, very drunk, at two in the afternoon. John hoped he would remember the conversation, so that John didn't have to have it again.

Next he had knocked at the door of the neighbor who put bread in Molly's father's cupboard and, after some discussion, arranged with her that her husband would look in on the man each night, just to be sure he still breathed.

He stopped at the circulating library to get the first two volumes of a new novel before heading back home for a quiet evening. But as he passed through Market Square, he saw Sukey at a table by the window of a pub, sitting with… with Thea? When she loved her half-holiday of freedom from the vicarage so much? She was an angel.

He almost went on, not wanting to interrupt them, but he wanted too much to hear her voice, even for a moment. It was getting so her presence made all right with the world.

Earlier this afternoon he'd introduced her to Plumtree. She'd stayed half an hour, in which space she and Plumtree had thoroughly charmed one another, and then she'd left.

And John had been shaken to discover he was—not less at ease, precisely, after she'd gone. But he had felt, all at once, almost in a false position, as if he wore a favorite suit that still fit but no longer hung quite right. As if the man he was with Plumtree was himself, but not all of himself.

He felt more at home with Sukey than with a man he'd known all his life, who was as good as family.

That, he realized with a start, was marriage. *Therefore shall a man leave his father and his mother, and shall cleave unto his wife.* Sukey was his family now. He went inside.

"John," she said a little warily. She and Thea were sprawled about, shawls and bonnets in cozy disarray, nursing the dregs of coffee cups as if they meant to do it all afternoon.

"I borrowed these from the library." He showed her the volumes. "I'm on my way home to read them."

She smiled, evidently relieved he wasn't staying as well as pleased he was enjoying her gift. He nearly left at once—but he said, "Would you consider coming home early?"

Thea made an amused sound. Sukey blushed and, to judge from the girl's reaction, kicked her under the table.

His ears burned. "I meant nothing untoward."

Sukey hesitated, licking her lip uncertainly. "I would be delighted to spend a quiet evening at home with you," she said at last with great dignity. Thea giggled at the word "quiet".

John was too pleased to be much embarrassed. "I shall expect you at half past six?"

She nodded.

He arrived home, thinking to mull some cider for them, and found the door locked and a note from Mr. Summers on the hall table. *Gone to use Lord*

Wheatcroft's library. Will likely stay for supper. He had the house entirely to himself for the next several hours. The sad visit to Molly's father still clung to his skin.

Honest labor cleared the mind and the heart. John had an idea.

* * *

As half-holidays went, Sukey had had very little of it to herself. She'd spent a nice half-hour with John and his friend Mr. Plumtree, a good-humored man with a tongue sharper than her own. She'd paid her usual visit to her mother, and then she'd stopped at the vicarage to collect Thea.

She'd feared regretting her kindness, but it had been a very pleasant afternoon after all, Thea being perfectly content to sit in the window at the Robin Hood without talking much, nursing a cup of coffee and watching the world go by. Now here they were, throwing snowballs at each other on their way home, two precious hours earlier than usual. She ought to regret it, but she didn't. John was waiting for her.

"Race you," she told Thea, and they fetched up at the back door with a thump, laughing and gasping and covered in snow.

John opened it in his shirtsleeves. "You're early."

"We can come back later," she teased, and he tugged her inside and held her tight against him as he locked the door.

"Can I borrow your book?" Thea asked, kicking off her pattens. "You won't be reading it, right?"

"It's on the kitchen table."

Thea vanished into the kitchen and then up the stairs.

Sukey noticed that John was frowsy and wilting a little. And the house smelled odd. "Have you been working?"

He gestured for her to follow him and slipped into the butler's pantry. "Shut the door quickly behind you."

Chapter Fifteen

The uncovered brazier was full of hot coals, the room so warm that Sukey was reaching for the buttons of her pelisse before she recognized the smell.

Roses, fragrant and luxurious in the heart of winter.

She breathed them in, disbelieving. Over a dozen lit candle stubs made the copper bathtub in the center of the room glow brightly and turned the steam rising from it a warm yellow.

Sukey knew that tub. They carted it up the stairs to Mr. Summers's room once a month, along with dunnamany buckets of hot water, and he took great pleasure in soaking in it.

She drew near to it. At least twenty-five gallons of water steamed inside, smelling like roses. "For me?" She reached out to touch the water, almost nervesome.

He caught her wrist. "It might still be too hot. You were early. Let me." He dipped a finger quickly in, and when this proved safe, submerged his hand. "Give it another five minutes."

"I've never taken a real bath before." She used a basin and sponge most days, and on Saturday nights the vicarage servants took turns filling a hip-bath before the kitchen fire. But soaking in a tub? That was for ladies and gentlemen. The labor it took to draw and haul and heat and haul again so much water, only to have to empty it out… "You shouldn't work on your half-holiday," she protested.

"I told you. It isn't work when I do it for you."

"And I told you it is."

He stepped up behind her and unbuttoned her dress. "Imagine an artist who paints society portraits all week," he said in her ear. "On Sunday he comes home and paints his wife. Is there really no difference?"

She let him pull her clothes over her head. He unlaced her stays so nimbly it seemed a professional skill, but he was no ladies' maid. He'd learned it undressing women, dunnamany of them. But the way he said *his wife*, it sounded special. As if she was the only one.

At the ball, he'd called it *doing something for love*. He'd said it without fanfare, probably meaning only to make use of the expression. *For love or money*, people said that all the time. People said *love* all the time, and then they left. Why was she fussing about a stupid word?

Don't get in that bath, she thought with sudden urgency. *You've done without it all these years. You don't need it.*

But when he knelt to untie her garters, she let him do that too. There was a lump in her throat and her chest tingled. At first it was fear, but it turned to happiness and she couldn't turn it back. She felt like an air balloon trying to take flight, straining at its ropes. Her throat trembled with wanting to laugh. He rolled her stockings down her legs in a manner that had nothing professional about it.

He wavered, eyes on the triangle of hair between her legs, inches from his mouth.

Sukey wavered too, but she pulled off her shift and danced past him towards the rose-scented water. "My bath is getting cold, and so am I." Actually, the water near scalded her cold toe when she dipped it in. But while she debated whether to pull it out again, the heat dimmed, becoming bearable.

She lowered herself into the tub, hopping with the heat. "I'll be boiled like a lobster!" But soon the pain faded. "Oh my. I see why the vicar likes it." The everyday words didn't measure up to the miracle of liquid heat right up to her breasts. She slid down the back of the tub, nipples dipping beneath the surface. She'd be *warm* soon, warmer than she'd been all winter. She breathed in rosy steam, finally finding the courage to lift her hands from the sides of the tub. She did not, as she half feared, slip helplessly into the water and drown.

She looked at John. He was smiling and—to her surprise—watching her face, not her tits. He knelt beside the tub to remove her cap and draw the pins from her hair. Sukey grimaced. She hated washing her hair.

Because it's always chilly! She dipped below the surface, hauling herself up sputtering a moment later, terrified of drowning. John laughed openly at her, brushing drops of water from his waistcoat.

Having wet hair felt nice, actually. She lowered herself slowly into the tub again, this time enjoying the water creeping up over her cheeks and forehead, and the way it poured down her shoulders when she sat up.

"Do you want me to stay?" he asked. "Or shall I leave you to soak?"

She could not believe it. That he'd go to so much trouble and not even expect to ogle her?

At the ball, when he offered, she'd refused to allow him to repair her dress alone. She'd thought it too great a gift to accept.

This would put her in his debt, and she didn't know how to repay him. But maybe that only meant she ought to stretch her brains and think of a way. She'd found she liked giving him things.

Maybe there was no limit to what you could take from your spouse, if it was offered freely. Maybe some gifts were too great to turn down. "I'd like to soak on my own a little. Thank you."

He nodded. "The water will be cooling in half an hour. If you want me before then, shout."

It was a marvelous half-hour. Sukey splashed about, humming to herself, exploring the tub, glad no one was looking at her. She liked John looking at her, of course, but sometimes you wanted just to be yourself. She floated, drowsy and dreaming, until she was half afeared she'd fall asleep and drown. Sitting up exposed her breasts and shoulders to the cooler air. It felt nice. She was pink all over, flushed with heat.

She grew almost bored, but she resisted calling for John. This was a pleasure she'd have only once, or at least only once in a very great while. She ought to wring the last drops from it. Washing her hair with soft soap, she marveled at how much cleaner this felt than bending one's head over a little washtub. Curious, she soaped her breasts, liking the way her hands slipped over them. Behind her, one of the candle-ends guttered out with a hiss and smell of smoke.

John knocked. She laughed and ducked under the water, washing her bosom clean. "Come." She stood, water dripping down her. John froze for a moment before he remembered to shut the door behind him. He leaned against it, silent and still.

Paralyzed with lust, she thought. For her.

Then he rushed forward and handed her a towel. "You mustn't catch a chill."

"I'll not be this warm again till June," she said as she stepped out of the tub, although in that moment she felt she'd be warm forever. There was snow on the ground outside, but she was burning up. Even putting on her shift would smother her. "Isn't there anything you'd like me to do, now I'm naked in the middle of the room?" She dried her hair as well as she could, glad it didn't fall much past her shoulders. She'd finish it before the kitchen fire later.

He wound a damp tress round his finger. "You smell like roses." When he let go to spread out their bedroll, her hair retained the curl, remembering him.

All of her remembered him, was homesick for him. The air stroked and petted her when she moved, curling around her shoulders, her belly, the back of her knee. John lay down on the pallet. "Come here."

He arranged her upright and straddling his thighs, only the insides of her knees brushing his pantaloons. She liked the way she towered over him. "It's not often I'm taller than you."

"Are you wet?" His voice was hoarse.

"Of course," she said innocently. "I just got out of the bath." She'd never felt so clean, as if she'd emerged from the water new-baptized and he was christening her with his eyes. Marking her as his own.

"Answer the question."

She slipped her middle finger between her folds, testing. "Yes, a little."

"Make yourself wet enough to take me." Unbuttoning his pantaloons, he drew his cock out. Stroked it until it was hard enough to spear her with ease.

She watched him watch her, finger circling her pearl, slow at first, then faster, rougher.

He held his cock upright in his hand. "Now."

She crawled forward and lowered herself onto him, feeling her cunny stretch. He took his hand away and left them joined just there, between their legs, making no move to touch her. "You like to watch me, don't you?" she asked.

His mouth curved. "You said it yourself: you won't be this warm again until June."

"Do you think you'd like to watch another man fuck me?" she asked, very daring. Too daring, maybe. "You wouldn't miss a detail then."

He lay still beneath her, but his cock twitched.

She leaned over him. Drops of rose-scented water fell from the tips of her hair onto his shirt. "Or a woman, maybe?" The idea of John fucking another woman had made her furious at the servants' ball, but if she was there too... "I'd like that, I think. Suckling at her tits while she cried out from your cock in her."

Yes, she thought, she *would* like that. To make the other girl mindless, desperate, pushed beyond the bounds of ordinary sensation. She'd like to touch a female body that wasn't her own and see how it responded to her. She'd like to feel John's eyes on her while she did it.

John's hips began to move. Sukey fumbled, but soon they were moving in harmony, grinding against each other. He kept his hands clenched at his sides.

Another candle-end guttered out. It made her feel very fond of him, somehow. She loved the way he wrinkled his nose. "Would you like that?" she murmured, still touching herself.

The sound he made was half a laugh, half a moan. "Where would we find this obliging person?"

Sukey shrugged. "I could ask a likely looking woman to help carry my basket home from the market. That turned out well for me last time."

He shut his eyes. "You wouldn't really, would you?"

She cuffed him on the arm. "Of course not! I *do* think of my reputation, you know." She leaned forward so her pearl was pressed between her finger and his belly with each stroke. Shutting her eyes, she teased her nipple with her free hand and imagined that another woman was doing it, that another woman was crouched by them, watching her shake, coaxing her to her peak, eager to see her wracked with pleasure.

"Then yes," he growled. "I'd like it a great deal, as you very well know. Then I could see what you look like with someone's tongue between your legs. God knows it always *sounds* terribly impressive."

She nearly fainted with the force of her pleasure. She awoke leaning over him, arms trembling as they held her up. She was hot and worn out, and her hair was drying at the tips, waving slightly. John was watching her.

She did love him. It was just a stupid word and it didn't mean *forever* or *sure* or *safe*, but it meant how she felt.

Well, there was no use in crying over spilt milk. She smiled at him—or meant to. Her mouth wobbled a little. Her second try was better. "Did you see everything you wanted to?"

He shook his head. "I never will." He held himself back from spending with an effort, every muscle tensed and unmoving save his hips, tilting up barely at all with each thrust. "There'll always be more of you to see."

"You shouldn't be so sweet. You'll encourage me to henpeck you."

He bent his knees and sat, startling her. She nestled in the cradle of his lap now, his thighs at her back. "Kiss me," he said.

He was too tall. She had to rise up on her knees to do it, half off his cock. But she kissed him, her tongue against his. He wrapped his arms tight around her naked body and spent like that, only half inside her but all around her anyway.

* * *

Hal! John almost said to the footman in green-and-gold livery standing on the vicarage steps. But remembering himself, he only said, "Good day," and held out his hand for Lady Tassell's calling card. He had handed over hundreds of these in his life. Thousands, probably. Strange to be receiving one, and to say, "Shall I inquire if the vicar is at home?"

"If you would, sir." As the countess, standing at the foot of the stairs, could see John's face and not Hal's, he could only bow in answer to the footman's friendly smile.

"Lady Tassell is here to see you, sir," he told the vicar, who was lingering over his luncheon with a new book from London. "Will you receive her?"

"Indeed I will. I have been expecting her. Ask Mrs. Khaleel to make up a tea tray, will you? Is the fire lit in the living room?"

John felt that the vicar might have mentioned this expectation. "Yes, sir."

"Then I will receive her there."

So John took his former mistress's muff, tartan pelisse and furs and showed her into the living room. "The Right Honorable the Countess of Tassell," he announced her, and depositing the overclothes by the laundry fire to dry, he hurried to the kitchen to inform Mrs. Khaleel about the tray.

Hal accompanied him, removing his wig with relief and swinging it by its queue as he walked. It was a habit in footmen John's father had always deplored, as powder inevitably got on the hand and leg and from thence, everywhere else. "I heard you got married. We all wish you joy."

"Thanks," John said, after which any delicate attempt to inquire into the countess's business was forestalled by Mrs. Khaleel's eager questions as to the type of sandwiches and cake her ladyship preferred.

He knew more about her preferences than he did about the vicar's.

As he carried in the tea tray and laid out the cups and plates, he felt her watching him, as serenely triumphant as if he marched before her in chains through the streets of Rome. He strongly disliked knowing that she must think him come down in the world since leaving her employ, as if his present home and his marriage were a wretchedness she had forced him to.

Larry, settling the urn on the cloth, contrived somehow to press his hand to the hot silver and made a pained hissing noise. John kept his face impassive as he dropped two slices of lemon and a lump of sugar into an empty cup, but he saw the corner of Lady Tassell's mouth quirk up and felt hot with embarrassment.

"Just how I prefer it, thank you, Mr. Toogood," she said in a surprisingly friendly way. "I should like to speak to you before I go, if your master will allow it."

John pantomimed polite surprise, mind racing inwardly. Surely she wouldn't go so far as to request Mr. Summers to dismiss him from his post. But then what could she possibly want? Perhaps she merely wished to convey his mother's greetings. That seemed long odds, but he could think of no other innocent reason. "Sir, if I may?"

"Naturally, Toogood. I know better than to stand in her ladyship's way." The two gentlefolk laughed as if it were a joke and not the literal truth.

John waited in an agony of impatience for the vicar's ring, and then waited another count of thirty; promptness was a virtue, but in this case, he wished to avoid any appearance of listening at the door. Mr. Summers's face was long, but he kissed the air above Lady Tassell's hand as he stood, old-fashioned and courtly. "I cannot wish you luck, my lady," he said, "but I will wish you a fair hearing." He made a good-natured flourish to John in her direction and went out.

John came to stand before her, hands behind his back. "My lady."

It had been so long since he'd seen her that he had forgotten the full force of her. She was small, but it was not only her petticoats and frills and tall hat that gave her the appearance of height. *Ice-cream faces*, Sukey had said of Dymond boys. *Nothing to stick in the mind.* Lady Tassell was blonde, fair-skinned and even delicate of feature, but the angular jaw that gave Lord Lenfield the air of a capably executed statue of an Olympian was unforgettable on her, and pleasantly so. John had always liked her. She was autocratic, but she was good company and her rules were simple. Until recently, he had followed them and got on well with her.

But he admitted to himself for the first time that Nick Dymond had always been his favorite of the Dymond boys precisely because he did neither.

She smiled, gesturing to the vicar's vacated chair. "Sit, Mr. Toogood. I don't plan to give you orders."

John didn't like it, but he sat.

"Please allow me to wish you joy on your marriage. Your wife is Susan Grimes, isn't she? My daughter-in-law's maid?" She shook her head, laughing at life's absurdity. "Like master, like man."

"Thank you, my lady."

The countess's face grew grave. Eyes on her hands, she crumbled a piece of cake in her fingers. "You look so much like your father," she said at last, and then was silent another half a minute. "He was at Tassell Hall before my husband was born, you know."

John felt a sudden pang of fear. "Is he—is he well?"

She pushed away her plate of crumbs and met his eyes. "He has had no sudden decline, and he isn't ill. But he is becoming an old man. I'm an old woman, and he has a score of years on me at least."

John said nothing. It was only what he already knew.

"I know I can't expect such an active man as your father to sit in an easy chair by the fire, any more than I'd do so myself. But I've asked him and your mother to go and manage our house in Rye Bay. It's lovely there, and there's only a small staff. Not much larger than the one here."

"That was very kind of you, my lady."

As he spoke, he remembered Sukey's imitation of an upper servant: wooden face and silence. His wife probably imagined that great folk expected the demeanor as a show of respect. That it was a suppression of oneself to please one's employer.

He'd always thought of it differently. The larger the staff, the smaller the importance of each member in his mistress's eyes. How much less inconvenient to replace one among dozens! Better to present a smooth surface with nothing to snag or seize upon. The less Lady Tassell knew, the less she had to use against him.

He wondered if that explained the Dymond boys' ice-cream faces.

"Your father can't manage Tassell Hall anymore," she said. "I'll muddle through one more summer if I must, but after that... I don't wish to hurt his pride. More than that, I want to repay him for his years of loyal service. He wants you to replace him. Will you?"

John could not have been more astonished if Lady Tassell had thrown herself into his arms and embraced him.

He wanted to refuse at once, unequivocally—but how could he? "It is a position of great trust. Is your ladyship certain you wish to offer it to me?"

She sighed. "Here we come to it," she said frankly. "You're angry, I suppose, at my treatment of you."

"I understood your reasons."

She laughed unhappily. "Until your child refuses to see or speak to you, until one of the suns of your existence informs you that it will henceforth be dark to you—no, I don't think you do."

"I'm sorry matters between you have come to such a pass."

"I thought he was susceptible, and you failed to protect him. Susceptible, ha! I never would have thought he could hold a grudge so long."

John thought Nick Dymond had resolutely turned his face away from his mother long before he stopped speaking to her. That she hadn't recognized it was not to her credit—but hard truths were hard to face, and perhaps she was right that he wasn't a parent, and could not understand.

She leaned in, distracting him from wondering if he would ever be a father himself. "Your talents are wasted here. You were an exceptional footman, and then an exceptional valet, and you are quite clearly an exceptional butler. But as good-hearted as these people are, one day you will want more scope for your genius than a quiet vicarage. I know you, John. You read the papers, you follow the debates in Parliament. You and I, we want to put our stamp on the world. Elections are won and bills introduced at Tassell house parties. *That* is what you were born for, and you know it."

As simply as that, doubts crept in. He knew all the reasons why he wanted to refuse her, and yet he hesitated, tempted. He tried to form his next sentence. *My wife is not accustomed...*

No. He would not tactfully warn the countess of Sukey's failings. He refused to imply in any way that he was not entirely proud of her. "And my wife?"

She shrugged. "I won't make her housekeeper, but if you want a place for her at the Hall, we'll find one." Then she told him the wages she offered. He wondered if she knew he knew they were ten pounds more per annum than his father's. "You might even set her up in lodgings nearby and start a family."

His heart failed him at the thought. Sukey in a snug cottage, singing and entertaining her friends. Cheerfully living her own life—one in which he naturally had some small place, but not a particularly essential one.

Greedily, he wanted more than that. He wanted what they had now. They had fought hard for it, sniped and confided and quarreled and kissed their way to it. Things were going so well between them, and here Lady Tassell was, to set everything on its ear again.

If the countess hadn't, out of spite, told her friends not to let their sons hire him, he'd be valeting for some rising MP. It would be a more peaceful existence, even, in some respects, one with more gaiety in it. But he'd made the best of things, and the best had turned out to be better than he'd dared hope. Why should he accept her offer?

His conscience readily supplied the answer. His father was ill and old, and had persuaded Lady Tassell to humble herself before John.

It didn't surprise him that she'd agreed in the end—though he noticed she'd put it off until the very last week of her stay. Repaying loyalty with loyalty was both principle and policy with her, and no one could have been more loyal than Mr. Toogood senior.

No, he was surprised his father had argued with her. Plumtree had told him, and John hadn't believed him. Privately, he'd been sure his father would never side with him against the Tassells. That he could never again be proud of someone who had betrayed Lady Tassell—and who, perhaps worse, had embarrassed him before her.

To say no was to throw his father's olive branch in his face. It was to refuse his mother her retirement. And it was to deprive his hardworking wife of a chance at leisure.

The chance was unlikely to come again.

"I don't know, my lady," he said at last. "I would need to discuss it with my wife."

"Good man. This concerns her as well." She settled her skirts more comfortably about her legs. "Mr. Summers informs me that he will be in London for most of February."

The vicar planned to see his children and to present a paper to the Society of Antiquaries. Things were complicated by the defection of his curate, but the rector of a nearby parish had agreed to make a loan of his. John had been looking forward to a restful month of catching up on everything.

"He has agreed that while he is away, you and your wife may journey to Tassell Hall to visit your parents. I will be glad to cover your traveling expenses, if it means I may have your answer by Lady Day. But then I would need you to come at once to Tassell to help your father with the summer house parties."

It was an overpoweringly handsome offer. "If I might have a moment to speak privately with Mrs. Toogood, my lady?"

She flapped a hand at him like an indulgent mother. "Don't be silly. Ring for her. I would be delighted to meet the young woman."

John lacked the courage to flatly contradict a countess, though he knew she had only asked to make it harder for them to plot escape. "She will be grateful for the honor, my lady."

Larry answered the bell and went to fetch Sukey. The boy was still visibly nervous. John would have to discuss the importance of unblushing aplomb with his staff—if they remained his staff. Sukey's brow, too, was tight with nerves when she came in. John went to her and took her hand. "My lady, may I present my wife, Susan Toogood?"

"It's a pleasure to meet you, Mrs. Toogood."

Sukey bobbed a shaky curtsey—deep, but not deep enough. "Thank you, my lady. I'm that sensible of the honor."

Lady Tassell blinked at the thickness of her accent, and John—he hated it, but his first instinct was to wish she talked properly, so Lady Tassell would have no excuse to sneer, and be obliged to recognize her worth. What did Lady Tassell's opinion matter?

"Mrs. Toogood, I want your husband to come and work for me again," the countess said without preamble. Sukey's eyes flew to John in shock before she fixed them respectfully on the hem of Lady Tassell's gown. "His father is ill, and I have asked John to come and help him and then, after a little while, if we find it suits us, to take his place."

"I see, my lady."

John was unsettled to see his irrepressible wife so awed. Lady Tassell laid out the whole proposition, and Sukey grew stiller and stiller as she went.

"You seem a good girl," Lady Tassell said finally. "If you wish to better yourself, there is a place for you at the Hall. But as I told John, you would be able to leave off working altogether and start a family, should the two of you so desire."

Sukey's eyes were like wary saucers. "I see, my lady," she said, trying for less of a burr this time. "I suppose I'd need to learn to speak better, to work at a place like Tassell Hall."

Lady Tassell smiled. "Not by much. Don't get an inflated idea of our grandeur, I beg you."

"Do you wish us to go, Mr. Toogood?"

"It is a great opportunity," he said, "and one which I am grateful to be offered. And my father…" He couldn't finish the sentence with Lady Tassell listening. "I thought we ought to consider very carefully. But if you feel differently, I am quite willing to be guided by you." *Say no*, he thought, knowing himself for an unfilial son.

"Now that is a bettermost sort of husband." Lady Tassell used the provincialism with a grin and a wink in Sukey's direction.

Sukey's sly, crooked smile flashed out a little uncertainly. "Only a fool would say no to a free journey," she said, meeting his eyes. "My mother didn't raise any fools."

As grateful as John was for this feeble attempt to pretend enthusiasm, he was afraid it would strike Lady Tassell as a very frivolous sentiment. But she seemed entirely satisfied. Soon everything was arranged, the money was in John's pocket, Sukey curtseyed herself out of the room, and John was left with the countess, itching to escort her out and speak with his wife further.

"Mr. Toogood," she said instead, sounding hesitant. "My son wrote you a letter of reference, I believe?"

He didn't want to bring her wrath down on Lord Lenfield if she didn't already know he'd helped John. "Mr. Nicholas did, yes, my lady."

"Might I see it?"

I wasn't aware you would require references, John almost said blandly. But he didn't have the nerve—or the heart. She looked so afraid of his refusal. "Certainly, my lady." He brought it to her, and waited while she read it—and then while she read it a second time.

John had read it many times himself during the anxious fortnight when he feared never finding another position. The letter had gratified John's vanity very highly, but he couldn't imagine there was much in it to satisfy a mother's craving for news of her son, being filled with *He is handy with a razor* and statements of that ilk. The most personal thing—indeed, the *only* personal thing—Mr. Dymond had written was *He is undemanding company, and managed a sad change in my circumstances (on the occasion of resigning my commission due to injury) with matter-of-fact delicacy.*

"That's more words than he wrote to me all the time he was in Spain." She folded it up and handed it briskly back. "Thank you, Mr. Toogood. I do hope you'll come and work for me."

John collected her dry things from the laundry room and went to fetch Hal, trying to decide what to tell the rest of the staff. He shrank from informing Mrs. Khaleel and Thea and Molly and Larry that he was thinking of abandoning them.

The next moment he scolded himself for exaggerating his own importance. But if their faces *didn't* fall at the news, he didn't want to see that either.

On entering the kitchen, it was obvious that Sukey had already told them. Four faces of forced good cheer were turned to him—no, five, for Sukey had rather the same expression.

"It's only a visit," he said.

"For now," Molly muttered.

He didn't even want to go. He wanted to stay and help Molly with her father, make sure Mr. Bearparke didn't harass Mrs. Khaleel, hear Thea sing disgusting ballads. At least he'd still be able to help Larry refurbish his livery before the footman accompanied Mr. Summers to London.

"Hal, it was good to see you." He handed the countess's things to the footman. "Give everyone at Lenfield my good wishes. Her ladyship is ready for you." And he still had to escort them out and shut the door behind them with a bow before rushing back to the kitchen.

"Mrs. Toogood, if I might speak with you a moment?" He looked round at the rest of them. "It's merely a visit. My father..." He tried to think how to explain. "It is my father's wish that I replace him. He isn't well. I owe it to him to talk to him before I..." *Say no* was too cavalier. "Make a decision."

"You don't have to take the position if you don't want it, only because your father isn't well," Molly said fiercely.

John smiled at her, though he wished it were that simple. "Thank you, Molly. It helps to hear that."

Mrs. Khaleel swatted her with a towel. "It's a much better position than this one, goose. If he wants to be rich and important, we'd ought to be understanding."

"It's merely a visit," he said again. If only he knew what to do. "Mrs. Toogood?"

She followed him to their room. "I thought Lady Tassell hated you."

John sighed. "Maybe she does. But she loves my father. He must have begged her."

Sukey twisted her hands together. "You told me you never wanted to be a butler."

"I *am* a butler." He fell into the chair, and then stood back up to offer it to her. She rolled her eyes and sat on the edge of the table. Lord, he wanted them to stay here. "I'll tell her no if you wish it. I only thought we should give it serious consideration before we do anything final. As you said, it's naught but a free holiday at the moment."

"How long has it been since you saw your parents?"

"I went home last July." He could see from her face she thought it a long time, though it had become usual to him.

"Home," she repeated quietly, and sighed. "Tassell Hall is your home. We should go."

He regretted his use of the word. This was his home. Their home. Reluctantly, he said, "I'm not only thinking of myself. Lady Tassell said I would make enough money to support you at home. You could leave off working."

She looked as if she couldn't quite decide if she'd bitten into a lemon or a cream puff. "So you'd be busy all day and I'd—I'd…" It was clear she couldn't conceive of a life without work, that she could think of nothing to fill so many hours. "I'd keep out of the way?"

He'd thought it would be hard to offer her this, but after all it was easy. "Sukey," he said, taking her rough hand, reddened with work. There was a scar on her right forefinger, where she'd once cut herself chopping beetroots. "You've worked ever since you were a child. So have I. My life has been pleasant enough, I don't say it hasn't. But sometimes I look back, and I can't understand where the years went. Day after day of waking, working and sleeping again, and somehow I was forty. You deserve the choice."

If you want children, you deserve not to wait another ten years until it's prudent. You could even keep them at home, instead of fostering them out until they were old enough to work with you. He couldn't say that. She'd said she wouldn't even think about children with him until a few years had passed. There was no reason yet to think anything had changed.

She took her hand back. "Could you really work for her after what she did to you?"

"It turned out well enough," he said. "I don't need to hold a grudge."

"Tassell Hall is near Chichester, isn't it?" She said it after a long pause, with an odd note in her voice.

He was taken aback. Did she have nothing to say about the idea? "We'll take the stagecoach there, and the Hall will send a cart to bring us the rest of the way." Then he remembered. "Your father lives in Chichester, doesn't he?"

She didn't answer.

"Do you know his direction?"

Slowly, she nodded.

"We could visit him, if you like." He gave her a small smile. "Or not, if you don't like."

She took his hand again, holding it tight. "Don't mention it to my mother. I don't know—I don't know how she'd feel about it."

Chapter Sixteen

The stagecoach was trapped on the road just inside the Chichester city walls, a line of carts and carriages stretching as far as Sukey could see before and behind. And she'd thought there was nothing worse than market day in Lively St. Lemeston.

She was unnerved by the city's size—thrice as large at least as her home—and by its self-assured modernness. The ancient cathedral soaring above them was hemmed in by brand-new brick and plaster, like a shabby pastor in his pulpit ignored by his well-dressed flock below.

Sukey'd been excited to ride the stage. Pfft. She was never leaving home again. She was never going *outdoors* again. All that kept her from a cruel death by frostbite was John's muffler over most of her face, and a fur rug an inside passenger had lent her. Sukey thought this piece of charity would get the woman through the Pearly Gates with never-so-many murders on her conscience.

John had warned her not on any account to fall asleep. As if she could, when she had to clutch the seat and brace her feet to stay upright. After an afternoon and a morning of travel, her legs were good and sore.

And last night they'd had to share a room with three other travelers. She'd been hoping against hope for some privacy on their journey, wanting, just once in her life, to hear John not worry about who might be on the other side of the wall.

If you stay at Tassell Hall, you won't have to make the return journey.

A home of her own, John had said she could have. Not so long ago, she'd have jumped at the chance: mistress of her own establishment, without even a husband underfoot. Financial security and leisure. Maybe she was a fool, to think drudging away in the Tassells' palace might be better because John would be there.

But it frightened her that he'd even suggested living apart. That he'd been able to say it so calmly and easily. She thought of the servants' ball, him telling her to go have fun while he worked. She hadn't only been angry because he'd treated her like a child, she let herself admit. She'd been hurt that he didn't want her to stay. She'd been glad to be with him, and he'd told her to go.

She'd forgotten all about it. But in the cold and snow and jostling, she suddenly couldn't stop turning it over in her mind.

She wanted to go home to the vicarage and eat Mrs. Khaleel's dinner and talk to her friends, and sleep in her own hard bed with John.

She shivered and told herself it was the cold. She dwelled on the cold in loving detail, because it was better than remembering that she might never go home and that soon she'd see her father. For Mr. Grimes had replied to her letter and promised to be home. He'd said he couldn't wait to see her.

He'd waited a good long time without noticeable complaints.

People acted as if they loved you—they drew you baths, for God's sake, baths that smelled like roses—but maybe it never really meant anything.

What would Mr. Grimes look like? What would she talk to him about? Did his new wife even know he had another? Sukey'd go along with her father, she decided for the thousandth time. If he'd lied, she'd be silent. She'd gain nothing by cutting up the poor woman's peace.

Poor woman? Who was she to deserve Sukey's pity when her children had been looked after by Sukey's father all these years?

What did she look like? And would it be better if she was prettier than Sukey's mum, or better if she wasn't?

A snowflake whirled past the brim of her bonnet and stung her forehead. Sukey made a sorrowing little noise no one could hear over the wind, and went over every bit of her body and how cold it was.

When her feet and hands had gone good and numb and the clock had struck half past eleven, the coach pulled off the street into an innyard. Sukey was afeared to stand. Her legs might not hold her, and then she'd fall to her death and they'd have to fish her out of a snowdrift and bury her in this strange town, away from all her people.

But John helped her up, holding her elbows until she found her balance. He clambered down into the unsteady snow and caught her when she jumped, his hands strong and familiar at her waist.

Leaving their luggage at the inn, they made their way to Mr. Grimes's lodging-house, a blindingly white building not far from the North Gate. Even the stairwell was brilliantly whitewashed. Sukey took in a deep breath, and another, and before John could say something kind, she gave him a wry shrug and rapped briskly on the door.

It was flung open at once by a pretty, dark-haired girl in her early teens. "It's Susan, Dad," she called excitedly over her shoulder. "Come!" She took Sukey by the arm and dragged her into the house. "I always wanted a big sister," she confided. "I hate that you live so far away."

Sukey blinked about at the charming family scene. The room was small and bare, but the fire was big enough to be cheerful. A woman rose from darning socks by the window, nervesomely checking the ribbons on her cap, and four rosy-cheeked children disported themselves about the place, besides the excited girl. *Big sister.* She'd never thought of these children as her sisters and brothers.

"Susan's aunt would miss her very much," a shockingly familiar voice said. "We hadn't ought to be selfish." She was engulfed in a hug before she had time to look at him.

She leaned instinctively into his well-known scent, but when he pulled away, it was more like wracking your brains—*Don't I know him from somewhere?*— than it was like seeing your father. She recognized his cobbler's bench and tools in the corner, though, the only messy thing in the room.

No one calls me Susan, she thought. *No one ever called me Susan but you.* She'd missed it when he left, but at some point it had stopped being her name; instead of something special they shared, it was a sign he didn't know her. "My aunt?"

"I mean Lizzy, who took you in after your mother died. But I'm sure my sister Kate would miss you as well." Mr. Grimes's smile...she hoped hers didn't look like that. Twinkly and false. She could feel her breathing go strange and shallow. Aunt Lizzy had died of typhus ten years ago. And every week in church she wished she could speak to Aunt Kate.

He'd told them her mother was dead. Her mum, who'd loved her and brought her up with no help from anyone.

Sukey had friends whose mothers put them in the workhouse a few times a year when things got bad. She'd been sure Mrs. Grimes would do the same, sooner or later, but she never had. Sukey was fiercely grateful for that, because going hungry or barefoot had never scared her as much as the idea of her mother leaving too.

She was ashamed of every uncharitable thought she'd ever had about her mother. Of how angry she'd been about Aunt Kate. Of wishing her mother would smile more or be kinder. Mr. Grimes's kind smile was awful. He'd said her mother was *dead*. He'd probably wished she *would* die and leave him free.

Sukey looked at the new Mrs. Grimes, who wasn't Mrs. Grimes at all. By the pleading way she was looking back, she knew the truth and her children didn't.

John stepped closer, his hand on the small of her back. She could feel the tension in his arm. He was angry for her, she thought, but he was waiting to see what she wanted to do.

"I'm sorry, I think I ate something that disagreed with me." Sukey bolted from the room. John followed without stopping to be polite.

Mr. Grimes followed as well. "Wait, Susan, please!"

Sukey didn't want to, but she stopped. She turned round, hating the horrible hope in her heart that maybe he would say something to make it better.

"I had to say that about your mother," he said earnestly. "It was that or say you were a bastard."

"I think this was a mistake." John was looking at her father, but his gentle voice was meant for Sukey. "Let's go."

Her father darted around them to block the street door. "Please don't go. Susan, you can't know how I've missed you. Tell me how you've been. I want to get to know this new man of yours." The way he said *new man*, it was as if they'd seen each other just a bit ago. As if only John was a stranger to him.

"I want my little girls to get to know each other," he cajoled. "Julia's talked of nothing else since we got your letter."

Sukey had lied to her mother to come here. She wished she hadn't come.

She at once envied Julia bitterly and pitied her for the blow that was bound to fall sometime.

But maybe it would never fall. Maybe Mr. Grimes's new family was better than his old one.

He tipped up her chin. "My blue-eyed Susan, all grown up."

Sukey stepped back sharply. John placed himself ever so slightly between them.

"You look just like I did at your age. Prettier, of course—"

Sukey trembled. She *didn't* look like him. "I'm going to be sick."

Her father tried to block the door again, but somehow he was brushed aside by the unstoppable progress of John's shoulder. They were in the street. Sukey walked faster, ran around a corner and felt safe.

Funny, to be afeared he'd chase after her, when all these years... "I'm sorry I made a scene. I'm sorry I wasted your time coming here in the first place. I'm sorry I couldn't—"

John gathered her in his arms, shaking his head. "Shh, don't be sorry. Time's never wasted when I'm with you."

It was too sweet. She sobbed wholeheartedly into his coat. "I should go back. I'll regret it if I don't. We came all this way."

She knew she could go in and act as if none of it bothered her. If she kicked up a shindy, would that happy girl guess her parents were liars, that she was a bastard? Would she be afraid Mr. Grimes could leave *her*?

"If you want to go back, we will," he said. "But we needn't. What can happen in the next two hours that will make such a difference to you? What's he going to say that's so vital for you to hear, after so many years of silence?"

"I want him to say he loves me," she wept angrily. "I want him to say it was a mistake to leave me, that he regrets it every day, that he's proud of the woman I've become."

"If he did say that, how would you feel?"

She imagined it and recoiled from the memory of his face. "No different," she mumbled. But she *wanted* to feel different. People said forgiveness was wonderful. She wanted to know what it felt like, wanted to know how other people felt. She wanted their confidence and grace, and their generosity.

She'd wanted to be somewhere where folks were generous with each other, but she was the stingiest person she knew.

"You're remarkable," John said, arms tight around her. "You're extraordinary and splendid. You always have been and you always will be, no matter who does or doesn't love you."

And she recoiled from *that*, feeling all at once as if he were a stranger too.

If he'd told her she was unbearable sometimes, that her father had left because nobody wanted to be bothered with a mouthy little girl, she'd have felt *closer* to him. She'd have felt as if he knew her. She couldn't forgive her father for making her this way.

Other people forgave. They sat down to dinner and laughed and talked with men who'd done much worse things than leaving.

Not your mother, she thought. *She never forgave or forgot. She never looked at a man again.*

Sukey desperately didn't want to be like her mother.

"I don't know what I want." She wiped her frozen tears away fiercely with her glove, wool and ice scraping her skin. "What did you think of him?"

"I think in other circumstances, I might have liked him," he said carefully. "In these, I very much did not."

She felt a roar of relief. John didn't think she was being a shrew. "Do you think I look like him?"

He considered the question solemnly. "There is a certain family resemblance. When you smile, your cheeks turn into little circles, here." He traced a circle below her eye with his finger. "You both have a mischievous air to you. But I don't think the similarity is as striking as he made it out to be." He sighed. "I'm afraid the same may not be true for my father and myself."

"Handsome old codger, is he?" Sukey didn't understand how John's face went from grave to smiling with almost no movement. A bit of softening about the mouth and crinkling about the eyes, and he might as well have been grinning ear to ear. But it was *better* than grinning, because it was just for her. "I'll regret it if I don't go back. I don't want to be a coward."

"Then we'll go back."

* * *

Speaking strictly for himself, John had sat through worse dinners. But he thought Sukey had not. She talked amiably with the second Mrs. Grimes, laughed and joked with her adolescent sister, played with the children, and shared reminiscences with her father. But at John's lightest touch, she twanged like a spinet wire. She ate ravenously, as if her ordinary demeanor was a great feat of strength that demanded fuel.

"Red is my favorite color too!" the oldest girl said—Julia, her name was— eyes shining at the marvelous coincidence.

Sukey smiled. "It's our coloring, that's all. We Grimes girls know what suits us."

Julia's eyes shone brighter.

He had wanted to say to her, when she'd wept in his arms, I *love you, and I will never leave you, and I*'m *proud of you.* It had leapt to his tongue. He was glad he hadn't said it. It wasn't relevant. She would have been equally perfect if she'd never met him. And if he'd said it then, she wouldn't have believed him.

He looked at her father, beaming with pleasure at his two little girls getting to know each other. His brown hair had only a few threads of gray at the temples. It was true: in other circumstances John would have liked Mr. Grimes. But what disturbed him most was that in other circumstances, he'd have thought of Mr. Grimes as a man of about his own age. John couldn't be his junior by more than five or six years.

She'd been so afraid to see her father's face in the mirror. But did she see him when she looked at John?

* * *

"Are you sure you want to go in?" John asked. "We could go back to the inn and talk. I'll get us a private room if you like."

Sukey didn't want to talk. She'd been talking for what felt like hours. She'd wanted to go to a real theater for as long as she could remember. They were doing a version of John's Shakespeare play with fairies. She'd put on her best dress and she wasn't going to let her father ruin it for her, even if she kept thinking of her sister saying, *Can I write you letters?* and hearing her own unconvincing *Things are so unsettled, I don't know where you'd ought to send them.* The girl had looked crushed.

Her father had smiled at her as they left, Julia leaning her head trustingly on his shoulder. He'd said he was sorry to see her go, but he wasn't really. She didn't matter.

"I thought you were famous for tactfully ignoring it when someone was unhappy." The joke came out sour.

John frowned. "If you mean Nick Dymond, he was my employer and I followed his wishes. And yes, I do try not to pry unnecessarily into others' private griefs. But, Sukey, you're my wife."

"What does that mean, then?" she said rashly. "That my wishes don't matter? That I haven't got anything private of my own?" What did he want? For her to rip out her heart and put it in his hand? Well, she only had so much kindness in her and she'd already wasted it on strangers.

John's eyes flashed. She waited, trembling, for the storm to break. It would be a relief.

But after a moment he shrugged, mouth tightening. "I apologize. If you'd prefer tactful silence, I can oblige you."

The knowledge that she was in the wrong squirmed in her stomach like a snake. But she didn't apologize, because then he'd talk to her again and she didn't want that. She'd opened herself up so she could be cheerful for her sister, and now she needed to shut herself off before she bled to death—or maybe she'd closed herself off and now she couldn't get herself open again, she didn't know.

She'd feel better after the play, and they could go back to the inn and talk about what everyone had been wearing.

The theater was a neat brick building, not especially pretty. John held the door with a courtly air, not quite meeting her eyes. "Two tickets for the pit, if you please," he said, and led her into…

The theater.

Sukey's breath caught. Everything was red and pale blue and gilt, finer even than the Assembly Rooms in Lively St. Lemeston. The ceiling was painted to look as if it opened onto a summer sky, while the boxes curved and swooped about the edges of the room, with two more tiers of seats above them.

Ahead was the stage. They could see a few feet of bare planking, with a plain door to either side flanked by flat, painted columns. Everything beyond was hidden by a great red curtain that fired Sukey with curiosity.

Rows of benches filled the sloping pit. She and John were early, and took the one closest to the stage. Before them, in a strange little box set into the floor, seven men tuned two fiddles, a cello and oboe-like instruments in various sizes. The fiddle players seemed to be quarreling, continually poking each other with their bows and elbows and wincing at the sounds from each other's instruments. Sukey watched them, and for half an hour the tightness in her chest felt like eagerness.

She didn't look at John, but now and again, out of the corner of her eye, she saw his face turn towards her.

At last the overture began, the curtain rising grandly on a Greek sort of palace, all painted columns and marble. A string of actors and actresses came through the doors in a peculiar assortment of tunics, sandals, headdresses and fluffily draped white dresses. A craggy fellow in ermine robe and coronet—he must be the Duke of Athens—began rather pompously,

> Now, fair Hippolyta, our nuptial hour
> Draws on apace: four happy days bring in
> Another moon; but O! methinks how slow
> This old moon wanes; she lingers my desires,
> Like to a step-dame, or a dowager
> Long withering out a young man's revenue.

Well, that's rude! thought Sukey. *You don't look poor to me, I should think you could afford to support your mother.* That was dukes for you, she supposed.

She remembered from John's account of the play that one of the girls eloped with her lover to escape the match her father made for her. This must be the father now, making a speech about the pretty gifts his daughter's lover gave her. Sukey was thinking that really, they did sound cheap, when he said,

As she is mine, I may dispose of her;
Which shall be either to this gentleman,
Or to her death, according to our law.

Sukey's entire body went stiff. He wanted his daughter *killed* if she didn't marry the man he liked? John hadn't mentioned that. And the duke didn't even blink, just knabbled on to poor Hermia about how she was nothing but a form her father had stamped in wax, while the girl trembled with fear. This was supposed to be a *comedy*.

After a dozen or so scraps of song so formal and fussy they'd be no fun to sing, the curtain came down on the first scene. "What do you think?" John asked.

"That jealous *sneak*," Sukey said furiously. "Why would Helena tell Demetrius about her friend's elopement? If he brings her back, they'll *kill* her."

He looked surprised. Hadn't they been watching the same play? "Don't worry," he said, smiling. "No one dies."

The second scene was in a cottage—a neater, airier one than Sukey had ever seen, but the actors wore smocks and soft country hats. A sturdy fellow with a hammer stuck through the ties of his leather apron said, "Is all our company here?" in a thick Sussex burr, and the audience exploded into laughter.

A cocky, tall young man strutted to the center of the stage, and *he* spoke in a Sussex burr. Gales more laughter, and there hadn't even been a joke yet.

John laughed too.

Sukey had heard people put on burrs before to be funny. She'd been hearing it all her life. Mrs. Humphrey's boarders did it sometimes, and laughed fit to split their seams. It had never troubled her overmuch. Sometimes she thickened her burr a little herself to tell a ghost story.

But tonight, with gentlefolk in satin gowns and silk stockings guffawing in the boxes, she *seethed*. She was sure some of those actors weren't even from Sussex. One of them had on a hat just like Larry's when he was helping the gardener, and you could tell it was supposed to be funny. The hat was a joke all of its own.

John was laughing, his face alight. Did he think how she spoke was funny? *He's seen the play before*, she reminded herself. *He likes the jokes.* But somehow she couldn't laugh at a single one. Her heart was small and hard as a cherry stone, and every time John laughed, she felt further away from him.

The curtain fell again. John turned to her, clearly expecting enthusiasm.

"What's so funny about artisans trying to act, anyway?" she burst out. "Obed Wickens from the Carpenters' Guild plays St. George every Boxing Day, and he's splendid. But of course actors think what they do is so important, you'd better be a gentleman before you try it."

"We should leave," John said. "If you're not enjoying it, let's leave."

The awful, terrible truth was that she wanted to leave without him. She looked at him, handsome and familiar, and she could imagine not loving him. She could imagine looking at his face and feeling nothing. As if he were a stranger.

That girl had smiled at her as if they were sisters, and she hadn't felt a thing, when she knew she'd ought to. What if her heart just stopped working?

She'd never felt so frightened. She nodded hurriedly, clutching at his sleeve. "Let's go," she said, fingers tight on the twill. "I'm so sorry, you were having fun but I want to go home." Nothing here was home, though, and tomorrow they had to go on to Tassell Hall.

John helped her on with her pelisse while a fairy sang, the silk moth-wings tied about her head fluttering foolishly. He pushed their way to the aisle, murmuring polite apologies with as much calm self-assurance as if he cleared a path for a duchess. Sukey's head hurt.

He asked for the private room at the inn. She pulled him down on top of her in the bed, straining to get as close as she could, to be swept away by passion. She wanted him in her, on her. But he kept saying, "You're not ready, Sukey, I'll hurt you. Easy, sweetheart. Relax, it's just me." He kissed her cheekbones beneath her closed eyes, and her jaw. His hands knew what she liked, and he did finally arouse her, make her want him. She even spent while he was inside her.

But it wasn't like it always had been before. He was so close, his eyes on her face and his body warming hers, his cock inside her, but the more she tried to open her heart up, the more she felt as if she might as well have picked up a stranger in the taproom and let him fuck her.

He held her afterwards. She barely breathed; she'd forgotten how to do it in a natural way. If she tried, he'd notice there was something wrong with her, that she couldn't even take in air like other people.

"I shouldn't have done that," he said. "I'm sorry I did."

"I wanted you to," she insisted.

"I know," he said slowly. "And earlier, you wanted me to be tactfully silent. But you're my wife, and I'd like— Please talk to me, Sukey."

But she couldn't. She hated the idea. She knew instinctively that it wouldn't make her feel better, that trying to make him understand would only make him seem further away than ever. This grief was hers and she wanted, perversely, to hoard it. *It's nothing to do with you*, she thought. *You don't even know if you mean to keep living with me.*

He stroked her hair away from her head. She held herself perfectly still so she wouldn't jerk away. "Tell me what you're feeling," he said softly. "You never talk to me."

"What do you mean? I chatter like a magpie."

He rolled away to look up at the ceiling. "Not about yourself. I look back on the talks we've had, and I told you far more about myself than you ever told me."

She knew it was true. When he'd told her all that about the Dymond boys, and getting coddled when he was ill, the best she could manage was *I had the measles once*. "I don't feel anything," she said. "So he's my father. What of it? Half my friends at home don't even know he's alive. He's nothing to do with me anymore."

"I'm sorry, sweetheart. I'm sorry it wasn't what you wanted."

Nothing is what I wanted, she thought.

Chapter Seventeen

"The countryside does look pretty in the snow," Sukey said. "What a darling windmill."

She wasn't talking to John, however. She was talking to Abe Tomkin, the groom who'd been sent to fetch them in the wagon. She'd barely spoken to John all morning, and then with constraint.

Not that she was precisely easy with Abe. John knew her well enough by now to know when she was making polite conversation and when she was really interested. But Sukey enjoyed even polite conversation more than he did. She seemed glad to have a stranger to talk to, so as to avoid looking at John.

He didn't understand what he'd done. He'd tried so hard to say everything right, and yet everything he said was wrong, and everything he did. Silence felt like abandoning her, but she'd said it was what she wanted. This morning while they waited for the cart, she'd even snapped at him, *Stop* watching *me!*

When Mr. Dymond was miserable, he'd only ever wanted his valet to be silent. But he'd chosen a wife he could talk to. John had thought...hoped...he'd wanted to be someone Sukey could talk to, instead of who he'd always been: someone whose presence, while a necessary evil, was at least unobtrusive.

They had reached Tassell land, though they weren't quite in the park. The winter landscape *was* pretty, now Sukey called his attention to it—canopies of bare branches giving way to snowy fields, and every so often a half-frozen millpond—but it was so familiar that John saw it without seeing it. He'd traveled this road countless times, first as a little boy helping with the parcels on market day, then as a liveried footman clinging to the back of the Tassell coach, and still later accompanying one of the Dymond boys on a trip home.

They traversed the home farm now. There was the old elm where he and the coachman's son used to play at Robin Hood, and here was the gatehouse, where they were obliged to stop for tea with Mr. and Mrs. Halfacre, who'd known John since before he was born. Mrs. Halfacre fussed over Sukey, calling her a "pretty young thing".

Sukey expanded gratefully under the attention, but she still didn't really look at John. She ignored him subtly enough that the Halfacres didn't remark it, but John knew his mother would.

He'd been looking forward to showing her off. But when he'd pictured the scene, he'd put Sukey hanging on his arm, teasing him, their happiness glaringly obvious. That must be what every delusional middle-aged man imagined when he took a beautiful young wife.

Pull yourself together, he told himself. *She's just upset about her father. Things were going wonderfully until this journey.* But somehow, knowing his parents were going to be looking at them made every hair-thin crack in their marriage gape and yawn in his mind.

What if she—what if everyone—thought Sukey was a pretty young thing who'd married an older man to get ahead in the world, and didn't have the time of day for him now the ring was on her finger?

And wasn't it true, in a way? She'd never have married him if she hadn't been dismissed from the boarding house.

He'd been selfish to accept her change of heart. He should have told her she'd feel better in the morning and escorted her home, and talked Mrs. Pengilly into having her live in. He should have had some damned self-control, but she'd put her hand on the front of his breeches and he hadn't been able to rush her into things fast enough.

John worried his way through tea (just enough time for the snow on their coats to melt and soak through the lining, not enough for it to dry again) and down the drive to the Hall.

Sukey gasped when they turned the corner. "It's enormous," she breathed. "Bigger than Wheatcroft."

Abe snorted, having adopted wholehearted the rivalry between the Whig Tassells and Tory Wheatcrofts. "Lord Wheatcroft's a country squire. The only place in Sussex bigger than Tassell Hall is Goodwood."

Goodwood was the nearby seat of the Duke of Richmond. Abe was probably exaggerating, but Sukey looked suitably impressed. Certainly Tassell Hall was huge, but only when judged—as Sukey no doubt did—as a home for a single family. John saw it rather as a small fiefdom. It had grown up around the lord and his family, who spent a part of their year occupying the state apartments and filling every room with their guests, but it had a rich and active life of its own. The main house with its bay windows and Dutch gables was blank, the snow on the drive undisturbed by carriage wheels, but smoke drifted up from chimneys in the servants' wing and the hothouses. Before John began to travel with the family at fifteen, he'd loved times like these when the servants had the house to themselves.

Abe drove them around the side and deposited them at the kitchen door, opened by Mrs. Toogood before they could reach it. John swept his mother off her feet, grinning, for the moment just happy to be home.

"Johnny! Oh, it's so good to see you. Here, put me down before I start to cry. Are you hungry?" She kissed his cheek, smelling of charcoal and the kitchen, and John's own eyes stung.

"We had tea with the Halfacres, thanks. Mama, this is my wife." He drew Sukey towards him, hoping she wouldn't push him away.

She nestled closer and held out her hand shyly. "It's an honor, ma'am."

"Oh, please, call me Amanda," Mrs. Toogood said, her manner so unaffected and motherly and welcoming that John felt a rush of pride and gratitude at his mother's superiority over other people.

"Then you shall call me Sukey," his wife said, sounding pleased.

John prayed his mother wouldn't say, *Oh, wouldn't you prefer Susan? It's so much prettier and more feminine.* She had rather a bee in her bonnet on the subject of nicknames, refusing point-blank to let anyone call her Amy.

"Come inside and let me get a good look at you." Mrs. Toogood took John's other arm and led them into the kitchen. John went and hung Sukey's coat and hat by the fire in his mother's sitting room, thinking it was time he gave her boots a thorough cleaning.

When he returned, Sukey was still gazing about the great kitchen, awestruck. John's pride in the Hall mingled with a sort of unease. This was his home, but to her it might have been one of the wonders of the world.

And John knew the look on his mother's face. She was, thus far, highly skeptical. His stomach lurched. He should have bought Sukey a new dress, and those boots…he loved them, but to his mother… At least he might have cleaned them.

Mrs. Toogood's expression melted into a warm smile as Sukey turned towards her. "You must come and meet my husband, and then I'd love to give you a tour of the old pile. I show visitors about as part of my duties, you know, and I can tell you the whole history of the place."

In the butler's pantry, Mr. Toogood was in the midst of a careful inventory of the silverware, polishing tarnish off a fork with a pronounced look of distaste. But he took off his glasses, smiled and embraced John.

His father had been of a height with him until a few years since, when he was abruptly two or three inches shorter. It always amazed John that a human being could shrink. "Mrs. Toogood, this is my father."

"Mr. Toogood." Sukey bobbed a curtsey.

"So you're the young woman who finally turned my sensible son's head," Mr. Toogood said with a smile. The underlying message—*so you're the hussy who ruined his career*—was probably obvious only to John and his mother, so he tried to ignore it. "A pretty little thing you are too. Are you sure you're not *too good* for him?"

Sukey ducked her head. "Oh, it's more likely to be the other way round." Her accent thickened with shyness. He saw his parents exchange glances.

"Not at all," John said rather sharply. "My father has the right of it."

Mr. Toogood laughed. "I should thank you. That's probably the first time my son's ever said *that*."

Sukey twinkled at him. "Make the most of it, for it's *too good* to last." A few more tired puns were exchanged before Mrs. Toogood shepherded them out for the tour.

"I never knew you were such a punster." John was instantly sorry he'd said it, and sorry for the edge in his voice.

"They do spring to mind now and then, with a name like yours," Sukey said rather tightly herself.

He'd always been glad she didn't joke about his name, but it hadn't occurred to him that she was actively resisting temptation, to be kind. He leaned down to whisper in her ear, "You're too good to me."

He wanted her to smile, and she did. But the expression was uncertain, her face turning to his with wide, startled eyes. It tugged at his heart, took him by surprise, made him see her as if for the first time: how slight and angular she was, how elusive, how beautiful. How likely to melt away with one last over-the-shoulder smile.

He wanted to tug her around the corner into a library alcove and kiss her, gripping her hips hard enough to bruise—something to prove that she was a flesh-and-blood woman and that he had touched her. He wanted to tease her until she lit up.

"John?" his mother said.

"Sorry. Shall we start in the great hall?" It was strange walking with his mother and his wife. Offering his arm to both would be awkward, and he could hardly leave Sukey. But it made him feel sorry and distant, not to do what he would have always done before as a matter of course.

He kept on expecting his mother to *need* his arm, but her carriage was as brisk and graceful as it had ever been. He hoped desperately that it would last. "Tell Sukey about the inlaid floor," he said as they entered the hall. "I love that story."

"Well, the present earl's grandfather had it put in. The workman was a French fellow…" John listened with half an ear, crossing to the staircase to run a hand over the handsome carved banister and down the corkscrew posts of the railing.

It came away dusty.

He looked closer. Dusting corkscrew spirals took time, and time had not been taken. There were innumerable pockets and streaks of dust, a week's worth at least in some places. Examining the room, he saw that though the furniture was safely covered in dropcloths in the family's absence, the tall mirrors had not been cleaned to the edges, and dust clung to the plasterwork reliefs on the walls, dulling the gilt.

He waited until the final joke of the French inlayer story. "Mother, there's probably no need to bring Father into it yet, but you ought to speak to whoever's been dusting in here."

His mother's face twisted unhappily. "Is it dusty?"

He nodded. "The plasterwork—"

His mother made an anguished sound. "Oh, Lady Tassell loves that plasterwork!"

John was taken aback. Of his parents, she'd never been the one who ranked cleanliness just above godliness in the catalog of virtues. But if she was upset, there was an easy solution. "It's all right. I'll take a paintbrush to it and have it clean in a trice."

"Thank you." She twisted her hands together. "I don't think it's just in here, though. Your father...well. His eyesight isn't what it used to be, and his back and knees have been bothering him so he can't always bend down or get at things the way he did. I think the servants take advantage."

John couldn't reply. He felt as if he'd been winded by a swift kick in the stomach. Everyone had warned him, but all at once it was real, and it was dreadful. His father had always been so proud, such a petty tyrant, and now he had lost the power to exact obedience. When he met his mother's eyes, tears swam in hers.

What was he going to do?

As Mrs. Toogood led them into the enormous dining room, its long table swathed in white sheets, for a moment John saw ghosts. Gentlemen and ladies of summers past talked and laughed; silver clattered and china clinked. He remembered laying out piping-hot dishes on that table according to his father's design, and woe betide him if Mr. Toogood's eagle eye detected an inch's asymmetry.

He had loved those evenings, flanking the sideboard or standing behind Lady Tassell's chair, listening to talk of politics and the opera. "Do you remember when Mr. Sheridan thought the roast was overcooked?"

His mother sighed. "That roast was perfectly tender."

"What happened?" Sukey asked, charmingly ready to be fascinated by the answer.

"Oh, it's not a very interesting story. John has such a memory for trifles."

Mrs. Toogood waved it away. The animation faded from Sukey's face for a moment before she pasted on a determined smile. John gritted his teeth and did the same. "This fireplace was preserved from the Old Hall…"

After the tour, Sukey went to help his mother with her pickles so John could be initiated into the mysteries of buttling at Tassell Hall.

"And this is where I record each social occasion for which invitations are sent, who attended, the menus and entertainment provided, and what could be improved in future." John's father flipped open a notebook to show him closely written pages. "I keep separate notebooks for occasions above a certain size. And here in this box is an alphabetical list of guests with their preferences and a history of their visits…"

John wondered what the women were talking about in the stillroom. He pulled the first book off the shelf and opened it at random, finding a menu card in his mother's writing attached to the page with a bit of thread. He lifted it to read his father's notes.

Mrs. L's gravy-soup much admired; refilled tureen in kitchen. Next time, 2 tureens. Ices: 2 per guest too many, 1½ will do. Bread well handled, served warm, compliments.

The date was some two years before John's birth. It took him a moment to recognize "Mrs. L" as his mother, before their marriage, the *Mrs.* a courtesy to a head cook.

John had seen his father's system before, and since he left the Hall had always used a similar one when entertaining for his employers. But there could be no comparison between this and chronicling Mr. Summers's rare dinner parties. The thought of continuing his father's labor of love, spending hours closeted in here writing, filled him with something like dread.

His father cleared his throat emphatically. "This is important, John. Stop your woolgathering."

"I beg your pardon, sir. It's just strange to think of you and Mother working together before your marriage."

"The situation had charms of its own." A reminiscent smile briefly illuminated his face, rendering it curiously soft and amorphous. Only when he frowned did the features come into focus, the broad planes of his cheeks and forehead acquiring shape and purpose. John wondered if that was innate to their shared lineaments, or if over time an accustomed expression had engraved itself. "Which is not to say we didn't get impatient from time to time. Still, you might have learned from our example." Mr. Toogood turned back to his boxes, pulling out a roll tied with ribbon. "This is—"

"Father, I'm forty. How long was I supposed to wait?"

"Until you were established in your profession! At least you might have chosen someone who wasn't a hindrance to your advancement. It's plain you got her with child, but I shall undertake to act surprised when you break the news to your mother."

"Sukey is *not* with child. And she *has* helped me to my present situation, and in it. Our employer adores her."

His father shook his head, looking sorrowful. "I've always been so proud of your levelheadedness, your ambition, your love of good hard work. And now to see you risk what you've worked for… Marriage is the gravest decision a man makes in his life. I don't want you to see you regret yours."

"*Proud* of me? When were you proud of me?" He swallowed the rest. Forty years old, and he still allowed his father to provoke him. Perhaps they were too similar, too quick to quarrel and too eager to be in the right.

Mr. Toogood sighed. "I know I've been hard on you. I haven't enjoyed it any more than you have, but I never shrank from it, because I knew it was all to your good. The proof of the pudding's in the eating, John. Look at you. Not every man could take this over, but you'll do it superbly."

John felt, all at once, an overwhelming sadness at the decisions his father had made, and their consequences. A man's son should be a comfort to him when he was old. But while John did love his father, it was not much like the way he loved his mother or Plumtree or Sukey. It had little of joy in it, no rushes of affection or desire for nearness.

I've always been proud of you. His father had never said it when it would have mattered; now John felt nothing when he heard it. He remembered Sukey sobbing and railing, *I want him to say he loves me.* But it was too late.

Yet Mr. Toogood was no monster. He was just an old man who'd valued perfection and correctness over people. A man who had thought he could turn a home into a clock.

It hadn't been easy to be his son, to hope for his love and pride. After a while, John had kept himself braced for the criticism or anger he knew would come eventually, unable to adapt himself to his father's moods the way his mother did.

But plenty of the other servants, even, liked Mr. Toogood, leavened with casual wariness and a wry acceptance of his faults. They shrugged and said, *That's just his way.*

And John remembered now—his father was at his worst when the Tassells were in residence. He'd forgotten, because from the age of fifteen he had traveled with the family and come to the Hall with them, but in between the strain and bustle of public days and balls and house parties were periods of calm and kindness, punctuated only by occasional outbursts.

He might like to think that he had become the man he was in spite of his father, but it was far from the truth. His father had taught him discipline, and the quest for beauty in small things. He had taught him how to perform domestic service, and that there was honor, even glory in it.

"I know I owe you a great deal," John said quietly. "I love this work that we do."

His father clapped him on the back, and he tried not to wince.

He thought of Mrs. Khaleel and Molly and Larry and Thea, of how happy it made him to have earned their trust at last. The house was cleaner and more cheerful now that they worked by lists they had written themselves. The difference had been immediate and palpable. The only place in Tassell Hall that felt like that was the kitchen. His father had never experienced it, and John wished—he wished he could show him what it was like.

I could bring that to the Hall, he thought suddenly. *I could make it shine.*

But could he? Or, shut up in this pantry surrounded by plans and papers, putting on dinners for two hundred on which rested the fate of the nation, would he grow ever more crabbed and disappointed and fanatical until there was no generosity left in his heart?

* * *

Sukey could not stop watching John's parents at dinner. Mr. Toogood made up his wife's plate with the fussy deliberateness of an old man and handed it to her with the devotion of a lovesick youth. They clinked glasses before drinking their wine, finished each other's sentences and smiled at each other with the matter-of-fact comfort that came from loving each other for…well, at least since John was born forty years ago.

Sukey stole a glance at her husband, who didn't look much moved by his parents' affection. He took it for granted, she supposed. No—now he sighed with impatience, his forehead wrinkling. He was annoyed by it.

In forty years, where would she and John be? She supposed if they strove for it they could be right here, clinking wineglasses. But she couldn't believe in it. John, for all his flowery speeches, had never said so much as one word about the future, until he said that if he went to Tassell Hall, they could live separately.

Would she want to live here anyway, amid this grandeur? John seemed to view it as she did the woods near Lively St. Lemeston, lofty and pleasant but naught to wonder at. He'd walked past gilt and painted ceilings, tapestries and marble floors, and seen only the dust. His mother had shown her a vase worth three years' wages. How could Sukey dust a thing like that?

"This is very fine," she lied, swallowing another bite of asparagus on toast. "What's in it?"

"Oh, it's just a light fish béchamel. With poached eggs, obviously. I like the undercooks to practice their techniques while the family is away. I hope your asparagus isn't mushy."

Sukey didn't like asparagus, mushy or not. She'd never heard of béchamel, but supposed it was the white, fishy sauce coating her tongue. She gulped the mouthful down. "No, it's perfect." *I just hope I don't get indigestion.*

At Tassell Hall, there'd be a parade of sophisticated French ladies' maids under John's nose, whose accents were elegant and who liked eating fish sauce. What if he… She couldn't even think about it.

I want to go home, she thought. *Take me home. I want* my *mother, who serves me penny pies for dinner.* But not every responsibility could be pleasant and a source of saintlike rapture. John had come with her to see her father. She had to stick it out here, not push him to turn his back on his parents and a small fortune besides.

Would he even do it if she asked him?

* * *

"The other day I was cleaning Lady Tassell's portrait by Sir Joshua—I clean the best paintings myself, and I learned that from harsh experience, I promise you—and the cramp in my foot put me in such agony I nearly tumbled off the stepladder. I'm just glad I didn't pull the painting down."

The blood froze in John's veins. He set down his forkful of poached egg. "You were on a stepladder?" His father had been catching John up on everything that had happened to annoy him in the last six months, ranging from his favorite pencil manufacturer going bankrupt to a nasty pamphlet written about Lord Lenfield during the recent county election.

"I'm sure her ladyship would rather pay to repair the painting than your skull," Mrs. Toogood said sharply. "That's false economy if I ever heard it."

Mr. Toogood waved this away. "You worry too much."

"My grandmother was a martyr to cramps in her foot," Sukey said, as if oblivious to the tension in the air. Ever the peacemaker, his wife. "She found that folding a strip of red flannel seven times and wrapping it round her next biggest toe did wonders."

John winced inwardly, knowing how his parents would take this.

Mr. Toogood regarded her blankly for a few moments. "That's an old wives' tale, my dear. I don't credit it in the slightest."

John opened his mouth to defend her, but before he could speak Sukey said, "Oh, no, but it cured my grandmother. There's naught magical in it. She said it made her hold her foot differently."

"Then why must it be red?" Mr. Toogood inquired sardonically.

Sukey paused, then laughed good-naturedly. John was in awe at her restraint. "I suppose that part is superstition. I never thought on it, for it's the easiest color to get anyway. The grocer sells bits of red flannel for just such a purpose. If you want to hear real old wives' tales, I could oblige you! My mother's aunt, you know, saw a friend cured of a wen on her neck by the touch of a hanged man's hand."

"And was she really cured?"

Sukey grinned. "Well, everyone said it was much smaller afterwards."

Mr. Toogood snorted. "Amanda, do you remember when your sister gave Johnny powdered mouse ash in his jam?"

Since that was a traditional remedy for pissing the bed, John flushed and put a hand over his eyes. When he dared to look at Sukey, she was watching him, eyes dancing.

"I was five," he said hopelessly.

Mrs. Toogood shook her head ruefully. "Well, it didn't do him any lasting harm."

"Tell that to the marines, for the sailors won't believe it! The poor lad had nightmares for weeks that the mouse was crawling about inside of him. Of course you helped matters splendidly by pointing out that he ate cows and chickens all the time."

John had forgotten that until this moment. But now he could clearly picture the cedar wainscoting in the chapel, and hear his father's voice explaining with absolute authority that no matter what anyone said, there were no ghosts; souls went to Heaven or Hell. A mouse once dead could not be resurrected except by the direct intervention of Christ, and Christ would not put a living animal inside a person. No, not even if they were very sinful.

It was startling to remember that his father's firm assurances had once been enough to quiet any doubts. John had ceased fretting over the mouse that very hour.

"Since none of them had ever crawled about inside him yet, you can see how I thought it would reassure him," his mother said, laughing.

"You thought? Ha! You said the first thing that came to your mind, as always."

John had decidedly not missed family meals. "Leave her alone. Don't you ever get sick of being right?"

"Oh, don't mind your father," Mrs. Toogood said. "He can't help himself."

"He might help himself, if you didn't take his side."

Below the table, Sukey put a restraining hand on his leg. "Don't speak to your mother that way," Mr. Toogood snapped.

Your hypocrisy beggars belief, John thought.

After supper, they sat eating Portugal cakes with hot cider. John tried to include Sukey in the conversation, but despite his best efforts and her heroic readiness to try again after each rebuff, talk kept turning to the past or to news of mutual acquaintances. When her cider and two cakes had vanished, Sukey pushed back her chair. "I beg your pardon, sir, ma'am, but I'm asleep on my feet."

John stood, but Sukey gave him a wan smile and said, "No, no, you stay."

"Yes, do stay, John," his mother said. "It will give us a chance to get reacquainted without boring your wife to tears. Do you remember which room you're in, dear?"

Sukey nodded.

"If you need anything, Tamar and Camilla's room is just down the hall. Some of the girls are in the habit of sewing there in the evenings."

John was about to insist on accompanying her, at least to unlace her stays—but he caught her relief as she headed for the door and hesitated, afraid she might be eager to escape him as well as his parents.

The door closed behind her, and her footsteps retreated through the kitchen. John knew he should go after her, but he felt ashamed—of his parents, and of himself for not knowing how to manage them.

"Poor girl, she's so intimidated by the house," Mrs. Toogood said. "I tried to make her feel at home, but I know it's not at all what she's used to."

"I suppose not many people *are* used to a house like this. You like her though, don't you, Mother?"

"Ye-es. Of course I do. She seems a very sweet, well-meaning girl."

"Mother." They both knew that in Mrs. Toogood's lexicon, that translated to *It's not her fault she's empty-headed.*

"I just always imagined you'd marry a bluestocking."

"*Mother.*"

She shrugged resignedly. "I suppose I was naive to think I'd brought up a boy who would care about his wife's *mind.*"

John set down his Portugal cake, queasy. "Sukey isn't stupid. Don't be snobbish."

"I don't care about her accent, John," his mother said indignantly. "You know me better than that. But she doesn't *read*. And she's so young. A man doesn't—" She stopped talking. "Never mind."

"Yes?"

"A man doesn't marry a woman half his age because he imagines her his intellectual equal," she said flatly. "You never said she was so young in your letters."

She isn't half my age. But the calculation was only off by two years. "You—" John tried to clear the fury from his voice. "You think I just married her to have someone to feel superior to?"

Her eyes widened. "Of course not. That isn't what I said at all."

"Isn't it?"

"You tell me why you married her, then."

"Yes," his father said. "Enlighten us."

He didn't know what to say. If he told them about Mr. Summers and the job, it would hardly be the defense of Sukey he wished. If he tried to explain that she was beautiful and witty, that she'd looked like a fairy and made him feel that life could be exciting, it would only sound to his mother exactly how she imagined it: that he had married a pretty girl out of lust and a pitiful desire to feel young and looked up to.

"I married her because I fell in love with her," he said tightly. "And because I liked her better than anyone I'd ever met. She's a marvel, and you'd see that if you bothered to look."

"Then I'm sorry to have misjudged you," his mother said, not very apologetically. "I'll try to be more open-minded tomorrow."

"Thank you." John stood. "It's been a long day. Good night, sir, madam. I'll see you in the morning?"

"Oh, Johnny, don't be angry," Mrs. Toogood implored at once, catching at his hand. "I didn't mean to hurt your feelings."

"You see your mother for the first time in half a year and you're going to go off and sulk?" his father said.

"I've had a long journey," he said, conscious that he *was* sulking. "I'm tired.

Besides, how often do I have the luxury of going to bed early?" They all laughed rather awkwardly, and he made his escape.

He entered their room quietly in case Sukey was really asleep. She was curled up in the bed, so small and wistful that John was ashamed of the wave of desire that went through him at the sight of her tip-tilted blue eyes, her bedgown tied shut across her small breasts, and the lithe angles of her body.

In truth, she was five and a half feet tall, taller for a woman, even, than average. But her elusive air, the way she had of darting a wicked glance up through her lashes—she always seemed more diminutive than she was.

"Sukey, are you sure it doesn't bother you that I'm older than you are? You don't feel that I've taken advantage of you?"

She rolled away from him. "Why, is that what your mother thinks?"

He was appalled by the bitterness in her voice. He wished he hadn't said anything. "Yes, rather."

"She thinks I'm stupid," Sukey spat out. "Just because I don't know a load of Frog words or like eating cream and butter in *everything*. My piss stinks from asparagus, and I've been sitting here trying not to be sick. The cows for that quaint little dairy we saw today must have sore tits from all the milking!"

"Do you want to go?" *Please say yes.* "We'll leave first thing in the morning if you do."

She rolled back to face him, curling into a tighter ball. "No," she said, sounding defeated. "I'm sorry. I didn't mean to say anything. They love you and they just want what's best for you." She plucked at the pillowcase.

"They don't want what's best for me. They want me to have exactly what they had. I'm sorry they haven't been more welcoming."

"They love you," Sukey said stubbornly. "Why do you quarrel with them? It only makes things worse."

He felt as if a door had been slammed on his nose. He'd been defending *her*. "You'd like me to sit quietly while they—" He snapped his mouth shut before he could repeat his mother's comments. It might get Sukey on his side for a moment, but later she'd realize he had been unkind and spiteful. He *felt* unkind and spiteful. How easily anger rose, and how hard it was to stuff it away again!

"They're your parents. It can't have been easy for them to bring you up themselves, here. Not everybody would have done that."

"So I'm ungrateful?"

Sukey's crooked mouth pursed. "My father left me, and my mother had to send me out to work when I was twelve. You're asking me to be up in arms because your parents are a little crotchety?"

His head pounded. "I have never told you how to behave towards your own family," he said, jaw tight. "I might easily have excused your father's conduct, but I did not. And now you—"

"You might have *excused* him?" Sukey said incredulously. "For bigamy? *How?*"

"Anybody can think of reasons to defend anything. That's not the point. A little crotchety? Do you remember that story my mother said was a trifle, about the overcooked roast? He brought it down to the kitchen, gathered the entire staff around, and made my mother eat a piece! And then he said, 'Perhaps you ought to have done that before you sent it up.' She *wept,* and the damn thing was perfectly cooked. I have been trying to get along with him for eighteen years longer than you've been *alive.* Staying is not the only measure of a good father."

And there went all the insight and compassion of the day. His father wasn't a monster, yet John realized he had half-hoped Sukey would think him one. He'd wanted, finally, someone who would take his part once and for all as his mother never had. But a wife wasn't an echo.

"And how long ago was that?" Sukey asked.

"More than twenty years ago," he admitted grudgingly.

"I'm sorry." Sukey's eyes filled with tears. God, now he'd shouted at her and made her cry. He hadn't been able to help himself. A chip off the old block indeed.

That was the worst part. As he told her the story, he could imagine himself in his father's place, fancying himself an avenging angel of roast beef. It seemed a small enough step from things he *had* done.

"It's only that I'm jealous." Her tears spilled over. "I can't help it, it's eating me up."

Chapter Eighteen

John went and gathered her to him.

"I'm sorry," she sobbed. "I can't believe I'm doing this *again*."

"No. Don't apologize. I should apologize for my stupendous selfishness."

Sukey snorted. "Selfish? You?"

"Yes, me. Cry as much as you like, please." John felt awful. Sukey had hurt his feelings last night, and he'd barely spoken to her since. He'd been wounded and self-doubting because he couldn't make her feel better—but how could he have expected to? Her father had left her and she was sad, and he'd wanted that to be healed in a day, so he could feel proud of himself.

And then he'd wanted her to heal *him*, to say what he wanted to hear about his parents and thereby make forty years of love and resentment go away.

His parents, this position as butler, Tassell Hall: they were his burdens and—despite his virtuous resolutions never to do so—he'd divided them with her without thinking twice. He'd dragged her somewhere *he* didn't even want to be, hoping she'd make it bearable.

Even now, weeping and miserable, she comforted him. The heat and weight of her in his lap, her hair tickling his chin, her long legs arched over his made him feel that something, at least, was right with the world.

His mother knew him better than anyone. She was entirely wrong about Sukey, but she was right about him. He'd married Sukey for his own gratification.

"Will you clean my boots tomorrow?" She sounded uncertain. Surely she couldn't think he'd refuse her such a small favor.

"Of course. I meant to anyway."

She tilted her head up. "Will you kiss me?"

He obliged her. "Ask me something harder," he murmured against her mouth.

She ground her arse into his cock. "I will in a minute." She twisted round so her back was to his chest. "Hold my breasts."

"If you insist." He squeezed them in his hands. They ought to talk, but God, he couldn't stand it. He wanted to forget everything. He wanted to feel that she wanted him the way he wanted her, that she was his family, that they were one flesh. He wanted to join with her.

She dragged his hand between her legs under her nightdress. When he drew his fingers lightly across her most sensitive place, she moaned and spread her thighs wider, her sharp shoulder blades digging into his chest. "Tell me you want me," she said.

"I want you." It wasn't enough. But everything he thought of was poetic, mannered, nothing to do with this need to be close to her that scorched his throat and stopped his breath. "I want you desperately." Woefully inadequate.

She pushed him farther back on the bed, following so she sat snugly in his lap, facing away from him.

"I w—" He undid his buttons and drew out his cock—and before he knew what she was about, she pushed herself up and sank down onto it.

He choked on his words.

"John," she said intently, pushing herself up with her feet and letting herself fall, her hands on the back of his neck holding him close. "John, *John.*" She speared herself anew each time she said his name, until she was bouncing, chanting furiously. The bed creaked noisily, and there was a bevy of maids just down the hall. He almost stopped her—but he didn't want to. Let them hear.

"Sukey," he answered, quietly but not whispering either. "Sukey." His pleasure was brutal, ripped from him. "I want you." No, it was all wrong, and he knew what he wanted to say instead. "I love you. I love you, I love you, I adore you, Sukey."

She gasped for air, arching her back with a keening moan, and he didn't know what that meant but he didn't care because it was the truth. The only word that would suffice.

He ran his hands up her arms to where she clasped his neck. Taking hold of her wrists, he held them in place, held her so she couldn't get away. He turned his head to kiss her forearm. Her movements gentled and shallowed; she rocked insistently against him. "I don't want to spend. I just want this."

He struggled to breathe. "I'm sorry. I can't last much longer."

"Can we go on afterwards?"

"Anything you want."

"I want you to tease me until your cock can stand again, and then fuck me again."

"I can—I can—" The word turned to a gargling noise as he spilled into her. He fucked her through it, going until he started to soften. Then he laid her on the bed, kissing, licking and stroking her everywhere but between her legs. When she squirmed, he held her down, suckling at her tits until she sobbed. He rubbed a thumb over the crease of her inner thigh and kissed her just above her triangle of hair.

"It feels so good," she whispered. "I'm on fire."

"You're so brave," he said, dipping his tongue into her navel. "I always feel foolish talking about this."

She smiled, running her fingers through his hair. "You shouldn't. I like it when you growl at me."

Growl? John had always thought of his voice as—stentorian, he supposed. Suitable for cutting through a busy servants' hall or announcing callers in a clear, dignified manner. Animals and sailors growled. But if she liked it... He pressed his open mouth to her belly and made a mortifying, animal noise low in his throat. She giggled and shivered at the same time.

When he entered her again, her head fell back and she mewled. "Oh, God, it's too much, it's—damn, I'm going to, no, I don't want to—" He slowed, but she wrapped her legs around him. "Harder, harder, I want to feel it—"

A moment later she convulsed around him, her nails scoring his back.

"Should I stop?"

She shook her head. "It's too tender, it hurts, more..."

Christ. "You don't know what you do to me," he told the pillow. It was maddening, her hitches of breath, her little sobs, the way she twitched away from him and curled her dainty feet around his ankles. He was glad he had spent once already, so he could enjoy it a little longer.

* * *

Sukey lay there, tired out with pleasure, and somehow her face still felt tight. For a few moments she'd felt close to him again, so close nothing could come between them.

He'd said he loved her, and she was afraid to say it back even though it was true. That was a false economy, that was. Hearts weren't meant to be pickled and kept on the shelf for a hard winter. "Remember when I told you I was sick of living at Mrs. Humphrey's, of everything being weighed and measured?"

She felt his nod in the pillow. "You said you wanted to be where people were generous with one another."

He remembered. He'd listened to her. That seemed like a good sign. It hurt to swallow, her jaw was so stiff. "I don't know how to be generous," she said quietly, tears welling up in her eyes again. "I don't know how to share."

"Darling, that isn't true—"

"It *is*," she said fiercely. "Don't tell me what's in my heart. You said I never talk to you, and you were right. I don't know how. I don't want to. I want to keep my heart for myself, because I feel as if, if I give it away, I'll—I won't have it anymore, and I need it."

"That isn't how love works," he said, low and kind. "The more you give, the more you have."

And she remembered that, how much she'd loved taking care of him, how every time she did something for him or gave him something, she felt strong and rich. She took a deep breath. "When I think about my father…I know he didn't want me, and no matter what I do, I can't change that. It doesn't matter, it shouldn't matter, but it's awful. I feel as if the awfulness could drown me, as if I'm fighting to stay above water."

"That sounds frightening," he said, not making any sudden movements.

"Aye."

He tried to put his arm around her. She twitched away, and he pulled back.

Part of her had hoped, secretly, that he'd know how to make her feel better. But he couldn't. Nothing anyone said could do that. Still, she thought suddenly of what it would have been like to see her father without him. Of how she'd feel if she were sleeping alone tonight. He was here, and he'd listened, and he wanted her. He loved her.

She turned and buried her face in his chest, curling into him. He was warm and solid and didn't try to put his arm around her again because he knew she didn't want it, and all at once she loved him again. Her heart overflowed with it and it felt good, not as if it would drown her at all.

"Thank you," she whispered.

"No, thank *you*." His voice was tender and amused.

"No, no, sir," she said, starting to smile, "it is I who ought to thank you."

"I really must insist, madam—"

They started giggling, the bed quivering with their relieved laughter. John buried his face in the pillow, but high-pitched sounds emerged at odd intervals.

She'd wanted to make him giggle, at the servants' ball. She'd finally managed it, here at Tassell Hall where everything seemed to make him frown. She felt very proud.

"I do love you," she said. "I do. Dunnamuch."

He pulled her tight against him. "Who cares what our families think? You're my family now, and I'm yours."

She nodded. That sounded nice.

* * *

John woke long past his usual hour, feeling cheerful and very hungry. He dressed, took up Sukey's boots, and made his way to the larder, where he cut himself a slice of bread and slathered it with butter and jam. His mother was in the kitchen, training the kitchenmaids in the proper preparation of consommé.

John did not envy them the orgy of cheesecloth that was to follow. "Good morning, madam. Is there coffee?"

She smiled at him. "Yes, in my sitting room. I'll pour it for you." Giving the girls instructions to occupy them in her absence, she let him escort her into the next room, where she poured his coffee and settled herself in a chair. He ate quickly and self-consciously, sensing that she wanted to talk to him on a significant subject.

At last he couldn't take the silence. "What is it, Mother?"

"I'm sorry if I was slighting to your wife yesterday. She seems a very nice girl, and I should have got to know her better before forming any opinions."

"Thank you," he said warily.

"John," she appealed to him, leaning forward. "I'm not one of those mothers who are always asking their children for things, am I? I don't earwig you to visit more, or demand you produce grandchildren to suit me? When you decided you wanted to be a valet and not a butler, I supported you, didn't I, even though it meant I never saw you?"

"You've supported me in everything." Fear and love struck John's heart together. Was she sick? "I've never met anyone with a better mother. Mama, what is it? What's wrong?"

Her face set. "You *must* take over your father's position. You must."

John went numb with shock, pins and needles as if his heart had stopped pumping blood to his extremities. On the one hand, he'd been plagued by a growing sense of inevitability ever since speaking to Lady Tassell. On the other, he'd almost made up his mind to tell his father to stop showing him notebooks, because he wasn't staying. He'd thought of them as the ones it would be hard to tell, not his mother.

"I know you made up your mind not to want it when you were a little boy, but you're a grown man now. Johnny, I want to retire. I'm seventy-five, I've worked my whole life, and I *deserve* to retire. So does your father. He's given his life to this house, and he deserves some peace and rest."

"Mother, I'm going to be honest with you. Sukey and I came because Lady Tassell agreed to pay our way, and I wanted to see you. I didn't wish to reject the position out of hand. But I don't—"

He didn't know what to say. *The idea of the position makes me feel as if I'm made of lead?* Would he really give his mother pain only because he wanted to *enjoy* his work? "Besides, I'm married now, and I ought to consider my wife's comfort. I don't think Sukey would be very happy here."

"I knew it," she said bitterly. "I knew she'd poisoned you against the idea. You listen to her, when you've never listened to me about anything."

"That's entirely unfair," he said, losing patience. "You know I've always had the highest respect for your opinion."

"You don't. You're just like your father. Neither of you listen to me." Her mouth trembled. "I've begged him to leave, but he won't, not until you take his place. He's always been so proud of giving you a good start in life, and a sure future, one you didn't have to fight and sacrifice for the way he did. The work he does is an honor! Lady Tassell and the Whigs rely on him. Why don't you want it? I know you, John. You might be enjoying an easy, idle position now, but you'll be bored in a twelvemonth and wishing you'd listened to me. And by then it will be too late. Your father will be *dead*."

"He'll be what? Why?"

Her answer was forestalled by his father's shouts echoing through the house. It was a familiar sound, but Mrs. Toogood was up and racing through the kitchen. John followed, soon outpacing her. He found Mr. Toogood in the great hall, red-faced and screaming obscenities at a cowering maid who was mopping up a spilled bucket of soapy water. The sound of his father's anger still made John's hair stand on end—but he'd never heard his father curse in the presence of a woman before.

"What happened?" his mother demanded, coming up behind him, breathing hard. "Are you all right?"

"This stupid slut left her pail in the middle of the floor where anyone could trip over it, that's what happened. *Think* before you do things, for Christ's sake. If you've *got* a brain rattling around in there. I'll be black-and-blue tomorrow." There was a great wet stain all along the old man's side.

"I'm that sorry, Mrs. Toogood," the maid said, tears in her eyes. "I tried to warn him of it, but he was going so fast. He took the fall with his body to save the decanters, madam. I'm that sorry. Let me see your arm, sir, please, I—"

Even through John's horror, part of him noticed that she was just spreading the water around.

"Why would I trust you to see to my injuries when you can't even see to a floor? Look at this mess. The whole thing will warp." Mr. Toogood snatched the mop out of her shaking hand and set to efficiently containing the spill.

"Let me, sir." John reached for the mop, afraid his father would slip a second time on the wet floor.

"I can do it. I'm not in my dotage yet, thank God."

John would have liked to wrest the damned thing out of his hands.

"Don't worry about it, dear. That will be all, thank you," his mother told the maid, who darted from the room.

"You always coddle them," Mr. Toogood said. "Just like you coddled John all these years. I might have smashed every decanter we own." He wrung the mop out fiercely—and dropped it, cursing viciously and clutching at his shoulder.

"You should have let them smash," Mrs. Toogood said shrilly. "It's just money, John. The Tassells can buy new ones. But you can't buy another shoulder. You aren't twenty-five anymore."

"I'm fine."

"You're not fine. Johnny, he's not. He's going to kill himself. He's going to kill himself, and what will I do without him?" She began to cry.

His father snorted. "So you're after the ungrateful brat to stop shilly-shallying and let me end my days in peace? I wish you luck. We could have been living by the sea for ten years now if he weren't determined to spite me. He doesn't care two pins for you, me *or* the Tassells. He'd like to behave like Mr. Nicholas and cut us off completely, I don't doubt." He sighed. "There, there, Amanda, don't cry. I'm not hurt." He put his arm around her, wincing at the movement.

Part of John *would* have liked to walk out and leave them there, would have welcomed never speaking to his father again. His own cold selfishness appalled him. A Dymond could indulge himself that way. John could not, and did not want to. "Father, please let me finish this. Your coat is frizzing."

His father looked down in surprise. "So it is. I'd better see to that. Bring the decanters to the pantry when you come, would you?"

Finally his parents left. John would have liked to sit and put his head in his hands, but the inlay would be damaged. He cleaned the mop water doggedly, trying to calm his racing pulse.

He couldn't stop hearing his father say, *I nearly tumbled off the stepladder.* His mother had not exaggerated. His father would break his neck, and there was no reasoning with him. There never had been, and there certainly wasn't now.

John would have to take the position.

It won't be so bad, he told himself. Looking about the empty room, he imagined himself announcing a glittering assembly of guests, stationed between hall and saloon with bright silks and a hundred wax candles to either side of him. He tried to drum up some enthusiasm for it. But his heart was in his boots, and all he could think was, *I can't make Sukey do this. I won't let her do this.*

* * *

Sukey, looking about for someone to do up her stays, at last admitted nobody was left in this part of the house. She'd slept far too late. *Lucky I brought my old self-lacing corset,* she thought, more pleased with herself than the little thing warranted. She felt very hopeful as she squirmed and contorted to fasten her dress buttons.

Her boots were missing, which meant John must be cleaning them. Sukey made her way to the kitchen, where she found most of the staff at their elevenses. Stomach rumbling, she helped herself to a fresh roll.

"Good morning," she said to the crowd, astonished anew at how *many* people worked at the Hall. She'd introduced herself to them yesterday and ought to know their names, but she barely remembered a one.

There was a chorus of answering good mornings. "Try the pickled tongue," a freckle-faced girl told her. Her name started with a *C*, Sukey thought. Camilla, that was it. She obeyed, glad to find that not everything at the Hall was cream sauce. The pickled tongue was indeed delicious.

"It's *too* good, isn't it?" Camilla said in a friendly way. Sukey faltered, remembering John had told her that people said that to make fun of his father. Hadn't she ought to discourage it somehow? But a circle of girls whose aprons were finer than Sukey's gown clustered around her, smiling, and she didn't want to ruin it, even if they were just currying favor with the wife of a man who might be set above them. Lady Tassell had been right, they didn't speak much better than she did.

"Is it true you were Mrs. Nicholas Dymond's maid?"

Sukey nodded, and then, not wishing to be a liar, she explained, "Not a lady's maid. A maid-of-all-work."

Their eyes went round with horror. "Mrs. Dymond had naught but a maid-of-all-work?"

Sukey wished she'd kept her clapper still. Now she'd lowered poor Mrs. Dymond's consequence in their eyes.

A brown-complexioned girl with a dreamy smile said, "She must be very beautiful, to have captured Mr. Dymond anyway." She had a biblical name, one of the unfortunate ones—Tamar.

"If he wanted a poor girl, he might have chosen me," Camilla mourned, putting a hand to her bosom in the best dramatic style. They all giggled.

"Did she seduce him?" a girl asked eagerly.

"Yes, is she in the family way?"

"No, and it would be wrong of me to gossip," Sukey said firmly.

Disappointment was plain. A stout redhead crossed her arms and said bluntly, "I wouldn't have thought a maid-of-all-work would be so nice in her views."

The other girls shushed her furiously, but one or two hid nasty smiles. Sukey would have liked to give them a piece of her mind—but if Mrs. Toogood caught her at it, she'd die of shame. She set down her plate with what she hoped was a queenly smile. "Thank you for a lovely breakfast," she said, and swept past them.

* * *

John gently rubbed tallow into Sukey's boots. This was what he enjoyed in service: watching things take on the shine they were meant to have, dulled for a time but brought forth with a little labor and a little love. He loved providing small comforts that eased someone's path through life. Mr. Summers's dinner was hotter since his arrival. That was something he could be proud of.

Here at Tassell Hall, he'd spend his day mediating quarrels, scribbling in notebooks, keeping accounts, sorting out difficulties and finding things that were lost. Struggling to hold on to his temper.

He could hear the murmur of Sukey's voice now among the chatter of elevenses. He hoped she would linger over her meal, so he could put off telling her. But the door to the sitting room opened, and there she stood. He wanted to strew her path with rose petals—not by proxy, but with his own two hands.

She had pasted another bright smile on her face. She could not even get through breakfast here without something happening to distress her. He had no doubt the other servants had been snobs.

The false smile dimmed—what did she see on his face? But she recovered it with an effort and sauntered into the room. "Good morning." Her eyes fixed on her boots in his hands.

"I've got to stay here," he said without preamble. "My mother—I can't tell her no."

The smile vanished altogether. "All right," she said at once, leaning her hip against the table. "I don't suppose I can go straight to upper housemaid here, but I don't mind working my way up."

No, he tried to say, but his voice cracked. He swallowed to wet his dry throat. "You don't have to do that."

She frowned. "John—"

"We'll find lodgings for you in the village." He nodded, trying to believe she'd agree, that at least he'd get to see her on his half-holiday. "You can even hire a maid-of-all-work of your own."

Her lips parted. "What?"

"I know you couldn't be happy here." He set down her boots, fully sealed. "I know you hate it. I can't ask you to stay."

She stared at him. "You don't have to ask. I've already said yes."

He could not answer her. He let his silence speak for him.

She crossed her arms. "You said we were family. You said you were my family now, and I was yours. And now you're putting me out of the house?"

John wiped his hands, not looking at her. His chest was hollow, his heart a small hard thing rattling around inside it. "I'm not putting you out of the house. The village is only a little ways off. Even if you were here, I'd barely see you. It's a demanding position, and—I just want you to be happy."

"I'm happy with you! I've *been* happy with you."

"And I've been happy with you," he said with finality. "But this house would eat you alive."

She went white. "You really do think I'm a child. Plucky little Sukey from the boarding house—isn't she pert? God! Flirting and a humorous accent are not the sum of me. I could do this. I could work my fingers to the bone, learn to speak, make friends with a gaggle of snooty chambermaids who can't even bake a pie or darn a sock. I could be housekeeper here someday if I'd a mind to. I'd do it for you, because I *love* you. And you said you loved me, but you don't."

He met her eyes, steadfast. "I do love you. I've been wanting to say it for weeks."

"What good is love, then?" she demanded. "You *promised* me last night that you'd be my family. I want to have a family for more than one half-holiday a week!"

So do I. At least you'd *get to live with our children.* But she hadn't even agreed to have children with him yet. "It would be more than that," he argued hopelessly. She was going to leave, he could see it. "We could write to one another as often as we wished, and dine together sometimes, and when the family isn't in residence, I could—"

Her jaw dropped. "Bugger you! You'll ask me for *that*, but you won't ask me to stay?"

"Sukey, for God's sake. I'm just trying to salvage a bright spot in this damned mess."

She pressed her lips tightly together. "The bright spot's not having me around to embarrass you, I expect."

He refused to rave like his father—but his anger flared. He could not bear to lose her, and yet he was so angry with her. "You don't embarrass me."

"Oh, no?"

He flushed, knowing it wasn't entirely true, and even angrier, that she would twist his small, unwilling, carefully concealed betrayal into something monstrous and throw it in his face. "*No.*"

"Liar," she hissed. "Just admit you don't want me anymore."

His calm began to crack like fine china, just a spiderweb of lines, and soon it would be smashed to powder. "I will miss you every day," he said as steadily as he could. It was an understatement so vast it confounded him. He could not bear the thought of her going. She must know that. He had made no secret of it.

"But it would be selfish of me to ask you to stay."

Sukey felt ready to vomit blood. "You think I should be grateful for this, don't you? Yes, you're a regular martyr, for taking a position that pays a king's ransom and getting your common little wife out of the way. It was a kindness to marry me and now it's a kindness to kick me out. I'm sick of your kindnesses. Tell the truth for once in your mealymouthed life. Do you think I haven't seen you caressing the wallpaper? Just say *you* want to stay, and you want me out of the way because I'd spoil the pretty picture."

He laid his hands flat on the table by her boots. "You *know* how much I admire you," he said through stiff lips.

"Oh, aye, I'm beautiful and perfect and time with me is never wasted. Tell that to the marines," she rudely mimicked his father. "But I ate it up, didn't I? How did you know all you had to do was polish my boots and I'd follow you about like a duckling? Was it just that I'm poor and young, or was there something about me that—"

"I cleaned your boots because they were *dirty*," he burst out. "And I wouldn't describe your behavior as having much in common with that of a duckling, either. Be reasonable, Sukey. Are you going to tell me you *want* to live here?"

"Yes," she shouted. "Yes, if you're here, I want to be here. So send me away if you like, but don't try to pretend it's because you're so damn *good*."

"I never said that." John screwed the lid onto his jar of tallow, tightening it with a jerk. "I am not good, nor is this position likely to bring out the best in me. You mayn't think asking you to leave is a kindness, but it is almost certainly kinder treatment than you'd receive if you stayed."

"When have you ever been unkind to anyone?"

He slammed the lid shut on his box of brushes and polish. "I've been unkind to you," he said, bite in his words. "And you know it."

"You've been angry! Everybody's angry sometimes, for pity's sakes. I'm so angry right now I could spit. But taking your father's job isn't going to magically transform you into him. This is *ridiculous*."

He pressed two fingers into his temple. "Perhaps you can agree I am best qualified to know my own heart. If you could understand how angry I am at you, only for disagreeing with me—this morning my father was bellowing filth at an unfortunate maidservant and I was actually annoyed with her because it caused her to clean inefficiently."

"Your father was what?"

He sat down. "He tripped over her bucket of water and chose to injure himself rather than drop some crystal decanters. I have to take the position, Sukey. My mother begged me. I have to."

"All right," she said. "Then you have to. But if we're family, then they're my family too, and I also have to."

"I won't ask you to do that. If I let myself, I'd ask you for *everything*, and you'd let me do it."

Sukey looked at her boots, shining side by side on an old newspaper, and wanted to throw his coffee cup at the spotless wall. "So now you're best qualified to know *my* own heart too? At least my father didn't pretend he was leaving for my own good. He just went clean away. You say you don't want to live together anymore, that you want me to idle about in lodgings, listening for your step on the stair, and I'm to believe it's because you *love* me? Why, because you say so?"

"Yes. Yes, because I say so."

She shrugged. "Then I suppose you love me, and I was right all along and love's just a stupid word that doesn't mean anything." She pulled her ring off her finger. "You like to polish things so much? Polish this." And she threw it at him.

He went on his knees to pick it up, examining it for scratches.

The room blurred. She blinked back the tears so he wouldn't see them. Crying just hurried men out the door that much faster. "Give me my boots. I'm going home."

"They're not ready." He came around the table, taking her by the shoulders. "Please, Sukey—"

She stood stiffly in his grasp, unable to look at him. "Bring the boots when they're ready, then. And tell Mr. Tomkin I want to go back to Chichester. Now." She said the cruelest thing she could think of. "I'll spend the night at my father's and catch the coach in the morning." And she stomped out.

The crowd of servants was gathered around, watching the door. She wondered what they'd heard. Although once again, she'd been the only one being loud. "Don't bother toadying," she said, raising her voice so John could hear. "I'm not staying."

* * *

John sat without moving, waiting for the tallow to dry on Sukey's boots. Perhaps if he moved them farther from the fire, it would take longer.

That was it, then. The end of his independence and his happiness. He had thought he'd neatly escaped the lot planned for him by his father, but here he was.

She just wants you to ask her to stay at the Hall. You might see her, and dine with her, and sleep with her at night. You might even be happy here, if she were here with you.

Yes, he might be happy. He might squeeze from her whatever happiness she had to give him, with no regard for her own. He might behave like his father, considering it his wife's duty to care for and comfort and cheer him, and when she said, *You never have time for me, we never talk to each other, I'm unhappy, you aren't kind*—then he would say, *Can't you see the strain I'm under in my work?*

He could do all that, but he wouldn't. He refused to. Servants at Tassell Hall didn't sing while they worked. He wanted to know that she was somewhere, singing.

He went to the stables to find Abe. "I'm very sorry to bother you again so soon, and on such short notice, but would you harness the carthorses? Mrs. Toogood wishes to return to Chichester."

Abe frowned. "What's the matter? Has she had bad news from home?"

John turned away. "She can tell you all about it on the journey."

Chapter Nineteen

When Sukey finally put on her pelisse and bonnet and ventured back to the kitchen with her bandbox, there was a neat stack of traveling gear by the door. None of it was hers. She watched, bones aching as if she had the influenza, while John settled an enormous hamper in the back of the cart.

He gave her a purse full of small coins next, enough for four such journeys. She'd have liked to refuse it, but arguing would make her headache worse, and besides, she had only a few shillings of her own and probably no position when she got back to Lively St. Lemeston without him.

Last he handed her her boots. She knotted the laces hastily and climbed into the cart, eager to be off. But he arranged hot bricks under her feet and handed her up a worn velvet muff. "Don't go," he said. "It isn't safe for a young woman to travel alone."

She put her hands into the muff, astonished at how warm they at once became. She felt about and found a hot water bottle at the bottom of it. "Whose muff is this?" She'd ought to give it back. She hadn't ought to take anything from him.

"I bought it from one of the maids." He wound a bulky shawl round her shoulders. She started violently when his hand brushed her breast, her eyes stinging anew. No, no, if she cried the tears would freeze.

"Sleep with your money on you," he said. "And don't let anyone see where you keep it. Don't give the coachman and the guard a tip of more than a shilling for every stage of thirty miles, no matter what they say, and when you stop at the inn, the chambermaid should get sixpence—"

"I'm *not a child*," she hissed.

He pressed his lips together, more advice clearly humming on his tongue.

"Will you send me word that you've arrived safely?" he said at last.

Why should I? But the driver was standing by, and she didn't know what John had told him. She nodded once.

"Be well," he said quietly, and kissed her. It was a sad kiss, as full of goodbye as the stiff way he held himself, but she could smell his shaving soap and she wanted it to last forever. Instead it lasted about a second and a half, and he went into the house.

Her hands and feet were toasty warm but she felt numb, numb and spongy, as if a poking finger would go right through her. Surely this wasn't happening. In a moment he'd come running back outside and beg her to stay.

But he didn't, and she sat carefully straight as Mr. Tomkin clucked to the horses and sent them down the drive, away from the house.

* * *

She was gone. John shut himself in the tiny room they'd shared, hoping no one would come and try to talk to him. But at last, as the afternoon wore away, his mother knocked on the door. "Let me in," she said peremptorily.

John, who had been lying on the bed, sat up and rubbed at his temples. "Come."

She carried a tea tray. "What happened?"

He shook his head at a cup of tea, then a biscuit, then a piece of toast. "She left," he said flatly. "What else is there to say?"

His mother frowned, setting the tray on a chair and sitting beside him. "She left you because you wanted to help your father?"

"No, because I told her I wanted her to live in the village instead of the Hall."

His mother's eyebrows went up. "And she didn't take it well?"

"She thought I was embarrassed by her."

His mother's mouth quirked as if to say, *What did she expect?* "And here I thought you'd leapt to her defense at every opportunity. She didn't make much of an effort to change your mind, did she?"

John remembered well the long-fought campaigns his mother had led to change his father's mind. Weeks or months of murmured conversations in the butler's pantry, occasionally punctuated by shouting, tears or both.

The words sprang at once to his tongue, to tell his mother that a marriage shouldn't be like that. A loyal but determined courtier, intriguing endlessly to alter the king's course by a hairsbreadth, powerless if he refused…

Because his word was law.

"I told her my mind was made up." Like his father. Even when he tried not to be his father, he ended up behaving just like him.

What would his father *not* do in this situation?

Walk away from Tassell Hall.

That was the one thing his father would never, ever do. Go live quietly and happily with his wife? God forbid! And it was all John wanted. He wanted to go back to the Lively St. Lemeston vicarage and lay out the vicar's clothes and have dinner with Mrs. Khaleel and Molly and Thea and Larry.

He also had responsibilities to them, responsibilities he *wanted* to fulfill.

He looked at his mother, her face tight with concern and sympathy. He loved her so much. How could he tell her no?

You don't have to take the position if you don't want it, only because your father isn't well, Molly had told him. She'd said it because he'd said the same thing to her. He believed it about her, but when it came to himself— He knew in his heart that he did have to take the position. That he'd be a bad son if he didn't.

So you're obliged to work sixteen hours a day for the rest of your life in a job you don't want, or you're a bad son? You're obliged to turn your back on your own wife, or you're a bad son?

What kind of example would he set for Molly if he stayed? What kind of husband would he be to Sukey?

He took a deep breath. Yes, he had it in him to behave like his father. But he'd never believed in destiny. He believed in care and hard work, and with care and hard work, he could behave differently.

"I don't want this job."

His mother drew back. "But, John, you promised me—"

"I know, and I'm sorry. But I never wanted it, and I don't want it now. It's too much strain, too little leisure, too long hours, too much supervising others and not enough using my hands."

"But if you don't take the post, your father won't leave it."

"You married him, Mama," he said gently. "That's up to you. If you can't make him retire, Lady Tassell can. Write to her."

"He won't forgive me for that."

"After everything you've forgiven him? He'd better."

She didn't return his hug. It felt awful to stand up and leave her sitting there. Who was he, if he wasn't a good son to his mother? Who would be proud of him if she wasn't?

"I love you," he said. "And I love him. But I'm going after Sukey."

He hadn't wanted to love Sukey, because he'd felt somehow that it was selfish, that love overpowered and dominated and demanded. He'd held himself back all this time because he didn't want to burden her.

He'd treated her like a child, just as she said. But he *wasn't* her father—or his. He was her husband and she was a grown woman. They were helpmeets, and it wasn't wrong to ask her to share his burdens.

He could ask her for whatever he liked, and she'd decide for herself whether to say yes. He'd have to accept her answer, that was all.

He'd start by asking her to forgive him.

"Take a night to think it over. Don't decide right away."

"No. I've thought it over long enough. If Abe can be bribed to take me, I'm going as soon as he gets back."

"You're as stubborn as your father," she said despairingly.

It occurred to him that she'd always said that when he argued with her. "I do listen to you. I thought very carefully about what you had to say. I nearly stayed. But listening doesn't always mean agreeing. Neither of you have ever understood that."

She sighed. "Do you want me to give him the news?"

She'd been their go-between so often over the years. So many times she'd shielded him. "No. I'll tell him myself. But thank you." He wondered, suddenly, if he'd ever complimented her. "You're the best of mothers."

She shook her head, laughing a little. "Oh, don't. I know I'm not."

"And I know you are." He kissed her hand. "Thank you. I'll visit you at the

Rye Bay house as often as I can."

* * *

Sukey didn't really go to her father's. She went straight to the coaching inn and bought her ticket for the next morning and space in a bed, huddling in it all afternoon with her hamper instead of venturing to the coffee room. She dined on pickled tongue and rolls that were only a little stale, conscious of stares of envy from the other women in the room. She thought of offering to share, but sadness made her closefisted. *Get your own food,* she thought, touching everything in the hamper like a miser caressing his gold. There was a roast chicken, a packet of biscuits, a little hard cheese, a small basket of roasted eggs—even a whole seedcake nestled in brown paper in a corner, round and golden with a crisp layer of baked sugar flaking off the top.

Tears blurred her eyes. *Pitiful,* she told herself. *Crying over a lousy seedcake. It's not as if he'll miss it. His mother will bake off fifteen more tomorrow.*

But she gouged out a piece of cake with her thumb and put it in her mouth, its pungent sweetness making the tears leak down her cheeks.

"Would you like a handkerchief?" an adolescent girl in a neighboring bed asked shyly. Her bronze skin, strong nose and deep brown eyes reminded Sukey of Mrs. Khaleel.

Sukey shook her head, sniffling. "I'll stop crying any second now."

"What's wrong?"

She glared suspiciously. "I'm not going to give you any cake."

"I can't eat your cake," the girl said scornfully. "Christian cake always has brandy in it."

"Not *always,*" Sukey protested, startled. What difference did that make anyway?

She gave the cake a dismissive glance. "So why are you crying?"

"My husband left me." Sukey stopped. "Well, not exactly. I suppose I left him."

"What did he do?"

"He took a swell job and then didn't want me to live with him. I expect

I'm not swell enough."

"Muckworm," the kid said. "Can you at least make him send you some of the money?"

She didn't want or need his money. She wanted *him*. She needed *him*. He'd given her a ring that said, *Let us share in joy and care*, and then he'd refused to let her share in either. And he'd refused to even admit he was doing it! "I don't need him or his money," she said sharply.

The girl shrugged. "He cared for money over you. So take what he'll miss most."

Sukey looked at her beautiful seedcake with an ugly thumb-hole in the top. "He didn't care for money over me. That's not fair. The job's his father's and his father hasn't been well."

She knew that. Oh, he loved the house, just as he loved his father, but he hadn't had a nice thing to say about either of them. She'd said he wanted her out of the way, but...

She admitted to herself that it wasn't the truth. She'd said it to hurt him, because his mind was made up and she couldn't change it.

This house will eat you alive. He'd said it so intensely. A sharp pain had stopped her breath, to see him so convinced she didn't belong there. With him. But if she'd paused to think, she'd have seen straightaway that he expected the house to eat *him* alive.

You couldn't be happy here, he'd said. *You hate it.* But really, *he* couldn't be happy there. *He* hated it. That, he didn't know how to say. If she was honest, she'd understood that all along. But she'd been so angry at his stubborness, his eagerness to get rid of her. He'd made her feel...

Like a child, powerless in the face of her father's decision to leave. That drowning feeling she'd told him about had poured up her throat, and she'd panicked. But a feeling couldn't really drown you.

As a seven-year-old girl, she couldn't understand what was happening. Her father had been half her world and there'd really been nothing she could do. She wasn't a child anymore. John *had* treated her like one, but she'd acted like one too. She hadn't tried sincerely to change his mind. She'd thrown a tantrum and left him, while he begged her to stay and gave her a basket full of cake. And what had she proven? That she was grown now and she could leave too? Did she really think that was news?

Nothing is sure in this world, he'd said when he first proposed. But you had to muddle on anyway. There was one thing she was sure of: John loved her today. He'd said so, and she believed him.

And she'd left him there. He'd tried to save her from the responsibility that was drowning *him*, and she'd abandoned him to it. She'd said she wanted to be his helpmeet, to take care of him, and she hadn't tried to help him at all.

He might leave her someday, yes. He might stop loving her and he might die tomorrow—

Sukey was filled with horror. She had to get back to him. She had to get back right away. He could fall down the stairs or be trampled by a horse at any moment and she'd left him!

"I'm going back," she told the girl. "Is there anything in here you *can* eat?"

The girl peered into the basket. "Ooh, eggs!"

Sukey let her fill her handkerchief while she buttoned her pelisse and jammed her bonnet on her head.

* * *

"You're going back to that poky vicarage when you could have all this?" Mr. Toogood was at his desk in the butler's pantry, so the sweeping gesture (with his uninjured arm) mostly encompassed his notebooks and the big silver chests and china cabinets. Maybe that was all he meant: not the great and beautiful house, but this small headquarters.

"You had the right of it," John said, determined to be civil, even kind. "I wasn't fully employing my talents as a valet. I enjoy being a butler. I enjoy having people who depend on me, and on whom I depend. I enjoy managing a household. I only don't want to be butler here. I want more peace and quiet than that. I'm sorry."

His father slammed some ledgers on their ends on the table, probably more to make an angry noise than to align their edges. "How any son of mine could have so little ambition!"

"I do have ambition. I want to be the best at what I do. I want to be the best man I can, and the best husband. And I want—" He almost said he wanted to make Sukey happy. But he was more ambitious even than that, his desires more lofty, reaching for all the kingdoms of the world and the glory of them, and not caring that it was sacrilege. "I want to be happy."

"Happy? Christ spare me your generation and its selfishness. 'Why is not man a god, and earth a heaven?'"

Ah, they had reached the part of the argument where his father quoted Pope. Wonderful. John's heart beat faster and his cheeks heated, but he spoke slowly and evenly. "You could have been happy. You still could be. Mother adores you. She wants nothing more than to spend the rest of your lives together in a bit of ease. You've both earned it."

"If I could have been happy here, then why can't you?" He pointed a finger at John in a familiar *I've got you there* gesture. "You love this house. You love the Dymonds."

It was easy in an argument to get caught up with winning, and not with sharing one's desires or speaking the truth. It was awful to watch his father seize on any apparent inconsistency in his speech without acknowledging the heart of what he'd said, and to know that he'd done the same to Sukey. "And I love you," John agreed. "But I'm leaving for Chichester." He went to the door.

"Can I give you a piece of advice?" his father called after him.

John turned back.

"If you want to be happy, don't have children."

John wished it didn't hurt.

* * *

As much as Sukey wanted to rush back to John—well, the odds were against his actually getting trampled by a horse in the next few hours. It wouldn't hurt him to spend a little time missing her. And there was something she had to do first.

She'd always wanted a sister. It had never occurred to her that she already had one. And as afeared and tense as it made her, walking up the stairs and knowing she'd see her father—she knew now that last time she'd been here, she'd closed herself off, packed her heart away in mothballs, so she could pretend she was glad to be there. She wanted to try out really being generous, really feeling things, and see how it went. She wanted to prove to herself that the sky wouldn't fall.

As she neared the door, she could hear the familiar childhood sound of her father's hammer. She almost turned around and went back. How could she befriend her sister and lie to her? Could she pretend her own mother was dead? But how could she tell the truth? She had no notion what the girl might think or do, or who might be hurt by it.

She set down the hamper and bandbox and knocked on the door.

"Juliana, will you see who that is?"

Her sister opened the door. Sukey smiled weakly. The girl's eyes grew round. "You came back. Dad, Susan's back!"

There was a clatter, and her dad appeared in the doorway, trying to put his arms around her. Sukey pulled away. "I don't—I'm sorry, but I don't know if—"

The girl glanced over her shoulder at her younger siblings. "He and Mum told me the truth," she whispered. "So you don't have to be mad at him anymore."

"The truth?" Sukey felt as if the floor had shifted under her. Was this another lie?

Mr. Grimes nodded. "I told her about me and your mum, and…I told her everything." He put an arm around Julia, who sniffled and leaned into him.

"Hush, kids, leave them alone." The new Mrs. Grimes herded her younger children into a corner, with many a worried glance. "I'll tell you a story."

"Tell us about the sweating pharisees," the littlest boy shouted.

Sukey was having trouble breathing again.

"I was so sad after you left," Julia explained in a hushed voice. "I hoped we'd be sisters, and I was sure I'd made a nuisance of myself."

Mr. Grimes dropped a kiss on the top of her head. "I couldn't let my little girl be unhappy and not know why. I hope she'll forgive me someday." He looked at her with double meaning as he said it, and Sukey felt herself shrinking inwards. *Julia* couldn't be unhappy and not know why? What about her? What about all the years she'd spent wondering why he left?

She supposed she could ask him. But she didn't want to know. Not yet, anyway. Probably he'd say it was something wrong with her mother, and she'd smash his nose in with his own hammer.

"I'm sorry." She still couldn't get out the word *Dad*. "I came to talk to Julia."

Julia brightened, but she looked anxiously at her father to see how he'd take this.

Mr. Grimes nodded reluctantly. "All right, Susan."

"And please—I go by Sukey now."

"Don't be daft." Mr. Grimes broke out in a smile. "I'm your dad, I can call you whatever I like."

"*Dad*," Julia said in an undertone.

Mr. Grimes gave in. "Sukey, then, if you insist."

"*Thank* you," she and Julia said together, and Julia smiled at her. "I'm so glad you came back."

"So am I," Sukey said. "Or I think I will be, anyway."

"Can I take your portrait?" Julia made her money cutting profiles out of black card for a penny apiece at the Chichester markets. When Sukey agreed, she ran to fetch her scissors and paper. "When I'm a little older I want to travel to fairs and such," she confided. "Does the fair come to Lively St. Lemeston?"

"Twice a year. We're not so small as that, you know."

Julia beamed. "Maybe we'll see each other again soon, then."

Sukey was obliged to hold still to display her profile, but out of the corner of her eye she saw Julia's scissors pause, her head turning curiously towards Sukey's baggage. "I thought you were staying at Tassell Hall for a few weeks."

Sukey sighed. "I had a row with John. I'm going back, though. I only stopped by to… Well, I was sorry for the other day."

"No, I'm sorry," Julia said earnestly. "I know Dad was only trying to protect me and the children, but he shouldn't have done it. He shouldn't have— I expect he should have stayed with your mum, actually."

"I wished he had for a long time." Eyes straight ahead, Sukey had a clear view of seven profiles tacked to the wall: Mr. Grimes and his new family. "But you're so happy. Happier than we would have been, maybe."

She'd been furious when John said, *I might easily have excused your father's conduct.* But now she could think of a dozen reasons Mr. Grimes might have left. She could see he hadn't had any money to send, that it wouldn't have been easy for him to come and visit.

It didn't hurt any less, but it was less frightening. It felt less like the end of the world and more like an everyday awful thing.

She was still jealous of her sister, who could forgive such a betrayal at once, in the sure and certain knowledge that she was still safe, that her father had only done it because he loved her. She still didn't know whether to envy or pity that much innocence. Like crossing an abyss on a plank bridge and not even knowing the abyss was *there*.

"I don't mind turning out the way I did," she said, and meant it. But she supposed the world was as full of kindness as it was of cruelty. It wasn't so bad to expect kindness from people. Maybe it made you turn away from cruelty when you saw it, instead of spending years licking Mrs. Humphrey's shoes. "I hope you're not angry with me, for being…"

"Legitimate?" Julia whispered.

Sukey nodded.

"You can move now." The girl took up a second piece of paper. "I'm not angry with you. I suppose it might matter to a suitor, someday. I'd have to be honest with him. But if I work hard and save up a dowry, I expect he won't mind too much. Unless he's stuffy and then I won't want him." She glanced at Sukey in alarm. "I mean, not that Mr. Toogood—not that there's anything *wrong* with being stuffy—"

Sukey laughed. "Abuse him as much as you like, please."

Julia smiled at her, beginning to paste Sukey's profile onto a sheet of white paper.

"What's the other one?"

Julia flushed. "It's me. So you can carry me with you. And I'd like to copy yours for our—" She gestured at the wall of profiles. "If you wouldn't mind."

Sukey picked up the floppy black outline of her sister's face. That was her own pointed nose, she realized, her sharp chin. She looked at her father's likeness on the wall. She could see the resemblance—not as striking as he'd made out, maybe, but undeniably there.

That still made her stomach turn over, but she didn't mind looking like Julia. "I don't know. Why don't you keep it in a drawer for now, and I'll think about it?"

* * *

"I'll take you in the morning." Abe warmed his hands at the kitchen fire. "It's nearly dark out."

John thrust a hot poker in a glass of ale and handed it to him. *It wouldn't be so late if you hadn't dawdled at the pub in Chichester,* he thought. He'd been waiting in an agony of impatience for hours, occupying himself with cleaning the plasterwork reliefs as he'd promised his mother, and only prevented from hauling a farm cart out of winter storage himself and bribing one of the younger grooms to take him by his expectation that Abe would be back at any moment.

"I will give you anything," John said. "The bidding may commence at a guinea, and any bed you like in Chichester for the night."

"I'll take you there in the morning. I promise we'll catch the coach."

"We might be snowed in by morning. I'll pay one of the boys to take me if you don't want to go."

Abe threw his head back in frustration. "There's none of the boys left at home trained well enough to drive my horses in the dark in this weather without me watching him. I trow, between you and your wife I'll have no toes left, and neither will my horses."

"Abe, *please.*"

Abe threw up his hands. "I'll put on dry stockings. But I want a featherbed at the Dolphin, a roast pheasant and a bottle of Madeira."

* * *

"You can't possibly go." Mrs. Grimes blocked the door. "It's nearly dark out, it's starting to snow, and you'll never get a cart this late. You'll stay here and share with Julia and Lou."

"Then I'll walk. My boots are newly sealed." Sukey would have liked to snap, *You aren't my mum,* but tried bribery instead. "Here, you can keep the hamper. There's a whole seedcake in it."

"Take the seedcake, Mum," Lou urged in a loud whisper. Sukey smiled, because her ploy was working and because Lou was darling.

A knock came at the door. Mrs. Grimes turned, startled, and opened it. John stood in the doorway, his hat in his hand.

Mrs. Grimes fell back. Sukey's feet felt nailed to the floor. How had he found her?

Then she remembered she'd told him she was coming here. She stifled a nervous giggle, thinking what would he do if she'd stayed at the inn?

Mr. Grimes pushed himself forward. "Now see here. I don't know as I'd ought to let you in after you made my little girl unhappy."

John looked at him, raising his brows slightly, allowing the silence to lengthen and the room to fill with, *After* I *made your little girl unhappy?* Mr. Grimes flushed.

Sukey loved him. She ran and threw herself into his arms. "I'm sorry. I'm sorry I left, and I'm sorry I let you stay. I'm sorry I didn't take care of you. You don't want to stay there, John, you don't and I won't let you—"

"I know," he said. "I was coming away just now. To go back to the vicarage with you, if you'll agree to it. Look, there's my trunk." It stood on its end on the landing.

Sukey's family— *No*, she corrected herself, *your father's new family.* But her heart wasn't in it. The Grimeses crowded in, eager to see what she'd say. "Keep your pointy little noses out of this," she told them with mock severity and shut the door, leaving her and John alone on the dim landing.

"I mean it," John said. "We can go and not come back. I told my mother to write to Lady Tassell and ask her to make my father retire. I'm not going to do it."

She couldn't stop smiling up at him. "Believe me, I'd like nothing more. But we planned to stay a fortnight, and I expect we'd ought to do it. Just to help at the Hall until Lady Tassell writes back."

He hesitated. "Are you sure?"

The fun would wear off this particular piece of generosity long before two weeks were up, but just now, it felt wonderful. "I don't say I'll enjoy it." She brushed melting snowflakes from his hair, painfully glad to be touching him. "But that's all right. Better that than your father falling off another ladder."

He let out his breath. "Thank you."

"You're welcome. Let us share in joy and care."

He felt inside his greatcoat and drew out her wedding ring, new polished. It caught the fading sun from the window, dazzling her. She tugged off her glove, and the ring was warm from his pocket when he slipped it on her finger.

"I'm so sorry about this morning," he said. "I should have listened to you. I shouldn't have presumed to make the decisions for both of us. I haven't wanted to ask you for things because I really do need so much. It was easy to give you up. It was easier to behave like my father than to face myself as he sees me, the weak, clinging, clumsy adolescent whose hands shook when he watched me work. God, my hands are shaking now."

He held them out, and to her shock it was true. She took them hard in hers, yanked his gloves off and kissed his fingers.

"I didn't want to tell my mother that I wouldn't be butler at Tassell Hall because I've counted on her all these years to tell me, *No, your father's wrong, you're a good, clever boy.*" His deep voice was shaking too, a slight, low tremor that made her heart tremble with it. "I didn't—Christ, this is embarrassing. I didn't want to admit that the job was beyond my capabilities. It was easier to be unkind to you than to face that. But there can be no reward without labor. So I'm putting my shoulder to the wheel."

"I understand," she said. "I do. It was easy for me to leave too. Easier to throw your ring in your face than tell you how hurt I was, how afraid, how much I didn't want to live without you. Because if you still didn't listen to me *then*—I've spent so much of my life trying to feel brave, trying to look brave, but I've never *been* brave. I've never wanted to risk anything. I'm afraid even to be happy because it will hurt too much to lose it. But I want to try with you. I want to be happy with you. I want to trust you. I want—"

Frustrated, sure her words weren't explaining it, she dug her fingers into the front of her pelisse. "I want to put my heart in your hand," she whispered.

He caught his breath. "Yes," he said. "Give me your heart. Give me *everything.*"

For a moment it was almost more frightening than being left, because at least that was over and done. This was every day for the rest of her life, her heart wandering about in his pocket where she couldn't keep her eye on it.

But she looked at his dependable face, at the lines smiling had cut in it, and she wanted to see them deepen and multiply until she and him were both old and there was a whole wrinkly history of happiness there. "I will. If you give me everything back."

"It's going to be ugly and discomfiting," he warned her.

"It's going to be beautiful too."

He nodded. "My joy and my care. I swear it."

* * *

John hired them a small private room at a nearby inn, Sukey's stepmother having promised them the sheets there would be clean. "I think we'd ought to talk about things," Sukey said, sitting on the edge of the bed. "What we want. What we're going to do."

John, having rather expected to fall into bed at once, was taken aback. He took a deep breath. Whatever she said, he would listen. They would talk it over and decide together. "Very well."

"I think..." She flushed. "I think sometimes I want...to feel close to you. I want to feel as if you like me. And the best way I know how is to go to bed. But I ought to talk to you instead."

It felt almost unseemly to see her with her bravado stripped away, no toss of the head or sly smile—only words trickling painfully out, one by one. How much more naked honesty was than nakedness. "I'd like that. I hope you know you always can talk to me, and that I always like you."

She nodded uncertainly, and he wished for the millionth time that he never made her feel as if he didn't like her.

"Sukey, can I ask you a question?"

"Of course."

"Are you afraid of me?"

She blinked. "No. Is this more about how you're like your father?"

Her easy answer should have reassured him. Maybe one day it would. "Partly. But whenever I speak sharply to one of the girls at the vicarage, you always try to protect them from me."

She frowned. "Do I? I'm sure I don't. I reckon I'm mostly worried one of them will say something they hadn't ought. And I've never liked quarreling."

He took a deep breath. That made sense. "I've worried too that you were hiding behind the other women. Molly brought in the new lists, and when I first wrote them, you let Mrs. Khaleel speak to me about my forgetting market day."

She sighed. "I thought you said it was all right that Mrs. Khaleel was head of the female servants, not me."

He had said that. He hadn't thought of it in that light.

He remembered again how his mother used to try to manage his father, the whispered conversations and the pleading and the shouting. Sukey, on the other hand— He smiled. Sukey kept her own counsel, as was every woman's right.

He didn't need her to be his ambassador between him and the other staff. He didn't want it. He could talk to them himself. To be honest, he probably should talk to them a bit more.

"Very well," he said. "If that's all it is."

"You do want to go back to Lively St. Lemeston?"

"I do." He sat beside her. "I like the vicarage, and our friends there. I'd rather not leave it. What about you?"

"I feel the same," she said firmly. "I want—John, I want to be with you forever. Every day until death us do part. I want us to be old together like your parents. Is that what you want?"

He could feel his face light. *Perhaps not just like my parents,* he thought, but he didn't say it. "Yes. I do." He hesitated. "Sukey, I know you aren't ready for this, but I want you to know that I'd like to have children with you. Sooner rather than later, if you'll trust me to stay and bring them up with you. I've been turning it over and I'd rather not wait ten years like my parents did."

She gave him a startled shove. "I don't imagine you do, being so ancient."

She sat, considering it. John held his breath. "I reckon I'd like that. But let me think about it, will you?" She sighed. "It would be easier to manage babies if we stayed at Tassell Hall and I didn't work."

He almost said, *We still can.* But he didn't want to, not even if it meant he could have a baby with her tomorrow. "Would you like to not work?" He couldn't believe they hadn't discussed it before.

She hesitated. "Maybe? I like having money of my own, though. And I don't want it so much that I'd— You're a servant. A servant isn't like a banker or grocer, who takes his midday meal at home and spends every night with his wife. I'd rather work and really live with you than live a life of leisure in a cottage a little ways off and never see you. I don't mind it, now I'm working in a nice home."

He gave silent thanks. "In a few years, who knows? Maybe we'll want to open our own boarding house. Or maybe Mr. Summers... Well, he can't live forever."

She nodded, looking sad. "Our own boarding house. Do you think you'd like that?"

"Maybe. Would you?"

Sukey's mouth twisted thoughtfully. "I don't know. It's an awful risk. It'd be grand if we found nice lodgers, I expect. And we could have all the babies we wanted, with folk always around to help look after them. Do you think we could really afford it?"

"I have some money in the bank," he said. And for the first time, he told her to the penny how much. "If we start putting money by now, if we decide to have children, we can choose for ourselves how to go about it."

She smirked. "There's only one way to go about having children, didn't you know?"

He pulled her into his lap. "Theoretical knowledge is so different from practical. Perhaps later we might run it through, so I'm prepared in the event."

She smiled crookedly up at him. "John, I—I don't know how to ask this, because your wages are so much greater than mine..."

"It's our money," he said firmly. "*Our* wages are fifty-two pounds per annum, excluding vails and Christmas boxes."

"I want us to put money aside for my mother. An annuity, maybe."

John was ashamed he hadn't thought of it before. "Of course we can."

She bounced up and kissed him. "Get out your little memorandum book, and we'll make a plan."

* * *

"Where are we going?" Sukey grumbled. "Haven't I tramped about in the snow enough this week?"

"Just a little farther." John's lantern swung in his hand. "I want to show you one of my favorite things about Tassell Hall."

Sukey didn't really mind. With John at her side, the full moon shining on the snow was beautiful. He led her down something that, from how it wended through the trees, might be a path in summer.

Something pale and unearthly rose up ahead: a circle of columns topped with a stone ring. A proud statue in flowing draperies stood in the center, a curious helmet on her head. In one hand she carried an iron spear tipped with gold, and in the other a tiny, golden woman with outstretched wings.

There was magic in the white snow on white stone in the white light of the moon, snow drifting over the still figure's helmet and breasts, snow piled about her shield and hiding her marble feet. Dark tree branches shot up overhead, nearly invisible against the sky.

"What is this place?"

"An imitation Greek temple built by the present Lord Tassell's father," John said. "I always loved it. There are other follies scattered about the grounds, but they're gardeners' sheds in disguise. This one is...useless, I suppose."

His impractical side startled and charmed her every time. She snuggled closer, pointing at the statue. "Who's she?"

"Pallas Athena, the Greek goddess of war. When I was very small there was a naked Venus, but Lady Tassell had her replaced."

Sukey giggled. "Of course she did."

John touched a finger to the tip of a tiny gilt wing. "I thought she was holding a fairy. Eventually I learned that this is Nike, a winged personification of victory. But I used to come here at night to see if I could catch the pharisees dancing."

Sukey shuddered. "Be glad you never succeeded. They don't like it."

He drew her past the temple, to where the path dropped off steeply to a frozen lake. "I suppose people in Lively St. Lemeston bow to their first sight of the new moon?"

Sukey nodded.

"The underservants do it at the Hall. I always believed it extra lucky if I saw her first from this spot."

Sukey drew in a deep breath of night air. "Did you know a girl can catch a glimpse of her future husband if she watches the first new moon of January rise?"

He shook his head.

"You have to sit across a stile and say a charm, and you couldn't tell anyone you were going to do it." Sukey looked up at the moon, serene and round-faced and whispering of love, and wondered why anyone thought she was chaste. "All my friends did it at one time or another, but I never did."

He was silent, but she knew he was listening. He did always listen to her, in the end. He always would.

"I never played any of those games," she said, not looking at him. "I never put nuts in the fire on Halloween to see how my affections would fare. I was afeared if I told anyone the names of the boys I liked, or even if I wrote them on a bit of paper—I might really have to marry them."

He took her hand. "I love you."

"I love you too. And I'm not afraid anymore. We're going to be married forever, and I'm glad of it. Gladder than I've ever been of anything." She climbed up on a picturesque rock, careful not to slip, and kissed him in full view of the moon and God.

He held her steady and kissed her back.

Epilogue

March 1813

"And you're not angry?" Sukey asked her mother for the tenth time.

Mrs. Grimes sighed and patted her on the arm. "You'll do as you like, I suppose. But don't you dare take money from her!"

Sukey smiled. "I wouldn't dream of it, Mum." She clung tightly to John's arm as he pushed their way through the crowd leaving church, the boys racing and shouting, excited because it was marbles season. They passed Molly, kissing her father on the cheek before he went back to the workhouse and she went off to Sunday school at the Quaker meetinghouse. There were Mrs. Khaleel and Thea on their way home to make Sunday dinner, and Larry holding a stack of papers and books for Mr. Summers and the new curate he'd found in London. (The curate was a shy and very young fellow who'd been allowed to move into the vicarage after a number of dire warnings as to the fate that would befall him if he dared take a fancy to any of the women servants, and who had so far proved entirely unobjectionable.) They passed Sukey's friends and Mrs. Humphrey and her boarders and the farmers from the market.

Sukey had always felt pushed to the edges of things, slipping by unnoticed, as if she and her mother could be swallowed up by the earth with no one the wiser. But plenty of people greeted her as she went, and anyway here was most of the town in church, and the church needed the vicarage. And the vicarage needed John, and John needed her, so there you were.

John fetched them up just behind Aunt Kate. "Are you sure you want me here for this?"

She held tight to his arm. "Don't you think of leaving me." She tapped her aunt on the shoulder.

The woman turned and stood, perplexed.

"Maybe you don't know who I am," Sukey said, terribly glad of John tall and steady beside her. "But I—"

Aunt Kate broke out in a smile. "Of course I know who you are, Susan."

"Everyone calls me Sukey now." She straightened, twinkling back, because she supposed that was what Grimeses did when they felt nervesome. "I've been wanting to talk to you."

Aunt Kate's eyes misted over. "So have I. Every Sunday for fifteen years. Introduce me to your husband, won't you?"

"Aunt Kate, this is John Toogood." *Gentleman's Gentleman*, she almost added, but he wasn't anymore. He bowed over Aunt Kate's hand, quietly growling something polite and making this as smooth and easy as he made everything else, and Sukey thought she'd get him new calling cards for Lady Day.

About the Author

Rose Lerner discovered Georgette Heyer when she was thirteen, and wrote her first historical romance a few years later. Her writing has improved since then, but her fascination with all things Regency hasn't changed. When not reading, writing or researching, she enjoys cooking and marathoning TV shows. She lives in Seattle with her best friend.

If you'd like to know when her next book is available, you can sign up for her newsletter at www.roselerner.com, follow her on twitter at @RoseLerner or find her on Facebook at www.facebook.com/roselernerromance.

Visit her website at www.roselerner.com for free short reads, deleted scenes, historical research, and more about the world of Lively St. Lemeston. The first book in the series, *Sweet Disorder*, is about John and Sukey's old bosses Nick and Phoebe Dymond, and the second, *True Pretenses*, is about Lydia Reeve and Ashford Cahill, whose banns Sukey hears read. (Spoiler: Ashford Cahill isn't his real name!) More books are on their way.

Political intrigue could leave his heart the last one standing…alone.

Sweet Disorder
© 2014 Rose Lerner

Lively St. Lemeston, Book 1

Nick Dymond enjoyed the rough-and-tumble military life until a bullet to the leg sent him home to his emotionally distant, politically obsessed family. For months, he's lived alone with his depression, blockaded in his lodgings.

But with his younger brother desperate to win the local election, Nick has a new set of marching orders: dust off the legendary family charm and maneuver the beautiful Phoebe Sparks into a politically advantageous marriage.

One marriage was enough for Phoebe. Under her town's by-laws, though, she owns a vote that only a husband can cast. Much as she would love to simply ignore the unappetizing matrimonial candidate pushed at her by the handsome earl's son, she can't. Her teenage sister is pregnant, and Phoebe's last-ditch defense against her sister's ruin is her vote—and her hand.

Nick and Phoebe soon realize the only match their hearts will accept is the one society will not allow. But as election intrigue turns dark, they'll have to cast the cruelest vote of all: loyalty…or love.

Warning: Contains elections, confections, and a number of erections.

Never steal a heart unless you can afford to lose your own.

True Pretenses
© *2015 Rose Lerner*

Lively St. Lemeston, Book 2

Through sheer force of will, Ash Cohen raised himself and his younger brother from the London slums to become the best of confidence men. He's heartbroken to learn Rafe wants out of the life, but determined to grant his brother his wish.

It seems simple: find a lonely, wealthy woman. If he can get her to fall in love with Rafe, his brother will be set. There's just one problem—Ash can't take his eyes off her.

Heiress Lydia Reeve is immediately drawn to the kind, unassuming stranger who asks to tour her family's portrait gallery. And if she married, she could use the money from her dowry for her philanthropic schemes. The attraction seems mutual and oh so serendipitous—until she realizes Ash is determined to matchmake for his younger brother.

When Lydia's passionate kiss puts Rafe's future at risk, Ash is forced to reveal a terrible family secret. Rafe disappears, and Lydia asks Ash to marry her instead. Leaving Ash to wonder—did he choose the perfect woman for his brother, or for himself?

Warning: Contains secrets and pies.

Honesty can be the deadliest policy of all.

A Lily Among Thorns
© *2014 Rose Lerner*

Lady Serena Ravenshaw is one of London's most prosperous women, but she's never forgotten the misery that set her on the path to success. Nor has she forgotten the drunken young gentleman who gave her the means to start her long, tortuous climb out of the gutter.

When he knocks on the door of the Ravenshaw Arms to ask her help in retrieving a stolen family heirloom, she readily agrees to help, and to let him stay rent-free. After all, Serena prefers debts to fall in her favor.

Still grieving the death of his twin brother, Solomon Hathaway just wanted to be left alone in his dye-making shop—until his highborn uncle sends him to the infamous Lady Serena to scour London's underworld for the missing bauble.

He's shocked to discover she's the same bedraggled waif to whom he once gave his entire quarterly allowance. Yet as they delicately tread common ground, they must negotiate a treacherous world of crime, espionage and betrayal before they can learn to trust—and love—again.

Originally published Dorchester 2011.

Warning: Contains toasty warm pastries, scorching hot chemistry, and a web of treason that just might see England in flames.

SAMHAIN
PUBLISHING

It's all about the story...

Romance

HORROR

Retro
ROMANCE

www.samhainpublishing.com

Made in the USA
San Bernardino, CA
05 June 2016